INTERLOPER

Realms and Realities Series

C.L. Merklinger

<u>INTERLOPER</u>

A person who becomes involved in a place or situation where they are not wanted or are considered not to belong.

DEDICATION

To my dad, who taught me the joy in stories

and the love of reading them

C.L. Merklinger

ACKNOWLEDGEMENTS

To the following - I am forever grateful:

James for his unwavering support during the maiden voyage in my journey.

My sister, Tracie for being a sounding board and reality check when needed.

My daughter, Gillian, for being my cheerleader and fellow weirdo.

My dear friend, Bruce, for lending me his brain during the editing process.

My editor B.K., my eagle eye, for his kind and thorough lessons.

C.L. Merklinger

PROLOGUE

The sky shifted from the blues and whites it had been painted with most of the day to its current palette of lavender with hues of pink and orange. Astrid walked from the modest home she shared with her father, Barnabas, and her maid, Mary, taking in the beautiful canvas as she tied her apron around her waist. It was time to secure the livestock for the evening, a chore she took on herself even though her father, who traveled often, made sure help surrounded her for anything she may require. This was *her* time, and no servants were needed.

As she collected the day's eggs from her chickens, she hummed softly and thanked each one for their gifts. Placing the bounty into a small basket she was carrying, she maneuvered over to a lantern kept just outside the coop. Astrid lifted its dome and brought a small flame to life under its glass captor. Carrying the lantern across a small path which led to her family's barn, she made sure the livestock were secure, then settled onto a mound of hay in the corner. Placing the lantern safely on a hook nearby, she reached deep into her skirt pockets to retrieve a small fabric bundle tied with a ribbon containing a crude pencil and paper.

She flipped through the sheets of paper one by one, examining sketches of plants and herbs she had discovered in the woods near her home. Detailed instructions on how to manipulate, measure, and blend them into remedies for various ailments plaguing the inhabitants of her small village accompanied her sketches. Arriving at a blank page, she set upon sketching her most recent find from memory. Even though the villagers desired the temporary relief her potions brought them, they would be the first to accuse her of heresy if it came to it.

They were religious folk, as she was, and strict believers in their Lord and his will. Such things as the herbology Astrid dabbled in could surely be considered the work of the Devil's hand. Astrid learned firsthand at the tender age of eight how quickly people will turn on those providing services such as hers. Her mother was taken from her in her original home in the Massachusetts Bay Colony, hung to death as a witch by those claiming to serve the Lord.

It was from her mother's early teachings that she learned the basic knowledge of what plants were safe and which were not. There were times she failed, and as part of her experimentation, she would suffer horrible side effects from what she created. Already successful in creating tried-and-true remedies for slight pains that would plague the head and body, Astrid was working on a simple potion to remedy stomach aches and ailments.

She picked up the pencil, a new instrument which released her from the quill and inkwell that her father had brought home from one of his travels. He was told it would revolutionize writing. Astrid took to it immediately, as it allowed her to be out in the barn and not confined to a desk. It also allowed her to blend her shading if she wet her finger and, with slight pressure, rubbed the pencil marks.

Placing the tip down on the sheet of paper, she brought to life an image of wormwood with finger-like leaves, bearing tiny teeth and grooved, rigid stems. Finishing the image, she added fluffy balls that would eventually spawn the loveliest yellow flowers.

Were she to grind the elements of this specimen in her mortar, she would add a touch of mint and lemon balm, creating a powder that one would ingest with a healthy tin of water. She wrote her findings from ingesting this concoction, noting the importance of limiting the amount of wormwood, as too much had caused delusions which took her days to overcome.

She placed the final embellishments on her entry, gently folded the paper back into the cloth, and wrapped it with the pencil, binding it with the pale green ribbon that had once been her mother's. She said goodnight to the cows, grabbed her egg basket, and made her way back to the house before the staff started to worry about her.

Upon entering, she was greeted by Mary, a woman of three and twenty hired to be Astrid's main caretaker after they arrived in Rhode Island. She placed her lantern and egg basket in the center of the small table in the kitchen and asked Mary what she had prepared for their evening meal.

As Mary slowly stirred the contents of a cast-iron pot over the flame, she replied, "Rabbit stew, Miss Astrid. Jeremiah caught us two lovely rabbits early this morning. Better take to washing up now. I will have it plated for us soon."

Taking her cue, Astrid rounded a large stone wall housing the sizable fireplace and ascended a set of stairs directly behind it to her small quarters. Removing her apron, she hung it on the post of her bed, then removed her pouch from her skirt and placed it in the small hiding spot she had created in the wallboards next to her bed. She then walked over to her wash station, which overlooked the small apple orchard her father had started soon after their arrival. Pouring a small amount of water in a bowl, she washed her hands with special care for her nails, which had collected quite a large amount of soil in her day's adventures. She splashed her face and patted it dry with a linen from the right of the bowl. Hanging it to dry, she turned to look in the mirror that was once her mother's.

Tidying stray black hairs curling around her temple, she sighed at the overwhelming hole left from her mother's death. How she wished her to be there.

Heading back down to partake in dinner with Mary, Astrid put on a smile to not worry her caretaker. No mother was Mary, but she was all Astrid had.

As Mary set the table, she thought about the changes that had taken over Astrid through the years. The once giddy and happy girl had been frivolous, like most children of eight years of age. Even after her mother's tragic death and a treacherous move to Rhode Island with her father, Astrid came to Mary as a ray of sunshine. She would remain that way until the third winter after their arrival.

Astrid became ill with a fever that brought her visions of white, ghost-like figures. The doctor excused the visions as symptoms of the fever, nothing else. It was during the height of the fever that Astrid exclaimed to her father and Mary that she knew her condition would soon change, as if a child with no education beyond her years would know such a thing. The next morning, to Barnabus' and Mary's horror, the child lay motionless and would not wake for several days. Then, as if stricken by no maladies, she awoke, telling tales of having been dead, entering the netherworld, and returning with a purpose she could not share.

From that day forward, Astrid was not the same carefree child. She seemed to know things that no one her age could know. She became more solemn and tended not to be enticed by those of her own age, instead spending her hours alone in the woods. Mary and the hired farmhands, Jeremiah and Caleb, were Mary's only true family, as her father almost immediately took to travels which kept him away, sometimes for months at a time. Recently, Mary noticed Astrid had become even more serious, giving up her fancier clothing and what remained of her childlike behavior for a deeper understanding of religion and how it pertained to her mother's death. Mary expressed her concerns to Mr. Fayerweather, and his only response was, "Well, she is her mother's child, isn't she? And for that, I can only give her a more tolerable place to live. What comes of it, time will only tell."

Feeling a slight breeze over her shoulder, Mary turned to face Astrid, who had a surprising smile upon her face. "Now that's better, child," Mary stated as she laid her hand upon Astrid's cheek.

Nodding, Astrid sat before her dinner and waited for Mary to join her before bowing their heads and joining hands to thank the Lord for what they were about to consume. A low rumble of horses approaching interrupted their prayer. Mary looked at Astrid, but before she could say a word, Astrid's face went pale, and she spoke words that would haunt Mary until her death some years later.

"It's time."

They released hands, and Astrid told Mary to retreat to her quarters. She said they were after her, and her alone, and Mary need not get involved. Barely making her way behind the curtain to her room, Mary turned to see three of the more influential men of the village enter the premises.

Thomas Greene was the first to speak. "Astrid Fayerweather, you are to come with us. You are being charged with heresy and murder and will be brought before the church elders this very evening."

Astrid didn't put up a fight. The other men took her out the front door and placed her in a small wagon hitched to Thomas Greene's steed. As they made their way into the night, Mary couldn't help but wonder why Astrid did not struggle, nor was she surprised that they had come for her. Knowing Barnabas would never forgive her for letting his child be taken alone, Mary quickly grabbed Jeremiah from his small dwelling, and they rode to the church at the center of the village.

Upon their arrival, they found a crowd had gathered. So many were there, in fact, the small church could not hold them all. Mary made her way to the steps of the church, not noticing the crowd that was busy assembling a small torture device to the right of the church. Pushing through the villagers, she made it approximately halfway down the aisle, close enough to witness charges being brought upon Astrid, who was tied at the hands and standing between the clergyman and Mr. Greene.

Again, Thomas Greene spoke with an authoritative tone. "Astrid Fayerweather, you are hereby charged by the council of the church with one count heresy upon the church and one count of the murder of young Sybill Smith. How do you plead before your fellow townsfolk?"

Astrid, whose head stood high and blue eyes showed no fear, stated her facts. "I did not murder the child. Her family approached me to help with the child's head pains, which plagued her at night. I supplied a natural remedy, taken by myself and proven to be safe. Her death was not a result of my influences. It was her time to go into the Lord's hands and nothing I did or could do could stop that from happening."

Mary stood as still as a mouse caught in the gaze of a cat as she heard the church explode with villager's voices screaming for Astrid's head. "She's a witch," someone yelled from behind Mary. It was then the clergyman stepped in and reminded the crowd that their village does not bring charges of witchcraft, which was why so many of the villagers, including the Fayerweather family, had come to make Rhode Island their home. It was a safe haven for those exiled from Massachusetts Bay Colony.

He then was quick to counter his statement with, "We do not, however, as servants to our Lord, tolerate heresy, and herein lies the charge we are placing upon Mistress Astrid. Her willingness to go against the Lord and take healing into her own hands will be marked as heresy. To prove that she is pure and willing to accept the Lord as her savior, we have devised a simple test for her to submit to. Should she prevail, she will be cleared of all charges and welcomed back into our Lord's arms."

With that, the crowd cleared a path for the clergyman, Mr. Green, and their guilty party, Astrid. Once outside, they walked her up a few stairs onto a wooden box in the center of a well of water approximately three feet deep. Mr. Greene took much pleasure in securing her hands and feet behind her back onto a wheel, then stepped down to her side. The clergyman then asked Astrid if she accepted the Lord as her divine savior.

When she did not answer, Mr. Greene placed his hand on the wheel and turned Astrid upside down so that her head was completely submerged in the water. Upon a count of ten, he brought her back upright and, as she spat water from her mouth, the clergyman asked her again, "Do you, Astrid Fayerweather, accept the Lord as your divine savior?"

Again, Astrid said nothing, and again Mr. Greene rotated her until she was submerged. That time, the count was thirty. When they brought Astrid upright this second time, Mary could only hope that she would take heed of what was being done here and have her wits about her to say the correct words. Upon being asked yet again, Astrid stayed silent, knowing from her visions what her fate was set to be. Mary swore she heard a faint "goodbye" come from Astrid seconds before she went under. This last time, after sixty seconds, Astrid would not be brought upright alive.

As she separated from her physical body, the world below Astrid's feet slowly disappeared until there was only darkness.

CHAPTER ONE
THE NEWS

The warm sun beamed down on Charlie's fair skin. She could feel her freckles popping through her epidermis like mini kernels of popcorn from the heat of a stove. To keep from burning, she flipped over onto her stomach to start the process over again. Those last few days of summer—not the calendar days, but the days from one's youth, the hot sticky days spent eating cherry ice pops and sunbathing in tube tops and short shorts—were her favorite. Her hair was twisted into a knot on top of her head, and the melodic sounds of Duran Duran telling a tale about a girl named Rio emitted from her lavender, pill shaped cassette player.

A breeze blew across Charlie, evaporated the tiny pool of sweat gathering in the small of her back, and caused her tiny hairs to stand on end. A small bumble bee, hovering at the smell of the sweet coconut oil she had slathered herself in, greeted her with the buzzing of its wings. The far away sound came closer, the buzzing growing louder.

Charlie awoke to an incessant vibration coming from her nightstand. Soaked in sweat, she realized the large oscillating fan meant to control the stifling heat in her dorm room was obviously not doing its only job. Her cell phone stopped vibrating long enough for her to wipe droplets of sweat from her brow. She still hadn't gotten used to having a cell phone, a gift from her dad to make sure she was safe walking around the campus alone.

"You never know," he chimed, handing it to her.

Cursing her dad for his overprotective ways, she scooped up the small device to see ten missed calls in the tiny window. Flipping the phone open, she miraculously managed to answer it at the same time. It was her dad, and she immediately felt dread emanating through the headset. In her fog, she heard between his deep sobs, "Charlie, she's gone".

She? This word had no meaning in her pre coffee brain.

"Charlie? You there?"

The words started to form meaning to her. In a hoarse voice, she said, "Huh? Oh… Yeah… She? Gone?"

"Yes, baby girl," her dad repeated "Your mom. She slipped away in her sleep last night."

Charlie was bewildered. Her mom was dead, gone? She had been the picture of health. It seemed unfathomable that she was gone. Charlie and her mom, Birdie, defied most mother-daughter relationships. They were friends—best friends, to be exact. Frik and Frack, her dad, used to tease. Most girls rebel against their mothers in their teen years. Charlie and her mom defied those odds. Charlie told her mom everything, and she was pretty sure her mom did the same. Spending their free time pursuing something artistic or out in nature, Charlie loved her time with her mom. She often thought about how this was surely a direct result of her mom's not so happy upbringing.

Birdie had been born to super religious parents, Joseph and Dorothy: True small-town, southern idealists with narrow-minded beliefs. The no-nonsense household did not spark nor nourish a creative and loving environment. Despite this, with Savannah as her backdrop, Birdie grew up to radiate the free spirit vibes one would expect from a female thriving in the sixties and seventies. Tall for a woman, Birdie was slight in build and fair skinned with the longest auburn hair set off by emerald green eyes. Charlie inherited her mother's auburn hair, but unlike Charlie's, Birdie's hair was as curly as the ribbons on a present's bow. Upon seeing photos of her mother sitting commune style with her female friends on a tie-dyed, quilted blanket in the middle of Forsythe Park on what one would only deduce was a one hundred percent humidity day, Charlie was grateful she did not inherit that particular trait from her mother.

Birdie strayed as far from her strict upbringing as she possibly could. She read everything she could get her hands on, hiding the forbidden texts of *To Kill a Mockingbird*, *Lady Chatterley's Lover*, and *The Catcher in the Rye* behind jacket covers taken from the dozens of religious books given to her by her parents. However, her hopes of becoming a worldly designer were cut short after the death of her father, leaving Birdie to care for her mother. Taking a job at a local optician's office as a file girl, she would eventually meet a handsome, practical young salesman named Dale. Dale and Birdie hit it off after a long discussion of form versus function in eyewear and were soon inseparable. Dates to the historic Savannah Theater to see *Love Story*, *The Graduate*, and even *The Sound of Music* on the big screen followed up by shakes and burgers at the local five and dime would lead to a whirlwind of a marriage proposal just six months later. Married in true Birdie fashion by an ordained former classmate of hers in front of the Forsythe Fountains, they embarked on a quick "honeymoon" across the Talmadge Bridge to Tybee Island. Dale then moved his new bride and her mother to Brighton, a small town just outside of Rochester, New York, where he was employed as a salesman and eventually became a product development specialist at Bausch and Lomb.

The complete opposite of Birdie, Dale was analytical and purposeful in his demeanor. Practicality ruled Dale while whimsy ruled Birdie. This proved to be the recipe for an almost idyllic and certainly loving marriage. Birdies' chaos balanced by Dale's structure suited them perfectly. Soon after moving to Brighton, Birdie found out she was pregnant with what would be their only child. Eight months later, on June sixth, Charlie Alaina was born. She was a perfect baby girl with Birdie's auburn fuzz and a rare trait called heterochromia, which solidified Charlie being the perfect blend of Birdie and Dale with one green eye and one brown.

She had her mother's love and zest for life. Birdie nurtured her artistic abilities daily. They spent Saturdays taking hikes to find natural materials with which to make art. Birdie also was never known to shy from what most would consider alternative ways of thinking. She believed in the paranormal and considered herself to be an empath. Charlie didn't necessarily believe in the full spectrum of the paranormal since she was also her father's child, but she recognized those moments when she could feel something was different or sense something was about to happen. Her mom always said it had to do with heterochromia and that as she got older, she would see the world differently. Charlie always just nodded.

Although a stay-at-home mom, Birdie continued the passions she nurtured during her time at Savannah College of Art and Design. She started an in-home business—a boutique of sorts which allowed her to be with Charlie—where neighborhood women could bring their "tired" closets to her for reinvention. Birdie had a knack for dissecting articles of clothing to create something new and unique. "Hybrid fashion" is what she proudly touted her aesthetic to be. She taught Charlie to be creative and freethinking, and Charlie used her Barbie fashions to mimic her mother's talent.

Even in college, Charlie still had a vintage Midge on her dorm shelf, sporting an outfit she created when she was six—a cheetah-trimmed gold lamé skirt with a hot pink, lace-trimmed top.

Although it was one of her earliest creations, with crooked sleeves and an uneven hem that reminded her more of Frankenstein than Ferragamo, Birdie still oohd and ahhd and praised her daughter's talents to the other moms on the street, stating they had the next Vivienne Westwood among their midst.

Reality sank in as Charlie finished that impossible conversation with her dad. Hanging up with tears in her eyes, Charlie realized she needed coffee, her lifeblood, but was in no mood to trudge down to the local coffee shop in her condition. Thankfully, she had the best RA ever, who had set up a coffee station in the common area.

Charlie donned her purple robe and kitty slippers and shuffled down the hall, hoping not to encounter any other souls on her journey. As she approached the center of the hall with its well-worn couches, the aroma of the true nectar of the gods filled her nose, and she smirked at the *This Shit Ain't Free* and *You Use it You Brews it* signs with arrows pointing to a can on the counter containing a few flimsy dollar bills and a small pittance in change. Charlie added her donation and snagged her cup of joe.

Once securely back in her dorm room, Charlie had never felt so lucky to have a space to herself. Her prior roomie decided college was not her thing and left early in the second semester. Curled up on her bed, Charlie took a big swig of the warm goodness and proceeded to cry. She and her mom bonded even deeper in her teen years over many a cup of "hot bean water", as her dad would tease. Charlie never felt there was anything she needed to hide from her mom. That cup, with its sugar and cream, had a bitter tinge to it that day. Gone was the sweetness that came with the memories. Crying for what seemed like hours, Charlie realized that she would need to reach out to the Dean to see what the protocol was for missing school due to a life event such as this. She was lucky in one aspect that the timing did not fall during midterms or finals. She would have to make sure to adhere to the syllabus strictly while she was back home to not fall behind. However, when it came to academics, Charlie had always been a sponge, absorbing any subject she was presented with. That was her father's influence for sure, as her mom was not, in the least bit, a planner.

Charlie finished her coffee and, out of pure emotional exhaustion, closed her eyes for a rest. Packing could wait.

As she moved on again, and again, and again, Astrid sat back, trying to remember her journey. At first, she didn't realize she was dead. She could hear her surroundings as her spirit separated from her physical body. Fear, she remembered that—even though she thought she had been prepared to die—she wasn't actually ready for it. She feared what her death would do to her father and Mary. Before she could think anymore, she was ascending.

Her first few stops were very brief. The first was exactly like home. In fact, it was home. She was home and could see daily life unfold before her, however, she could not interact with it. She could hear, see, touch and smell, but could not speak. How long this lasted, she could not tell, because there were no full days. It was as if she were reliving brief episodes of her life.

Then, just as quickly as before, she entered the next realm, where yet another thing was taken from her—smell. This broke her spirit, as she was so accustomed to smelling the world and its wonders. The flowers, trees, animals, food, and even something as simple as the oils Mary would use upon her neck. Again, how long this lasted, she did not know. Each time losing a little more of herself, more of her connection to the world she so dearly loved.

Upon her last ascension, a form introducing himself to her as the Master greeted her. He explained she could not proceed further until she proved to the others she was worthy to ascend to the seventh and final plane. Before the Master could explain to her the ins and outs of what was happening, Astrid realized she was devoid of any physical form. She was her thoughts and memories, but no physical body or its necessities. She no longer felt hunger, pain, sorrow, or anger.

When Charlie woke, the sun was lowering in the sky. It was not quite dusk, but her stomach informed her she had missed a meal or two. She threw on some jeans and one of her favorite concert tees, which she picked up at a Bangles show the prior year, then slid a parka over that. The campus was ripe for walking and the weather at that time of year was unpredictable and could be brutal at a moment's notice.

After arriving at the campus cafeteria, she ordered a burger and fries, then sat at a window rail table and stared at her cell phone, trying to remember the last conversation she had with her mom. She was sure it was something trivial like the ratio of peanut butter to jelly for a sandwich. They traveled down the obscure tangent road now and then, and to be honest, Charlie preferred that. The world was quickly becoming too serious of a place.

As she inhaled her food, Charlie made notes in her constant companion—a notebook about how the next week or so was going to work. She knew her mom had specific requests for her interment.

Birdie had always been open and vocal about her death so that would not be much of a to-do to work through. Charlie couldn't stop thinking, however, about how and why it happened. As she looked down on her notepad, she realized it was at the core of what was bothering her, thanks to her doodles—one of those quirks that drove her father crazy, as he would find random rabbits and other small animals throughout the home she grew up in. Doors, in between patterns in the wallpaper, kitchen cabinets—wherever there was a surface, she would doodle. Mom never once tried to discourage her, but her dad seemed to think of it as a form of vandalism, which had made Charlie giggle. The same could not be said this time.

She slurped down the rest of her Coke and bundled back up for the walk back to the dorm. Since she had her trusty security device tucked in her pocket—*Thanks, Dad*—Charlie decided to take the longer route back to the dorm from West Campus through Sorority Row along Fall Creek's edge. As she looked up at the night sky, she was amazed at what the universe provided as artwork. Wistfully, she remembered how, as a family, they would pitch tents in the yard and gather on a blanket to stare up at the constellations and quiz each other on astrology and deep space. Dad provided factual details as to why a constellation was named the way it was while Mom created completely new constellations by drawing outside the box, allowing her and Charlie to come up with names like Giant Pudding Cup and Lady Pouring Kool-Aid. Her mother believed in all things most considered fantastical and occult driven. Astrology, palmistry, life after death, ghosts, and so on. If it was mystical, her mom was intrigued. Although Charlie would ride the bandwagon at times, she mostly fell on her father's side when it came to things like that. She, like her father, was more of a seeing-is-believing type of person. Still, she couldn't help but wonder: Wouldn't it be nice if her mom was right just this one time?

With a full and content belly, it was going to be a list-driven night for Charlie. After deciding which basics would work for her time back at home, she packed what she could, scanned her syllabuses, and set aside the appropriate texts. A conversation with her advisor and the Dean earlier put her stress aside regarding taking time away. They would communicate with her professors, and she could make up any missed work upon her return. She plopped on her marshmallow of a bed, where the ratio of blankets to people was a solid ten to one. To distract her mind, she found some reruns of *Three's Company*, and to her delight, it was one of her favorites: the one where Chrissy gets mistaken for a call girl. That did the trick. Later, after a bit of channel surfing, she landed on MTV, slid into her footie pajamas, made sure the fan was on, and closed her eyes for the night.

Startled awake by a knock at her door, Charlie bolted upright, placing both feet on the floor. She attempted to shake the fog from her brain as she shuffled across the generic square tiles, yellow and aged. She opened the door just as Tabitha from two rooms down came in for another knock, almost contacting Charlie's nose.

"Oh, uh, hey, Charlie," Tabitha said in a way-too-energetic voice for that time of the morning. "I have professor Tighman's philosophy class today and was wondering if I could borrow your notes from the last lecture?"

Charlie shook her head to feign off a yawn.

That must have come across as a no, because Tabitha immediately said, "Oh, okay. It was a shot in the dark."

Charlie quickly realized the error that just transpired and immediately rectified it by saying, "OMG, Tabs, of course you can! As a matter of fact, I was going to ask you a favor, too." Charlie explained the situation with her mom and how she had to go back home for a bit and asked Tabitha if she could take notes for her on the next few lectures so she wouldn't fall too far behind.

Tabitha squeezed Charlie's arm with a sad look in her eyes and said, "Of course I will."

Charlie handed over her notebook and they said their goodbyes. Shutting the door, Charlie caught a whiff of herself and realized that she had completely forgotten to shower since hearing the news of her mom. She gathered up her towel and shower caddy, complete with soap, Noxema, and her favorite Herbal Essence shampoo and conditioner.

Finishing her shower, she quickly dressed in a pair of sweats and a pullover, threw her long Auburn hair in a ponytail, and headed down for a quick bite at the cafeteria before her dad was set to pick her up to take her back to Brighton.

After inhaling her breakfast, Charlie made the short trek back to her pickup spot. As she wound herself through the paths of the campus, she truly hoped the almost two-hour ride home wouldn't be too painful or awkward. There had never been a drive without her mom planted in the passenger seat. A hiccup brought up the taste of a sausage she had pretty much eaten whole, and plopped herself on a raised planter next to the entrance of the lot. She sighed at the thought of how hard this must be on her dad. Maybe he would have some productive news as to why, or at least how, it happened. A familiar honk grabbed her attention, and she looked up as her dad drove up in his trusty Jeep Grand Cherokee. She stood up and stuck her thumb out, pretending to hitch a ride, knowing that would be a great way to start the trip: A laugh and a lecture on how many young people, especially pretty girls, go missing from that exact action, followed by percentages and statistics galore.

The car came to a stop and her dad rolled down the passenger window. "Hop in, Kiddo," he said in a tone Charlie knew was an attempt to hide his pain. She tossed her belongings in the back seat and joined him in the front. America's "Horse with No Name", halfway through its melodic story, came through the speakers. He turned down the radio as the chorus ended, put his hand on hers, and nodded her direction.

She could see that was all he could muster at the moment, tears welling up in the corners of his eyes. *No percentages or statistics today*, Charlie thought. She took a quick inventory of her dad's appearance. He was dressed, which was a plus, in jeans and a sweater—nothing in excess of what he needed to be "decent". Just like Charlie, he too appeared to have forgotten to shower, as his hair was disheveled and not its usual coiffed locks.

His first attempt at small talk started about three songs into the drive.

CHAPTER TWO
THE MASTER

Astrid meandered through her first few days, months, or years; she couldn't tell how long passed, as there didn't seem to be actual time where she was. It was as if yesterday, now, and tomorrow were happening all at once. Her basic lessons started shortly after her arrival. The Master explained who he was and how he came to be, that he started just as she did, a soul released from its physical confines upon his death and rocketed through the realms until he met his Master. He then explained their purpose in the universe, which left Astrid with an enormous amount of questions, which he did his best to answer.

The Master took her under his wing. He explained he had been watching her since her birth and had his fellow divas step in as best they could to help her. He asked her if she remembered almost being trampled by a workhorse when she was a young girl.

Astrid thought back and was surprised she did. She remembered her mother was tending to the garden while her father was away on one of his many trips. Astrid wandered off past the gate, drawn to the chickens on the other side. Not noticing or knowing there was a large workhorse grazing in the field just to the left of the coop, she continued on her chosen path. Later, the adults would tell the tale that the horse had been spooked by a hornet, and that is why he took off towards Astrid. The real reason, no one ever knew. Astrid remembered the sound of the hooves approaching so fast she could not avoid the trampling. She remembered crouching, giving up to fate. She then was lifted out of harm's way and set down several feet from near death just in time for her mother to comfort her.

The Master explained to her that it was them, and, as he mentioned when she first arrived, she would be trained and would eventually be given her own charge to watch over and protect. She would, as most do, have many charges over time, and shouldn't get connected to anyone. He then went on with simple explanations of the timing of the training. It would consist of a probationary period, a pledged discipleship, and finally an ascension to her final form.

When the time came, she was introduced to others. There were infinite souls in that realm. Once she was introduced, she could feel both her own energy and the energy of the others simultaneously. It was as if they were a connected hive, like bees, with the Master being their "queen". They all buzzed about completing their levels of training. Astrid found it interesting that even though their energies were connected, their education and knowledge were not. Somehow, they remained individuals in that way. The Master explained to her that it was because each of them were on their own journey to becoming something more.

Years, decades, then a century and two went by. She shared the Master's ability to move about through the realms. He helped her learn how to create a visual home there using her powers.

"You can take the sights you see, memories you are fortunate to keep, and make your space here into whatever you wish." He showed her how to use her thoughts to project her reality.

Over time, as she journeyed, she found new worlds and sights that enticed her heart. With most of her own energy being expended in her lessons, she had little to work with regarding her environment, so it was always simple—a forest, meadow, or a beach. No belongings or actual home. One thing she learned there, wherever there was, was that physical needs and desires had no purpose. However, she still yearned for her mother. The sorrow of not living her own life the way she had envisioned or planned also pained her. She was surprised how that feeling never left her in her time in that realm and throughout her training. The Master explained the things that one leaves unfinished or unresolved drives their energies in that realm. She experienced this time and time again. Her charges were almost always young people who experienced great loss, whether it be the loss of a parent, a sibling, or a pet. In her efforts, her pang of sorrow grew. It was as if it were its own beast which needed feeding.

As part of her lessons, Astrid learned how to open the doors of the mind—what The Master explained in layman's terms as the "nine states". He told her that to achieve each of these states, she would need to master several techniques and realizations. Broken down to their most simplistic form, they were to do right merely because it's right with no consideration for gain or loss; honorable conduct; acceptance of purity and calmness; complete subjugation via purity in actions; true tolerance; endurance; resist being turned away from one's path by temptation; faith, confidence, and trust in her Master and herself; and finally, the intense desire for liberation from earthly life.

He taught her to be mindful, that even in their realm, they were not precluded from experiencing evil. He further warned her of those who follow the Dark Magician. They were those souls who were lost in suicides or violent deaths. Those who were snatched from a dark place were destined to continue to a dark place. Astrid asked why her death was not considered violent, for as she remembered it, it definitely was. The Master explained even though her death came from a violent act, it was because she was a child along with the purity in her actions and her innocence which spared her from that path and led her to him.

CHAPTER THREE
HOME

As they pulled onto the familiar street, Charlie made note of the changes since her last visit home. The Carter's changed the colors of their shutters and front door, black and bright red respectively. *Bold choice*, she thought. The Miller's had invested in a gleaming RV proudly parked in their driveway.

She wistfully noted that was something that her mom always wanted for them as a family. Hands and head moved fervently as she embarked on tales of the adventures they could have. "Just imagine it", she would say, "the three of us, footloose and fancy free. Traveling the country. Seeing all the wonders and beautiful sights. I could check the big ball of twine and Lucy the Elephant off my list too!"

Her dad made the swirl around the corner to their cul-de-sac, and before them sat the building they called home: a blue, shaker-shingle craftsman with a quirky green door courtesy of her mom. Would this still be a home without her mom, or would it be just a box that only housed memories from then on, like one of those old cedar boxes kept by a widow?

The car came to a stop just in front of the garage. They gathered Charlie's items from the back seat, walked up the stone path under the breezeway, and entered the house. Charlie took a deep breath. It still smelled like home. Remnants of her mom's incense, embedded in the curtains, couches, and other soft surfaces reached out to Charlie's olfactory axons and hit her heart.

"Welcome back Charlie," her dad said as he hung her backpack on the decorative hook to the left of the door. They both sighed deeply and took steps simultaneously into the small hall that led to the kitchen. "You hungry at all?" he asked as she mounted the stool at the kitchen island.

"Kind of, but not really."

As if he were a mind reader, her dad reached into the pantry and pulled out a red and white can of her favorite soup, double noodle chicken, and his classic tomato.

While he prepped the soups in saucepans, Charlie got up and meandered to the fridge and pulled out cheese slices, mayo, and bread. "We can't have soup without a dunking device," she chirped. "Mom's recipe, of course. We don't want to commit heresy by using butter." They both chuckled.

Charlie wanted to simply enjoy their food and save the more serious talks for later, and her dad seemed to agree. They caught up on the happenings from Dale's job, the neighborhood, and Charlie's college as they dunked and sipped their respective delicacies.

After cleaning up, Charlie excused herself so she could unpack. Loading up, she ascended the staircase, taking deep breaths as she knew she would have to pass her mom and dad's room in order to get to hers. Taking a brief pause at the top of the stairs, she could see her mom's favorite quilt peeking through the doorway, neatly folded at the foot of the bed. She could only assume that her dad had taken up residence in either the guest room down the hall or, even worse, the couch in his office.

"One foot in front of the other," she murmured to herself as she slid past the master bedroom.

The second level of the home had a unique feature called an oculus, which meant she had to circle around the hallway to get to her room. She had many memories of sailing origami swans, cranes, and other creatures of flight over the railings of the oculus to her mother below. One time, her mom sent sixteen very large helium balloons floating up the center to deliver her sweet sixteen birthday wishes.

As Charlie approached her door, familiar signs from her youth greeted her—*Artist at Work* and *Top Secret* surrounded by pictures of Simon LeBon and Rob Lowe carefully clipped from her Teen Beat subscriptions.

Turning the knob, a recognizable creak resonated through the second floor as the door slid open. She stood in the doorway and immediately smiled. No matter what changes she had or would go through, her room, that house, would always bring her complete solace, even during such a sorrowful time. She walked in and scrunched her toes deep into her shag rug that lay before her childhood bed.

Her mom had picked out the furniture for her daughter before she even was certain she was having a girl. She just knew. She seemed to always *just know* things, Charlie noted.

The bed was a dainty four poster which could hold a canopy if desired. Charlie remembered a time when it did, but mostly it was without one, which allowed her and her mom to create whimsical forts to hide out, explore, and dream in. Many a night was also spent under the covers with her "trusty rusty" flashlight, one of the few items she inherited from her mom's dad, Joseph. It was a military green tube with a curve at the end that housed the light, and it was as heavy as a small anvil. Even though her mom didn't talk much about her childhood, Charlie gathered that this was Grandpa Joseph's from the war and had made it back in his rucksack. She and trusty rusty would tell many tales—from heroic adventures to spooky stories—to her stuffed entourage, and it illuminated creative works from drawings to diary entries when she got a little older. She set her bags on her bed and let out a sigh. Every inch of the room breathed her mom's touch, from the paint colors and pillows to the band posters they systematically tore out of Charlie's Teen Beat magazines.

Upon getting things settled in, Charlie knew it was time for her and Dad to have the hard talks. She changed into sweats and slippers and scooted downstairs. She found her dad in his office, staring out a window framing Mom's garden. They had purposefully chosen this as his office so he could, as he would say, "Watch his Birdie in her natural habitat."

With a hitched breath, he turned to Charlie and motioned towards an oversized leather couch by the fireplace. Grabbing a blanket from one of the side chairs, she curled up cross-legged on the sofa. It screamed masculinity in a home that most definitely had the feminine touch. Her dad sat catty corner to her on the couch and whispered, "I don't even know where to begin."

Charlie said, "From the beginning."

CHAPTER FOUR
THE DAY

There was nothing particularly special about that Friday. It started the same as ninety-nine percent of most Friday's do. Dale awoke slightly before dawn to his alarm clock furiously ringing and the smell of coffee wafting up the stairs from the kitchen. Birdie, of course, was already awake, having always been a restless sleeper. He imagined she was down in her studio working on her most recent designs after setting the coffee to brew. He silenced his weekday nemesis, sat up, planted his feet into his slippers kept at the side of his bed, and reached for the sky. Taking a moment to assess his surroundings, he heard Birdie singing, of all things, "Blue Moon".

The woman normally couldn't carry a tune in a basket, but she honestly sounded like a sultry songstress. It was almost as if there were a stranger in the house. He smiled to himself as he shuffled to the closet to decide which corporate prison suit he was going to wear that day and thought to himself, *Don't be silly, she probably just found her sweet spot.* As he slid the clothing back and forth on the rods, he mumbled, "Man, I can't wait until the only clothing decision I have to make is gray sweatpants or jeans." Choosing to go with the navy-blue pinstripe suit, pale blue dress shirt, and geometric tie, he carefully laid them on the bed and made his way to the bathroom.

Twisting the shower to its on position and making sure it was set on scald, he postured in front of the medicine cabinet mirror. He wasn't raised to be vain, but he found he was paying more and more attention to the lines and sags around his eyes. Birdie threatened to shave his beard in his sleep quite often, but he liked it, as it made his skinny face seem more manly. It always amused him how it never seemed to have a single gray hair, unlike his head, which started showing signs about two years prior.

"Okay, get to it," he told his reflection as the mirror steamed up from the shower. Ten minutes later, he descended the stairs and greeted his lovely bride in the kitchen.

Birdie, in an attempt to get him to eat healthier, had been substituting his bacon and eggs over easy with egg whites and bran muffins. That day was no exception. He accepted his plate, thanked her, and sat down at the table. As he took a sip of his coffee, he slathered his muffin with some I Can't Believe It's Not Butter in an attempt to lube the dryness of the bran. He folded his morning paper for easy access and the best working platform for his daily crossword. Birdie sat across from him and began stating her plans for the day.

As she worked systematically through her agenda, Dale piped in with an occasional, "Mm hmm," "Uh huh," and "That sounds wonderful." Most women would take that as him placating or humoring her, but both he and Birdie knew better. He learned early in their marriage when she was on a roll, it was best just to let her go with it. An occasional question would make its way through the chatter, requiring an actual answer, but mostly it was just her way of sharing her to-do list and organizing her many thoughts.

After confirming what they would have for dinner and running through her grocery list, she opened the door for actual conversation. They talked about his workload for the day and, of course, Charlie—which one had communicated with her last and what she was up to. As they wrapped up the small talk, Dale grabbed his unfinished puzzle and a coffee for the road then planted a kiss on his wife's apple-hued cheeks.

Something made him take an extra moment to step back and admire her. All those years, and she still had it. Even in her robe and crazy curls, she radiated beautiful energy, and when she smiled, it melted him like a sundae on a hot summer day.

They said their final farewells for the morning as Dale hoisted himself into his Grand Cherokee for the whopping fifteen-minute morning commute down Monroe Avenue to his office. He had considered biking once or twice over the years...but who was he kidding. He waved and exited his cul-de-sac not knowing it would be the last morning spent with his love.

Getting up without the aid of any external devices, Birdie slid out of bed and quietly donned her robe and fuzzy socks, as slippers always made her feel like she would trip at a moment's notice. She made it down the stairs and into the kitchen, where she brewed a pot of coffee. Seconds later, she was humming her way to her studio to work on some designs. Carla Murphy had dropped off a few outfits for her to reimagine. Sketching her designs for the outfits would be the focus that morning. Before sitting down at her makeshift desk, she opened the blinds at each side of the box window. That window normally would have an amazing view of her favorite lilac tree. However, in true Rochester form, the calendar said one date, and the weather deemed it to be another. Despite the persistent winter's delay of blooming lilacs, she enjoyed the crispness that came with the early morning air and loved seeing moonlight dance across the dewy grass.

She hung the first outfit for consideration in front of the window and, after an initial shiver, took a long sip of her coffee and set to work. Although she never got to finish design school, she obtained basic skills which paired with a natural talent school could not provide. As she ruminated over the first outfit—a large, floral print, almost floor-length dress with a Peter Pan collar—she thought about the warmer days that would be coming.

Grabbing her pencils and her sketchbook, she quickly put her vision to paper. A romper is what she saw. First, she visually removed the sleeves and collar from the dress. She drew a blouson-tank-style upper bodice tapering in at the waist with… with…. While chewing on the end of her pencil, it came to her. She jumped up and rummaged in her scrap pile. "It's here somewhere," she mumbled to herself. As she snatched the brightly colored swatch, which was once part of a terry cloth short set she had reimagined for Barbara Colton, she sang, "Bingo!" That would work perfectly to show off Carla's waist and allow for any stomach sins to be hidden. She flung it on her desk and continued the sketch.

The long, dreadfully too long, skirt would be cut and brought up above the knee to form the skort portion of the romper. She would actually have enough to make a matching headband, as well. With outfit one figured out, she slid the second outfit into place in front of the window. As she stared at the dizzying pattern of the suit jacket, *it* happened.

Needing to strengthen her abilities, Astrid slid past Birdie through the layers of the realm. As she sat in the room, which she learned over time was a studio, she took in her surroundings, grounded her thoughts, and, in her happiness, sang one of her favorite songs she had learned of over the centuries. She remembered when she first heard it.

She had been practicing moving between realms with her Master when she was drawn to an energy resonating through the ether from a particular spot. With instruction from her Master, she hovered at the rear of the space in her ethereal form as a black woman in a beautifully beaded yet risqué gown walked up a set of stairs onto a platform. She introduced herself as Billie Holiday and thanked the Cotton Club for having her that evening. Her sultry voice then released the song "Blue Moon" into the air. Many memories had faded from Astrid over the years, but that one stayed with her.

Continuing to belt out the song, she drifted around the room, being sure to touch and manipulate various items as she did. As her Master had taught her early on, her kind only has a minute amount of energy to expel, and one must balance it. She had to choose wisely what she wished to accomplish. Using her energy to travel only from one space to another would allot her more time in a space. However, as soon as she touched, communicated with, and manipulated the space around her, she cut into her allowable energy. As she practiced and grew in strength, she obtained more energy, but even then had to be mindful. Everything must be in balance.

She remembered the story he told of himself and a student of his, Pasquel. "Looking over the realms, Pasquel and I were startled by a horrible scream of pain. In a moment, as we are able, we were on the spot, where we found a young boy who had fallen over the edge of a cliff to the rocky gorge below. He was terribly injured with a broken arm and leg. More concerning to us was the sizable open wound in his upper thigh, which was discharging large amounts of blood. Pasquel cried that we must help the boy quickly or he would surely die. In emergencies such as these, Astrid, you will have to think fast. We needed to stop the bleeding and somehow alert a physical being to his predicament. I was obligated to materialize either Pasquel or myself, as we needed physical hands to tie a bandage and give the young boy someone to have at his side to help him through the trauma he was experiencing.

"I materialized Pasquel since I could do so and have energy left over to procure help. You see, Astrid? Pasquel would not have been able, at his neophyte stage, to perform either task on his own. We were able to save the boy as Pasquel bandaged him properly and I summoned his mother, through telepathy, alerting her that something was terribly wrong with her son and she must go find him."

Her memory was cut short by the sounds of shuffling in the area above her, Astrid stopped singing. Making note that she was able to maintain her presence for a full thirty Earth minutes that time, she again passed Birdie, returning to her realm. With darkness surrounding her, she mentally thanked her Master for the basic knowledge, then the Dark Magician for teaching her those ideas were limited in their good intentions.

Settling in for reflection, she smiled.

The snapping of the pencil between her fingers startled Birdie back to reality. It was daylight. *How?* As she glanced at the clock on the wall, she realized she had lost time yet again. That time, it was a solid thirty minutes. Rattled, she realized Dale was in the shower. She abandoned her project and scurried to the kitchen to start breakfast. In an attempt to follow Dale's doctor's suggestions, she had recently switched his eggs over easy and bacon to egg whites and bran muffins. Dale was not amused by this change and thought she didn't know he was covering up any healthy aspect of this switch with a slather of butter, hence her sneaking I Can't Believe It's Not Butter into the rotation.

As she worked diligently towards this goal, she could not shake off the fog still clouding her brain. She made a mental note to review her journal entries and add the instance to the more frequent occurrences she had been having. As she poured herself another cup of coffee, she heard Dale rounding the corner of the staircase.

After she waved goodbye to Dale and waited for his exit from the cul-de-sac, Birdie shuttled herself back into the house, shaking off the chill that followed her in. She decided to abandon her aforementioned schedule. She was fooling nobody, least of all herself; her and schedules rarely worked as planned. Instead, she ran up to Charlie's room—abandoned for the time being, traded for dorm life and independence.

Birdie smiled at the signs posted on the door warning her to keep out and marking the room as Charlie's, then turned the handle and went in. Walking across the shag rug lying at the foot of Charlie's bed, she picked up some serious static electricity. Her curls danced erratically in the air and her robe clung to her in all the wrong places. She reached the window seat on the opposite side of the room, then received a large electric shock when she slid Charlie's boom box over to access the panel beneath.

As she repositioned the cushion and raised the plywood panel, she noticed one of Charlie's doodles. A cat's head with crazy, long whiskers and a horse's body. She sighed like most mom's do when their kids get older and leave behind their childish ways. Peering into the well below the panel, Birdie pulled out a decorative box that housed her many journals, tarot cards, and other spiritual dabblings. Since Charlie moved out, this was Birdie's new hidey-hole, established so Dale couldn't find and read about the instances that had been going on over the years.

She wasn't keeping secrets, per se. She just knew Dale and his overprotective ways. He would read them and insist on helping, which to him meant analyzing what had transpired to make it logical. What she experienced, however, was far from logical.

She pulled out the most recent bound journal and jotted down an account of what had happened earlier that morning. Over the years, she found it most helpful to outline the episodes with when they happened, where she was, how long the episode lasted, what she had recently eaten, how tired she was, and finally, what was she doing when it happened. After documenting her answers, she set the book down on the floor next to her and meditated.

She closed her eyes to place herself back prior to the missing time, remembering the pattern in that hideous suit jacket with the dark sky behind it. As she continued to meditate, she pulled more details. As if in a dream, she faded into another room, one darker and lit by a single candle in a glass lantern set by a window. She assumed this was another lucid dream, which she had only recently begun to research and only partially understood. She had complete freedom of movement in the new space and took time to assess her surroundings. In the dim candlelight, she made out the features of the room itself.

It was not at all modern, with slatted wood walls and a stone fireplace. A variety of modest furniture was available to her: a table and chair, a small bed with a crude mattress, a tri fold screen in the corner, and an oddly useless mirror which created a fisheye effect when she peered into it. Unfortunately, this obscured her from seeing herself and what physical state she must be in.

Looking down at herself, she saw youthful hands lacking adornment of rings or even nail polish and some sort of lace-trimmed nightgown. As she performed a second scan, her eyes adjusted to the darkness, and she noticed a small book of sorts with a quill pen and inkwell next to it. She moved closer, but "moved" seemed to be the wrong choice of words. It was almost as if she thought about moving and was there. No physical movement seemed to have taken place. She skimmed the writings on the page, then sat. She picked up the pen in her right hand and thought, *How curious*, as she was left-handed. She instinctively continued the written train of thought before her on the paper.

I have never felt so weak as I do now. What I am afflicted with, I do not know. Neither, it seems, does Father, Mary, or Doctor Tuckerman. The fever is the worst of it. It keeps me lethargic. I feel heavy, like a lead balloon. It feels as though I have no tether to the world when I am in my fever-induced sleep.

I can hear the muffled voices of Father and Doctor Tuckerman speaking as if I were soon to be dead. The doctor keeps telling Father that the only saving grace is that I still have a faint heartbeat. Why they are unable to wake me is a mystery. He says I am in the Lord's hands, and they are to wait patiently and continue to cool my body as to bring my fever down.

I cannot wait to wake and tell Mary and Father of my adventures and stories of visiting worlds beyond what we can fathom. I see the inhabitants as if they are real, but I cannot touch the figures that roam freely amidst my travels. They are our equals in shape and physical traits, but unlike us, they seem to be made of a thick, mist-like fog. Most will not communicate with me, but there is one, a pleasant gentleman whose age is undeterminable. He has explained to me through some sort of telepathy that he is what this place calls a Master.

He says I see them because my earthbound body has created a thin veil between our realities which allows me to move about between them. Upon the death of my physical form, if my Karma is positive, he says my ethereal form will continue on to gain more positive energy and be a helper to those left behind.

He equated it with what I know as an angel. As real as these dreams feel, it is almost impossible to distinguish what is truly real or more insidious, the work of a more malevolent entity attempting to lure me to a certain death. This Master does not feel nefarious in his explanations, but I cannot help but wonder.

Nearing the end of documenting the experience, Birdie heard a loud chime in the distance from outside the window. It sounded like a church bell. *There is no church for miles*, she thought.

Feeling the most peculiar falling sensation, Birdie's eyes snapped open to reveal daylight. Looking around the room, she had a sense of shaking, but was not. Taking a few deep breaths, she centered herself in the moment, stood up, and gathered herself and her thoughts. She lifted the journal, smacked it closed, and stacked it in the box that was housed in the hidey-hole. As she exited Charlie's room, a sense of dread filled her heart.

She decided to carry on with her plans for the day and, in order to shake off the negative energy, maneuvered herself to the bathroom to shower and get ready. Setting the shower on hot, she dropped a cup of eucalyptus Epsom salts onto the floor of the tub, hoping to soothe her senses. While the room steamed up, she glanced in the mirror. As she stared at her reflection, the mirror hazed over with steam. A very intense déjà vu moment hit her and she flashed to her reflection in the fisheye mirror.

She took a deep breath to inhale the minty air and stepped into the shower, allowing the hot beads of water to flow over her. She tipped her halo of curls back, saturating them and releasing the tension she had been holding in her head and neck. Closing her eyes, she mulled over what had transpired that morning and the years and years of lost moments. The frequency had definitely picked up over the past twelve months.

She drifted back to her childhood, remembering when the moments were blamed on youthful peccadillos, and how, back then, they had always seemed to coincide with her imaginary friends appearing. In particular, Astrid. She, of course, documented these episodes as best she could at such a young age. She only wished she had learned early on to never speak of it due to the level of trouble she would be in with both her mother and Joseph for being such a remiss and irresponsible child. As the years went on, she stifled the urge to let adults know, so as to not incur the punishments that came as belts and switches coupled with hours of scripture recital.

Wrapping up her shower, she turned off the water, stepped onto her plush bath mat, towel dried, and twisted her wet locks up in a hair turban. As she passed the fogged mirror, it happened again. Déjà vu. Quickly exiting the bathroom, she got dressed, massaged some mousse in her curls, and padded down the stairs. Gathering her purse and keys, she hopped in her car and headed to Wegmans to grab what she needed for dinner.

After a successful outing, Birdie loaded up her arms with bags and, in one trip, brought in her haul. Of course, she almost knocked over her favorite vase in the hallway as she plowed through. She set down the bags on the island, placed the items in their respective homes, and set to make a quick lunch.

One tuna salad sandwich later, she poured a cup of tea and retired to her studio to finish up Carla's second outfit. Still in its prime spot, hanging in the center window, Birdie rummaged for a new pencil and began to sketch her ideas. It was exponentially more difficult than the first, mainly due to the head-spinning pattern. She thought long and hard about Carla's personality and soon the ideas began to flow.

No longer would it be a stiff eye hazard of a suit. She envisioned reversing the fabric to reveal a softer palette and a more unique pattern. She would cut the sleeves into thirds after removing them at the shoulders, then reverse the jacket, bringing the high collar to the front and leaving a low reveal in the back. Taking the leftover strips from the sleeves, she would make a connection across the center of the back for some modesty and design elements. Carla had a great back for a look like that. She then scooped the high front down into a sculpted, almost square heart to reveal just the slightest amount of cleavage. Sexy without being trampy. That connotation reminded her of her mother. She hated it when Dorothy would use that word and its close cousin, harlot, to describe her friends in high school and college.

Continuing the sketch, she suspended the circular cuffs cut from the sleeves in stacks of three with a brushed gold micro chain to add an element of whimsy. Her final tweak would be to attach the skirt to the waist of the jacket to transform the two-piece suit into a cocktail dress that would set off Carla's long hair and shape.

"Wow! Toot, toot," she quipped as she pulled on an imaginary train whistle line. If one couldn't toot their own horn, who could? Feeling satisfied with her creation, she set down the pencil and leaned back in her chair. Glancing up at the clock, she saw she had time to take in a guilty pleasure before she started dinner preparations.

"Robert Scorpio, here I come."

After brewing a fresh cup of tea, she curled up in front of the living room television, she listened to the closing credits of *One Life to Live* in anticipation of the only hospital she ever found comforting: *General Hospital.* Sipping her tea, she allowed her brain to melt into the drama between siblings Bobbie and Luke.

Dale, distracted by thoughts of Birdie, stared out his office window overlooking the park. Nothing stood out as being wrong that morning, but his gut couldn't convince him otherwise. An unsettling feeling was nagging him. *Stop it*, he thought to himself. *This is Birdie's influence. You're the logical one*. He chuckled. No one could ever blame him for being an illogical person, but still, something felt wrong. It had all day. Deciding he couldn't focus on work any longer, he left for home.

Dale pulled up to the house. It was odd there were no lights on anywhere in the home, just the familiar flicker from the television. That was another oddity, because outside of her three o'clock program, Birdie was not a slave to the TV.

He walked up the path, let himself in, and bellowed out, "Hello, I'm home." After removing his shoes and coat, he veered to the right and saw the back of Birdie's head. She was seemingly staring at the local news. Glenn Johnson was giving the week's weather report. Dale cleared his throat, but there was still no movement from her.

Circling around to block any view of the television, he found she was in, of all things, Charlie's clothing. Her eyes were open but not responding to either the light from the television or his hand motions. He ran to the kitchen to grab the phone. Dinner was started, but it was all wrong. Dishes were strewn about, the oven was cocked open, and food mess was everywhere, including what seemed to be chocolate handprints on the fridge. His Birdie would *never* let the kitchen get like that. As he was about to press the final one in nine-one-one, Birdie appeared behind him.

"Dale, why are you home so early?"

The phone handset hit the floor with a resounding thud.

Dale scrambled to pick it up as Birdie entered the kitchen. He laid the handset on the cradle, turned to her, and enveloped her body with his arms.

Stunned by the exuberant display of affection, she said, "Welcome home, babe."

Pulling away, Dale shivered as adrenaline continued to pulse through his veins. "Birdie, honey, are you okay?" he asked with a concerned look on his face.

"Of course. Why wouldn't I be?" She opened her mouth, seeming about to comment further, but glanced over his shoulder at the kitchen instead. "Dale... What were you trying to do here?" She ended in a nervous giggle, then looked into his eyes and reality seemed to slam into her like a Mack truck. She urgently motioned towards the island stool and settled half on, half off.

"Sweetheart, what was the last thing you remember?" Dale asked, taking her hands in his.

Birdie described her day, ending her tale with the scene where Bobbie and Luke Spencer were at the hospital after her daughter B.J. had gotten hit by a bus. She looked over at the clock on the range, and her voice quivered as she said, "Dale, that was almost three hours ago!"

Looking around at the kitchen explosion, Dale said, "So you don't remember *any* of this?" He gestured in a large, swooping motion.

She shook her head as a tear ran down her flushed cheek onto Charlie's GoGo's *Beauty and the Beat* t-shirt. At that moment, she looked down at the outfit she was wearing. Charlie's pink Chuck high-tops, jorts, and the aforementioned t-shirt. This seemed to send her into full panic mode, and she buried her head deep into Dale's chest.

Feeling completely vulnerable and useless to his wife at that moment, Dale pulled her in tighter and gave a few pats for reassurance.

Lifting her head up, Birdie sighed and excused herself from his arms.

Knowing a reset was needed, Dale suggested he walk her upstairs so she could change and take some time to center herself. He offered to tackle the kitchen clean up after he changed, adding a suggestion of Chinese delivery to allow them time to talk about what had happened further.

Birdie accepted all the offers and, hand in hand, they ascended the staircase.

After a stop in the guest bath to gain her composure, she joined Dale in the master bedroom and they both stripped and donned more comfortable and age-appropriate clothing.

As Dale headed back down to the kitchen, Birdie folded Charlie's clothing while attempting to remember anything she could about the past three hours. As to not let this large of an event slip away undocumented, she made a beeline for Charlie's room and, as she had done earlier that day, set forth to record her event. That time, however, she would not lock the journal in its enclosure. It was time at last to share at least the most recent events with her husband.

Astrid remained still in the shadows of her current realm. Looking around, she knew achieving her goal would mean no more creating and casting realities for herself when she felt bored with her surroundings. She must save her energies for the goal. The idea of truly being free was worth the sacrifice. No more being confined alone for eternity. If the final steps worked, she would be free.

The two trials proved her plan was possible. Controlling the exercise for as long as she had, manipulating the motions and finalizing the influence needed to master the transformation, was exhilarating. However, it was also exhausting. She needed rest, for the time had finally presented itself and the full capacity of her energy would be needed.

As Astrid closed her eyes in that realm for the last time, she dreamed of the island she had once seen in one of Birdie's photos.

CHAPTER FIVE
THE DARK MAGICIAN

The Dark Magician, taking pleasure in the complete absence of light, relished over finding Astrid and the growth he was seeing in her. It seems like it wasn't that long ago that he felt her essence—he was drawn to the pain she carried over along with her deep desire to be human again and live a life to fulfillment. It was like a cry in the night, echoing through the realms until it had reached him.

Introducing himself was the most challenging part of the process. She was ferociously devoted to the Master and their cause. He introduced himself as a vision so as not to alert the Master. From there, he took his time, showing her she could have the things she desired, that he found her from the deep desires she was communicating throughout the realms. He drilled into her that it was never too late to feel alive. Once she asked her first question, he knew he was in and would never be asked to leave.

He continued to reveal others to her, proving that he had the power to make her desires a reality. He promised all the human traits, the feeling and belonging she desired and felt she was robbed of, but said in order to achieve these, she would have to train in his ways.

As with all his neophytes, he allowed them small *wins* to show he had the power to provide what he was suggesting. He showed her how to use the basic skills the Master was teaching her and amplify them, allowing her to manipulate her charge and other objects on a much greater level. Astrid asked how the Master could not see or sense these actions, and the Dark Magician explained the Master feeds from and taps into pure energy. Neither he nor the Master could inhabit a neophyte's energy at the same time.

He explained that these actions would require great energy, energy she may not always have, and therefore she may have to feed off him. He explained that if she followed him and his teachings, she would be human again and get to live her life. However, due to the finite energy a human holds, she would have to commune with others like herself.

She accepted his offer, but he left out the most crucial clause: that *he* ultimately feeds off the energy they expel as a group and that although she will be free, the cost of living would be losing her soul to him forever.

CHAPTER SIX
BEGINNINGS AND ENDS

Birdie descended the stairs and bellowed, " Marco." She heard Dale's "Polo" and followed the reply to the sunroom. The room spanned the back of the house and had access from both a door in the family room and kitchen. Even though it was set up for all four seasons, they rarely used this space outside of the summer months.

Typically used for entertaining, there was a seating area with two small loveseats and a coffee table on one side of the room and a large, circular table and chairs for dining on the other. Dale had started a bar project, which was located in between the two. She chuckled to herself as she accepted it was a two-year project so far with no end in sight.

Dale was at the table with at least half a dozen red and white Chinese takeout containers, plates, chopsticks, and a bottle of merlot breathing next to the Reidel wine glasses. Not being fancy people, the Reidels were definitely out of place in the scope of their life. However, being a gift from Dale's cousins for their twentieth anniversary, they were brought out on special occasions.

She made her way to the table, nervously clutching her journal. She sat down, and Dale poured her glass first, then his. "We have sweet and sour chicken, sesame chicken, teriyaki beef, vegetable fried rice, dumplings, and for dessert, your favorite, cookies d'fortune," he said in his best fake French accent. Having just recently mastered the use of chopsticks, Birdie helped herself to a little bit of everything, realizing as she did how famished she actually was since she had nothing to eat since her tuna salad sandwich earlier in the day. Dale repeated his selections and, after a moment of silence, lifted his glass to her. She did the same, and they toasted to, "Getting through this together."

As they ate, Birdie recapped her day as best she could for Dale. She then slid the floral-patterned journal over to him and said, "Today is not new. I have been having episodes as far back as I can remember. I started documenting them in my teens, and this, here, is the most recent journal." She explained the current layout and why she documented the way she did. She explained how she hoped that in doing so, she could figure out a pattern or maybe why it was happening. She described how the lost time would range in length from seconds to minutes, but until today, never more than an hour.

Flipping through the pages, Dale seemed flabbergasted and hurt. "Birdie, why would you—no, *how* could you keep something of this magnitude from me?"

She hung her head low to her chest, eyes welling up with tears. After a deep sigh, she replied, "Dale, honey, you and me are so different when it comes to these types of things. You are logical, statistical, a seeing-is-believing type of person. You also are a huge worrier, and I didn't want to put that on you. I truly didn't make too much of this. I knew it wasn't physical or medical. It's something that has been with me my whole life. It never felt harmful or evil—never truly disruptive. If it had been, that would have been a different story and required a totally different approach."

As Dale continued to flip through the pages, he pointed to the journal and asked, "So, there are more of these?"

Birdie nodded. "About three dozen more, if I had to guess. Since Charlie left for college, I've been keeping them in her window seat."

Again, she hung her head in shame. Not for having a lifelong curse, but because she hid it from him.

Tapping his fingers, Dale took a large swig of his wine and said, "Okay, this is what we are going to do. Monday, we will call Doctor Schneider and set up an appointment. This could very well be medical, honey. I know you would love to believe otherwise, but let's be realistic here. The supernatural stuff is a fun thing to believe in and have as an interest or a hobby, but there just isn't any factual basis for these beliefs. Science, however, is real, tangible. Once we see the facts, we can get you some help and relief from this. We will continue to document…." Dale's voice faded.

As Astrid peered through the eyes of her friend, she saw the human she learned to be Dale gesturing and talking. Astrid knew that doctors could louse this up for her. She took in what he was saying and instantly knew that it had become a now or never situation. *Tonight*, she thought. *It would definitely be tonight.*

"Birdie, sweetheart, are you okay with this?" Dale patted her hand.

Alerted, she instinctively said, "Um, why of course, Dale, whatever you think is best." Taking a bite of her dinner, she tried fervently to recollect what Dale's plan was and couldn't. They took time to finish eating and cracked open their respective fortune cookies, revealing their prospects for the future. Birdie giggled at Dale's fortune—*Deep thoughts will lead you to great riches*—and the stark contrast to her more cryptic one—*An old life ends and a new world begins.*

Deciding to finish their evening on a pleasant note, they opened a second bottle of merlot and took their personal party to the living room couch to watch one of their Friday night rituals, *Full House*, a tradition started with Charlie. The Tanner family felt like home to them, and they rarely missed the opportunity to see the parenting style of Danny and Uncle Jesse. Another bottle of wine finished, they eventually dozed off in each other's arms. They awoke long enough to make their way to their actual bed.

Loitering in the darkness, Astrid began the final steps of her plan. There would be no goodbyes and no regrets or second thoughts about leaving the beyond. There would be no one to miss that version of her. She began the spell, using the knowledge she collected in over two hundred years. Knowledge she remembered solely from repetition, so as to not forget anything that might ruin these crucial moments.

"This is it," the Dark Magician chimed in her ear. "You will be free! Congratulations."

With no remorse for Birdie, Astrid chanted the final words and took over the woman's life force. She moved past her and briefly felt the pang of Birdie's confusion and sorrow. Laying there in the newly vacated shell, Astrid dreamed of what her life would soon be like.

She was not completely out of the woods yet. She continued her work, conjuring her final human form, and decided that it would be fitting to continue on as Birdie.

Not knowing how much time had passed, she eventually heard a panicked voice followed by cries. There had been none of that in the realm she just left. There had been no one to grieve her, just total, deafening silence. Settling her thoughts as Dale's face came into focus, she took the moment to relish that the first phase of her grand plan was complete.

As Birdie's awareness was torn from her body, she realized she was not prepared to die. She hadn't been able to say her goodbyes. What would her death do to both Dale and Charlie? Just like that, her life subsided and her spirit lifted from her body. *Peculiar feeling*, she thought to herself as she rushed towards a light. As she did, she felt a presence move past her—a familiar presence. Birdie knew it well. *Astrid! Why was Astrid—* But before she could complete the thought, Astrid was gone, and Birdie was alone.

Passing Birdie sent a whirl of excitement through Astrid. This was what she had wanted. It was what she strived for and planned for ever since meeting the Dark Magician. Out of the din, he had picked up on her overwhelming desires to live, love, touch, dance, eat, and laugh. He sensed her overwhelming desire to be human again and showed her how to achieve her goals. She played the game and never questioned his instructions. She obeyed, and this was her reward!

Slowly waking to the sun creeping through the sheers covering the windows, Dale groaned and rolled over towards Birdie. She was turned away from him, curled in a relaxed fetal position. Her crazy curls were strewn over her pillow. He reached over to cuddle with her. Her skin was cold. Why was she so cold? He moved his hand up and down her exposed arm, and concern turned to panic.

Bolting upright, he shouted, "Birdie! Honey! Baby?" as he attempted to roll her onto her back. Not being able to, he took to the air instead and hurdled over her lifeless body. Reaching the side of the bed, he saw her beautiful face and her eyes laid open. Gone was the twinkle of life. Placing his ear to her nose, he felt no breath. He cried, then screamed. Reaching for the phone on the bedside table, he dialed nine-one-one, knowing his Birdie was gone.

Charlie leaned across the couch and hugged her dad. Both ineffectually wiped tears from their eyes. After holding their hug for what seemed like an eternity, they separated and sat still. So many questions lay before them both. Initial preparations would have to be followed up on, of course.

Dale broke the silence again by saying, "The coroner deemed the cause of death to be natural, a possible aneurysm."

He may believe that, Charlie thought, but she felt in her gut otherwise. They would get through it together, but first they needed to sleep.

"I'll handle cleaning up," Charlie said, then hugged her dad goodnight.

CHAPTER SEVEN
PREPARATIONS

Charlie awoke to the smell of coffee and fresh-baked…something. Knowing her dad didn't know the difference between flour and baking soda, she was curious what it actually was. Forgetting for just one moment why she was in her bed in her parents' house to begin with, she stretched her arms above her head and gave a quick mental kiss to the Corey Haim poster across the room. One can never be too old to throw some love at one's former teen heartthrob.

Slipping socks on her bare feet and her hair into a ponytail, she padded to the kitchen. Her dad seemed deep in thought before a pad of paper, pen in hand and glasses perched on the end of his nose. She held off the urge to call him *old man* and poured herself the biggest cup of coffee she could manage. Tucking a carton of milk under her arm, she scooped up a small container of sugar off the counter and sat down across from him.

"Good morning, Pops," she joked.

He peeked over his rims and said, "Mrs. Connor brought us a blueberry muffin basket." He gestured towards the oven, which was set to "warm.

Ah, Charlie thought. *I knew it!* She stood up and asked, "Can I grab you one?"

He nodded.

Swiping two saucers from the upper cabinet, she snatched muffins for each of them, making sure not to scald her fingertips. Placing the goodness on a tray that she grabbed from the top of the fridge, she then retrieved the butter dish for herself and the I Can't Believe It's Not Butter for her dad. One knife and two napkins later, she carried the tray to the table.

Slathering the muffins with an exorbitant amount of butter, she remembered how her mom used a buttercup flower to predict Charlie's butter predilection. Charlie was about four and was out in the yard. Mom called to her and had her sit on the garden wall next to her. She ever so sweetly explained to Charlie how generations of women all over the world could predict whether their children would love butter. As she continued the sentence, she lifted the tiny yellow flower to Charlie's chin and said, "If you love butter, your chin will glow as yellow as this buttercup."

Charlie, not knowing enough to realize the sun and reflection had everything to do with that magic instead of a person's love for butter, repeated the act on her mom, who also shared her love for the creamy goodness. The mysterious witchery failed her when she attempted it on her dad later that night. He did not glow.

Taking a sip of his coffee, Dale read what he had been working on regarding their plan of action. The funeral home had asked for some photos of Birdie, as well as a small statement to post with her obituary. He tasked Charlie with the photos. They took time to discuss flower options, keeping in mind what Birdie would have wanted. The obvious choice of lilacs was out, as they were not in season at the moment. They wrote a list of relatives to notify and a few area hotels to consider as suggestions for those coming from out of town. Dale's parents would stay with them at the house, of course, but they would discourage others, claiming the inn was full.

With their rough plan down on paper, Charlie decided to make the most of the rest of her day. She would take her newly assigned duties on the road for a bit, but first she would satisfy the deep, deep craving in the pit of her soul that only a Nick Tahoe's garbage plate could fill. As a bonus, she would give her friend Ramona a call to help her sort through the photos at the local library.

She explained her plans to her dad, hopped up from the table, gathered the few dishes there were, and placed them in the sink. After ascending the stairs two at a time, she showered and got dressed in her favorite jeans and a gray, wool, cable-knit sweater. That would allow her to go sans coat, since it was a balmy fifty-five degrees.

Once she was ready to head off, she stopped at the door around the corner from her room. It was the access to the attic. Finding the light switch, she gave it a flick and headed up the narrow and steep stairwell before her. At the top, she examined a shelving unit where her mom had placed a few flashlights, knee pads, pairs of gloves, a cobweb remover thingy, and, as a joke, a construction hard hat. This obvious jab was towards Dale's overprotective tendencies. *Funny*, Charlie thought. *All of Dad's protective steps, and he couldn't protect mom at all in the end.*

With a deep sigh, she grabbed a flashlight, turned it on, and gave a quick scan of the attic. As far as attics go, it was pretty organized. The far right corner housed old furniture handed down to her mom from Grandma Dorothy. Plastic and canvas drop cloths covered most of it. The far left corner had a plethora of decorations for various holidays. To the left of that were familiar childhood items of Charlie's: boxes of Barbies and other dolls, the Barbie Dream House—still intact with a working elevator, an old red and yellow

Big Wheel, a rocking horse, and a half dozen or so miscellaneous boxes.

Charlie rounded the corner and found the items she was seeking on the back wall. Lined floor to ceiling with shelves, the wall contained dozens of boxes labeled with a person and suspected years on the outside. Charlie scanned them until she reached the two labeled *Birdie Childhood* and *Birdie 1960-1970*. Pulling the two boxes from their dusty perch, she carried them one at a time to the top of the stairs, then maneuvered each down and carried them to the front door.

She found her dad at his desk, presumably working on the obituary draft. "Hey, Dad," she chirped, "I'm about to head out for a bit. Can I borrow your Jeep?"

Seemingly without thought, he reached into his top right desk drawer, stood up, and said, "I have a better idea. Follow me."

Charlie followed him through the back door, along the walkway, and to the side door of the detached garage. After opening it and pressing the dimly lit button for the main, automatic garage door, Dale gave her a set of keys. She instantly recognized the flower keychain as her mom's.

"Use her all you want, kiddo. This way, we can each run our errands without sacrificing time."

Charlie took the keys from his hands and stepped down to lean her hip on her mom's prized possession, an over-the-top orange Karmann Ghia she had named *Juicy* because it reminded her of an orange. Charlie hugged her dad before they both went back inside to gather the photo boxes.

Once loaded up, she made her way downtown to Nick Tahoe's for her desired garbage plate. Maneuvering around the outside of the historic brick building, she found a parking spot in the rear. She entered the space, which at first glance would make the faint of heart question their choices. However, she knew how amazing Nick's was. She slung her backpack over her right shoulder and went up to the worn Formica counter and placed her order. "I'll have a plate - cheeseburger, white hot, mac salad, home fries, cheese, mustard, ketchup, and meat sauce, please. Oh, and a root beer." Her order complete, she took a seat at one of the tables by the front window, letting the intoxicating aroma of meat and french fries surrounded her.

While waiting for her lunch, she splayed open her backpack to tackle a few school items she needed to go over. As she wrapped up reading a small chapter on rationalism for her Philosophy class, they called her number. After grabbing her plate, some additional toppings, napkins, utensils, and a straw, she settled in and, between bites, mulled through her notes, prepping for the next paper due when she returned.

After satisfying the garbage plate monster in her belly, she gathered up her textbooks and notes, shoved them in her backpack, and headed out to Juicy. Even though she was a convertible, it was still way too chilly in Rochester to even think of going topless. Looking at her watch, Charlie hoped she wouldn't be too late meeting Ramona. Driving down Mt. Hope Avenue and Elmwood to the Brighton Memorial library, she enjoyed the views and thought about how great it was going to be to see her friend, even given the circumstances. It had been months, but they never seemed to miss a beat.

Charlie turned into the library parking lot to find Ramona waiting for her, her dark, wild, curly hair springing from her head like coils. Charlie smiled at her friend. She and Ramona had met one fateful day in kindergarten when they both reached for the burnt sienna crayon and were pretty much inseparable since. Charlie parked two spots down from her and, without even taking time to turn Juicy off, Charlie popped out and ran into her friend's open arms.

Burying her face in Ramona's shoulder, Charlie finally felt she could release her sorrows and wept for what seemed like an eternity as Ramona stroked her hair and consoled her. Stammering, Charlie opened up to her friend "I—I—I'm sorry, Ramona. I haven't been able to f—f—f—feel all the feels because of Dad. Mom being gone, it's like I'm dying inside. I can't breathe sometimes, you know? I feel like I can't breathe." Releasing one final, hitched breath, Charlie stood back, wiped the snot from her nose on the back of her sleeve, and said a bashful, "Thank you."

Ramona nodded. "You're welcome."

"Now, let me take a look at you," Charlie said.

Ramona took a step back and did a slow twirl. Standing a head shorter than Charlie, Ramona was also slimly built, but unlike Charlie, she had the most beautiful olive skin and an adorable pattern of freckles that speckled her apple-shaped cheeks.

"You look mahvelous," Charlie said in her best Billy Crystal impression.

"Why, thank you," Ramona replied with a tiny curtsey. Laughing way too hard at herself, Ramona sobered up the banter just long enough to give her friend the *it's okay to be sad* speech. With the mood elevated just past complete and utter sorrow, Ramona helped

Charlie unload and carry the boxes of photos. The pair entered the library and found a large table tucked away in the corner to work on.

As they opened the first box marked *Birdie Childhood*, Ramona took the opportunity to nose into any details about what had happened. Digging through the top layer, Charlie explained the scenario to her friend.

Dale quietly sat at his desk and stared at the few words he had managed to put on paper. "Well, that only took two hours," he mumbled. Frustrated, he dropped his pen and decided he needed to get out for a few. Maybe some food and fresh air would help. He could even stop at the local florist to help narrow down the floral arrangements. It would kill Birdie all over again if they allowed the standard bouquet of white lilies at her funeral. Grabbing his keys and a coat, he headed out the door.

Timing is everything and the only thing. The two gentlemen poking and prodding Birdie's body were testing Astrid's patience. As they talked and talked about the cause of death, prepping the body for interment, and what they were going to have for lunch, she seethed. She needed the body for her final transformation. The spell given to her required her to be near the form she would replicate, and Astrid knew that with it tucked away until its internment, she could finally start the second phase of her plan.

With an incantation acquired from the Black Magician's teachings, Astrid would manifest her soul into its new form. Finally, the two men relinquished their post and exited the area. It was her time. Closing her eyes, she called upon the Dark Magician's powers and recited the incantation. A bright light enveloped the corpse, and Astrid was suddenly standing in the corner of the mortuary, using the wall to steady herself.

Looking down at her newly acquired form, she reveled in her success and almost immediately thought to herself that this new body would take some getting used to. Noting her nudity, she found a pile of discarded clothing in a bin on the far side of the room. After dressing herself, she would need to find a spot to rest, then she would head to collect the items she had squirreled away in preparation for her triumphant transformation.

Charlie and Ramona emptied the first box and started about twenty piles based on estimated time frames, thanks to hints written on the backs of the photos. They giggled at the clothes in the photos.

"Imagine all the layers under that dress," Ramona said as she pointed to Charlie's grandmother Dorothy wearing a traditional fifties housewife-style dress—complete with stockings, heels, and pearls—bible firmly clutched in the crook of her arm. Since the photos in the pile were black and white, they could only guess as to the colors. That one, they determined, was either a pastel yellow or peach.

Charlie had no memories at all of her Grandpa Joseph, as he passed way before she was even a spec in the universe, but she had some memories of Grandma Dorothy, both her own and those imparted by her mother. Dorothy always had a bible of some shape or form on her. She had a round face with helmet hair that she kept up with weekly visits to the salon to have it set. She spoke with the thickest, most syrupy sweet southern accent, making it almost near impossible to understand her as she got older and lazier with her speech. Charlie learned very young that "bless your heart" was not a phrase you wanted to hear if she was referring to you.

Grandma Dorothy couldn't have been more opposite of Birdie if she tried. She always insisted on saying grace before they ate anything and lectured Charlie's mom and dad for not attending church services on the regular, making sure to let them know Charlie was doomed from infancy as she was not received in the light of the Lord. From what Charlie remembered from her mom's descriptions, Dorothy was just as strict, if not more, than Joseph.

He evidently was the physical enforcer of order in the household and adhered to roles the Church set forth, but Dorothy was the mental enforcer. She scolded Birdie if she were to do anything inappropriate, anything that would hinder her chances with prospective husbands, and most of all, anything that might tarnish her soul in the eyes of God and the church. Things like television, music, books, and social activities that were not religion based were strictly forbidden and banned from making their way into their household. Of course, Birdie being Birdie, she would find ways to skirt around these restrictions. Knowing her mom like she did, Charlie could imagine the battles that would have ensued during those ripe teen years.

Mindlessly stacking photos into the piles, Charlie drifted off in thought. *What could possibly have happened to make Mom just fade away in her sleep like she did? The coroner's guess of aneurysm could be right, but that just didn't make sense or feel right.*

With a sudden "Ahem!" from Ramona, Charlie was snapped back to reality. "Charlie, did you even hear a word I was saying?"

Charlie instinctively shook her head from side to side and said, "Um… No, I'm sorry. You were saying?"

Ramona took a breath. "I was just letting you know that you were mixing up the photos."

Charlie looked down and, sure enough, she had. Realizing she also had not thought ahead as to how to keep the photos sorted, she placed her head in her hands and said, "Fuck!" An all too quick shushing resonated from the librarian's central station. With a tiny flush of embarrassment, Charlie explained to Ramona her error.

Ever the optimist, Ramon replied, "Totally fixable, Charlie girl! You got any paper?"

Relief filled Charlie's brain. "Yes!" A stern shushing followed, so in a quieter tone, she continued, "Yeah, I have my backpack in the car. I'll run and grab it. Be right back."

The rest had done Astrid some good. She explored her surroundings as she prepared to begin the next part of her plan. After several breaks in her travels, she had found park benches and landscaping walls were her friends. She had not anticipated the large energy draw simply walking would consume. She had been told that her strength and stamina would continue to build with every day she remained human. Until then, she would have to be mindful of the levels and plan accordingly.

Finally arriving at her destination, she walked along the darkest side of the structure and found a potted bush next to the rear entry door. Reaching her hand between the pot and the soil, she felt the key she had hidden some months ago. As part of her teachings with the Dark Magician, she had learned that once she transformed, she could no longer manifest ethereally. She could continue to scout and communicate telepathically, but her movements would be limited just as a human's would be. Entering the home, she glided through the halls, following the path from her many visits, and made her way up the attic stairs to find the bag she had stowed away.

Peering into the suitcase, she took inventory. A small amount of cash, Birdie's license, and clothing she had taken from the daughter, Charlie. "No offense, Birdie, your body will do, but your daughter's fashion style is more up my alley."

Knowing she would need all the cash she had set aside to get out west, Astrid exited the attic with the suitcase and made her way throughout the second floor to gather the other items she had stashed around the house. Reaching the doorway to the master bedroom, she realized that her energy levels were depleting quicker than she had anticipated. As she made her way down the stairs to the foyer, she heard the rumble of a vehicle approaching and scurried down the hall to the rear of the house, carelessly knocking over a blue vase in the process.

Arriving back at home, Dale shed his coat and shoes, dropped his keys into the dish in the foyer, and proceeded down the hall towards the kitchen. Within three steps, he stumbled and winced as a sharp pain shot through his foot. Immediately backing up to rest on the hallway wall, he looked down to see Birdie's favorite blue vase shattered to pieces all over the floor.

Lifting his foot up to assess the damage, he found a sliver of blue glass protruding from it, blood having already turned his white sock crimson around the wound. He yanked the shard, successfully removing it from his foot, then hobbled over to the kitchen sink to wet a towel with hot water. Taking a seat at the kitchen table, he removed his sock, wiped off the blood, and inspected the opening further for any splinters of glass that may have been left behind, but found none. The bleeding had stopped, and the small opening would not require any bandages.

Placing his sock back on temporarily he opened the pantry door and grabbed a broom and dustpan. As he swept up the glass from the hall, he couldn't help but wonder how that happened. The vase had been intact when he left; he knew it. Maybe Charlie had come home and gone back out, knocking into it and not noticing? No, that would not only be improbable but most certainly impossible.

After dumping the glass into the garage trash can, Dale returned to the kitchen and poured himself a glass of apple juice. He decided to wait for Charlie to get home before making any dinner decisions. Dale shuffled to his office, turned on his stereo, and placed a Creedence album on the turntable. He then grabbed his glasses, a pen, and some paper from the desk and sank down onto the couch. He jotted down the few options he had noted at the florist, then turned his brain back to the task of writing the obituary.

Charlie and Ramona had successfully sorted all the photos into groups which they wrapped in sheets of paper torn from Charlie's notebook, creating makeshift envelopes. Each was labeled and placed neatly in their respective boxes. Ramona stood and stretched her arms above her head, then from side to side. "Well then," she said, "wanna get these back to Juicy and take a walk around the corner for a Slurpee?"

Nodding almost too eagerly, Charlie said, "Heck yeah," in a tone acceptable to the librarian, therefore avoiding the dreaded shush.

The pair sat at a bench under a tree, and after taking the last sip of cherry goodness from her cup, Charlie said, "Well, Ramona, I have to head home and help Dad with the rest of our list. We have a lot to get through in the next twenty-four hours. Thank you so much for your help today."

"Of course," Ramona said. "What are friends for, if not this?"

They squeezed a few hugs and made plans to have a sleepover before Charlie headed back to school. Pizza, chips, candy, and a horror movie marathon were immediately put on the agenda.

Sliding in behind the wheel, Charlie turned the key in the ignition, switched the radio channel to her favorite pop station, and headed towards home. As she drove, she began thinking about her mom. As she passed by Wegman's, she slammed on her brakes. To her right was a woman carrying a suitcase walking towards the 7-11.

She looked just like her mom. She would bet her life on it. Aside from the wardrobe, she could have been Birdie's twin.

Charlie proceeded forward, fighting the urge to turn around and confront the woman. She had heard that everyone has a twin, a doppelganger, but she had never truly believed it. Continuing her journey home, she couldn't shake the eerie feeling she had on the back of her neck. Turning the corner into her neighborhood, she finally convinced herself that it was just her mind playing tricks on her. A manifestation brought on by deep grief.

Astrid quickly realized how tired the physical form could get and decided to secure a room at a local motel. Using Birdie Bauman's identification, she paid with cash and took the key to the room labeled as 11. Inserting the key into the slot on the door, she entered and spread out her items to check one final time before her journey to meet the others. It was then she noticed that in her rush to leave, after knocking the vase over, she had forgotten a crucial piece: the envelopes containing the extra cash she had Birdie hide over the years. She would have to go back to retrieve them. But when? With so many more family members sure to descend on the home, she couldn't risk being seen. As she laid on the pitiful, flowered spread, her last thought before dozing off was, *It will be during the funeral.*

CHAPTER EIGHT
A GIRL AND HER DAD

As Charlie and Juicy cruised up the street towards home, she contemplated if and how she would bring the strange sighting up to her dad. She pulled up the driveway just outside the back door and put Juicy in neutral, engaged the parking brake, and got out. Opening the mudroom door, she bellowed for her dad.

Dale came around the corner from his office and greeted Charlie. She gestured to the car and asked, "Can you help out a meek, fair maiden by bringing in some boxes?"

He chuckled and said, "There is nothing meek about you, Charlie."

Each carrying a box, they headed to the sunroom, which had a table that offered the most usable workspace. Charlie let her dad know she had sorted through all the photos with Ramona, and they had categorized them into groups. They would just need his eye to make the final decisions.

Dale nodded and asked, "Can I hijack the conversation for a moment to discuss something very important?"

Charlie gulped, and even though her mind went to dark places wondering what he was going to say, she squeaked out, "Sure."

"Hawaiian or meat lovers?" he asked, using his hands to mime holding pizzas on a tray.

She let out a huge sigh and giggled. She was a Hawaiian girl, through and through, and it was so silly to even ask. Pineapple and ham, who would ever eat anything else?

Dad headed to the phone in the kitchen to order the pizzas. After he set the phone back in its cradle, they agreed to take a break, go change, refresh, and gather the tools needed to tackle the mission at hand.

Charlie jogged up to her room to change into some sweats and a pullover. Moving towards the dresser, she noticed something odd. From the second drawer, she saw a sock dangling like a wet noodle. Then, on the floor, laid another random sock. She was certain they were not like that when she left this morning. Tucking the items back into the drawer, she shimmied out of her clothes, went into her bathroom, splashed water on her face, and threw the hair back into a ponytail.

Joining her dad in the kitchen, Charlie filled up a glass with ice and grabbed a can of Coke for herself and a can of Welches grape soda for him from the fridge. She teased him over his love for all things grape, reminding him they could still attend the grape festival together in the fall.

Since the pizza was still about twenty minutes away, she went back to the sunroom and laid the bundles of wrapped pictures out on the table. The table was getting more use than it had in decades. While she worked, she noticed her dad's draft of the obituary. *I'll never get used to this*, she thought. She also knew that once they no longer had tasks to keep their minds busy, they both would have the appropriate breakdowns neither had seemed to experience yet. At least, she hadn't, and she doubted her dad would admit it if he had.

Charlie watched her dad move about the kitchen, worried about him. Her mom had literally been the caretaker. It was obvious at that moment she may have to go as far as checklists or a book of where things are to help him until he got his bearings.

With that thought, the doorbell chimed. Dale answered and paid the pimply faced teen. While he took the pizzas, Charlie grabbed the plates and napkins he had spent ten minutes trying to find before the doorbell rang. She confirmed a list of where items were located would definitely be needed.

While they devoured their dinner, Charlie filled her dad in on Ramona's current life adventures and some of the interesting finds from the photo boxes. Dale returned the favor with a breakdown of his trip to the florist. Since lilacs were out of the question, they agreed to do a mix of pink, orange, and yellow gerbera daisies with a healthy smattering of mixed dahlias. Dale then read the obituary he had worked on to Charlie.

Birdie Bauman, forty-two years old, passed away in the early hours of March 18th. Birdie was the only child of Joseph and Dorothy Doucette. She was a 1962 graduate of Effingham County High School and attended the Savannah College of Art and Design briefly before meeting her future husband, Dale, in 1965.

As a mother, she was generous, loving, and kind. In her free time, Birdie loved designing, gardening, and spending time with her family as often as possible. She believed it was very important to stay active in both mind and body. Birdie truly lived life to the fullest through simple pleasures like chatting with friends and family, snacking, and spending time with her art in her garden. Birdie had an uncanny ability to reach people in a deep and positive way. She will be greatly missed by her family, who adore her with all their hearts. She is survived by her husband, Dale, her daughter, Charlie, and a large and loving community in Brighton.

Family, friends, and others whose lives Birdie touched are invited to join the family at Lilac Memorial Gardens on Thursday, March 23rd at 11:00 a.m. to support each other. A celebration of life to follow at the Bauman residence. Please wear bright colors, as requested by Birdie's family, in honor of her colorful spirit.

After a long hug and a much-needed cry, they moved on to the photos. After choosing their respective favorites from the paper envelopes, they moved about the house to grab a few of the more recent photos of Birdie. Charlie suggested they could send a few for larger prints, but that she would like to take them and a few others to Fotomat and have them converted into slides. That way, they could have them playing before and after the ceremony. Dad agreed, and they formed a new pile.

With a collective sigh, they briefly discussed the last items they needed to work through before the service. Birdie's wardrobe and music choices, Charlie would handle. Dale would follow up on any paperwork for the insurance companies and the funeral home. They both would write their own eulogies.

Cleaning up, they decided to end their night with a tradition from when Charlie was a teen. Ice cream sundaes and *The Goonies*. Charlie dug through the VHS tape collection while her dad scooped the Neapolitan ice cream into sundae dishes. After inserting the movie in the VCR, Charlie joined her dad at the kitchen island to finish building her concoction. She added chocolate syrup; chopped nuts; chopped cherries; more nuts; and chocolate syrup. Then an obscenely large cloud of whipped topping and a healthy dose of Reese's Pieces, one of her favorites since the *ET* craze from her youth.

Her dad, who opted for the more traditional nonpareils as his final topping, held up his sundae glass and toasted Charlie. "To getting through this together, kiddo."

They took their masterpieces to the living room, and before plopping on the couch, Charlie hit play on the VCR. As the Fratelli chase unfolded, they both shoveled in a spoonful of goodness and laughed. For the next two hours, they each recited their favorite lines, reenacted the truffle shuffle, and played sporadic games of "remember that time".

With a sugar coma in full gear, Charlie said goodnight and got up to put the kibosh on the closing credits, pushing the eject button on the VCR. Dale simultaneously clicked the remote to give the television its rest for the night.

Before heading up, Charlie grabbed the envelopes she would take to the Fotomat in the morning. As she did, she made an unwritten plan to go back to the location on Monroe where she saw her mom's doppelganger. Once upstairs, she entered her bedroom, scrunching her toes in the plush shag rug then placed the envelopes on top of her dresser. She then meandered into her bathroom and filled the tub for a hot bath, adding a few drops of lilac oil and Mr. Bubbles for relaxation.

She stripped down and threw her clothes through the bathroom door into a pile. Looping her arm out of the bathroom door, she snatched her Walkman from the top of her dresser, knocking the papers on the floor and scattering the photos. "Shit," she exclaimed with an exasperated motion. "I'll get it later." Placing the headphones over her ears, she slid into the tub of bubbles. Once submerged, she clicked open the Walkman to see which cassette she would have the pleasure of listening to. The marker informed her it would be an episode of Kasey Kasem's Top 40 she had recorded when she was younger. She set the Walkman on a small table next to the tub and closed her eyes. As Kasey introduced Olivia Newton John's "Physical", holding onto its number fifteen spot, Charlie slid deeper into the bubbles.

Laying in her motel room, Astrid's projected consciousness watched the daughter, and she felt a pang of melancholia. She remembered missing her mother upon her death, as well. Only a few choice memories survived the centuries, and that was one of them. So far, being human again was not at all what she had imagined it would be. Bored, she knew that until she was at strength again, she was confined to those four walls, and that meant passing the time the only way she knew how. Leaving Charlie to her bath, Astrid decided she would head out to nourish the body with food, something she was not used to having to do, then rest. Then, she could contemplate heading back out to the home to gather the rest of her belongings.

CHAPTER NINE
DISCOVERIES

As side one of the cassette came to an end, the sudden click of the play button startled Charlie awake. She sat up, confused as to where she was for a moment. As she did, a chill ran over her. It could have been due to the temperature difference between the air and the water, but the chill went deeper and seemed more ominous. Deciding to stay in a bit longer to warm up, Charlie released the drain plug with her toe and then, with her feet, twisted the faucet to the on position and maneuvered the black triangle to the red dot that indicated hot.

After a third of the water emptied, she closed the drain with a push of her heel. She reveled in the super-hot water which enveloped her yet again. After flipping the tape, she set both the Walkman and headphones back on the table. She completely lowered herself into the tub, the woosh of the water from the faucet and the swirl of her hair as it flowed weightlessly around her head bringing her immediate comfort. Catapulting herself back up above the waterline, she turned off the faucet and placed the headphones back on her head, making sure to complete a head tilt to either side, ensuring no water was lingering in her ears. She tapped and hummed along to Huey Lewis and The News, then finally decided it was time to exit when she noticed how pruned her fingers were getting. Releasing the drain, she stood up and wrapped her hair in a twist with a towel, dried off with a second one, and puttered to her room.

Opening her top drawer, she grabbed her purple undies and tossed them on the bed. She then moved to the drawer below it, which housed her cozy sweats and shirts. Digging around, she furtively looked for her favorite sleep shirt. *Curious*, she thought, *it's not here*. She knew she hadn't worn it since returning home. Choosing her Cornell shirt instead and a pair of pajama shorts she had fashioned from an old pair of sweats, she plopped on her bed to get dressed.

Releasing her hair from the twisted towel, she gave it a quick tousle and re-wrapped it into a tall pile on her head, tucking the end in for security. Not feeling very adult at the moment, she tossed the second towel so it landed next to her previously discarded pile of clothes. She then gave a quick scan of her room. Her backpack, which housed a few reading assignments she knew she had to complete soon, sat on her desk chair. Papers and photos were scattered from when she grabbed her Walkman. She sighed and looked over to the window seat.

Light from a full moon seeped in from below the window valence. She followed its beam down to the seat itself. To carry on the theme of no adulting that night, she decided to play hooky from her reading assignments. Instead, she stood and sauntered over to the window seat.

Sliding her boombox and collection of stuffed animals and pillows over, she reached for the L-shaped latch, which served as a lock for the hinged top. She lifted the top up and slid a book into the corner to keep it propped open. Peering down into the large well of storage space, she found several of her favorite board games: Clue, Battleship, Operation, and Life. Next to those were five stacks of Teen Beat, Bop and 16 magazines, most of which were no longer fully intact due to the large collages she used to make with the faces of Simon Lebon, Corey Haim, Rob Lowe, and Madonna. A few other miscellaneous items, including Mr. Honey Bunny and her baby blanket, which was more of a ribbon by then, snuggled up to the magazines.

What she was after lay in front of her: Decorative boxes stacked in sets of four which housed what she knew to be the years and years of journaling her mom had done. She slid her bean bag from the corner, sat, and lifted each box out of its holding place, stacking them to each side of her, keeping room in front of her for workspace. Some of the boxes had little slips of paper taped to them with date ranges, others did not. She organized them as best she could, deciding to start with the unlabeled boxes which she assumed to be from her mom's childhood. Opening the first box, she found journals of various sizes and colors stacked neatly on top of each other, secured with a ribbon.

She pulled the end of the ribbon to release the bow, plucked a journal off the top, and opened the leather cover to expose her mother's handwriting. Mom had the most unique and, for lack of a better term, historically dainty style of writing. Even in her childhood pen, this was true. Charlie flipped through the pages, revealing hundreds of entries varying in length. They all started with a day, date, and year.

As she skimmed the contents of the box, she deduced it was from Birdie's high school years. Wanting to go in chronological order, she started a pile to her right and continued to do the same for the other undated boxes, organizing from Birdie's childhood to the more recent.

Needing some auditory distraction to keep her heart from beating in her ears, Charlie pushed the tiny power button on her boombox and the red indicator light glowed, letting her know it had power. She rolled the tuner until it stopped on 88.5 WRUR,

Rochester's local college station. The eerie voice of Suzie from Suzie and the Banshees sauntered through the speakers.

Charlie leaned back in her beanbag with the first journal in the lifelong series. The handwriting was that of a child and told a tale of innocence. Birdie described her friend Astrid, who would stop by to talk to her or play games of hide and seek and hopscotch. From the writings, Astrid was just as mischievous as Birdie, if not more at times. Birdie described her in a variety of ways, sometimes as a small girl her own age, with dark, curly hair and blue eyes. Sometimes she described an older child with red hair and green eyes. One particular story in that journal stood out to Charlie.

Astrid just left. She made Mother mad at me. She looked so pretty. Her dress was frilly and white like the one I wore to church today. The one that is ruined. I tried to tell Mother that it wasn't my fault. That my friend Astrid and I were playing with my dollies in the churchyard when Tommy Spangle started to tease me, calling me a retard for talking to myself. I told Tommy that I wasn't talking to myself, that my friend Astrid was right there! Tommy called me a "liar, liar, pants on fire," and before I could say anything back, Astrid shoved him into a puddle, splashing mud all over my dress. I don't like that Mother doesn't believe me. I hate being punished.

As Charlie read, she could sense the frustration in this child version of her mom. Evidently, Grandma did not approve. There were dozens of instances where Astrid would do things, and Birdie would incur the brunt of the blame. Documented also were instances of corporal punishment, used to deter those outbursts of "heathen" behavior. Even though an obviously young child, Birdie had a way of conveying the little world she lived in. Charlie sensed the confusion her mom was experiencing by the blatant anger she had towards her friend. Then, some days, it would just say, "Astrid didn't visit today. I'm sad."

Charlie dropped the last journal to the floor and let out a roar of a yawn. Her dad's grandfather clock, in his office, chimed four times. "Shit, fuck, damn! It can't be four am," she exclaimed. She looked over at the fuzzy digital clock on her nightstand and, sure enough, four had snuck up on her. Leaving the journals as they lay, she climbed into bed and switched off the lamp on the nightstand. She laid her head on her pillow, and before she knew it, she was asleep.

Charlie woke to her dad knocking on her door. "Hey sleepy head. You sleeping the day away?"

Charlie sat up and looked over at her clock. To her dismay and surprise, she saw it was ten thirty. "Uh, no," she replied, then threw back the covers, slid out of bed, and shuffled groggily to the door. She gave the knob a swift turn and tug. Her dad stood in the hall with a cup of tea in one hand and her Oscar The Grouch mug full of coffee in the other.

He made his way past Charlie and took a seat at her desk after offering up her beverage. Giving a quick thank you, Charlie climbed back onto her bed, twisted her legs over each other, and pulled her fuzzy blanket up around her shoulders. She took a long sip of the coffee, letting the warmth and delectable flavor sit in her mouth for a second or two. Swallowing, she choked off a hitch in her throat as she thought about her mom.

Her dad must have noticed the tears welling up in her eyes. "Penny for your thoughts, kiddo."

She sighed and stared down at the coffee in her hands. "Dad, it's all sinking in. We've been so busy, I haven't really let any of it sink in, but just now, here, drinking coffee, I could feel her. I miss her so much, Dad." With that admission, it was like the flood of emotions she had been holding back burst through a levy, and Charlie wept.

Dale stood up, set his tea on the desk, and walked over to join her. He sat on the bed next to her and enveloped her with his arms. She buried her face into the small of his shoulder. "Let it out," he said.

After several minutes, Charlie sat up and used her blanket as a makeshift tissue and wiped her face and eyes. Then, with one final inhale and release, she said, "Thank you, Dad. That really helped".

He smiled at her, a glisten in his eyes betraying that he was fighting back tears, although he'd never admit it. Instead, he patted her hand and said, "Let's get today in motion."

She nodded, and they reviewed the plan of action. Charlie would pick out Mom's outfit and drop it off at Lilac Memorial Gardens, then go to the Fotomat and get them working on the slideshow. Dale would call in the flower order and finalize everything with the obituary, then work on the house and guest room for his parents and get the incoming family members situated. The few traveling in would be arriving at hotels throughout the day, with his parents coming to the house around dinnertime.

With their marching orders finalized, Dale gathered the two mugs and made his way downstairs. Charlie sat a moment longer, slapped her knees, and said, "Let's do this." She got up and threw on jeans and a sweater, then ran her fingers through her hair, deciding to keep it free from the confinements of a hat or ponytail. She slipped on her Keds, dabbed some Bonne Bell strawberry on her lips, and slung her backpack over her shoulder.

She headed down the hall to her mom's closet. Dropping the backpack outside the closet door, Charlie entered the small space that held her mother's wardrobe. Her mom's personality presented itself in the contents. Each piece was unique, eclectic, and colorful. *Just like Mom is,* Charlie thought, then caught herself. *Was.*

She exhaled and started on the left, working her way around to the right. As she slid each hanger to expose the next article of clothing, she smiled at the memories some of the garments held. Piece after piece, she pulled out the viable options and placed them on a stool at the back of the closet. Noting she was halfway through the first wall, she slid a dress over and noticed something odd. Taped to the wall, midway up, was an envelope.

Being careful not to take the paint with the tape, Charlie separated the envelope from the wall. *Curious,* she thought. She slid it in her pocket and continued down the line of clothing, determined to complete the task at hand.

Once she had what she considered to be a good selection picked out, she took a moment and laid the items systematically on her parents' bed. Standing back to eye her choices, she snickered, imagining that she must look like Sloane and Ferris Bueller in the gallery scene, hands on their chins in deep philosophical thought, attempting to figure out what the artist meant by his inclusion of some vague brushstroke. With one final circle and a "Tada"," she decided on a floor-length skirt with a bright floral pattern of purples, blues, and accents of orange. The top she chose to accompany it was a shade of robin's egg blue that would complement her mom's complexion. As that thought ran through her mind, the fact that her mom's natural complexion was lost to a deathly pallor which would be replaced by thick cake makeup applied by the mortuary cosmetologist struck her.

Shaking her head, she returned to her task and picked up the silver and bronze skirts, returning them to their place in the closet.

She then scanned the floor for a pair of matching slip-on shoes. She wasn't sure they would be needed, but better to be prepared. Adding those to the bed, she then walked over to her mom's vanity table. Taking a seat on the matching, tufted bench, she opened the lid to her mom's mahogany jewelry box.

Although not a huge or habitual jewelry person, Birdie held onto a few family pieces handed down to her from her mother: A pearl necklace, a few rings, a broach, and a pair of screw-back earrings that had totally befuddled Charlie when she was younger. She remembered how her mom attempted to explain the reasoning behind screw backs and why they were a thing versus the more modern pierced post style. Religion was such an odd control factor in so many people's lives.

After laying her choices next to the outfit she had picked, Charlie made her way down to her mom's studio and gathered two sheets of tissue paper and a bag to transport the items to the funeral home. She went to the makeshift desk to jot a note to remind them to return the jewelry after the service. Charlie tore the sheet from the pad and carried the tissue paper, bag, and note to the master bedroom. Folding the paper, she carefully wrapped the jewelry, then placed it along with the clothing and shoes, laying the note on top. After giving the room a cursory look, she gathered the bag and her backpack and made her way to the garage.

She opened the garage bay door and slid into Juicy's driver's seat, then placed her foot on the clutch and turned the key. After releasing the brake, she placed the vehicle into reverse. She pressed down on the gas pedal, but released the clutch too soon, and Juicy gave a hop and shudder before going dead. Charlie palmed her forehead in frustration. She forgot how finicky the clutch and gears could be, as she had dozens of memories of her mom shifting and grinding her way from second to third.

She pushed in the clutch again, making sure the gearshift was wiggling free in neutral, and gave the key a turn. She slid the shifter back into reverse and was mindful to balance the release of the clutch with a gradual application of the gas pedal. As the car rolled down the driveway, she patted the steering wheel and said, "Good girl." Once at the bottom of the driveway, she made the same mindful maneuvers to put the car into first gear. Now she was cooking with gas. Flicking the radio on, she made her way down her street singing the oh so appropriate lyrics of DJ Jazzy Jeff and Fresh Prince.

Dale finished up the phone call securing the flowers and proceeded to the kitchen. As he wiped the surfaces and scrubbed the few dishes he and Charlie managed to dirty up, he had a fleeting, happy thought about them having a home-cooked meal for a change. His mom had referred to a few of her infamous casseroles. Giving the counters a final wipe down, he made his way up to the second floor. After retrieving the vacuum out of the hall closet, he steered it towards the guest bedroom. He unwound the thick, gray cord from its tightly wound state and plugged it in, then switched the vacuum on with the foot pedal. He maneuvered the Kirby Classic, more lovingly known in the Bauman household as The Beast, in neat rows across the carpet. Birdie used to complain about The Beast constantly. Dale had promised her a lighter Hoover, and cringed at the thought that he could never keep that promise.

After steering The Beast to the corner, he tapped the pedal to stop the whir of the motor. Walking to the bed, he removed the decorative comforter from it, exposing its bare mattress. Removing a set of sheets from the armoire, he began to make the bed. Finishing up with a karate chop to each of the pillows, he laid the comforter back into place, gave a quick look around the room, and packed up The Beast.

Charlie made her turn onto Elm, then an immediate left through the entrance gates into Lilac Memorial Gardens' parking lot. She grabbed her delivery from the seat beside her and headed toward the building's entrance. As she approached, a man clad in blue-gray coveralls stopped raking the flower bed long enough to open and hold the door for her. Their eyes met, and she thanked him.

The lobby was clad in an overwhelming amount of mahogany wood paneling decorated with brass trim. The bulk of the room was filled with a dozen or so model caskets, ranging from traditional oak to a spaceship-silver bullet. The entire space smelled of a combination of old wood and chemicals. "Yep this is exactly how I pictured it would be," Charlie muttered. A reception desk was centered on the far wall. As Charlie sauntered across the cold, beige marble floor, she was greeted by a woman who was obviously hand-picked for her job.

Small in stature and pear-shaped, she had a beehive hairdo and very bold, striking choices in makeup that contrasted starkly against her gray wool suit dress. Her voice, almost too soft, reminded Charlie of the psychic in the movie *Poltergeist*.

Before Charlie could explain who she was and why she was there, the tiny woman before her said, "You must be Charlie, Birdie's daughter. We were expecting you."

Charlie nodded, shaking off a chill, and maneuvered over to a table that was to the right of the receptionist's desk. Noticing the woman's name tag, she placed the bag on the edge, filled Cora in on its contents, and reviewed the note regarding the jewelry.

Cora nodded in acknowledgement and let Charlie know they had just confirmed the floral arrangement delivery that her father had placed. "Unusual choice, if I do say so."

Charlie quipped back with, "My mom was an unusual woman."

Cora gave her condolences, which seemed like more of a line in a script than anything heartfelt.

Charlie made her way to the parking lot, and as she hit the fresh air, she took a huge gulp to clear the acridity from her nose and lungs. The groundskeeper noticed and said, "You never get used to the smell."

"I can only imagine," she retorted, said her goodbye, and headed to her car.

As she sat, letting Juicy idle, Charlie weighed the idea of going back to the area where she saw her mother's lookalike. She decided instead to head to Wegmans in Pittsford since they had a Fotomat in the lot between them and their partnering hardware store Chase Pitkins.

Pulling up to the shack, Charlie sang a line from "Love Shack" by the B52s and stifled a giggle just as the photo tech slid the glass panel open and greeted her. Handing over the packet of photos, she explained what they needed and the timeframe. The young man handed her a claim ticket and confirmed her pickup for the next day between ten am and one pm.

As she pulled away from the shack, her stomach gave a rude reminder that she had skipped breakfast. "Okay, okay. I hear ya," she said as she patted her tummy. Deciding on a slice or two of Wegmans' sinfully delicious pizza, Charlie parked Juicy and meandered inside, making a beeline for the pizzeria located in the cafe section of the store. Taking her bounty to a table, she sat and decided to work on a few school items that she had been neglecting.

Dale got confirmation of his parent's arrival time from his mom via a phone call prior to their leaving the hotel in Ohio. Even though he could make the trip in one day, his parents, in their golden years, decided to split the journey into two due to his dad's sciatica. It had been six months since he visited them last, and he regretted that this particular visit was under such sad circumstances.

Having little else to occupy her time while she recharged, Astrid decided to eavesdrop in on Dale. Projecting her mind into the kitchen, she found him on the telephone. The telephone amazed her—most inventions did, actually. Centuries of them. Some were useful while others were a total detriment to society as far as she was concerned.

She shook off thoughts of the damage caused by societal progress and set her attention on Dale. He was a basic, yet handsome man—nothing flashy, but no slouch, either. He was talking to someone, who Astrid quickly realized was his father. They were discussing their upcoming visit to witness the burial of Birdie.

Astrid listened to the small talk, then focused harder and honed in on Dale's emotions. His voice betrayed his guilt over not visiting his parents more. She remembered the last time he had done so. The daughter was in college, so that left Birdie alone. Astrid had a lot of time to practice her movements and put things into place for her transformation then.

Oh Dale, she thought *Little do you know your time away allowed this to move forward exponentially.* The time practicing, Astrid had no doubt, was what sped up Birdie's decline in health. Just as manifestation drained Astrid's energy, the Master taught her it also had adverse effects on the human they choose to interact with. One helpful, good deed is but a spec or blip. However, as each interaction happens, it takes life force away from its host. Without time to replenish, it can cause irrevocable damage. *If you had gotten Birdie to the doctor, you would have found clues,* Astrid thought.

Taking the last notes on her philosophy reading assignment, Charlie shuttled her trash to the bin on the far side of the cafe. As she packed up her texts, she decided to take a peek at the area where she saw the woman walking the day before. As she headed to her car, she took in the sun, thankful that Spring seemed to finally be coming into its own.

Once in motion, she cruised down Monroe Avenue and ran the event over and over in her mind. When she saw her destination ahead on the right, she pulled into the closest parking lot, gave a quick glance around to make sure the doppelganger wasn't around, and stepped out to start her investigation. *I mean, really, what am I even looking for?* she thought. She admitted she was on a mission to settle her brain more than anything else.

Walking along the path where she saw the woman yesterday, she swept the ground—again, for what, she had no clue. After making an almost complete circle around the block with nothing to show for it, Charlie let out a sigh. Content with not finding proof of her vision, she vowed to put it out of her mind.

Astrid sensed something was off. She looked over her shoulder as the daughter walked up the street, then dodged around the corner. *That was close*, she thought. She had to be more careful. She found an alternate way to her motel, completely avoiding Charlie.

CHAPTER TEN
THE GRANDPARENTS

Charlie arrived back home just in time to see her grandparents' Grand Marquis ascend the driveway. She loved her grandparents, and not only because they were her only living pair. They were the epitome of the grandparent moniker. Eleanor was all of five foot one and pear-shaped, with a round face and snow white hair. Walter, her exact opposite, was six-foot something, square jawed, and soft bellied with silver streaks in his hair. They shared the wrinkles of time.

With Dale's Jeep and their land-yacht blocking the garage entry, Charlie completed a round in the cul-de-sac and parked in front of the house, making sure not to block the mailbox.

She got out and scurried up the driveway to greet everyone. As Grandma set a casserole on the roof of the car, Grandpa pulled a suitcase from the trunk and set it to the ground. "Come give me a hug, Charlie Bear." He scooped her into his arms for one of his signature bear hugs and a quick peck on the cheek. Grandma was next in line to hug her as the garage door rose and Dale ducked under it.

"Hey, Mom, Pop," he said. He extended his hand to his father, and they exchanged a firm handshake, then Grandpa pulled Dad for a hug of his own, whispering into his ear. Charlie flashed them a curious look as they met eyes and nodded. "Okay," Dale exclaimed. Then, he turned to to open trunk of the car and asked, "What have we got here?"

As Grandpa went through the list of items to collect, Dad gave his mom a hug and kiss. "My baby, I am so sorry," she said in her soft voice. Dale held on for a moment longer, pulled away, and grabbed the casserole off the roof.

Eleanor pulled out two more large casserole dishes, one which she added to her son's arms and one she carried as she followed him up the walk.

Charlie assisted her grandpa with the bags as he filled her in on a story about the weather, and then, in true Grandpa fashion, he said, "Hey, Charlie, do you know why casserole dishes don't have wheels? In case 'ey roll away."

Laughing, they both entered through the mudroom door just in time to hear the familiar ring of the phone. Charlie's dad placed the casserole dishes on the island and said, "I got it." As Charlie set the bags at the foot of the stairs, he added, "Hi, Ramona. Yeah, she's right here. Nice to hear your voice, and thank you." Dad handed the phone to Charlie and mouthed *it's Ramona for you*. Thankful for the extra-long cord, Charlie excused herself and wound her way into the family room, the long golden coil following her as she did.

"Hey, Ramona, what's up?" Charlie listened as Ramona clamored on about Eric Patterson, her current crush.

"He invited you and I to join him and his buddy Christopher over at Silver Stadium for a Red Wings pre-season game. What do you say?"

Several factors made Charlie hesitate to immediately accept. First, her grandparents' arrival, and second, she hated the thought of being forced to entertain a stranger. But as she listened to Ramona's pleas, she gave in and said, "Sure, let me work things out on this end". An ear-piercing squeal on the other end of the line made Charlie pull the handset away from her ear. They solidified the times as she walked back to the kitchen, then she placed the phone on the cradle.

While her grandma's head was deep in the fridge, shuffling items to make room for the casseroles, her dad asked what Ramona needed. Charlie explained to the group and quickly stated she could stay home if they needed her to, as she didn't want them to think she was bailing on them. Collectively, they encouraged her to go, making points about her being young and enjoying it while she can.

"Besides," her grandmother added, "it will let us play catch up." She placed a soft, wrinkled hand on Dad's shoulder.

Charlie accepted and offered to get her Grandparents set up in their room before she prepped to go out. As Grandma set the oven to preheat, Charlie and Grandpa headed up with the bags they had abandoned at the foot of the stairs earlier. Setting them on the foot of the bed, he took the moment to ask Charlie how she was doing. He explained that it would be totally normal for her to feel the heavy loss and be sad. "You know my friend Martha lost her dog—"

"I'm okay, Grandpa. Really," Charlie cut him off, then gave him a hug.

As her grandfather started in on unpacking, Charlie headed over to her room to change. She chose a pair of Guess jeans and pegged the cuffs, then threw on her favorite Benetton sweater with abstract stripes of gold, purple, orange, and red. She slipped on a pair of black Capezios then took to the bathroom to attempt some makeup. Never really wearing eyeshadow due to her dual color eyes, she usually opted for black liner and mascara. She plucked a complimentary shade of Cover Girl lipstick from her aqua Caboodle and topped it off with her strawberry flavored lip gloss. After running a quick brush through her hair, she grabbed her small crossbody and dropped the gloss, her keys, ID, and some cash from her monkey bank into its opening.

She still had about ten minutes before Ramona and the guys would arrive, so she joined everyone back in the kitchen, where the aroma of her grandmother's cooking filled the air. She was a little disappointed that she was giving that up for ballpark hotdogs and popcorn, but friends must step up in dire situations. Chuckling at her last thought, Charlie sat on one of the stools at the counter. Her grandpa was mid-tale about their journey from Chagrin Falls to the hotel in Ohio, where they stayed the night before. As he rounded the end of the story, a horn sounded from outside.

Charlie got up, gave everyone a hug, and said, "Don't wait up."

As she bolted out the front door, her dad exclaimed, "Have fun! And don't get married!" She rolled her eyes at that last quip. It had been his go-to ever since she and Tony Hughes went on their first official date back in eighth grade. As her dad loved to remind her over and over again, Charlie and Tony had made plans to marry after one fateful roller rink slow skate.

Dale's mother turned to him and asked, "Can you believe that was our little Charlie?"

As she turned to pull her casserole out of the oven Dale offered a solemn, "She's all grown now. It's just me." His dad gave him a firm, knowing pat on the back.

While his mom wrapped up making dinner salads to accompany the casserole, Dale and his father set the table. Small talk ensued, chatting about things like how much Chagrin Falls was changing, the neighbors, and their overall health. Dale wondered to himself at what age discussing health became a thing.

He carried the salad bowl and dressings to the table as his mom placed the casserole on a trivet in the middle of it. His dad cracked open an ice-cold Budweiser for himself and offered one to Dale. "Why not?" he replied and accepted the can and glass. Mom opted for iced tea, and they all settled in at the table.

After the perfunctory compliments on the casserole, which consisted of beef, egg noodles, cheese, and some sort of cream of something soup, Dale's dad cleared his throat and looked towards his wife, who gave a nod and knowing smile. He then turned back to Dale and asked, "Son, would you like to talk to us about what happened? Things were so vague over the phone, which we totally understand, but we feel there is more."

Dale winced and reiterated the story he had told Charlie just days before. His parents listened intently. Walter got up to grab another beer for both him and Dale. As he sat and pulled the tab back on the can, he said, "Cheers."

Dale's mom then added, "So, Dale, honey. What will you do once this is over? With Charlie in school, this house will be such a huge responsibility for you financially and emotionally. Would you consider selling it and moving closer to us in Chagrin Falls?"

Dale knew he couldn't leave Birdie behind and needed to stay there for Charlie, at least until she finished at Cornell. He let his mom down gently and steered the conversation to a task-driven goal for them all. He and Charlie had plans to go through Birdie's personal effects, and they would love her help. She accepted, and with the prior topic all but erased for the time, they continued eating their meal.

Charlie sat in the stands at Silver Stadium, glad she wore her sweater, wishing she had worn her boots instead of the Capezios. She could have at least thrown on some socks, but she was a slave to fashion, as they say, so she shivered. Christopher sat to her left and Ramona to her right, followed by Eric. It was so cute to see Ramona swoon over the guy.

As a cheer erupted, Charlie looked down to the field to see the batter wallop the ball deep to the outfield, bringing runners from third, second, and himself over the plate, increasing the score in Redwings favor an additional three runs. As the cheering subsided, Christopher asked Charlie and the others if they were ready for another hot dog. With nods across the board, he flagged down a roaming guy with a large silver box, who made his way over to their row. Charlie wondered if the over-exuberant man in stripes would correct Christopher on his hot dog talk and make him say red hot. Christopher was originally from Maryland, and the Rochester area vernacular regarding hot dogs and hamburgers was not an easy transition to make. As he performed for them, adding mustard, ketchup and relish, he sang a verse of take me out to the ballgame and did not correct Christopher at all. *Classy move*, Charlie thought. As she bit into the beefy goodness, she was glad she came. Christopher wasn't that bad of a guy, and it was nice to have some normalcy. Reaching for her Coke in front of her right foot, she noticed Ramona and Eric holding hands and smiled.

After cleaning the dishes, the father, mother, and son trio made their way to the living room to enjoy a little Trebek, Dale's guilty pleasure and obsession. He recorded the daily episodes to rewatch at later dates. He popped in the tape from that day's episode, and they settled in to test their collective knowledge against the three contestants. As Final Jeopardy wrapped up and a middle-aged woman was deemed that week's champion, Dale's father said, "I think we're going to call it a night. Travel takes it out of you at our age."

Dale nodded and said, "If you need anything let me know." Then he hugged his parent's goodnight.

Not ready to call it a night himself, Dale grabbed another one of his father's beers from the fridge, settled in on the couch, and began flipping through the channels just in time to catch Billy Crystal typing *The night was* repeatedly as his character tossed paper after paper into the trash, agonizing over which words to describe said night. Dale threw his interjections at the tv. "Muggy, sticky, heavy." He laughed way too hard at himself. Taking another sip of beer and covering his legs with Birdie's favorite blanket, he changed the channel and settled in to enjoy *Throw Mama From the Train*.

Dropping Charlie off, the group said their goodnights, everyone expressing they had a great time as Christopher opened the car door for her. Charlie stepped out into the crisp air, and he leaned in for what she was assuming was going to be a kiss, so she maneuvered it into a hug. "Good night," she said with a smile.

"Good night," he said as she went up the driveway and across the path to the front door. Letting herself in with her key, Charlie gave a final wave to the departing car.

As she went inside, the all-too-familiar television static buzzed from the family room. To her surprise, she found her dad fast asleep on the couch, remote in one hand and the other tucked under his head. As she walked towards the tv to turn it off, she saw, to her amazement, four empties on the floor in front of the couch.

"Way to go, Dad" she whispered, half giggling, half snorting to herself. He rarely let go and relaxed, and she knew he needed it more then than ever. She tiptoed over to him and knelt in front of his face. "Dad," she whispered, "Time to head up." She pulled the blanket off his torso.

He grunted something unintelligible, sat up, and groggily made his way to the stairs. Charlie clicked the lamp off and followed him up, her hand in the small of his back in case he lost his footing. Guiding him to his room, Charlie said goodnight and smiled as she heard her grandpa's snores emanating from down the hall.

Quietly pushing her door open, being mindful that it occasionally squeaked, Charlie entered her room. She tossed her crossbody on the bed and sat in her desk chair to slip off her shoes. Realizing she wasn't tired yet, she changed into comfy clothes and socks and slid on her fuzzy robe in case she ran into any late-night roamers. Careful to be quiet, she descended the stairs to find a midnight snack. Opening the fridge, the soft glow of the bulb illuminated the cavernous space before her. She scanned each shelf for just the right item to fulfill her craving. Not finding what she wanted in the way of food, she grabbed a can of Coke and shuffled to the pantry to continue the hunt.

Upon opening the door, she saw her targets: a bag of Doritos and a package of Nutter Butter cookies. *Jackpot*, she thought. She grabbed both from their nesting places, maneuvered to the island, and found a large plastic bowl from the lower cabinet to put them in. She emptied half the Doritos into it and placed half a dozen peanut shaped goodies around the perimeter. Closing the packages, she returned them home, promising to visit them again soon. Scooping up her delicacies and a few napkins just in case, she climbed back up the stairs to the confines of her room.

Once in, she pushed the door closed with her tush and proceeded to her bed. Setting the bowl on the center of the mattress, she walked over to the media shelf at the right of her desk, snatched a *Sixteen Candles* VHS from its confines, and slid it into the TV-VCR combo on top of her dresser. She took a seat, propped a few pillows behind her back, and settled in and watched the misadventures of Sam's birthday unfold. Snacking away, she thought about her day and the crazy characters she had come across. She wished her mom were there so she could tell her all about the events and excitement during the game.

As she crunched her triangle-shaped treat, she recalled the various times she and Ramona had confided in Mom over boys, girls' stuff, and basic teen angst. Her mom would always point out how she'd always be there to talk, since she never had that luxury in her mother. If it didn't involve the Church or Jesus, that woman hadn't been interested in it.

It was then Charlie remembered the envelope she had found taped to the closet wall that morning. She hopped up, grabbed her backpack, and plopped in on the bed in front of her. Unzipping the tiny pouch, she slid out the envelope and examined it.

It was plain, white, and standard sized, sealed shut with no writing at all on the outside. Charlie ripped the top corner off and slid her fingertip in to run it open. As she did, the revealed contents bewildered her further: Twenty neatly wrapped, crisp one-hundred-dollar bills. What in the world would her mom be doing with these, and even more puzzling, why she would be hiding them?

Charlie knew her mom kept a Christmas fund going throughout the year, but this wouldn't be that. She crunched down on a Nutter Butter and chewed, deep in thought. She then set the envelope and its contents down on her nightstand, lifted her Coke can, and took a swig. Nothing could beat the combination of a fizzy cold Coke washing over the sweet and salty concoction she had created in her mouth.

She decided at that moment to document the strange series of events from the past few days. She grabbed a notebook from her backpack and wrote down: *Mom's unlikely death: natural? Mom's journals: apparitions and lost time. Woman on the street. Money. Misplaced and disheveled items in my room. The broken vase.*

Her mind clear for the time being, she flipped her notebook closed and returned her attention to the movie just in time to see the Donger riding an exercise bike with his sexy girlfriend.

Fighting the urge to call Ramona to see how the rest of the night went, Charlie took her last swig of Coke, repacked her bag, and made her way to the bathroom to pee and brush her teeth. On her way back to bed, she heard a noise in the hall. Thinking it was one of the grandparents, she cracked the door to say a quick goodnight. She found nothing, not a soul, but caught the slightest whiff of her mother's perfume.

Since acknowledging her earlier mistake, Astrid had attempted to come up with a plan to rectify it. The only thing she could foresee working would be to return to the home during the funeral and perform a more thorough search. Before taking such a risk, however, she needed to be sure the items she coveted were still in place. This would require calling upon an old friend of sorts. She needed to project her mind into the home. She could then move about freely and lay eyes on the items she sought confirmation of.

CHAPTER ELEVEN
WAFFLES AND BREADCRUMBS

Charlie awoke to the amazing smell of waffles wafting into her room. For a brief moment, she forgot her mom was gone and was excited to see what crazy topping she had come up with. Raisinets, M&Ms, fig jam, or something else? Sadness hit her in the face like a cartoon frying pan, and her heart sank to her toes as she snapped into reality and realized that would never happen again. Grabbing a tissue from her nightstand, she wiped tears from her cheeks and blew her nose. Centering herself, Charlie got up, slid on her robe, secured the thick tie around her waist, and followed the intoxicating smells down to the kitchen. As she did, she amused herself with another cartoon memory of Bugs Bunny floating in midair as his nose followed a delicious smell.

As she entered the kitchen, she stifled a giggle at her last thought and saw her grandpa at the table, head buried in that morning's edition of the *Democrat and Chronicle*, a steaming cup of coffee in his right hand. Grandma was stationed at the island with a waffle production line in front of her. A bowl of batter was on her right, the waffle iron, with its red beacon light in the center aglow, sat before her, and a stack of hot, yummy goodness on her left was covered with tin foil with the edges of waffles peeking through.

Charlie greeted them with a good morning and smiled as she reached for her coffee mug. "Smells amazing, Grandma." After filling her mug, she padded over to the table and asked if there was anything she could help with despite knowing the answer beforehand.

"Of course not, dear. Just sit and relax."

As if Charlie were the amazing Kreskin, the scene played out just as she had predicted. She sat at the table and said, "What's up, pop pop"?

Walter flipped the edge of the paper down long enough to say, "Good morning, Charlie Bear."

Smiling, Charlie perused the table, which had several bowls filled with strawberries, chocolate chips, butter, and, even more exciting, Grandma's homemade whipped cream.

Taking a test sip of her coffee and helping herself to the comics section of the paper, Charlie asked, "where's Dad?"

Her grandma replied, "We figured we'd let him sleep in. He's had a rough couple of days, and from the looks of the empty cans by the couch, he may have a touch of a hangover." They both giggled at that, knowing he was not a drinker, so even a few beers could accomplish said hangover.

As the three of them enjoyed their breakfast, Charlie filled them in on college life and her goals for the next year's courses. Being the only grandchild, she often wondered what it was like for other kids who had to share their grandparents. As she wrapped up her anecdote about her biochemistry professor, she heard her dad's footsteps coming down the hall.

"He awakes!" Walter exclaimed, provoking laughter from Charlie and her grandmother.

"Let me get you a coffee, darling," Eleanor said as she gave her son a hug and kiss.

"Mornin' Mom, Dad, Charlie," Dale said, nodding in their direction as he took a seat at the table.

Eleanor set a mug in front of Dale and slid the cream and sugar his way. "Would you like some waffles, hon? I still have some batter left."

"Coffee will be fine for now, thanks, Mom."

"Rough night, eh, son?" Walter asked, tapping his fork on his plate.

"Yeah, me and my old buddy Weiser haven't hung out in a while." The table's occupants let out a cacophony of laughs. "Glad my pain brings so much pleasure," he added.

Charlie got up and offered to get her dad some Tylenol. He accepted, and she rounded the corner to the half bath. Returning with two tiny white pills in her hand, she said, "Here you go."

Her dad slapped them into his mouth and swallowed.

"So, what's on today's agenda?" Walter asked.

They discussed the final follow-ups needed leading up to the next day's service. Charlie's one task would be to secure the slides and deliver them to the funeral home. Dale and his parents would verify the rest of the family members arrived and tackle getting the house set up for the celebration of life after the funeral. They had decided on a less sullen celebration to match Birdie's zest for life.

With her marching orders in hand, Charlie took that moment to excuse herself, as she needed to get dressed, but more importantly, she wanted to sneak a peek in her mother's closet one more time in case she missed another oddity the day before. Taking a detour to the guest room, she entered her mom's closet, inhaling the all too familiar smell that sent her olfactory nerves into nostalgia. She flicked on the light and pressed further in, following the same flight path she had previously.

Starting with the first article on the left, she was careful to look at the actual garment *and* its surroundings. She found nothing around the first piece. Second, *nope*. Third, *nada*. She continued until she got to a romper. She looked at the wall behind the hanger then patted down the garment like it was a perp. As she reached the hip area, she heard a crinkle. Going over it again, this time reaching inside the garment with her right hand and pressing with her left, she felt another envelope-shaped object, seemingly sewn in between the outer layer and the shell.

She took the hanger off the rod and hung it over the door frame, then ran to her room to grab a pair of scissors, returning posthaste. Cutting a slit just above the top edge of the hidden object, she reached in and pulled out yet another envelope. She slid open the flap and found another stack of bills.

Wanting to continue the search, she shoved the envelope into her robe pocket, placed the garment back in its place, and moved on down the line. By the time she examined the last garment, her robe contained a total of ten envelopes of various sizes. Turning off the light, she scurried to her room to assess the findings.

Two cups of coffee and a chocolate-chip-laden waffle later, Dale was feeling himself again. He and his parents took turns calling the relatives to ensure their arrivals. With two-thirds of the list down, Dale's mom popped up in true mother fashion, gathered the plates, and ran hot water into the left side of the sink. Reaching under the cabinet as if she had lived there for years, she brought up a bottle of Joy and squirted a little under the running faucet. As bubbles formed, she scooped leftovers into the orange and green Tupperware containers Birdie had purchased at a neighborhood party. After sealing them up, she placed them into the fridge.

Dale smiled to himself. Some things never seemed to change. His dad almost completely took over the phone calls, seeming to find it quite entertaining to talk to relatives he hadn't in a while. They were a captive audience, so to speak.

Dale took the opportunity to step away to his office to work on his eulogy. Pen in hand, he felt just like he had the night before. *Birdie was…* he began, then nothing. He laid his head in his hands, feeling completely defeated.

Entering her room, Charlie locked her door for the first time since eighth grade. She made her way to the bed, plucked each envelope from her pockets, and plopped them down. Her head was spinning. She went to the side of the bed and grabbed the original envelope from the nightstand. Taking out the cash, she laid it to the left of the pile. She then opened each envelope, counted the contents, and laid out each stack.

Upon tallying the hefty sum at the end, Charlie almost lost her footing. There was over thirty-thousand dollars lying before her, in all denominations, mostly fifties and hundreds. No two envelopes contained the same amount. Also, none had any identifying notes as to their purpose. She fell away from the bed and into her desk chair.

As she leaned back and stared at the stacks before her, Charlie contemplated what her next step should be. Tell her dad? Would it be worth the chaos it would stir up? No, she needed to do more research and find out what was going on. What was her mom doing and thinking when she stashed this cash? Charlie would continue her dive, and once she had gathered enough data to present to her dad, she would do just that.

Hopping to her feet, she walked over to her closet and found a shoe box she could put the money in. She grabbed an old grocery bag, slid the cash inside, and placed it in the shoebox. After taping it shut, she added it to the journals in her window seat.

Glancing at her clock, she realized she needed to get moving. It was turning out to be a warm day, so she opted for an ankle-length cotton skirt, a light t-shirt, and her white Keds. Not wanting to mess with her hair, she slid it into a banana clip, then grabbed her crossbody from the previous night and her backpack.

Once downstairs, she saw her dad at his desk deep in thought. As she was about to say her goodbyes, Grandpa Walter summoned them both to the kitchen table. Having finished playing phone reunion with relatives, he had reverted back to the *Democrat and Chronicle*, finding Birdie's obituary. He folded the paper in half, moved his reading glasses to the tip of his nose, cleared his throat, and began to read it aloud.

Once he was done, Grandma piped in with, "That was beautiful, Dale. You did a fine job."

Nodding and fighting back tears, Dale thanked her and added that Charlie had helped with the final draft.

Walter expressed that he and Eleanor wanted to be useful, so they were going to utilize the daylight to gather items that would be needed for the party. After writing a list and reviewing it with Dale, they prepared to leave for Wegmans.

One large round of hugs later, Charlie said she would be heading out as well. Her dad pulled out two twenty-dollar bills and handed them to her, and she grabbed a can of Coke and a Slim Jim on her way out the door. Charlie made her way down the driveway and steered Juicy in the direction of the Fotomat.

Pulling up to the photo-processing shack, Charlie dug in her crossbody for the claim ticket. Snatching it from the bottom, she looked at the crumpled mess and made a life decision to get better organized. Placed between her fingers, she flicked the ticket gracefully out the driver's window and into the clerk's hand. He scanned over a log book, made a tapping motion, turned around to face the rear of the small shack, and proceeded to open drawers. He plucked two small boxes out, and a few clickety clack motions on the register later, he said in a shaky voice, "That'll be twenty-one dollars and sixty-two cents."

Charlie pulled out the money her dad had handed her and slipped it his way. More computations, the sound of a drawer sliding open, and the wrestling of coins rang out as he retrieved her change. As she held her hand up to the window, he counted the money out to her, then placed the boxes in a tiny bag and, as he handed it over, recited, "Please think of Fotomat for all your future memory needs."

Charlie nodded, grabbed the bag, and said, "Have a great day." After placing the slides on the seat next to her, she decided to give Ramona a call to see what her plans were for the day. Parking, she thought about the cell phone she had in her backpack but quickly told herself that was for emergencies only and laughed at the scene that would unfold with her dad if she abused the privilege and racked up unnecessary charges.

She exited the driver's door, ran up to a payphone just outside the Wegmans, inserted a quarter, and punched in Ramona's number. After two rings, she was greeted by a cheerful, "Hello Lorenzano residence."

"Hello Mrs. L, it's Charlie. Is Ramona there?"

After offering a quick condolence, Charlie heard a muffled shout of, "Ramona! Telephone!"

Three seconds of silence was followed by the sound of a second handset being picked up. "Got it Mom!" Ramona belted.

Charlie waited to hear the familiar click to signal Mrs. Lorenzano had hung up, then said, "Heya. I'm out running an errand, then I'm gonna head back home to help set up for tomorrow. I was wondering what you were up to."

Ramona filled Charlie in on how successfully things had gone after the game, promising dirty details later. Finally getting to the matter at hand, Ramona said, "Unfortunately, Eric and I actually have plans to go roller skating and then see a movie this afternoon."

"That's fine, Charlie said. "I'm happy for you two. Just don't forget about the service tomorrow."

"Totally there Charlie. And I was hoping to cash in on our girl's night after the party to catch up and watch movies."

"Sounds like a plan," Charlie confirmed. "And don't do anything I wouldn't do."

"Well, that doesn't leave us many options."

Pulling into the Wegmans parking lot, Walter and Eleanor got the startle of their lives. Six spaces up was the orange glow of the Ghia, and peeking in the windows was a woman they would swear to their graves was Birdie. As Eleanor and Walter sat parked in their vehicle, they tried to make sense of what they were seeing. Clear as day, Eleanor was witnessing her daughter-in-law peering into the windows of Charlie's car. Walter admitted there was a resemblance, but didn't think it meant anything. Eleanor *knew* better. After what seemed like an eternity of rationalization, Eleanor looked up to find the Birdie lookalike was gone. With a shrug, they both exited the vehicle and set forth to complete the task at hand.

Charlie spun around to return to Juicy, then made a quick decision to visit the ladies' room, not wanting to risk having to use the funeral home facilities. As she exited a few moments later, she saw what had to be her grandparent's Grand Marquis pulling out of the parking lot. *Dang, just missed them*, she thought. After unlocking the driver's side door, she slid in and proceeded to Lilac Gardens.

Knowing the daughter would be returning to the little shop that day, Astrid patiently waited across the street until she saw the orange vehicle. Finishing the last few bites of her breakfast sandwich she got from a corner building called 7-11, she proceeded across to the target destination. She still was getting used to having to feed this physical body, something she hadn't had to think of in the centuries spent in her ethereal form. Taking inventory of her surroundings, she watched Charlie retrieve a bag from the small hut. She then watched as the vehicle stopped and Charlie walked up to the larger store.

Astrid crept up on the car and peered into the glass to see if she could find anything. She knew this girl had her items. She just knew it. If she could retrieve them then, she could avoid having to return to the house at all.

Seeing a large fabric sack on the seat, she attempted to tug on the levers that would give her access to the items she sought. They didn't budge. Frustrated, she looked around, not sure what she might find, but hoping for some flash of inspiration. In doing so, she noticed a large vehicle parked nearby with an older couple who seemed to be arguing, and the woman was pointing right at Astrid.

Giving up on her endeavor, Astrid scuttled through the rows of cars and back across the street.

As Charlie pulled up to the funeral home, she recognized the familiar face of the groundskeeper between a row of headstones in the distance. She pulled into a visitor spot out front, parked, and reached for the small Fotomat bag to her right. Making her way inside, she found Cora sitting behind her desk and braced herself for the woman's creepy voice.

As she handed the bag over, she explained what they were and how her dad had already spoken to Mr. Cuthwaight, the funeral home's officiator, about how they wanted them to be displayed. The tiny woman thanked Charlie, then read from a list before her, reviewing the schedule for 'the next day's interment. That word had a visceral cut that hit Charlie to the core. She nodded in agreement with the timeline as Cora made a few additional ticks to the boxes on the paper before her.

Seeming to sense Charlie's discomfort, Cora asked if she needed to take a seat for a moment and gestured to a small sitting area tucked behind several coffins. Declining, Charlie thanked her and turned to leave. Taking refuge in Juicy's front seat, she laid back her head and closed her eyes. She wasn't sure how long she sat that way, and was interrupted by a sudden rap on the window which startled her, making her bolt upright, causing her to hit her head on the visor.

Peering out the driver's window, she saw the face of the groundskeeper looking in at her. She cranked the window down and greeted him. He introduced himself as Mateo and informed Charlie that he didn't want to alarm her, but he sees a lot of strange things in his position and, most recently, he saw her mother roaming the grounds. He told her he believes in ghosts and spirits, but he did not believe what he saw was her mother's spirit, but another creature. His abuela raised him to believe in *otro yo*, or a ghostly double, and *gemelo malvados*, or an evil twin. He explained that he sensed something nefarious and diabolical in its intent and warned her to be mindful of her surroundings, then handed her a set of rosaries that his abuela had given him for protection. Charlie attempted to refuse the gift, but Mateo insisted. She thanked him and pressed that she had to get going. He bowed his head and said his goodbyes as he performed the sign of the cross.

Looking in her side-view mirror, Charlie wound her window up. That was not at all something she would have predicted would happen that day. As she drove home, she couldn't shake off what Mateo had told her. Was that what she had also seen?

Arriving back home before her grandparents, Charlie kept her spot in the driveway to allow them the access to the garage and the breezeway. She greeted her dad as she walked through the door, but decided to keep the events at the funeral home to herself. She followed his voice to the back of the house, where he had moved around the furniture in the sunroom and was currently setting up several six-foot-long party tables. Her mom had invested in them years ago for mini fashion shows she would host with the neighbors and other customers. They definitely had gotten their money's worth out of them.

Dropping her backpack on the small couch in the corner, Charlie reached for a set of legs, snapping them into an upright position. Securing the base, she let her dad know she successfully dropped off the slides and reviewed the schedule with Cora.

Dale interjected, "Oh, the woman that looks like that creepy psychic in Poltergeist?"

Charlie giggled. "Yep, that's the one"

"Go into the light Carol Anne," Dale mocked in his best creepy southern accent.

They both laughed as they flipped the table to its upright position. Sliding it into place, completing the large U-shape, Dale gave a palm slap to the top of the table and said, "Now to wipe these babies down and figure out where your mom kept the coverings for them."

Charlie filled him in on where to find the cleaning products and volunteered to go on the hunt for the table cloths.

She headed up to the attic, where she vaguely remembered seeing a box labeled table linens. She grabbed a flashlight at the top of the stairs and examined the writing on the boxes shelved to her far right. *Charlie's Baby Clothes. Dale's College Papers.* She continued to scan, moving on to the next set of shelves, where she noticed an odd, unlabeled banker box tucked in a dark corner between shelving units.

Lifting the lid slowly, she told herself, "Just open it...it's not like something's going to jump out at you." In the dim light, she found a pile of random pictures, a few stuffed animals, tchotchkes, and a few journals. The journals, however, were different from the ones she had already found. These were older looking, leather bound, and even had locks.

Placing the lid back on the box, she decided to leave it in its place. Ending her search for the tablecloths just a few moments later, she made her way back down to her dad, who was relaxing in a side chair, Coke in his hands. She set the material on one of the tables, slid into the kitchen, and grabbed a can of Coke for herself along with the opened bag of Doritos, to which she said, "I told you I'd be back."

As she entered the room with tiny little skips, Dad smiled at her and the contents of her hand. "Oh, to be young and be able to eat whatever you want with no repercussions." She unrolled the top of the bag and shoved the opening towards him. "Eat," she commanded. He reached in and drew back a handful of cheesy triangles. They sat together, noshing and sipping, as they discussed the final setup for the room and which room to tackle next.

Charlie filled her dad in on her date the other night, as well as Ramona's pending sleepover plans for after the party, then agreed to tackle the half bath on the ground floor and the guest bath upstairs in case there was a need for the overflow. Her dad said he didn't want to inconvenience his mom and dad and suggested that Charlie keep her door open this one time? Agreeing, she gave a soldier's salute and headed for the tiny linen closet in the mudroom that housed the cleaning supplies. Her dad would move on to the family room.

Deciding she needed a little musical motivation, she headed up and grabbed her Walkman from the small table next to her tub. Returning to the half bath dancing to Men Without Hats' "Safety Dance", she shimmied around the small room with the spray and cloth. She took a step back after several minutes, admiring her efforts, and headed to the linen closet to grab two clean hand towels. After placing them on the towel bars, she ripped open a Renuzit air freshener from its cardboard confinement and gave the top a twist to expose the weird, gelatinous cone beneath it. She remembered how she was always curious as to why it disappeared over time, and her mom's even more obscure explanation likening it to a snowman melting.

After setting the air freshener on the center of the toilet tank, she gathered her trash and cleaning supplies, then flicked off the light and proceeded to her next victim. "Dirty Dancing" her way up the stairs with her best Francis "Baby" Houseman impression, she made her way to her bathroom. She stood in the doorway and observed the scene before her. While she was in no way a messy person, she definitely inherited her mom's disastrous approach to organization. She grabbed her Caboodle, corralled the half-dozen or so makeup items strewn across the vanity top, and plopped them in the trays. She then picked up the hair clips, ponytail holders, and bobby pins and placed them in a wicker basket, which sat on a shelf above the toilet. Systematically, she worked her way around the room until it was presentable and pine fresh. Taking the trash and setting it outside her bedroom door, Charlie slid her headphones off her ears just in time to hear her grandparents making their way through the mudroom door. With a final scan of the bathroom, she turned off the lights, retrieved the trash, and went downstairs to see if she could be of help.

Greeting the group, Charlie offered to help Grandpa with bringing in the rest of the groceries while Grandma started the process of unpacking and sorting through the bags. By the time she and Pops made it in with the last of the bags, the kitchen had exploded with various items. Grandma and Dale stood ready to snatch the bags in their hands.

"Mom, I think you covered everything! And then some!" Dale said with a tone of wonder in his voice.

"The last thing we want is to run out of something," she replied.

All four of them tackled placing the remaining items in their respective spots. Charlie explained she had finished the bathrooms and was ready for the next task.

Her grandma chimed in with, "Why don't you help me get some lunch together for us all?"

Charlie accepted, and her dad and grandpa went outside and made sure things looked good and to discuss parking for the reception, leaving Charlie and grandma to their culinary artistry. As Eleanor ran through a few options, Charlie grabbed another Coke from the fridge, realizing she needed to wean herself off that stuff.

They landed on grilled ham and cheese sandwiches and tomato soup as their menu for lunch, and Charlie pulled four cans of soup from the pantry. Opting for the less manual way of opening them, she placed each can under the arm of the pea green can opener and pushed down hard enough for it to grasp the lip and begin its circular journey to expose their contents. Repeating this for each can, she then dumped the red liquid into a large saucepan from the lower cabinets. Taking one of the cans and the pan over to the sink, she added two full cans of water to the pot. It called for a one-to-one ratio, but Charlie and her dad liked it on the thicker side. Setting the pot on the rear burner, she turned the dial to low and set a wooden spoon across the top for stirring as needed.

Turning around towards the island, she found her grandma had assembled four ham and cheese sandwiches and was currently slathering the tops of the bread with mayo in preparation for grilling. Leaning down to grab the large skillet from the drawer below the stove, Charlie asked her grandma what she thought of Wegmans. Grandma waved her arms in the air as she described the sheer size of Wegmans compared to their tiny Piggly Wiggly store back in Chagrin Falls and how the choices were almost too overwhelming, but that she and Grandpa had enjoyed all the little shops within the store and the samples that came with visiting them. She also shared that they had splurged and gotten several pastries from the phenomenal bakery for them to have for breakfast with coffee in the morning.

As they grilled each sandwich and stirred the soup, Charlie pulled down four bowls and small plates from the upper cabinet. She took a peek out the rear window, but couldn't see her dad and grandpa and figured they were out front by then. Excusing herself to go gather them up, she opened the front door to find them both down in the cul-de-sac, chatting with their neighbor. Her grandpa had a long stick with chalk secured to the end and was marking out a makeshift parking spot on to the macadam. As she called them in for lunch, she noticed the dozen or so spaces they had created. She waved to the neighbor and turned around to head back in.

Astrid watched, contemplating a way to enter the home, as she listened to their plans for the day. Solidifying her window of opportunity, she withdrew her consciousness back to her body in the motel room. For her plan to work, walking would be out of the question. There was no way she could drive, so she decided she needed a bicycle. She rode them over the years when she would possess Birdie. She was no expert, and honestly, had no idea how to secure such a thing. Astrid opted to rely on some human help. Leaving her room, she went down to the desk clerk and asked if they knew how she could acquire a bike.

Dale and Grandpa washed up in the kitchen sink after threats of bodily harm from Charlie if they messed up her cleaning efforts, then took a seat at the kitchen table. Charlie carried over a gold

Tupperware pitcher filled with sweet tea and placed it down as Eleanor filled the bowls with the steamy soup. Each carrying a tray over with them, Charlie and Eleanor took their seats at the table. After dishing out the food, they began enjoying their lunch together. Dale and Grandpa filled in the group on the parking situation. Charlie noted how, for the first time since her mom's death, the house was showing tiny hints of being a home again.

As Astrid wheeled her find down the street after handing the previous owner ten dollars, she thought back to how she had once ridden one of Birdie's bikes. She had watched Birdie perform the task almost daily, and one day she used her limited energy to take control of Birdie and ride. The wind in her hair, the freedom gave her one of the first signs that she wanted more.

After wrapping up lunch, Eleanor announced she would clean the kitchen, then she would need help making some dishes for the next day. She asked Charlie to run up to the guest room and grab her recipe book from the dresser. Returning with the home-crafted recipe book in her hands, Charlie saw her dad and grandpa busy in the sunroom spreading the tablecloths. She set the book on the counter and grabbed her glass of tea from the table before joining her grandma at the sink. Grandma washed; Charlie dried.

They turned their focus on the recipe book as they heard the whir of The Beast in the family room. Her grandma explained they would be making deviled eggs, potato salad, and mini deviled ham and tuna sandwiches. Flipping to the first recipe, Grandma guided Charlie to pull down the items needed for the eggs. As Charlie did so, her grandmother filled a large pot with water, tossed in a handful of salt, and added two dozen eggs to the cold water. While the eggs came to a boil, they began chopping onions. The inevitable tears formed for both of them. Charlie took the moment to share her mom's trick to cure the crying. She handed her grandma a slice of bread and instructed her to bite down on it. Grandma was overjoyed at this discovery and was quick to share her excitement as the men made their way towards them.

"What in blazing hell are you up to, Eleanor?" Walter scoffed. Snatching the bread from her mouth, she explained the science, and, in disbelief, Grandpa attempted to disprove the theory.

Charlie and her dad laughed at him as he tried several variations to debunk the helpful hit. Finally convinced it was legit and not some crazy woman thing, he and Dad stated they were going to head out for a beer run, leaving the girls to their cooking.

An hour or so—and forty-eight deviled eggs, one large bowl of potato salad, and dozens of small sandwiches, later—the men trudged in with a few boxes of beer under their arms and bags of ice in their hands. They proceeded through the sunroom door. Charlie watched through the kitchen window as they systematically snatched coolers from the shed, hosed them out, and filled them with ice and beer. Closing the last of the coolers, the pair walked back in and explained it was cold enough outside that the ice would be fine.

In one final group push, they arranged Dixie plates and plasticware, along with napkins and cups, out on one of the party tables. Grandma then performed one final walkthrough and gave her motherly approval. Deciding they all needed some downtime before thinking about dinner, Dale went to his office to finish up his eulogy, grandma set herself up in his recliner in the family room with her cross stitch, and Charlie challenged her grandpa to a game of backgammon. With everyone in their spots, the next hour or so ticked by uneventfully.

With the sun setting outside, Charlie took the loss to her grandpa with dignity and went to wake her grandma, who had fallen asleep, cross stitch still clasped in her hands. With a gentle whisper, Charlie asked her grandma what temp to set the oven at for the lasagna that was on the menu for that night. Grandma shimmied to a more upright position with a few grunts and groans and let Charlie know three hundred and seventy-five degrees would be fine. After setting the oven to the temp requested, Charlie excused herself to go work on some reading for a bit while dinner heated up. Saying a quick hello to her dad as she turned up the stairs, Charlie made her way to her room.

Halfway through her biochemistry chapter, Charlie could smell the lasagna getting stronger in the house. Knowing from experience that when smells reach her room, the food would soon be done, she highlighted her last few lines and set her text and pen down on her desk. She stood to stretch, then went to her closet to pick out her outfit for the funeral in the morning. She knew it was traditional to wear black, but also knew her mom would have completely backed up a choice to be more vibrant. Finally deciding to have the best of both worlds, she picked a classic black sheath dress with a wide patent leather belt for the funeral. She selected a brighter, floral print dress with a fitted top and flowing skirt separated by a thick, hot pink, elastic clip belt for the party to honor her mom. Hanging her choices side by side on the rod, she went to her bathroom, splashed water on her face, dried off, reset her banana clip, and went to join the others downstairs.

Charlie entered the kitchen as Grandma lifted the foil off the lasagna for a final browning. "Do I hear the salad cavalry?" She asked.

Charlie replied, "You betcha."

Grandma pushed the lasagna back in the oven, lowered the temp a smidge, set the timer, and turned to a pile of salad ingredients on the island. Charlie washed her hands, grabbed a small knife, and stood opposite her grandma. She decided to tackle the tomatoes while the older woman shredded the lettuce.

"So, tomorrow, you're going to be okay?" Grandma asked.

"Honestly, I'm not sure," Charlie said. "I think we are set logistically, but I'm not ready to say goodbye. It's going to make it…" After a long pause, she finished with, "Real."

Grandma set the lettuce aside and placed her hands on Charlie's. "You are strong, you have us and your dad, and we will be here for you always."

Clearing a lump in her throat, Charlie said, "I love you, Grandma."

"As do I, Charlie. Now, let's show this salad who's boss."

The two worked together, dropping the ingredients into one large bowl, until the timer for the lasagna sounded. While Grandma lifted the steaming hot masterpiece out of the oven, Charlie looked for her dad and grandpa. Not seeing them, she asked her grandma if she knew where they were.

"Oh, those two?" She laughed. "They went for a walk. Your grandpa needs to get his steps in every day, but he has been slacking."

Charlie grabbed salad bowls from the edge of the island and filled each one, adding a few croutons as she giggled at the memory of her and her mom calling them cryptons. After setting the bowls at each placemat, she went to the fridge and grabbed a bevy of dressings. Thousand Island for herself, blue cheese for her dad, and, just in case, an Italian and ranch. *It's always good to have choices*, Charlie chimed in her head with Birdie's voice.

Astrid's face grew warm. This girl was delaying her final exit to the life she deserved, the life for which she had worked so hard for so many years. A pang hit her heart as she thought of her mother. So many of her memories had been lost over the centuries. Shaking it off, she chose to take a few deep breaths and returned to the present. She needed to focus. She needed her energy and strength for the next day. Forcing herself to rest, she closed her eyes and slept.

As Grandma sliced and plated the cheesy goodness, Charlie slipped a hand in and snagged a taste of a rogue noodle. She complimented her grandma as her dad and grandpa came through the mudroom door. "Wash up," Grandma commanded of them both. Quickly, Charlie added, "*Not* in the half bath. The kitchen sink, please."

Both men filled their palms with hand soap and ran them under the flowing water, drying off with the rooster tea towel hanging from the macrame holder on the oven door, then took their seats at the table.

The compliments began even before the first bites were taken. Between bites, small talk, and jokes, laughter ensued. They went through the list one last time to make sure the 'i's were dotted and the 't's were crossed for the next day.

As the team tackled the dishes together, they decided to settle in the family room for a little tv and relaxation. Grandma, again, chose her cross stitch, Charlie and grandpa set up opposite each other for some blackjack, and Dale opted for a scientific word search. With the day winding down and the realization of what was ahead of them set in, each said their goodnights and retreated to their rooms.

Charlie laid in her bed unable to sleep. She thought about the impending service and its meaning to both her and her dad. She considered the finality of laying her mom to rest. What she couldn't get out of her mind, however, was the nagging feeling that her mom wouldn't be at rest. There was something deep in Charlie's heart that insisted her mom was not completely gone.

CHAPTER TWELVE
GOODBYES

The alarm sounded way too early. Charlie's energy level matched the task at hand. She crawled out of bed and began preparing for her mom's funeral. Seemingly in slow motion, she showered and got dressed.

Realizing she was ahead of the others for a change, Charlie descended to the kitchen, brewed a pot of coffee, and laid the pastries out that her grandparents had picked up during their trip to Wegmans. While she was waiting for the coffee to brew, she had the horrifying realization that she had not prepared anything to say for the service. Maybe it was her subconscious taking over, because she was unable to face herself or to believe it was real. As the final drips from the coffee maker sputtered into the carafe, she determined she would just have to speak from the heart or wing-it, as her mom would always say. The woman was the reigning champion of the wing-it Olympics. Smiling a lonely smile, Charlie removed four coffee mugs from the cabinet and, needing caffeine STAT, rejected social etiquette and filled her mug to the brim, skipping the cream and sugar completely.

As the final drop slid into her mouth, she heard the soft murmurs of her grandparents making their way towards her. She stood up and filled two more mugs in addition to hers. Realizing they would need more coffee, she brewed a second pot. Not wanting to seem ungrateful, but also not truly hungry, she begrudgingly took a small bite of the cheese danish she had picked up from the serving plate. The delicious filling kept her mouth busy as her grandparents stirred their coffee.

Grandma was the first to break the silence. "Your dad just needs a few more minutes." They all nodded in empathy and drank in silence.

A few moments later, Grandpa ended the thick tension smothering the air by grabbing a cherry danish and saying, "Over the lips and past the gums, watch out arteries, here it comes."

The initial soft snickers erupted into nervous laughter. As Charlie took her second bite, her dad entered the kitchen and uttered a soft and meek, "Morning."

Grandma instantly popped up and poured her son a coffee, guiding him to a seat at the table. For the first time since her mom's death, Charlie saw her dad's fragility. The brave front he had been portraying was gone; in its place was a tired, sullen, disheveled shell of a man. His suit pants and shirt were on, collar open at the neck with his tie hanging unassembled and loose. Charlie assumed the jacket was still hanging in his room. She would check for it after they were done. His hair, although combed, still looked haphazard, and he had not shaved. None of them were going to mention this or force the tasks. Charlie lost a mom, but her dad lost his wife, lover, best friend, and caretaker all in one fell swoop.

With very little to no small talk, they finished their coffees and Charlie cleared the table. She then signaled to her grandma and whispered she was going up to grab her dad's suit coat. Reaching the top of the stairs, she felt a chill run through her. As she walked into her dad's bedroom, she could once again smell her mom. Returning to the kitchen, Charlie had the suit coat in one hand and her clutch purse in the other.

She set the purse on the counter and reached into the breast pockets of the jacket to make sure her dad had his eulogy notes. Confirming the paper was there, Charlie hung the coat over the door handle of the pantry. She grabbed her clutch and disappeared to the half bath to stock up on Kleenex. After filling the opening with as many tissues as she could squeeze in, she closed the clasp and returned to the kitchen. After a final check, they all headed to the Grand Marquis and made their way to Lilac Gardens to say their goodbyes.

Astrid rode up just as the car pulled away. She waited until it turned the corner and took the bike through a path along the rear of the neighboring homes. Tucking it between the shed and a tree, she made her way into the home to seek out the items she needed for her journey.

Instead of pulling up to the main building, the car was directed down a path between the headstones to a small chapel-like structure. As they wound through the path, Charlie saw the groundskeeper, tipping his hat towards her. She lifted her hand in a small wave. Reaching their destination, Grandpa dropped off Dale, Grandma, and Charlie with an attendant, who explained there was a golf cart service he could use to return once he parked back at the main building. Watching him pull off, Charlie hooked her arm through her dad's arm. Grandma took the other. They presented a unified front heading in, bracing Charlie's dad in case his footing should falter.

They were the first to arrive, as expected, and upon entering the small foyer, images of Birdie glided across a wall screen in synchrony with a playlist they had chosen. Stevie Wonder's melodic voice sang "Isn't She Lovely".

Charlie's dad, unable to hold back tears, began a soft weep. Before Charlie could grab a tissue, Grandma reached up with the corner of her handkerchief and dabbed his cheeks. The flowers, more than perfect, were placed around the foyer and flanking the aisles as they passed into the next room. Proceeding down a center aisle, Charlie saw both Mr. Cuthwaight and Cora waiting for them. Both standing tall. Each with their hands clasped in front of them like statues.

They guided the trio to the front bench seating, which was labeled *immediate family*, gave their condolences, and briefly went through the schedule of events. Mr. Cuthwaight explained that the spiritualist they had found for them would speak first, leading the room in a non-denominational meditation. Dale would then give his eulogy, followed by Charlie, and a short allowance of time for anyone else who may want to speak. The service would end with a final reading and short viewing period before they head to the internment area.

There's that awful and painful final word again, Charlie thought.

They sat together in silence, waiting for Grandpa to join them. When he arrived, Cora approached and said it was time to move to the vestibule to greet the fellow mourners. Charlie and her dad stood to the left side of the doorway, with her grandparents to the right. As family members and friends made their way in, each gave their own version of condolences. Charlie and her Dad received hands, pats on the shoulders, and nods of understanding. Few words came from either of them; it was all Charlie could do to keep from crying like a baby. As the last of the guests made their ways into the seating area, the family returned to their seats up front.

Soft, ethereal music played and a woman in a flowing gown made her way to the center of the stage. She requested the room to bow their heads and take a moment to bring forth their favorite memory of Birdie. This energy gave strength to Dale as he made his way up to the podium.

He reached in his breast pocket, pulled out his notes, placed them on the podium, and began to speak. "'Nobody sees a flower—really—it is so small it takes time—we haven't time—and to see takes time, like to have a friend takes time.' Georgia O'Keefe.

"I want to start off by thanking everyone for being here today," Dale continued in a soft voice, as if speaking louder would cripple his movement forward. "I feel my wife would tell me I was being rude if I didn't. She was very sweet and accommodating that way and would want me to mind my manners. That was my Birdie—always keeping me straight and in line. She was the kindest, smartest, most loving, and most compassionate soul on this Earth. She was everything to me, and I miss her terribly." This last revelation caused Charlie's dad to falter and hang his head. He took a deep breath and continued. "Birdie and I were fortunate enough to have spent many wonderful years together. However, I would give anything to be able to have more time with her. I am a broken man, and my better half is gone, but I can see her in the face of our beautiful daughter, Charlie." He gestured to the family seating, where Charlie watched with tears rolling down her cheeks. "Birdie was beautiful both inside and out. I was truly blessed to have a wife who loved me as much as she did, who had more talent in her baby finger than I do in my whole body. I don't know how I am going to move forward without her, but I know she is somewhere telling me to suck it up. I am trying, my love, but it is hard without you here. I know that everyone here loved her too and will miss her sweet soul as much as I do. Thank you again, and my darling Birdie. I will see you again soon."

Dale returned to his seat, almost inconsolable even in his mother's arms, as Charlie made her way to the podium. Lowering her head, she stared at the mahogany brown top, gripped the sides, and took a deep breath. Her goal was to not completely fall apart as she spoke about her mom. "I miss her," she started. "*We* miss her. My mom was the heart of our family. She was my best friend. She was always there when I needed a sounding board, a shoulder to cry on, or someone to celebrate with. I won't lie and say I am not angry with the world at this moment. I wanted to talk about all her wonderful attributes, but all I can think of is fair. Fair is a word that keeps coming to my brain. Nothing about this is fair. It's not fair to me to have to grow up without her. It's not fair to my dad to grow old without her. It's not fair my future children will never know her beauty, laughter, and hugs. It's not fair to any of you, her family and friends. I know she would be so happy to see all of us celebrating her, but I would give anything to have her back. I miss you, Mom." Charlie wrapped up and invited anyone else who might want to share up to the podium as she let go of it and stepped back. A small line formed, and one by one, sweet stories and anecdotes about Birdie continued until the last of the remembrances finished up. Mr. Cuthwaight stood and announced, "Before we begin the viewing processional and go out onto the lawn to take in this beautiful day, I would like to share a poem by Mary Elizabeth Frye with you.

"Do not stand at my grave and weep.
I am not there. I do not sleep.
I am a thousand winds that blow.
I am the diamond glints of snow.

I am the sunlight on ripened grain.
I am the gentle autumn rain.
When you awaken in the morning's hush
I am the swift uplifting rush
Of quiet birds in circled flight.
I am the soft stars that shine at night.
Do not stand at my grave and cry;
I am not there. I did not die."

Lifting his bowed head, he then gave instructions for the viewing processional. As the mourners took turns walking up to say their goodbyes to Birdie, Charlie was shaking uncontrollably at the back of the line. She then felt Ramona's arm slide around her to let her know she was there for her. Together, they walked up. Dale, just in front of her, had permanently snagged his mom's kerchief. Charlie, her dad, and Ramona stood side by side over the casket. Charlie wept like she had never wept before, barely able to form the words, "I love you, Mom." Dale squeezed her hand and Ramona guided her to a chair in the corner to help her catch her breath. Charlie watched from her seat as her dad reached in and grabbed Birdie's hand. He whispered his goodbyes between gut-wrenching sobs. Ending with a painful cry—the depths of which Charlie couldn't fathom—he released his wife's hand. No word other than anguish could be used to describe how he looked at that moment.

Charlie and her dad then walked out of the front of the chapel, following Cora and the grandparents. Slowly, they wound between headstones. The sun was shining and the day was warm, as if nature, too, wanted to say goodbye to its flower child.

Finally stopping, they lined up before a row of chairs and took a seat near a gaping hole of earth before them, surrounded by metal bars and a very large mound of dirt. It seemed barbaric to Charlie that they were about to lower her mom down into it.

With Cora at his side, Mr. Cuthwaight stood opposite those attending and recited a phrase from one of Birdie's favorite books, *Dandelion Wine*.

He paused before asking those gathered to stand for the committal. "To everything there is a season, and a time to every purpose on earth, a time to be born and a time to die. Here in this last act, in sorrow but without fear, in love and appreciation, we commit Birdie Althea Bauman to her natural end."

Hearing this set a fire in Charlie's heart. This was *not* a time to die, and it was anything but a natural end. She could feel that for certain. Watching the groundskeeper turn the crank to lower her mom into the ground, Charlie let out a guttural cry. It doesn't get more final and real than that. Her dad, unable to stand himself, fell to the seat behind him, sorrowful moans emitting from his soul. Once done, they all tossed final gerbera daisies down onto the casket and turned away to make the long walk to the car. There were, of course, golf cart shuttles, but they all needed the fresh air and time a good walk allotted them.

Ramona hugged her mom goodbye as she transferred her bags to the trunk of the Grand Marquis. Her mom had regretfully decided to not attend the celebration of life party, as she was needed back home for Ramona's two younger brothers, who had been left alone long enough. Grandpa and Dale took the front seats, and the ladies slid in the back. Grandma said, "That was a very nice service, dear." Otherwise, the ride was as quiet as, well, a funeral.

Arriving at the house, they made their way in through the breezeway door, being sure to close and lock it to guarantee guests would have to come to the front door. Everyone made their way up the stairs to change and wash up before the guests arrived. Charlie and Ramona shut the door to her bedroom behind themselves. Ramona gave Charlie a big best friend hug. Charlie accepted this emotional gift, then said, "Thank you for everything."

"You know it," Ramona quipped, giving two thumbs up. She then entered the bathroom to change and teased Charlie over its immaculate state.

Charlie went to change into the outfit that she had placed on the rod just inside the closet door and let out a yelp, which caused Ramona to run out from the bathroom. She maneuvered over to Charlie, standing at the closet door with her mouth gaped open, staring at a huge mess on the floor. Not having time to deal with it at that moment, due to the first of endless doorbell rings, they both quickly dressed, shut the closet door in case guests made use of her bathroom, and headed downstairs to see her mom's cousin Beth hugging her dad in the doorway.

Beth had made the formidable trip from Savannah, Georgia and was currently exclaiming how brutally cold the weather was.

Charlie thought to herself, *Lady, you don't know what cold is.* Taking a left at the bottom of the stairs to avoid the commotion in the hallway, Charlie and Ramona walked into the kitchen through the family room and immediately offered their services to Charlie's grandma. Each of them carried food from the refrigerator to the tables in the sunroom.

Through the kitchen window, Charlie saw Grandpa outside checking the cooler. Seeming satisfied, he sauntered back in just in time to be handed a crock pot full of meatballs from a neighbor from five doors down. He set it on one of the tables and leaned over to Charlie to ask what to do with the crock pot.

She excused her grandpa to go grab himself a beverage and plugged in the power cord into the nearest receptacle. After turning the dial to warm, she returned to the kitchen to continue her hosting duties. For every two guests, a dish of some sort was brought in. She decided to keep some aside for her dad once the tables were at capacity. Charlie figured if she handled it correctly, at the rate food was arriving, he could feasibly not have to cook for a month.

As she made her rounds, chatter continued and stories were told. A small gathering had formed around the family room coffee table where Charlie had laid out several stacks of photos of her mom that she and Ramona had picked in their visit to the library. Just like Charlie, everyone seemed to be having a hard time with the sudden death. Words like tragic, unfathomable, shocking, and unfair were tossed around. Food and drinks flowed. Eventually, music and laughter dominated the house. One thing Charlie could be sure of was that it definitely was the type of goodbye her mom would have wanted.

Making sure to keep an eye on her dad, Charlie slipped a plate in front of him from time to time. Although he never took more than a few bites, it was enough to satisfy Charlie that he wouldn't starve.

Afternoon turned to dusk, and eventually evening, with just a few stragglers lingering out on the sunroom couches, more due to intoxication than wanting to stay. That was Charlie and Grandma's cue to reimagine the drink table into a makeshift coffee bar. By seven-thirty, the remaining guests had caffeinated and sobered up enough to head back to their hotels. After saying their final goodbyes and offering thank you hugs, Charlie and her dad shut the front door for the final time that night.

Dale almost immediately retreated to his office and slid the pocket doors closed behind him. Allowing her dad his chance to grieve on his own, Charlie and Ramona joined Grandma in the kitchen to clean. Her grandpa, being the eternal caveman, said, "I'll head in to catch some news and leave you women to it."

Deciding a full cleanup wasn't needed that night, they each retrieved all the food from the tables and placed them in containers to be saved for future consumption. As they did, the round of dishes grew to a sizable tower. Thank goodness for Dixie plates and disposable cutlery, which cut the overall mountain down. After filling two large trash bags with those items, Charlie and Ramona took their sacks to the garage and placed them in the garbage cans located on the back wall next to Dale's Jeep.

Taking a final look around, Charlie and Ramona made a bilateral decision before heading up for the night. They grabbed two Jiffy Pop containers from the pantry and mimed a sword fight, then made their way to the stove. Removing the cardboard tops, they each placed the tin pans on the front burners and began the shimmy and shake, watching as the foil grew to resemble giant mushrooms. Slid to the back burners, the random pops of the remaining kernels continued as the girls placed several Cokes, a variety of cookies, and candies on a tray.

After giving her grandparents a goodnight hug and kiss, Charlie left them lounging in the family room, eyes fixed on Barbara Walters' latest report. Ramona carried the tray as Charlie gave a quick rap on her dad's office doors, saying, "Goodnight, dad, I love you."

"Me too Charlie Bear, me too"," he replied through the carved oak doors.

Sitting the tray on the bed, Charlie and Ramona made quick work of putting their pajamas on and twisting their hair up in t-shirt turbans. Charlie grabbed her nail caboodle from the bathroom and set it on the side table.

Ramona flung one of her bags onto Charlie's desk and exposed the contents within. "Go ahead, make the first pick."

Charlie evaluated her options: *Nightmare on Elm Street*, *Halloween*, *Puppet Master*, *The Exorcist*, or *Suspiria*. Charlie decided to start with the original *Halloween*. She slipped the video tape out of its plastic Blockbuster confines and placed it into the mouth of the VHS player. As the copyright warning came up on the screen, letting them know it was for "Private Home Use Only", and the previews started, she and Ramona climbed onto the bed and placed several pillows behind themselves for comfort.

Charlie peeled back the Jiffy Pops' foil mound first, excited about *hot* popcorn. Ramona did the same, and they tossed handfuls into their mouths. They crunched away and popped open their cans of Coke as, on the screen, unknown eyes peered through a living room window, watching two teens make out. Washing the popcorn down with a swig of the caramel bubbles. Charlie leaned over to Ramona and mimicked the spooky background music.

Between handfuls of popcorn, they bantered back and forth about the awful clothes Jamie Lee Curtis and her friends wore. They debated over how she should tame the frizz factor in her hairdo, and they each were on the opposite end of the fight-or-flight debate. Ramona insisted Curtis' character should get the hell out, while Charlie thought she should fight back. They both agreed one should never put themself in that kind of situation to begin with.

The last drops out of their Cokes drained, the movie wrapped up with Michael's mask coming off and six bullets erupting from Loomis' gun, knocking Michael out of a second-story window. The girls got up for a bathroom break and selection of movie number two as the ominous piano riff played in the background.

Ramona finished first and started digging through the stack of videos in the bag. As Charlie exited from the bathroom, Ramona held two videos behind her back and said, "Pick a hand".

Charlie chose left, and Ramona revealed with a verbal drum roll the movie they would be watching next: *Nightmare on Elm Street*. Situating themselves back on the bed, Charlie reached over and brought her Caboodle to the center between them. As they watched Freddy shred teens with his knife-adorned glove, they painted their nails. Charlie opened a bottle of flashing fuchsia as Ramona dug out a half empty bottle of blue polish called electric youth. Sprawling out on the bed to allow for their nails to dry, the pair dozed off to the sound of Nancy's screams for help.

CHAPTER THIRTEEN
FRIENDS AND FAMILY

Waking up the following morning, the girls gazed upon the plethora of empty containers that were scattered around the room. Charlie looked over to her closet door, which was still closed, and a chill ran through her.

Ramona asked, "What's going on?"

Charlie shrugged and said, "Probably nothing," and told Ramona about her dream. "Honestly, it was more than likely all the junk food before bed."

"Yeah, probably." Ramona popped up and scuttled to the bathroom.

Through the open door, Ramona asked, "Do you want to get this off your mind now and investigate the closet mess from yesterday?"

"Yeah, I think that would be a good idea. Get it out of my brain. We totally need coffee first, though."

As Ramona exited the bathroom, she and Charlie almost collided. They giggled and placed their fingers over their lips in a *shh* gesture, then Charlie opened the bedroom door and padded downstairs. The house was eerily quiet for nine in the morning. She figured her dad was still sleeping, as his bedroom door was shut, but her grandparents were nowhere to be found. As she approached the coffee pot, she saw it was already full of the liquid fuel and a note in her grandma's handwriting sat beside it. *Good morning! Enjoy! We went for a walk over in Highland Park.*

Pouring two large mugs of coffee, Charlie loaded a tray with sugar, creamer, and—to her joyous surprise—leftover Danishes from the morning before. She considered whether to nuke them, but decided that they were just old enough to be perfect dippers for their coffee. Carrying her spoils up to the room, she found Ramona had already cleaned up a good amount of the trash from the night before.

As they sat and dunked away, Ramona "said, "I really like Eric. I think this could be something truly long term. You need something like that. You just need to be more open to a connection, and it will happen."

"I don't know," Charlie replied. "I'm too wrapped up in school to put myself out there in the dating pool. Ninety-five percent of the dates I've been on since freshman year in high school, you set up."

The pair giggled and decided they needed to get focused on the day.

With a newly gained burst of energy and sustenance, the pair opened the closet door and peered yet again at the disarray before them. It was literally like someone had been searching for something. Pulling the string for the overhead light, Charlie entered the closet, stepping over the landmines of clothing and bags. Taking a spot at the end of the closet, she sat on the floor across from Ramona. They began picking up the pieces, analyzing if anything was missing. They marveled at the items that had been ravaged: old handbags, backpacks, and jackets—pretty much anything with pockets. Even shoe boxes were scattered about. *Shoe boxes!* That sent a bolt of electricity through Charlie. She sprung up, leaped from the closet, and ran to the window. She slid the items on her window seat to the right, clicked the latch open, and pulled out box after box, laying them on the floor between the closet and the desk.

Ramona finally asked, "What the what?"

"This is what they were after, I am sure of it." As Charlie patted the box, she explained further, as she could see the confusion on her friend's face linger. "I am not sure who, but I am one hundred percent positive someone was here, and they were after what's in this box." She slid a taped shoebox labeled *Charlie's Rock Collection* over.

"Um, Charlie, why would anyone want a box of rocks? Are you losing it?"

With a heavy sigh, Charlie pulled the tape aside, flipped the top over, and exposed the stacks of cash to Ramona.

"Holy shit balls!" Ramona yelled.

"Shh," Charlie urged.

"How much is there?" Ramona stammered.

Thirty thousand," Charlie whispered.

Mouth gaped open and eyes as wide as saucers, Ramona became a temporary mute. She pointed. She tilted her head. She slowly blinked a few times, then squeaked out, "What in the actual fuck?"

Nodding in agreement to that response, Charlie said, "I had the exact same reaction."

"Why do you have this, Charlie?"

"That's the more baffling part. I found these in envelopes hidden around my mom's closet. Taped to the walls behind clothes, in pockets, and even sewn between layers of the clothes themselves"

Ramona, still seeming to be in shock, asked, "Was your mom a spy? Or in witness protection?"

Tossing a small stack of cash she had picked up back onto the pile, Charlie said, "I have no fucking clue. My plan was to wait until things settled here before I attempted to figure this out. There are so many more moving pieces." With that, she showed Ramona the stacks and stacks of journals and mentioned there was a whole other box she found in the attic. "I'm pretty sure this is all linked somehow."

"Have you told your dad?"

Charlie shook her head. "I don't think I am going to until I can at least get some questions answered first. He has enough on his mind with her death. He doesn't need this on top of everything else."

"You don't think any of this is linked to your mom's death, do you?"

Laying the bike up against the wall outside her room, Astrid fumed.

I know the money is there, she thought. *I can't keep relying on these plastic currency cards. They will only tide me over for so long, and the small amount of cash I had in my first stash is dwindling fast.*

Patience was not one of her virtues at this moment. At her wits end, Astrid decided it was time to call on the Dark Magician. He would know what to do.

Charlie and Ramona made quick work of securing the cash and placing everything back in the window seat. "You know what I need to do today?" Charlie asked. "I need to take some of the burden off my dad and start processing some of my mom's items. Wanna help me? I'm thinking we start with her closet since my grandparents are out?"

"Of course!" Ramona said. "But first, let's wrap this closet up."

Charlie agreed, and expeditiously processed the mess left in the closet. Who made the mess would remain an open item for the moment.

When they were done, Charlie asked Ramona to go up to the attic and grab any empty boxes she could find, saying she would go grab some trash bags from the kitchen. Taking the tray with her, Charlie exited her room and noticed her dad's door was open. She found him sitting in his recliner in the living room with a cup of coffee and the *Democrat and Chronicle.* "Morning, Dad"

"Morning, Charlie Bear."

Setting the tray on the coffee table, she bent down and gave her dad a hug and kiss.

"Where's your sidekick?" he asked.

"She's up grabbing boxes from the attic. We are going to tackle mom's closet this morning. You okay with that?"

With a long stare and wistful sigh, he said he was and added, "These things must be done, I guess".

Giving her dad another hug, Charlie offered to top off his coffee. He declined the offer and said he would just rest for now. Charlie turned to get to the cleaning closet, but her dad grabbed her hand and said, "I love you, kiddo. Thank you"

Charlie nodded and met Ramona as planned in the guest room. They set up a box in the closet for donations, a bag for trash, and brought the vanity chair over upon which to lay anything to be kept. Charlie excused herself for a moment and returned with her boombox. Placing it on her mom's vanity, she slid the plug into the socket in the wall, pressed the power button, and rotated the dial until she found a replay of Kasey Kasem's Top 40. That episode took them back to 1986. As Kasey wrapped up the long-distance dedication segment, he let his audience know that on that day in 1986, Falco debuted in the number one spot with "Rock Me Amadeus".

Charlie sang along as she began sorting with Ramona. Making quick work of the first third of the closet, Charlie showed Ramona where she found the envelopes of money. The first donation box was reaching its limits, so Ramona slid it out by its flaps and tossed an empty box, calling out, "Heads up." She then asked, "Hey, you want I should go grab a Coke?"

Charlie answered with a resounding, "Heck yeah!" As Ramona disappeared down the hall, Charlie continued her sorting.

A few minutes later, Ramona bounded into the room singing in unison with Jackson Browne's "For America" Ramona handed Charlie a Coke.

"Don't quit your day job," Charlie taunted.

Feigning an arrow through her heart, Ramona landed her wounded body up against the half empty wall of the closet. As she hit the wall, a folded scarf slid off the top shelf and hit the floor with a light thud. Ramona's eyes grew wide in shock. Charlie reached down, unwrapped the scarf, and found another leather-bound journal tied lightly with a green ribbon.

"It smells funny," Ramona stated as they examined the outside.

"I found another one like this the other day, but it had a small lock on it," Charlie said with a sense of mystery in her voice. "These are completely different from the ones my mom used to journal with." Agreeing that wasn't the time to open that particular can of worms, they set the journal out with the boombox.

While sliding a box to the hallway, Charlie grabbed a marker from the desk in her room and marked *donations* on the sides. After Ramona secured the tops, the duo carried the items from the chair into Charlie's closet and hung them up. The smell of her mom filled the small space, and Charlie smiled.

Hearing several voices downstairs, Charlie and Ramona padded down in their PJs, each carrying bags bound for the trash cans with them. They greeted Charlie's grandparents who were sitting with her dad in the family room. With the greetings came a loud growl emanating from Ramona. As each of them turned their heads towards her, Ramona laughed and said "Oopsie."

"Sounds to me like you may be hungry," Grandpa teased.

Agreeing that they could all eat with the bonus of getting her Dad out of the house, Charlie suggested burgers and shakes at Bill Grays. With a consensus, the girls excused themselves to get dressed, leaving the adults to continue their conversations.

Looking out her bedroom window, Charlie could see it would be an overcast afternoon, which definitely meant chilly temps with the unseasonable weather. Charlie chose jeans and her Duran Duran *Seven and the Ragged Tiger* t-shirt, and completed the outfit with an oversized plaid flannel shirt.

Sliding a wool sweater over her head, Ramona made a quick exit to the bathroom to settle down the static that arose in her hair. Charlie stuffed a wallet in her back pocket and herded Ramona out of the bedroom door as she pinned up the sides of her hair.

Joining the group, they decided on Dale's Cherokee after he pointed out if he didn't run her every other day or so, she would give him fits. Climbing in and setting the path towards Webster, they all continue with a hodgepodge of conversations. The men talked sports and politics and the ladies discussed Grandma's walk and the lilacs peeking through. Grandpa, of course, piped in from time to time to give his two cents. As Dale pulled the Jeep up to the restaurant, they were informed by Grandpa that it would be his treat and he would brook no arguments.

All in agreement to the terms, they each supplied the cute, button-nosed teen with their orders. Taking their plastic numbered tent to a large booth, they rotated going to the drink fountains to grab their beverages. By the time Charlie made it back with her root beer, trays of food had been delivered. Taking a quick poll on the ketchup and mustard situation, Charlie made her way back over to the condiments and filled seven mini paper souffle cups with ketchup and one with mustard. Surprising herself with her dexterity, she made it back to the booth without dropping or spilling any on herself.

Lunch wrapped up, they headed back to the house, where Dale and Grandpa went into the office to work on the stacks of papers that had been accumulating the past week as a result of Birdie's death. Eleanor donned one of Birdie's aprons and set her sights on the kitchen and meal preps she wanted to leave for her son.

The girls raced up the stairs to Charlie's room to gather Ramona's bags. Giggling, they shoved ahead of each other, and as Ramona crossed the threshold to Charlie's room, she victoriously screamed, "Take that!" Winded, she plopped onto Charlie's bed.

Charlie entered the closet and returned to the room with a big smile on her face, presenting Ramona with a flowered mini dress that was her mom's. "I set this aside earlier to give to you. I was thinking maybe you could wear it on your date with Eric tonight."

Ramona sat up and tears trickled down her freckled cheeks as she looked at the vintage piece. "Charlie, it's perfect! Thank you!" Ramona squealed as she ran and enveloped her friend in a giant bear hug. Finishing up her packing, she placed the dress carefully in her bag and gave it a quick zip.

Charlie hoisted the video tape bag onto her arm, and they headed out to Juicy. Charlie drove out of the cul-de-sac and set out towards the Blockbuster near Ramona's house. They exchanged small talk and sang along with various melodies that made their way across the airwaves, then arrived at their destination. Ramona hopped out and entered the front door of the Blockbuster. Neither of them trusted the drop box method, Ramona always saying she was in charge of her destiny when it came to the *Be Kind, Rewind* rule. Presenting the tapes directly to the clerk to check was the only way to be certain one wouldn't get charged a fee.

As Ramona stood in line, Charlie zipped up and down the dial to find anything but commercials. Unfortunately, it seemed that all the stations were in cahoots with the local media market at that moment, and unless she wanted to listen to a sermon, she was stuck with a struggling artist ad promising no oil painting over thirty-five dollars. This was followed by a Genesee Beer commercial, stating, "It's not just a beer, it's a Genny."

As if on cue, Ramona slid back into the car just as "My Sharona" started. Turning towards her, Charlie sang, "ma ma ma my Ramona!" They both burst out laughing as Charlie backed Juicy up and out of the lot. When the song finished, Ramona asked Charlie what her plans were for the stack of stuff that had been building up from her mom. Charlie shrugged, hands in the classic ten-and-two position, and said, "I'm not one hundred percent sure. It just keeps growing. I think I am honestly going to have to sneak it all with me back to school and deal with it there. There are so many journals that will need deciphering and cataloging along with the creepy dreams, odd occurrences, and last but not least, all that money!" She shook her head rapidly, as if shaking the excess contents out her ear.

Smiling at Charlie, Ramona reminded her, "If you need to run anything by me, I am just a phone call away."

Juicy slid up the gravel driveway of Ramona's house, the duo gave each other hugs. "See you next break, Ramona the Pest," Charlie teased. "I'll miss you."

"Ditto," Ramona said as she hopped out. She waved goodbye to Charlie as she entered her front door. Charlie waved back, unable to shake the ominous feeling in her bones.

Walter and Dale sat across from each other in the office. Stacks of documents lay before them. Some, like the death certificate documentation and items for the funeral home, needed immediate attention. Others, like the bank and insurance, could wait. They sat together, sorting and filling out the necessary forms. Deciding to take a quick break to see how his wife was coming along, Walter stood, stretched, and excused himself for a moment. Receiving a minimal nod from Dale, he slid the pocket doors open and made his way to the kitchen.

Eleanor was buzzing like a bee. Containers and leftovers surrounded her like a plastic fortress. At the moment, she was scribbling furiously on a notepad.

"What did that paper ever do to you?" Walter joked.

Laughing, Eleanor explained she was writing down a meal plan of sorts for Dale. "What is in which containers, expiration dates, and instructions on how to reheat. Most, he can microwave, but there are just some that should never be subjected to that kind of torture."

Walter walked over and stood behind Eleanor, reading her instructions over her shoulder. "You do know Dale is a Penn State graduate on top of being a forty-six-year-old man," he reminded her.

"Of course, dear. He also is a man who is grieving the loss of the person who handled all these things for him, and with Charlie heading back in a few days, I just want him set up to not have to worry or struggle—or worse—starve to death." She tipped her face up over her shoulder and pecked Walter's cheek. "Why don't you take a little something back in with you to tide you over until dinner?" She slid over to the refrigerator and removed a container of devilled eggs and a pitcher of sweet tea. Filling two glasses with ice, she poured them each a drink. Nudging Walter to grab the eggs and a few napkins, she walked behind him with a tea in each hand.

They entered the study just as Dale threw his pencil down on the desk. "This is crazy!" he exclaimed in frustration.

Eleanor, in full mom mode, said, "Well, it seems like we come at a perfect time. Take a break, grab a snack, and refocus your efforts." She set the teas onto coasters before them.

"I bring good ol' American fart food with me," Walter joked as he popped a whole deviled egg in his mouth and winked.

Dale chuckled. "Yeah, sounds good. Thanks, mom and dad."

Charlie walked in through the mudroom to find Grandma closing the pocket doors to Dad's office behind herself. "Ramona all back safe and sound?"

"Sure is," Charlie sighed, nodding towards the office. "They still in there?"

"Sure are."

"Well, I am going to grab a snack and make my way to Mom's studio to start the next phase," Charlie said as she loaded her arms with a Slim Jim, a Twinkie, and a Coke. "You've gotten a lot processed here, Grandma. Impressive!"

Grandma thanked her and filled her in on what had been done so far so she could help convey the instructions to her dad if needed.

After that, Charlie entered her mom's studio, which felt surreal. She very rarely, if ever, went in there without her mom. With the door having been closed the past week, the air was a bit stale. Setting her snacks down, she flicked on two lamps and made her way to the picture window. Opening each side slightly to allow some fresh air in, she turned to stand and view the room in its entirety.

Charlie took a breath. This room was her mom. Every inch screamed Birdie. Slowly walking around, she slid her fingers delicately over the variety of surfaces and knick knacks, fighting back tears. She stopped facing a large bookcase on one side of the room, housing a variety of design and sewing books. There was also an entire shelf of Simplicity and Burda pattern packets that her mom had collected over the years. Why she did so always puzzled Charlie, as she knew her mom mostly sewed from the hip. A few small creations from Charlie's childhood served as bookends, such as the obligatory pottery fiascos from kindergarten and first grade. A smattering of family photos dotted the shelves.

Just as Charlie was about to turn her sights to the next area, her eyes caught the collection of books on the lowest shelf. Titles such as *The Art and Practice of Astral Projection*, *Control Your Dreams*, and *The Spirit World and Devils and Demons* were stacked on top of each other.

Charlie knew her mom was paranormal friendly, but she never talked about subjects like those. Picking up one of the texts, she saw dog ear after dog ear and let the cover naturally fall open to reveal a page on realms in the afterlife. Yellow highlighter and penciled notes littered the contents. Taking the spine in her left hand, she used her right to fan the pages as if she were viewing a flip art book. The number of untouched pages paled in comparison to the graffiti-ridden texts.

After setting the book on the windowsill, she repeated her efforts on the rest of the stack. "Jesus," she exhaled. "What the heck were you doing, Mom?"

Choosing to leave those for a more detailed examination later, Charlie made her way to a small file cabinet to the right of the makeshift drafting and craft table. Pulling out a few files that may be of help to her dad, she placed them on top and, in an effort to make her stomach stop rumbling, snapped into her Slim Jim and washed it down with a sip or two of fizzy goodness.

The Master smiled. "Good work Marcus," he said, adding that they need to come up with more ways to reach out to her. "We need to draw her attention to the possibilities of what is out there. She cannot defend herself against the unknown, and we can only do so much."

Marcus nodded, and the pair turned their attention back to Charlie.

From the cleaning closet, Charlie grabbed two handfuls of trash bags and headed back in to the studio. As she emptied the contents of the file cabinet, she kept the stack for her dad in place for the time being. Charlie methodically made her way around the rest of the room. Deciding to keep the material and sewing supplies for herself, she left those in their current locations for boxing up later. She took the garments her mom had started for Mrs. Murphy and hung them on the corner of the door. Placing the cover on the sewing machine, she cleaned up the scraps. She grabbed the photos of them at Niagara Falls and placed them on top of the books she planned on keeping. Making a few more donation notes, she packed up and escorted the trash to the cans, which had filled up fast after the party.

Tomorrow is trash day, she remembered. How she knew that was unclear, as time seemed to have stopped since being home. Opening the garage door behind the Jeep, she wheeled the cans to the bottom of the driveway, making sure not to ding Grandpa's Marquis. She then returned inside, hooked the garments on the coat rack by the front door, and carried the items she was keeping to her room. She placed them on the window seat and laid her untouched Twinkie on top.

Joining her grandma in the kitchen, she sat at the island, where she noticed Grandma had just finished the most ultimate game of refrigerator Tetris Charlie had ever seen. "What's your high score now?" Charlie joked.

Grandma squinted, tilted her head to the side like a Labrador, and gave a smile. Ignoring the question, she let Charlie know that they were going to have the chicken and dumplings the Nicholbees brought over for dinner, nodding towards the hot oven. "I'm thinking of mixed vegetables to have with it? You agree?"

Charlie nodded in silence, as she was *not* the person to ask an opinion of when it came to veggies. If it were up to her, she'd opt for none, ever, except potatoes with butter. Her imaginary side dish set her mouth watering, but she quickly recovered. "I'm going to set the table," she said, and started to grab plates.

Eleanor placed her hand on hers and said, "Let's make this an easy night for us all." She handed Charlie a stack of leftover Dixie plates from the party.

Charlie smiled and agreed, but insisted on real silverware. Something about the possibility of a plastic fork prong breaking off in her mouth gave her the willies. As Charlie set the table, Grandma hummed a little ditty. *This is nice*, Charlie thought. College definitely was not home.

Calling the men to the dinner table, Grandma led the parade down the hall.

Walter exclaimed, "Smells like you outdid yourself again".

With a wink over her shoulder, Grandma thanked him and let him know the Nicolbees were to thank for this meal. "Which reminds me, Dale, we all need to work on thank you cards before we head out."

Grandpa snatched two beers from the fridge, handed one to Dale, and said, "There you go son, we earned it!"

Dale smiled through his obvious exhaustion, which Charlie figured was ninety percent mental and ten percent Grandpa. Even more reason not to bring any of the weirdness up to him just yet. They each plated their dumplings and ate. Grandma told a story Charlie was sure her dad had heard at least fifty times about when she and Grandpa were looking for their first home.

Wrapping up dinner, Charlie was thankful her grandma insisted on the easy route, but since the silverware was her idea, she washed them while the others retired to the family room for some local news. Walking through the door from the kitchen, she caught the snippet of a conversation they were having about this house and her dad's plans.

They looked like three cats who ate canaries, so Charlie moved the conversation in a different direction, letting them know she was going upstairs to call Tabitha at school. She needed to see if there was any additional work she needed to be aware of before she returned. As she walked past them towards the foyer, Grandma let her know there would be mini strawberry shortcakes for dessert around eight-thirty if she wanted to join them. Agreeing all too eagerly, Charlie performed a quick mental calculation on the caloric intake her body had endured since she'd been home.

Once upstairs, she shuffled her backpack to the corner of her desk, pulled out her mini address book, and slid her finger to the "T"s. Finding Tabitha's number, she picked up the phone she had since early high school and chuckled at what she had deemed cool in those days. Pressing the number pads on the clear handset, she twisted the yellow cording between her fingers. On the third ring, a female voice answered, "Tori and Tabitha's room. Speak"

Charlie asked for the latter and waited as Tori yelled down the hall. "Yello," Tabitha chimed, sounding winded.

"Hey, it's Charlie. I'm checking in to see if you had any updates for me on classwork."

Tabitha informed her it had actually been a slow week, and other than her class notes and a tiny quiz, she had missed nothing. "How have you been holding up? Do you know when you'll be back?"

"Doing okay, considering," Charlie said. "Looking to be back by Monday."

"Awesome, see you then!"

Charlie heard the click of the line before she even had a chance to respond. Thankful no new workload was added, Charlie focused her attention on finishing the reading and outline for her next paper. Notebook splayed in front of her, she found herself in full procrastination mode. She tapped her pen, twirled her hair, and counted the boy band members that donned her walls. As she looked down to see literally two new words written on her paper, she decided that trying to write anything at that point was a task in futility. She couldn't focus, what with the small fortune in cash, a chest full of journals, and spooky themed books taunting the armchair detective inside of her. She knew she didn't want to tackle any of those things there. That was one hundred percent clear in her mind. So, she turned her attention to working on a plan of attack for the attic the next day. But first thing was first. Music.

Lost in the lyrics of the Eurythmics, Charlie looked up from her list and saw it was somehow already eight-twenty. Meandering down to join the others, Charlie heard a knife on a cutting board. Her grandma was humming to herself as Charlie walked in to explore further. Grandma, who was busy slicing strawberries, looked up and asked Charlie to hand her a colander.

As she placed the bright red slices in, Charlie went to the pantry and pulled out a package of premade shortcakes, tub of cool whip, and a can of her dad's favorite Redi Whip. Setting her armload on the island, she turned her sights to the cupboard and retrieved four dessert bowls. She then worked on opening the shortcake package.

"How did the studies go, Charlie?"

Waiting to answer her grandma until after the ear assaulting sounds of the cellophane ended, Charlie filled her in on how she was actually ahead of the game and felt things would go smoothly upon her return to Cornell. Plopping a shortcake in each bowl, Charlie waited for Grandma to finish stirring sugar into the strawberries, then watched as she spooned mounds of gooey, sugary goodness onto each yellow, spongy disc. Retrieving spoons for each of them, Charlie laid them on a tray she had retrieved from on top of the fridge. She then set the bowls, both whips, extra spoons, and napkins to the side.

They entered the family room with Grandma leading the way. As Charlie set down the tray, her dad grabbed the Redi Whip, vigorously shook it, popped the red cap off its perch, and, with a slight push of his index finger, rocketed a steady stream of whipped goodness into his mouth. "You can take the man out of the country but can't take the country out of the man," Grandpa chided as he reached for the Cool Whip. Charlie also went that route, and

Grandma ate hers naked, having already spooned extra sugar syrup on hers when in the kitchen.

The gang enjoyed their desserts as *Family Matters* played in the background. Licking the last of the cool whip off her spoon, Charlie challenged the group to a friendly game of Scrabble. To a chorus of agreement, Charlie retrieved the box from the bookshelf of the built-in credenza. She opened the box and dropped all the wooden squares in the lid, and as Grandma flipped the pieces face down, Grandpa opened the board and handed out the letter racks to each of them. One by one, they reached in and grabbed a tile, with an "A" giving Dale the starting move. They played a no holds barred game, contesting words, and feelings were hurt when Grandpa denied their validity thanks to the small paperback Webster's Dictionary he kept by his side like a trusty pistol.

Over an hour later, the final numbers were tallied, and Grandma claimed victory. After congratulations were given, the grandparents excused themselves to go pack and call it a night. Grandpa noted they would be leaving early, but Grandma quipped in quickly to say they should have coffee together first. Agreeing, in a huff, Grandpa kissed Charlie on the forehead before heading up the stairs. Grandma gathered her cross-stitch supplies that had made a home beside the recliner, gave Charlie a kiss and Dale a hug, and joined her husband.

Dropping the lid on the Scrabble box, Charlie gave her exit speech as well. After swallowing her dad in a bear hug, she lifted the tray and took its dirty passengers to the kitchen, placing them beside the sink. After one final goodnight, she headed upstairs.

Vulnerability set in. Dale thought to himself how odd it was that he was so strong throughout most of the experience, but reality was setting in. The reality of Charlie going back to school. She seemed to be handling her mom's death as best as could be expected, but he sensed that she was pulling away from him. He couldn't quite put his finger on what it was, but he knew something was off. Maybe she just needed a routine again. He wished that for her. He wished and hoped that school would be her solace and help her from missing her mother. With that thought, he hoisted himself up and set off to his study, knowing sleep was not in his immediate future. He began to work on the cards his mom had mentioned.

Soft tapping on her bedroom door woke Charlie. Opening her eyes, she saw it was still dark outside. Letting out a guttural growl she rolled to her side. The tapping persisted. "Charlie, honey, it's Grandma. Your grandpa and I are about to head out soon and wondered if you wanted to join us for coffee?"

Groaning again, Charlie managed a response. "Yes, Grandma. I'll be down in a minute." Charlie heard her grandma repeat the response in a whisper to her Grandpa, followed by soft footsteps. Rolling to her other side, she laid eyes on her clock—it was five-thirty in the morning—and let out one last, gruff growl. She slid out of bed, shuffled to the bathroom, and splashed cold water on her face, then wrapped herself in her robe. Thinking she would possibly regret the decision, she opted not to slide on her slippers, figuring the cold floor would force her to stay alert.

As she circled around the hallway, her dad joined her at the top of the stairs, looking just as perky as she was. They gave each other a mini high five.

"Here's to getting down the stairs unscathed," Dale joked.

Charlie thought that was almost funny enough to elicit a giggle. Almost.

As they approached the kitchen, a wonderful aroma of coffee hit Charlie's olfactory nerves. As she fixed herself a cup, Dale poured himself a large glass of orange juice. Grandpa, seated behind the paper, said, "Morning."

Grandma placed a coffee cake she had heated up on the table, and they all sat around it. Walter set the paper down, took a sip of his black coffee, and assessed the day's travel plans. They would head out 490 to 86 and would make their stop just past Salamanca, where he had booked a room at the Holiday Inn. He planned on having them home in Chagrin Falls by Sunday at noon.

Charlie's dad attempted one more time to remind his dad that the trip was less than four hours total, and they could do it in one fell swoop.

Grandma quickly chimed in, "Yeah, Dale, honey, but your dad's sciatica wouldn't possibly allow him to sit that long."

Charlie snickered, knowing that her grandpa sat at least that long in his recliner watching football on Sundays.

The grandparents assumed their traveling positions as Charlie and her dad stood side by side, waving goodbye to the Grand Marquis as it backed down the driveway. Turning to her dad, Charlie announced that since she was up, she was going to start packing and finish the attic. Dale nodded at the plan and expressed his intention to get some more sleep.

Charlie loaded up a large coffee mug and made her way to her room. After taking a sip, she went to the closet to grab her suitcase and large duffle bag. She placed them on the bed, unzipped them, and proceeded to her dresser. Drawer by drawer, she pulled out the items that would need to go with her since Spring was imminent.

With the duffel bag half full of intimates and sleep shirts and the suitcase feeling a bit jealous that all it got was some light jeans and shorts, she walked into her closet to see what additional items she would be taking. Making sure to include the items she snagged from her mom's wardrobe, she also added a few spring dresses and skirts and two lightweight jackets, one being her Members Only that she didn't have the heart to part with and the other more of a raincoat. She placed a few pairs of shoes into the duffle and zipped everything up. Having already secured the journals and cash in Juicy, she felt like that was it. She sat on her window seat and admired her little doodles as she finished off her coffee. With the last drop hitting her tongue, she stood and moved on to go grab the box in the attic.

Dale had resurrected by that time and started his version of breakfast for him and Charlie. She could smell the sweet aroma of the Eggos a mile away. Gliding into the kitchen, she propped herself up at the island and said, "Leggo my Eggo."

They giggled as Dale dropped four crispy disks onto her plate and slid it, along with butter and syrup, across to her. Loading up the stack with all the goodness, she asked for a glass for OJ since he had informed her that there was no Tang to be had. He pushed down his own waffles, grabbed the juice glasses, and sat next to Charlie to wait. She poured them both a tall glass. They sat in silence for a moment before Dale chimed in, "I was thinking about Juicy and your trip."

" "Oh?" Charlie asked, waiting for the clincher.

"School isn't too terribly far away, but just far enough to be problematic for a car of Juicy's age and, well, temperament. I was thinking you and I should go out and give her a once over, then head on down to the auto parts store and grab anything she may need. What do you think?"

Having just shoveled a large stack of Eggo in her mouth, all Charlie could muster was a fervent nod to show her approval paired with a thumbs up.

"Great," he said. "Let's wrap this up, and I will meet you out in the driveway. You may want to change into something you don't mind getting dirty in case we need to get up in the engine."

As they finished eating, they chatted about how they thought the grandparents' road trip was going.

After tossing her plate and glass in the sink, Charlie made a beeline for her room to change. She selected an old pair of jeans and an even older t-shirt from one of their many vacations to the Grand Canyon and swapped ensembles. Then, with a jaunty step or two, she met her dad in the driveway.

Rounding the corner of Juicy, Charlie saw her dad bearing a mischievous look on his face. Sliding his hands from behind his back, Dale revealed a set of keys dangling from a keychain labeled *Charlie*. Not quite sure what was happening, Charlie cocked her head and asked her dad what was going on. Taking a deep breath, Dale handed her the keys and said, "She's yours, Charlie Bear. Your mom loved you, and this car, more than the world. It's only right that Juicy gets passed down to you."

Tears welled up in Charlie's eyes, which her dad gently brushed away. "Enjoy her, honey".

Giving her dad a big bear hug, Charlie whispered in his ear, "Thank you."

"Okay, enough of that," Dale said. "Let's get her roadworthy for your trip back".

They checked the oil, Dale offering a brief explanation on the quirks of the Volkswagen having a strainer plate in lieu of a filter system if she ever felt the urge to change her oil. The pair laughed way too hard at that thought. They checked the other fluids and tire pressure. Charlie wrote down the items they would need, then Dad gave her a quick rundown on how the spare tire worked. "Most cars have a donut spare in the trunk, fully inflated. This crazy car of your mom's has a mechanism linking the spare to the windshield washer pump. So, just keep in mind that if you use your windshield washer fluid a lot, you will need to check on the spare tire's pressure, so you aren't left with an unusable spare." Charlie watched as her dad did his best Vanna White impression to solidify his statements in her brain.

With their shopping list in hand, they headed out in Dale's Jeep over to the local auto parts store. After acquiring the items needed, the pair headed to McDonald's for a quick bite. They returned home, wrapped up the maintenance items on Juicy, and loaded up the small compartment in the front with extra oil.

The rest of their evening was spent creating lists and menus for Dale to follow in Charlie's absence, dinner, and a couple of movie classics before saying their goodnights.

Not getting much sleep, Dale made his way quietly to the kitchen. *Today's the day*, he thought. *Charlie goes back to school, and I am left here alone to my own thoughts.* He would probably fill most of his days with work, but that left a lot of alone time at the house. Filling the coffee filter with a few scoops of Folgers, he padded to the sink and loaded up the carafe with water, which he methodically dumped into the Mr. Coffee. He pressed the brew button, and the kitchen soon filled up with the wonderful smell that reminded him of Birdie. While the brewing proceeded, he filled a glass with Orange Juice and walked down the hallway to the front door to grab the *Democrat and Chronicle* from the front stoop. Taking his OJ and paper, he settled in at his desk to catch up on current events. Unable to focus, he sat and stared out his window.

Charlie and her mom walked up Drayton Street, heading towards Forsyth Park. Her tiny hand in her mom's, Charlie stopped to stick her nose in a large cluster of Gardenia growing on a stone wall. It was such a wonderful and intoxicating smell. As she inhaled, she heard a bluebird nearby singing the happiest of songs. Mom explained to her that male Bluebirds are bright blue with a rusty belly, and the females were a more subdued gray blue. She continued to explain that some people believed the bluebird is a symbol of joy and hope, and that if you see one, it could mean good things were coming or it could also be a representation of a connection between the living and those who have passed away, like Grandma Dorothy.

As Charlie stuck her nose in for one final inhale, Mom let go of her hand, and the bluebird got louder and louder.

Charlie woke to a bird chirping. She squinted at the sun shimmering through her curtains. She immediately closed her eyes in an attempt to fall back into the dream she was having. After a few minutes of lying there, she realized it was a futile effort. Shifting herself up on her elbows, she took in the room. She was going to miss home for sure, but would be glad to get back to a routine.

She hoisted herself to a full upright position and swung her legs over the edge of the bed, letting them dangle. She inhaled deeply and quickly realized there was coffee. Sliding on her slippers and robe, she hustled to the kitchen.

Upon entering, she found her dad standing in front of the refrigerator, looking quite dumbfounded. "Mornin', Charlie Bear! I was trying to figure out what to make for your bon voyage breakfast and seem to be stuck."

Charlie sidled up to her dad to get a full view of what he was looking at. From top to bottom, she could see his conundrum. The fridge was packed with casseroles and salads galore, but nothing that would be a breakfast choice. Tapping her fingers on her thigh, she had an *aha* moment. "Dad, I'll take over," she said as she walked over to the pantry. She grabbed a loaf of bread, cinnamon and syrup, then pulled out a few eggs and milk from the fridge. "How about some French toast?"

"But, of course!" Dale retorted in a phony French accent.

Charlie began to whip up the batter, turning to grab a small griddle from the cabinet below her in the island. She plugged it in and retrieved some butter while it heated up. "The key," she started to tell her dad, "is to make sure the griddle is nice and hot." Dipping her hands under the kitchen faucet, she wet her fingertips, then flung the water onto the griddle. A sizzle and pop notified her that the surface was ready for her. She turned the heat down one notch and dipped and flipped the bread, making sure to coat it with the egg mixture. "How do you like your cinnamon?" she asked.

"Plentiful," Dad responded.

She laid the dipped squares of bread onto the hot surface and sprinkled extra cinnamon onto her dad's slices. Waiting for the flip, he said, "I am going to miss you, kiddo. I am so proud of you, but I am going to miss you."

Charlie nodded. "I know, dad. I'm going to miss you too." Flipping each square, she then turned to grab two plates. After placing the finished product on them, she wedged a good hunk of butter between each layer. Handing a plate to her dad, she then assembled hers. "Wait!"

Her dad froze, mouth open and a fork of French toast, dripping syrup, halfway inserted.

"Powdered sugar!" Charlie explained. "I almost forgot!" She spun back to the pantry and returned holding the small shaker containing the sugar delight. Dale watched as she shook a blizzard on his stack and repeated the sequence on hers.

After filling their bellies, they reviewed the list Charlie had created for her dad and her path back to college. Dale reminded her she was to call as soon as she landed back in her dorm room. Looking up at the clock, Charlie realized she needed to get going if she wanted to be back in enough time to settle in before dinner.

Dale agreed to handle the dishes, so Charlie whizzed up to her room to get dressed and grab her bags. After descending the stairs two at a time, she signaled to her dad to meet her out by the garage. "Let's keep the goodbyes civilized," he declared.

Feeling his sadness, Charlie leapt into his arms for a big bear hug. "Bye, Dad. Take care, try not to worry, and remember I am just a phone call away."

Dale chuckled as he replied with a simple, "Ditto." He hugged her tighter before releasing her to her travels.

Charlie slid into Juicy as her dad pushed the garage door button to start the familiar grinding, signaling the rise of the door. She cranked the window down, then started the engine. With a bit of resistance from Juicy, she finally got her in reverse and held her hand out the window to her dad. She gave her dad's hand one final squeeze, then made her way down the driveway.

This whole damn plan is imploding before me, Astrid thought *It's all because of her. And now she's off to college. I need to find a way to follow her. I will not let this stand in my way. I have worked too hard and too long.* With that, she screamed for the Dark Magician to appear.

CHAPTER FOURTEEN
BACK TO SCHOOL

The drive back to school was pleasant and uneventful. Top down, wind in her hair, sun on her face, and with great music playing, Charlie decided she could definitely get used to having that kind of freedom of mobility and mentally planned weekend mini trips. As she maneuvered her way down Route 366, McGraw Tower appeared in the distance. Making a right on Caldwell Road, she wound her way through the campus, ending her sojourn in the parking lot closest to her dorm. She made a mental note to stop by the administrative offices in the morning to obtain an official pass.

Snatching her suitcase and duffle from the front compartment, she took a deep breath, closed her eyes, and contemplated how good it felt to be back. Upon entering her dorm lobby, she greeted the student residential assistant at the front desk, then stopped at her mailbox to check on its contents. After slipping a few flyers and campus propaganda into her back pocket, she opted to take the stairs to her floor. Making the final swirl around to the fourth-floor landing, she heard the hustle and bustle of the other inhabitants of her floor in the common area.

When she pushed the door open, no fewer than five heads whirled around and announced, "Welcome Back, Charlie!"

With her hands full, Charlie mustered a nod and said, "I'll be back to catch up soon." Reaching her room, she inserted her key and turned the knob. She was immediately hit with a wall of stale, warm air and something most acrid. She dropped her luggage on her bed and set out to find the culprit, stopping briefly to start up her oscillating fan and crack the tiny case window she was allowed to open—as if *anyone* would want to jump to their death from the fourth floor.

Following her nose, she found the most unholy, black, fuzzy ball bathing itself in a sticky lake of goo. Realizing she had left an apple to rot on her desk, she retrieved a plastic bag from the small locker tower she had in the corner, pinched her nose, and surrounded the decaying sphere, making sure to get a good swipe in to rid the desktop of as much goo as possible. Trying not to heave, she grabbed a small spray bottle of cleaner and wiped the residual ooze off the surface, leaving behind a dark shadow that she was unsure would ever disappear. She dropped the paper towels into the bag and tied a knot, trapping the foul odor for good. Taking her bag of rancid apple carcass down the hall, holding it at arm's length in front of her, she opened the trash chute and dropped it down to the depths of the building.

Swiping her hands on her ass cheeks, she walked back to the common area where the gaggle of girls were still strewn along the vintage sofas and chairs that adorned the space. Plopping down next to Victoria, she said her obligatory greetings to everyone present. They responded with condolences and things like "I can't imagine" and "dish the dirt" from those with no sense of social niceties.

Wrapping up the social hour, Charlie looked at her Swatch and realized why her stomach was angry with her. Excusing herself, she went to her room and grabbed her meal card, her crossbody, and a light jacket, then made her way down to the dining hall.

Loading her tray with a plate of meatloaf, mashed potatoes, and a pea and carrot medley, she circled around the tray track to the deserts and grabbed a slice of yellow cake with chocolate frosting.

As she waited for the student cashier to ring her up, she swiped a Pizza-Hut-style plastic cup and placed it on her tray. She presented her meal card for payment, then bee-lined over to the beverage station. After taking a moment to swig down the first cup full, she refilled and wove through the tables, finding a spot next to a window.

Charlie stacked her first fork full of meatloaf and mashed potatoes, then bounced the stack into the carrots and peas, creating the perfect bite. An immediate panic set in as she swallowed the first mouthful; In the chaos of finding the apple ooze, she forgot to make the critical phone call to her dad. Reaching in her crossbody, she fumbled to find her cell phone, then quickly dialed the home number. Instead of ringing, she immediately heard the scolding tone of her father's voice on the other end.

After several apologies and a quick conversational rundown on how the trip went, Charlie and her dad said their goodbyes. Looking at her now-cold meatloaf and mashed potatoes, Charlie grabbed the red squeeze bottle on her table and shot a puddle of ketchup in the center of the latter. She then added the meatloaf, stirred, heaped it on a spoon, and quickly devoured it. Rinsing it down with a swig of her Coke, she then set her taste buds on the cake. *There's something special about cafeteria yellow cake that no fancy bakery could ever replicate*, she thought as she savored every bite.

As the chewing continued, she thought about her classes and drifted into what she was going to do with the items she had yet to retrieve from the car. She wanted answers as soon as she could get them, but she did not want it to interfere with her actual schoolwork. She mentally ran through her upcoming week and set a plan of action. The next day would be slammed, so she would take time that night to spread it all out, then she would have time Tuesday and Thursday between classes to start her research. Charlie took the last few sips from her drink and walked across campus to Juicy.

The air had definitely taken on a chill, Charlie was glad she had opted for a heavier coat. Charlie hopped in and drove Juicy to the front of her building. Exiting the driver's seat, she lifted a lever to gain access to the boxes in the makeshift back seat. Knowing she wouldn't be able to carry both in at once, she chose to grab one and drop it off in the lobby before heading back out to retrieve the other. After setting down the second box, she went back out to lock up her car, then headed back into the lobby. The student RA had switched shifts, and Mandy was now peering inquisitively at Charlie. "Those look really heavy," she stated as she cracked her gum.

"Mostly awkward," Charlie replied. "Hey, Mandy, didn't there used to be one of those old hotel type luggage racks here?"

Mandy seemed to delve way too deep in thought for such a simple question, then let Charlie know that it was in the closet to the right of the mailboxes.

Charlie slid the archaic contraption out of the confines of the closet and wheeled it over to her stack. After loading up the contents, she wheeled it over to the elevators and mentioned to Mandy that she would be right back down to move her car. She pressed the up-arrow button. When the doors opened, she stood back to make sure no human contents would come spilling out, then backed herself and her sleigh into the metal box. She pressed her floor and waited for the doors to close. Humming to herself as she ascended, she glanced over at the inspection sticker. She found it hard to believe it was correct, given the horrible moans the elevator ground out with every floor it conquered. As it pinged, she snapped out of her humming trance and pushed the luggage cart to her room, cringing as a high-pitched squeak accompanied every turn of the wheel.

Charlie unloaded her boxes just inside the door, returned the brass monstrosity to its hovel, and deposited Juicy back into the parking lot. Entering her building for the final time that night, she once again took the stairs. She entered her room, threw her bag and keys onto her bed, removed her jacket, and sat at her desk. Gnawing on her lip, she debated if she should satisfy some of her curiosities. *No*, she thought. *You have a plan. Stick to it.* She did, however, pull out the small safe, placed it in the rear of her closet, and buried it under the spare laundry basket she had. She decided to go wash the road trip grime off her, gathered her shower caddy and towel, and headed to shower.

All clean and relaxed, she selected her kitty pajamas, wrapped her hair in an old t-shirt, and climbed on her bed with her backpack. With a flick of her remote, she perused the channels until she narrowed it down to either *Magical World of Disney*, *Herbie Goes Bananas*, or *ALF*. The lovable, cat-eating alien won out. Charlie emptied the contents of her backpack on her bed as she watched his exploits. What she was about to do was definitely a result of her father's influence.

She took the texts and notebooks that were not needed for the next day and set them on the floor next to her bed. She then stacked her remaining texts and notebooks in order of the class and its time. As she did, she made sure to review the most recent notes. Charlie placed the stack neatly back into the large opening of her backpack, then checked in on the small pouch containing her pens, pencils, and highlighters to make sure she would have what she needed. Satisfied with her results, she zipped all openings closed, hopped up and over to her mini fridge, and slowly opened it, hoping she would not have a repeat of the apple ooze. "Phew," she said to herself as she pulled a cold Coke from the door. She then went to her locker and removed a fresh bag of Ruffles.

Taking her spot back on her bed, she looked at the clock, flicked to Fox and watched a Burger King, Chevy, and Budweiser commercial before the splatters of paint were tossed around and a group of hip hop dancers moving to Heavy D singing In Living Color. She nibbled and sipped attempting not to choke at the hilarious comedy skits playing out on her TV. She knew this would be a new Sunday routine for herself. With the closing credits rolling, she set her snacks and can to the side table and maneuvered under her covers. After turning off the light, she fell asleep.

Monday morning came way too early for Charlie's liking. Remembering she had to make her way to the admin office before her first class, she made quick work of getting dressed. That day's forecast called for jeans, a t-shirt, and a flannel shirt. Charlie was growing quite fond of them, especially when it wasn't cold enough for sweatshirts or warm enough for just short sleeves. She slid on a pair of Keds, then grabbed her backpack, crossbody, and a hat. She contemplated common room coffee, but opted to stop by one of the coffee carts by the admin building.

As she walked up the path, it hit her how many students took full advantage of later classes. Not quite a ghost town, the campus definitely was lacking student representation at that moment.

Pulling open the heavy wood door to the office, she saw a very tired-looking, middle-aged woman staring off into space. An enormous cup of coffee was steaming before her which looked untouched. "Ahem," Charlie vocalized, stating her presence. "Good morning. I need a parking pass for the Stewart and Williams lot. How would I go about obtaining one?"

Continuing her zombie impression, the woman, who based on the nameplate was Audry, took a deep breath that resembled more of a sigh and slid open a file cabinet to her left. Barely throwing eyes in its direction, she ran her fingers across the top tabs and stopped, opening a manila folder full of packets. "Take one of these," she said as she clipped it to a clipboard. "Have a seat there and fill it out. I will need a driver's license and ten dollars in cash."

Charlie did as she was instructed and filled out the pertinent information about Juicy. She snickered at one point, wondering if she was the only one on campus who had a car with a name. Signing her name and dating the form, she reached in her crossbody and pulled out a tenner. After handing the board and money to Audry, she sat back down and waited for the process to take place, wishing she had grabbed the coffee before.

Trying not to hum or whistle to the Musak playing in the background, she found a People magazine on the side table. She could hear Audry walking about as she read about the lives of the rich and famous. The woman's loafers shuffled to a stop in front of Charlie, and she handed her a laminated card labeled *Parking Permit 9176*.

"Keep this visible on your dash at all times when parked in the lot," she said. "It's only good for that lot and any lots marked as public throughout the campus. It is not, under any circumstances, to be used to park in faculty or emergency personnel lots."

Charlie nodded and accepted the shiny card. She stuck it in her back jeans pocket and exited the office, saying a quick thank you and good day to Audry, who had already settled back into her seat, this time inhaling the coffee before her.

"Outstanding idea, Audry," Charlie said as she made a beeline to the cart just outside. With a large coffee in hand, she looked at her Swatch and realized she had a few minutes to kill before her anthropology class. She opted to go display her shiny new pass on Juicy's dash.

With that done, walking towards McGraw Hall and her class, Charlie pondered her mom's mystery. It was as if the boxes were haunting her, calling her to action. She shook it off and entered professor Tighman's lecture space.

She heard a muffled, "Hey. Hey!" A fellow student tapped Charlie on her shoulder. "Class is over. Were you sleeping with your eyes open?"

Charlie looked around the lecture hall, then turned to the guy speaking to her and replied, "Uh, no. I must have been deep in thought. Thanks."

"No probs," he said as he turned to head up the stairs to exit.

Charlie sat still for a moment, attempting to take in what had just happened. Once again, she looked around the lecture hall, seeing no other students. She looked up at the institutional clock on the wall and realized that forty-five minutes had passed. She shook her head and looked down to see that she had not taken a single note in the class, but in front of her was a small paragraph, and its contents terrified her.

Listen to me you meddling fool. I have worked too hard and long to let someone like you stop me. You have no idea who I am and what I am capable of. Keep testing me though, you insignificant little girl, and you will find out the true meaning of misery. You think you are hurting now as you miss your pathetic mother? I promise you that is nothing compared to the pain and suffering I will bring upon you and those you love if you keep up your nosey ways. Turn your efforts and attention elsewhere before it's too late.

Grabbing all her belongings, she shoved them haphazardly into her backpack. Sprinting up the stairs and out of McGraw, she collapsed onto the grass, her heart beating as though it would pop out of her chest. She sat, a crumpled pretzel of a person, and just stared out at the sky. "What the actual fuck," she said to herself. Inhaling and exhaling slowly, she struggled to catch her breath. Once she had control of her breathing, Charlie looked at her watch to see she still had plenty of time for lunch before her next class.

Hitching herself to a standing position, she flung her backpack over her shoulder and started her walk to the dining hall. Still feeling shook up, but also knowing she had to eat something, Charlie grabbed a tray and loaded it with two slices of pizza and a can of Coke. She paid the student cashier, who was giving her the oddest stare. "You okay?" they asked. "You look pretty pale."

Stating she was fine, Charlie lifted her tray and proceeded to a lounge chair and a small table in the corner. She set the tray on the table and collapsed into the chair. After cracking the tab on her Coke, she took an enormous swig, almost choking on the bubbles that hit the back of her throat. Placing the can back on the tray, she raised her backpack up onto her knees. She unzipped the large opening and pulled out the notebook from class, which bore the scars of being mangled in the chaos. She flipped open to where her notes were supposed to be and examined what was written on the page before her.

It was her handwriting, for sure, but she had no memory of putting pen to paper. As she read the words before her again, tears came to her eyes. How could she have written that with no memory of doing so? To keep herself calm, Charlie picked her pizza slice up and took two huge bites. Chewing, she inhaled and decided the best course of action would be to stick to the day's schedule as planned, as she needed to be present for Professor Charmichael's class since she had missed the past two lectures.

Mentally thanking her dad for inheriting his sense of calm and rationalization, Charlie opted to approach the matter scientifically. When she got back to her dorm after class, she would assess everything before diving into the research on her mom. Having a plan allowed her to enjoy the rest of her lunch before shuttling off to the world of Bio-Chem.

Astrid was having difficulty adjusting. The past few days were beyond frustrating for her. She had to rely on her own devices and limited funds to figure out how to follow Charlie to college. The girl had everything Astrid needed, and she couldn't let her slip away. First, Astrid had to figure out where the college was. That was a feat in and of itself. She remembered mentions of it from Birdie over the past year, but in the end, had to use some of her energy to seek out Charlie's aura. Once pinpointed, she used her powers of telepathy to influence a stranger to give her a ride out to Ithaca.

Charlie twisted the key in the door to her room, entered, and released all of her belongings to her bed. She then headed for the small water closet that some of the dorm rooms had. That was a huge bonus she sought when selecting her room for the year. No more sharing toilets with the masses. If they only had enough room to put a shower. She sighed as she splashed her face with cold water from the tiny sink.

Patting her face dry with a hand towel, Charlie picked up her phone and dialed Ramona. She needed to soundboard the day's occurrence off someone before heading into research mode. As the phone rang, Charlie clicked on her TV and grabbed her last can of Coke from the mini fridge.

"Lorenzano residence," a crackly, pre-pubescent boy's voice said.

"Hey, Domenic, it's Charlie. Is Ramona there?"

With a huge, audible breath, Domenic bellowed, "*Ramona*! *Phone*! It's Charlie!"

Charlie pulled the headset away from her ear to keep it from ringing. Soon after she heard the click of the second phone picking up and an immediate "Get off the phone, d-bag," resounded.

"Bite me," Domenic retorted, followed by the bang of the handset slamming down on the cradle.

"Hey, bestie" Ramona sang.

Not quite in the same playful mindset, Charlie filled Ramona in on what happened during anthropology class.

"Holy fuck," Ramona said. "Think you just spaced out from stress or lack of sleep?"

"Maybe," Charlie responded. "But if that was the case, then why the message?" Filling Ramona in on her plans to spend the rest of the day researching the stuff with her mom, Charlie simultaneously pulled out the journals and laid them out. A few more minutes of small talk concluded with the obligatory status update on Ramona and Eric. The girls then said their goodbyes, promising a follow-up phone call if anything major came up.

Placing the phone on the cradle, Charlie stood before the stacks of journals and methodically piled them in chronological order. Standing back to take in the magnitude of what she had before her, Charlie walked over to her desk and pulled out a fresh spiral notebook to start her research.

She took the first stack of books and perused them. The first few were more like a child's musings and really couldn't be classified as journals or diaries. In them, Charlie read about her mom's days spent playing with church mates who lived nearby, as well as her "invisible" friends. From what Charlie could gather, there were several early on in Birdie's life. Thomas; Troy; Mary Kate; and Astrid. Skimming quickly through the stack, Charlie found childlike sketches of those friends and, with the few written details, she was able to compile mental images of them herself.

As the journals in that stack progressed along with Birdie's age, Troy and Mary Kate faded away, leaving only Thomas and Astrid. Thomas always seemed to be there for Birdie when she was in need, whether physically or emotionally, whereas Astrid seemed to be around for the more frivolous and fun times. She almost always was around when mischievous things happened, leaving Birdie to take the blame.

Charlie left a dozen or so blank pages after the notes on that set of journals for additional research. She then stood up and stretched, tossed her can in the trash, and decided to trek down to the vending machine for some M&Ms. After scooping some change out of the frog dish on her dresser, she slipped out of her dorm room and, in bare feet, padded down the hall.

Humming a song that had embedded its way into her brain, Charlie inserted the coins into the slot and pulled the knob for the M&Ms. Hearing the victorious sound of the bag hitting the exit tray, she bent down and snatched out her prize. Charlie re-entered her room and proceeded to the desk, where she laid out a sheet of paper.

Tearing the corner off the M&M packet, she emptied the contents onto the paper. Methodically, she slid the coated candy into colored piles. When they were sorted, she looked down and took count of which colors had what amounts. As usual, the dark brown won out. Followed by blues. Then almost equal red; orange; green; and yellow. The poor light browns came in dead last with two. She chuckled to herself that she still performed that ritual. It was something her mom introduced her to when she was a toddler and had carried on through the years, to the point where Charlie honestly couldn't just eat M&Ms out of the pouch. Snatching the browns in her hand, she grabbed the second stack of journals, changed position by crossing her legs indian style and continued her research.

An hour later, with her notes growing, Charlie closed the last of the books from the latest stack. She stretched her arms up over her head, then leaned over and grabbed the reds from their resting place and popped them into her mouth. Chewing slowly, she read over her notes. The timeframe for that set was late elementary to right before junior high. More of the same antics from Astrid prevailed. It was during that time that Thomas completely disappeared after a final act. Birdie claimed he pushed her out of harm's way as a car careened down her street. She mentioned she felt Thomas' hands shove her in the middle of her back. As she fell to the curb, she turned to watch Thomas disappear into the clouds, never to be seen again.

During that time frame, Astrid was at her most mischievous behavior. It was also when Birdie stopped confiding in adults about her friends, as she was drawing negative attention by doing so.

Looking up to see the sun had lowered in the sky, Charlie decided to wrap up the task at hand and head out to the local Wegmans to pick up some supplies.

It was definitely a top-up kind of day. Even with the sun out, there was a chill in the air. Turning into the parking lot, Charlie thought how she loved that Wegmans just as much as the one near home. It had been a prototype market when it opened, so just like the Pittsford Wegmans, it had all the bells and whistles she loved.

Charlie parked Juicy and headed in for the items she needed. Exiting with her arms full, Charlie slid the bags into the front passenger seat and drove back to campus. She managed to bring it all in with one trip and placed the bags on her bed. She loaded the mini fridge with Cokes; apples; oranges; milk; and cheese. Then she stashed bags of Doritos and Ruffles, along with a box of Rice Krispies and Bugles, in the locker.

Plopping herself on her bed, she aimed her remote towards her TV and clicked on ICTV, where she could find something to kill some time and free up some mental space before dinner. Charlie being Charlie, she couldn't help herself and picked up her notes from earlier.

As she read them, she wondered why her mom had been picked by those "friends". Was she special or just unlucky? Charlie also made some side notes in the margins as she saw patterns forming. It was too early in the research to be certain, but it was enough to make note of and consider through the rest of her research.

One thing was for sure, it was going to be a late night. With that thought, Charlie laid down her notebook and pen. She slid off the bed; clicked the TV off; grabbed her satchel and ID; and exited her room. She maneuvered her arms into her flannel, hit the button for the elevator, and mashed her hair into a beanie as the ding of the elevator's arrival resonated through the floor. Greeting the other students, who were surely on their way to the dining hall, Charlie stood in silence as the elevator carried them to the main floor. Escaping the metal box, they all sauntered out the front door and on to their destinations.

Prime dinner time meant longer lines. After grabbing a tray, Charlie stood with it to her side as the collective masses made their way, one by one, past the plethora of choices offered. Tapping her foot, as a mousy girl five people in front of Charlie hemmed and hawed over whether she should go for the salad or the boiled chicken. Charlie let out a sigh. After prodding from the guy behind her, the mousy girl settled for the salad, set it on her tray, and zoomed to catch up with a gaggle of sorority sisters already swiping their meal cards.

One thing Charlie learned quickly was that Cornell students loved their Greek life.

Finally reaching the rail, Charlie plopped her tray on top and started pulling her dinner choices onto it. Two cheeseburgers; tots; green beans; a small taco salad; and apple pie with vanilla pudding for later. Charlie slid a cup onto her tray and waited for the student cashier to total her haul. She slid her meal card and lifted her tray as the successful beep came through.

Balancing the tray in her left hand, she filled up her cup with ice and Coke, then made a straightaway to a round, half empty table towards the back of the room. After setting her tray down, she arranged her food in front of her.

Unintentionally, she overheard a conversation between two students. They were talking about a class they were taking, and their topic of discussion regarded dreams. In particular, they spoke of lucid dreaming and astral projection. In an attempt to not be obvious, Charlie kept her head down and unwrapped her overly steamed cheeseburgers. Dipping the corners in ketchup between bites, she listened as they went on about someone's recent dream travel. Feeling in her gut that this was something she needed to not only pay attention to, but take notes on if she could, she dug into her crossbody and retrieved a pen. She jotted key words, using arrows and circles to connect the trains of thoughts, as she continued to nibble her way through dinner.

Deflation hit her hard when the pair stood up to leave. Recognizing that Charlie was staring in their direction, the taller of the pair asked, "Can I help you?"

With a huge rush of blood to her cheeks, Charlie apologized for listening in, but let them know that she really needed to hear more on the topic they had been discussing.

An immediate body language shift transpired before Charlie, and the tall girl sat back down, scribbled something on a piece of paper, and slid it in Charlie's direction. "Be here," she said, tapping the paper. "Tomorrow night, Old Robert's Hall. We get together as a small discussion group. Join us if you like. All are welcome."

"Thank you," Charlie said as she slid the paper next to her napkin notes.

"See you tomorrow," the pair chimed as they walked away.

As she slid her pie in front of her, Charlie glanced down at the paper she was just handed. Written on the small square was the name of the hall, the time, and two names: Heather and Scarlett. Charlie slid the paper and her notes into her crossbody and, as she inhaled her pie, she had a gut feeling that gathering could be very important to her research on what happened to her mom.

Once back in her dorm room, Charlie assembled the next stack of journals to research. While doing so, she caught sight of the small safe and mentally acknowledged its contents. That would have to be dealt with, but she was hoping to find out where the money came from first. For the moment, it was safe and secure in her dorm closet.

Stacking her notebook and pen on top of the five journals she wished to review that night, Charlie plunked down on her bed and arranged the stack by date. She loved and admired the variety in the journals. No two were alike. It was as if she were getting a glimpse into her mom's personality at each point in time just by the journals she chose.

Flipping the pages in her notebook to a blank sheet, Charlie wrote down the first journal's description and the start date and end date, then dove into reading. Gone were Anthony and Mary Kate, but in their place, several new "friends" made their way in and out of Birdie's life. Astrid remained strong, instigating similar antics and punishments as before.

None were noteworthy until the third journal, where Astrid made her presence known to another one of Birdie's church mates. It seemed Astrid was becoming stronger and a definite liability in Birdie's life.

Soon after was when Birdie began to not remember things. She took punishments from Dorothy and Joseph for acts that she swore she did not commit, but in their eyes, could be the only culprit. They were tiny things at first, like missing bites out of a cake that Dorothy prepared for a church luncheon, rips and tears in clothing, a refrigerator door being left open, and so on. The punishments would fit the accusation, such as reading chapters in the bible, confession, or prayer time with Dorothy. During those times, Birdie grew more and more disenchanted with Astrid, to the point where she began to ignore her. Astrid, however, would not be ignored and retaliated against Birdie by escalating the acts.

After that, it seemed as if Astrid had disappeared from Birdie's life. Others would float in and out, mostly joyous and helpful. Months went by with no headaches or other ailments. Birdie excelled at school again and was brought back into the Church fold as a good girl. The stories she shared with parishioners about her friends and their acts of kindness were taken as proof that God has sent angels to Earth to help in times of need.

By the fifth journal, Birdie's entries were mostly smatterings of sketches. They were crude, appropriate to her age, but still conveyed a clear representation of the friends. Charlie found it interesting how they all seemed to stay true to the first descriptions from sketch to sketch, unlike Astrid's sketches. She appeared differently to Birdie throughout the years. Charlie decided to document a timeline.

With only one journal left in the stack, Charlie looked at her watch. She only had one lab the next day and no lectures so she wouldn't have to get up as early. Choosing to continue her research, she popped up, grabbed the next set of four journals, and laid them on the bed. She then tapped into her food locker and pulled out a bag of Bugles, then grabbed a cold Coke from the fridge. Cracking the tab open, she took a long gulp and crinkled her face as the bubbles hit her nostrils.

She set the Coke and the crunchy trumpets on the bedside table and walked over to the windows, raising her arms into a long stretch. She watched a group of students walking through the lot to the path that wound its way from Pi Delta Psi to Delta Delta Delta, past Zeta Psi, and eventually to her dorm. She chuckled to herself, thinking how she could have very easily been a sorority girl if it weren't for the incessant need to belong and crazy rituals. Her dad and mom had raised her to be too free thinking and independent for such a lifestyle.

After stretching to either side, she pivoted around on her toes, walked to the TV, and turned it on. Taking a seat on the bed again, she glanced at the timeline she had started.

Astrid bugged her. Knowing something more sinister was growing, Charlie opened the next journal and read on. Two Coke's later, Charlie wrapped up her research for the night. The last four journals offered little more than she already had documented. Setting them down with the other stack of completed journals, she closed her notebook and folded the timeline, then placed them both on her desk. Charlie needed a shower, so she gathered her items and headed out to the showers down the hall before getting ready for bed.

CHAPTER FIFTEEN
HEATHER AND SCARLETT

Charlie woke to her alarm buzzing, hit the snooze button, and rolled to her side. She was in the middle of a dream and desperately wanted to get back to it. After several attempts to capture the dream, she opened her eyes and succumbed to the daylight. Staring at the ceiling of her dorm room, she smiled to herself as the face of Simon LeBon smiled back at her. She didn't think she would ever outgrow that man. With a widened yawn, she sat up and inhaled.

Charlie planted her feet on the cold tile and maneuvered to the bathroom to pee. As she trudged back into the room, she ran through a mental timeline of her day. Peckish, she decided that sustenance would come first. Not feeling like impressing anyone so early in the morning, she threw her hair in a ponytail, slid on a jogging suit and parka, then slung her dining pass around her neck. Taking her notebook with her to review while she ate, she also grabbed her Walkman for some musical inspiration. Checking the cassette tape, she knew she could do better and dug around in her shoebox collection until she found just the right mix.

The weather that day suited her—moody and ominous. Charlie entered the dining hall and grabbed a tray. Deciding on cereal, she skipped the hot food line and went over to the cereal station. Grabbing a bowl, she stood before her options and went wild with a mix of Rice Krispies, Fruity Pebbles, and some Captain for his crunch. Not wanting to sog up her bowl, Charlie plucked two cartons of milk from the ice bin. Tossing an apple, a banana, and a coffee cup on her ray, she headed for the cashier.

Taking a spot in one of the more hidden corners, she set her tray down and chaotically opened her milk, pouring one in the bowl and setting the second aside. She covered her ears with the spongy headphones and clicked the play button on the Walkman, sending Joy Division through her brain.

Shoveling in the first spoonful of her concoction, she opened her notebook and began to read over her notes. While doing so, she started a list of questions on a separate page. Although she didn't have high hopes for the day's meeting with Heather's and Scarlett's group, she wanted to be prepared just in case she might gather some insights into what the heck happened to her mom. What was most curious to her so far was why her mom had an imaginary friend for so long.

Most kids relinquish those predilections early in life. She never heard of someone carrying them well into middle school. At least no-one she had ever known did.

Tapping her pen on the pad of paper, she let her thoughts expand back to the money. The journals were one thing; the money was completely another. Why would her mom have hidden that kind of money away? She couldn't have been planning to leave her dad. That she was certain of. So, what was it for?

Knowing no answer was going to fly into her lap, she finished up her cereal, shoved her fruit choices in her pockets, dumped her tray in the large plastic bin, and headed back to her room. She had all morning to continue her journal documentation before her lab in the afternoon, so she looked at her watch and decided a call to Ramona would be on the agenda when she got back.

Once in her room, Charlie scooped the banana and apple out of her pockets, placed them on her desk, grabbed her phone, and pulled the cord to give herself a good amount of slack over to her bed. Picking up the handset off the cradle, she punched in Ramona's number. Two rings in, she heard the handset pick up and Mrs. L state the all too familiar, "Lorenzano residence."

"Good Morning, Mrs. L, it's Charlie. Is Ramona in?"

"*Charlie*! How are you doing, honey?" Mrs. L said in a voice only an Italian mother could muster.

Charlie assured her she was good and getting settled back in, then asked about the family and waited patiently as answers flowed in. Likely realizing she had monopolized enough of Charlie's time, Mrs. Lorenzano finished with, "Let me get Ramona for you. Take care of yourself. *Ramona*! *Telephone*!"

Almost deafened, it surprised Charlie she could hear her friend pick up the line. Pleasantries ensued, followed by a story or two about Eric and seeing Charlie's dad at the Wegmans. "He looked well by the way." Ramona then asked the question Charlie had been waiting for. "How's the research going? You find anything?" Charlie explained to Ramona which journals she had already explored and gave a brief synopsis of her notes. Ramona informed Charlie that she and her brother Antonio both had imaginary friends as kids. but by the time we settled into school and made real friends, we grew past that."

"Oh! I almost forgot," Charlie exclaimed. "I have another odd thing to tell you." She explained how she ran into the odd couple and her plans to attend the meeting later.

"Man, oh man, I wish I could be there with you," Ramona said. "Do you think they are Wicca? Occultists?"

"They looked a smidge goth, with dark hair and way too heavy eyeliner, but they didn't seem to be much different than us. I guess I'll know more tonight. I wrote down a list of questions this morning. I'm sure more will arise from the meeting."

"Be sure to bring something to record the meeting. You don't want to forget anything," Ramona said in a mysterious voice.

"Yeah, I should have a mini cassette recorder for lectures somewhere in my desk."

With that, the conversation circled back around to their normal banter and ended with Ramona complaining about how she has no privacy between her mom and her brothers. "I need to decide soon what I want to do with my life and get out of here," Ramona said with a sigh. "Easier said than done in the 'Corleone' household."

After catching up on a little celebrity gossip, they said their goodbyes and ended the call. Charlie placed the handset back on the cradle and laid on her back, staring up at Simon again. "Take me away, you gorgeous hunk of a man," she said in a sultry voice.

A startling knock on her door interrupted her fantasy. As she opened it, Charlie was greeted by Christina, the self-proclaimed dorm social director, who wanted to discuss the dorm's contribution to Spring Fling that year.

Not having an opinion on the matter, Charlie listened to the options and voted for B, whatever B was, and ushered Christina back into the hallway. Charlie then closed her door and turned to her desk.

Looking at the journals left to go through, Charlie felt overwhelmed. She slid out the chair at her desk and plopped down, pulling the top journal off the stack and opening her notes.

This volume differed from most of the others in that it was simply a composition book. Nothing defined it as a journal upon first glance. She thought her mom must have done so intentionally, maybe to keep prying eyes away. Charlie fanned the pages to get a look at the date range she was working with. Based on them, it would have been solidly in her mom's middle school years.

Like the journals before it, nothing stood out as a singular concern, but Charlie noted the continued appearance changes Astrid went through. She also marked that her mother, in addition to missing larger chunks of time, also was suffering from more frequent illnesses. Nothing major, mostly headaches and fatigue, which the doctors labeled as migraines and for which they prescribed rest. Meanwhile, Astrid grew into more of a confidant for Birdie—a sounding board, so to speak. She was always there to listen to Birdie lament her ongoing battle with her parents over control of her social life.

This was also where Birdie started to document Astrid's fascination with the boys in her life. Birdie had no interest in boys by then. In particular, the local boys, finding them crude, mean, and just plain obnoxious. Several times in the journal, Birdie wrote how Astrid attempted to push her into experiences she was not comfortable or ready for.

Charlie wrapped up the journal, peeled open her banana and stared out the window. She really missed her mom, and the journals, however insightful, made the pangs of missing her stronger. She wished she had gotten this glimpse of her mother while she was still alive. They raised so many questions, and the only person who could answer them was gone.

Wistfully, Charlie slid the next journal in front of her and continued her documentation. The juxtaposition between her mom and Astrid blurred more and more as the journals carried on. It was as if Astrid wanted to *be* her mom. Charlie was ready to enter her mom's high school years when she noticed the time.

Crap, she thought to herself. *I have a lab in an hour.* Closing up her notes, she jumped up and changed into more class-appropriate clothing. Making sure she had the correct contents in her backpack for the lab, she grabbed her wallet and headed out the door to grab a quick slice before heading to class.

Analytical Biochemistry lab always energized Charlie. Something about documenting chemical reactions on living organisms got her brain jazzed.

After the lab, as she walked back to her dorm, she thought about her life and how much it had changed in such a short period of time. Not just hers, she acknowledged, her dad's as well. Possibly more so for him. She turned the key to her dorm door, released her backpack to the floor and stepped into the bathroom. Splashing a bit of water on her face, she noticed she physically looked different. Older? Perhaps. Different, for sure.

After taking long strides across her room, she picked up her phone and dialed home. She was hoping to catch her dad. She knew he was taking the week to work on some things at the house before pushing himself back into the office.

Just as she thought she was going to get the answering machine, her dad picked up, answering the phone with a soft, "Hello?"

Charlie returned the sullen greeting with, "Hey, Dad! It's your favorite daughter."

She could hear his smile as he corrected her. "You mean my *only* daughter."

She shared her first few days back with him, expanding on her lab from that day.

"Oh!" Dale blurted out, cutting her off with the promise of some profound revelation. "I ran into Ramona at the Wegmans the other day."

Charlie rolled her eyes at the not-so-new news, but said, "Oh, really? That's nice." Moving on. "So, have you been eating and taking care of yourself?"

"I have. It's a good thing your Grandma left so much food. What Mrs. Colrabi brought over was barely fit for human consumption. I relinquished that to the depths of the trashcan."

Charlie giggled. "A dog could have come in handy for that."

Dale shared an update on the grandparents' return home before they said their goodbyes.

"I'll be sure to stay in touch," Charlie said. "Promise me you'll get out and about and not become a recluse."

"I promise, Charlie Bear. Love you."

"Love you too, Dad."

After hanging up, Charlie stood up and caught a glimpse of herself in the mirror. Not normally nervous about meeting new people, she was curiously concerned about first impressions. She couldn't pinpoint it. Maybe it was because they were in a totally different world than she was used to being around. There were goth kids in high school, of course, but they were never part of Charlie's circle of friends. She enjoyed listening to Bauhaus and Clan of Xymox, but she did so in the comfort of her preppy bubble. Knowing she was going to have to change outfits before heading out, she started digging into her drawers to find something that would be appropriate.

After shoveling through her t-shirts, she opted for her Depeche Mode concert tee. It was black and moody without being too obvious. She laid the shirt on her bed and went to the sink in her bathroom, turned the water to hot, and patiently waited for it to heat up. As she looked in the medicine cabinet mirror, she focused in on her eyes.

Her mom used to tell her stories of how special it was to be a child with heterochromia. She explained she heard it meant the person was special, blessed with psychic abilities and good luck, and even more interesting, the ability to see into the spirit world. Charlie always thought it made her a freak, and as most kids do when something is different, they wish it wasn't real. Charlie definitely fell into that category with her eyes. She just wanted two blue eyes or two green eyes. Having two eye colors was weird.

Shaking off her old insecurities, Charlie dunked her head under the faucet to soak her hair. With her senses muddled by the flowing water, Charlie had a strange feeling there was a presence in the room with her. Dismissing it as her overactive imagination running away with thoughts of her mom's superstitions, she reached for a towel. As she did, she felt a hand and snapped upright, catching her head on the corner of the medicine cabinet mirror. As she thought, *how*, her world went dark.

Something hot and sticky trickled down the back of Charlie's head.she reached around to touch it, and winced. Seeing the dark red stain on her fingertips, she remembered hitting her head as she came up from the faucet. But how? She knew she had not opened the cabinet. She remembered looking at her eyes, but hadn't touched the mirror. She grabbed her towel, which lay on the floor next to her, and remembered the sensation of a hand touching hers just seconds before hitting her head.

Charlie wrapped her head in the towel and used some tissue to clean off her neck. After she struggled to her feet, she closed the mirror to the cabinet and realized her t-shirt would definitely need a thorough Spray 'n Wash treatment before washing, as the entire collar trim was stained red.

Trying to steady herself, she placed both hands on the sink. The pain was a dull thud, and her vision was retreating from the fog. Taking tiny steps into her room, she maneuvered over to her locker and grabbed a bottle of Tylenol before exhuming a can of Coke from the mini fridge. Swigging down the tiny white pills, she sat on the edge of her bed and glanced at the clock.

She had only been out for fifteen minutes, which was a good thing. She figured that ruled out a concussion. Unwrapping the towel, she shook her hair loose and opted to not put in any product so as to not aggravate the wound. The bleeding had stopped, but she would have a doozy of a headache, she was sure. Pausing long enough to finish her Coke, she donned her Depeche Mode t-shirt and set forth to get items ready for the meeting. With her backpack empty, she slid in her notebook and her mini recorder, complete with a fresh set of batteries. Noting she still had a large amount of time before she needed to head out, she opted to review her lab notes from earlier and rest her head a bit.

The setting sun was Charlie's cue to head out. If she left then, she would have just enough time to settle her nerves with a little food before heading over to the former Roberts Hall plot. She grabbed her backpack and a jean jacket, slipped her meal card around her neck, and headed out. As she walked to the dining hall, she couldn't decide if she was excited, scared, or just plain curious about the group of people she was about to meet and interact with. She hoped her questions wouldn't be deemed remedial. As that thought passed through her mind, her stomach told her the best way to get through the jitters was to load up on carbs.

Once in the dining hall, Charlie filled her tray with a healthy helping of baked ziti and garlic bread, then snatched a cup, paid, and made her way to an empty seat. Inhaling her food, she caught herself checking her Swatch way too often. Noticing her right knee was bouncing at an alarming rate, she took a few deep breaths and muttered to herself to keep it cool. The last thing she wanted was to stand out as the weirdo in a group of weirdos. Slurping down the last of her Coke, she looked one final time at her wrist and stood up.

After dumping her tray, she left the dining hall and wove through the arts quad, eventually coming upon a darkening field where Robert's Hall formerly stood. Several lanterns were planted in a circle, and just inside that sat Heather, Scarlett, and a dozen others. Upon reaching the group, Charlie's nerves settled a bit. The group was a wild mix of races, sexes, and proclivities.

Scarlett was the first to speak up and greet her. "Glad you could make it!" She then continued with introductions, involving too many names for Charlie to ever remember.

"Cop a squat," Heather called out as she patted the ground next to her.

Charlie claimed the spot and lowered herself into a pretzel. Opening her backpack, she set her recorder to her left and laid her notebook and pen on her knees. Small talk continued until Scarlett cleared her throat and started the meeting.

"Hello, everyone. Thank you for joining up this evening. As you all know, I am Scarlett and this is Heather." She pointed across the circle to her co-founder. "We already covered the introduction of the newbie, Charlie, so let's get to business. Who wants to start?" Her eyes skimmed the circle until a hand raised into the air. "Heck, yeah, Aubry. Go for it."

Aubry, a blonde girl with a slight build, stood up. Her pale skin almost glowed in the moonlight. Charlie could tell she was not a public speaker by the way she carried herself. In a demure voice, Aubry spoke about how she believed that an item she picked up at a flea market over in Geneseo may be haunted. "In case y'all don't know, I'm a collector of porcelain dolls and figurines."

That statement received several heckles from the circle, from a few *you know betters* to a *been there, done that.*

Aubry continued to describe the doll. "Guys, she's so pretty. I had to get her. She is small, only about eight inches tall. She has the most angelic halo of strawberry blonde curls, big blue eyes with milky skin, and peach cheeks. The person selling her at the market said she didn't know her origin, but that I could research the company based on the mark on the bottom of her foot." Most of the group nodded in unison. "I got her back to my dorm and set her up on the shelf with the others, and ever since, weird things have been happening."

A girl sitting near Aubry let out a low huff. If Charlie remembered correctly, her name was Callie.

"What?" Aubry asked, glaring at her.

Callie kneeled up to give her response. "You know that before you brought her near your room, you should have performed a cleansing."

Everyone in the circle expressed emphatic agreement to that. Another girl, Evie, piped in, "Aubry, how long is she awake for? Does she sleep? Has she moved?"

Charlie let out an exuberant giggle, which evoked a collective head turn in her direction from everyone in the group. "Um... I mean... What are you—?"

"Charlie," Heather cut her off, "for this group to work, we have to remain open to all the ideas and stories brought before us. Almost every one of us has been in contact with a possessed item in our lives. I'll recommend some things to read if you like, but let's allow Aubry to finish."

Charlie nodded, feeling admonished. She had a feeling her issue too was going to bring some disputes.

Aubry resumed her story. "She hasn't moved from her spot, but her eyes seem to move around the room, as if they are following you. She also seems to change expressions from time to time. But the most disturbing thing is that she seems to talk to me while I am sleeping. Sometimes she is sweet and soothing, but other times I can hear her chanting in what I am guessing is Latin or something. That freaks me out, for sure!"

After she sat down, the group offered advice on how to handle the doll. Charlie sat back and listened. With several options to try, Aubry thanked the group.

Heather then turned her attention to Charlie. "So, Charlie," she started, "Scarlett and I invited you here tonight because we noticed you taking an interest in what we were talking about the other night. Can you tell us why you came here tonight?"

Charlie's face grew hot. Before she stood, she made sure her recorder was on and aimed it out the corner of her jean pocket. "Hi, everyone. I'm not sure where to begin or how much you need to know, so I guess I'll start by telling you my mom recently died."

The group let out a chorus of condolences.

Charlie smiled, then continued. "The coroner told us it was natural, but I just don't know. She was healthy and young for a mom. She had migraines her whole life, but that pretty much was it. Anyway, after she died, I found journals she had kept her whole life. I mean, from like as soon as she could write until the day she died. I have been reading them since I got back and started documenting things that stood out as odd to me. The first thing is, she had imaginary friends. I know that isn't odd in itself, because I had them as well, and so did my best friend Ramona. What stands out as odd to me is how many she had and how one in particular was still around in her middle school years."

This induced a few gasps from the group, but Charlie continued. "Another odd thing is she seemed to become aggressive and change her appearance a *lot*. I guess I just need help understanding what I am dealing with here. My mom missed periods of time, and I just had something really spooky happen to me, too." Charlie filled them in on the occurrence in her bathroom.

Not knowing whether to continue based on the expressions on everyone's faces, Charlie turned to Scarlett, who looked intrigued. "Hey, everyone," Scarlett said, "we are coming to the end of our time here. Charlie, I may have someone who can help you understand this. Stick around after and we can talk."

With that, she led the group in an affirmative blessing and gave everyone a reading assignment, then disbanded the circle. A very tall girl with wild, multi-colored hair—Charlie couldn't remember her name—approached and sat next to her as a few people paired off for side talks. "Hey, Charlie, I'm Cassandra," the girl said as she stuck out her hand. "I may have someone who can help you understand this. I have an acquaintance, Jared. If you want, we can go pay him a visit. He was studying to be a priest at one point, but decided he liked certain proclivities too much to give them up." She let out a deep belly laugh. Likely recognizing Charlie's concern, she added, "Only if you want to and are comfortable, of course. I know this is a lot, but I don't think our little group here is going to be able to help you find what you need."

"Thank you," Charlie said. "I just need some time to think everything over." She took Cassandra's number and promised to reach out with an answer soon.

Standing up, she switched off her recorder and said her goodbyes to those left of the group. The night air had taken a cold turn. Charlie could see her breath as she crossed back through the campus to her dorm. By the time she entered the lobby, she had convinced herself that she needed a hot chocolate.

Charlie stripped her jacket off as she entered her room and set the recorder on the dresser before heading in to pee. Noticing the red light on her answering machine, she pressed play on her way past it.

"Hi, Charlie, sorry we missed you. It's Grandma Eleanor. Just wanted to check in on you. Please call us when you get a moment. Love you lots." She ended with her number before the long beep.

Charlie giggled to herself. She found it comical that her Grandma felt she had to identify herself by her name in addition to her relation. She was Charlie's only living grandmother, after all.

Feeling sticky from being out earlier, Charlie washed her face and hands, surprised at how exhausted she was. She reached around to feel the lump on her head and decided to use her hot chocolate to chase down a side of Tylenol.

Flipping open her locker, she squatted to peruse the bottom shelf. That was where she kept items she didn't dip into frequently. Sliding two cans of Vienna sausages to the side, she found what she was looking for: a can of Swiss Miss. Tucking it under her arm, she stood up and slid into her slippers, then opened the door and made her way down the hall to the common area.

Setting her can down on the credenza, she saw someone had left coffee to burn off in the carafe. With a deep sigh, she picked it up and made her way to the small sink on the opposite side of the seating area. After filling the carafe halfway with water, she swished and sloshed it around in circles, doing her best to loosen up the coffee that was stuck to the bottom. Realizing it was a futile effort, she gave up when no new residue released from the bottom.

She filled it with enough water to make her cocoa, shuffled back to the coffeemaker, and poured it in. Placing the carafe back in its slot, she hit *brew* and waited for the machine to heat the liquid.

While she waited, she put a few scoops of the Swiss Miss in a paper cup, making sure to add a heavy ration of dehydrated marshmallows in the mix. After the coffee maker clicked, she poured the scalding water over the mix and watched as her marshmallows inflated. She turned off the machine, grabbed a swizzle stick and stirred her cocoa. Definitely too hot to drink at this juncture, she carried her prize back to her room and shut the door behind her.

Between the head wound and the gathering, Charlie wanted nothing more than to take a hot bath. Dorm life sucked in those moments. Opting to enjoy her cocoa then take a hot shower, she settled herself at the edge of her bed and scanned her small VHS collection on the makeshift shelf she had on the side of her desk. As she scanned, she found the evening's feature flick: *Fright Night*. She had the biggest crush on Chris Sarandon. She wished Ramona was there to watch it with her, as between the two of them, they had the whole script memorized. Shoving the tape in the player she clicked on her TV. Flipping the dial to channel three for the VCR, she sat down on the edge of her bed just as the howl of a wolf indicated the start of the movie.

She took a deep sip of the hot, chocolaty goodness, which warmed her insides and helped take off the chill of the night. Enjoying the scene where Amy began her sultry dance with Jerry Dandridge, Charlie took the last sip of her not-so-hot hot cocoa. She licked her upper lip to savor the last of the flavor. She set the mug down on her desk; hit pause on the VCR; grabbed her shower caddy and towels, then headed off to the showers.

Once back in her room, she got cozy and settled in between her sheets to finish the movie. She watched the storyline unfold, and considered the offer from Cassandra. She would need to decide soon. Making sure her alarm was set, she laid back and fell asleep just before Peter Vincent slayed the werewolf that was Evil Ed.

Telepathic communication was the Dark Magician's power of choice at the moment. Having watched this Charlie, he grew nervous for his Astrid and her final plans. He summoned her, and almost immediately heard her thoughts.

She, too, was worried. She has been unable to secure the financial means to continue on her journey and felt herself getting weaker. Charlie was proving to be quite a thorn in her side.

He acknowledged Astrid's frustrations and compelled her to continue forward without trepidation. The girl was just a small wrinkle in an otherwise perfect plan. He offered a proposal, even though it carried risks.

She acquiesced and replied that it would be done.

This, the Dark Magician thought, could go one of two ways. It could make Charlie back off immediately in fear, or it could rile her up and send her further into researching her mother's death.

As Charlie slept, Astrid would use what energy she could muster and plant two additional journals in the room.

Charlie's alarm startled her awake. She maneuvered out of bed and slipped into a pair of jeans and her oversized flannel. She grabbed her keys and meal lanyard, paused to flip her hair upside down to insert it in a banana clip. Taking a quick look in the mirror, she mumbled, "Go get 'em, tiger."

Not wanting to sit and eat in the hall, she took her pancakes and sausage to go. On her walk back to her room, she thought about the meeting the night before and Cassandra. Should she take the offer to talk to her friend? Entering her room, she heard the tail end of a message being left by Scarlett, ending with the familiar beep as she hung up before Charlie could snag the handset. She pressed play on the machine, and Scarlett's voice let her know she hadn't forgotten about her and was around if she felt like talking more.

Charlie set her food down on her desk and called Cassandra. They exchanged small talk before Charlie told her she would be amenable to meeting her friend.

"As luck would have it," Cassandra said, "Jared's coming over to my dorm to hang before we head out for dinner later. Do you want to join us?"

Having not fully committed to the idea of meeting this person so soon, Charlie hemmed and hawed for a moment before realizing the only way she was going to find answers was to keep moving forward, seeking as much information as she could absorb. "Okay, sounds good. Where should I meet you?"

"Great. Come over to Balch Hall."

As Charlie sat in her room, the Master looked down upon her. He needed to find a way to protect her and to help release her mother's soul.

He watched a long-standing member known as Marcus rescuing a young mother and child from a boat wreck.

He will do, the Master thought. *I will send him to Charlie, and hopefully she will be open to hear what he has to say.*

CHAPTER SIXTEEN
HELP

Charlie entered Balch Hall and checked in with the Tiffany look alike at the front desk. After signing the guest book, the pop star's doppelganger made a swift motion towards the elevators and let Charlie know that she was going to the third floor, room three-seventeen. Joining two skater boys at the elevator, Charlie stood quietly until the bell dinged, notifying them of its arrival. The group slithered on, and after they hit five, Charlie hit three.

Exiting the elevator on the third floor, she walked out to get her bearings on the room numbering system in the dorm. She saw her target room would be down the right hallway on the left-hand side. Hitching her backpack higher on her shoulder, she felt those pesky butterflies. It wasn't about meeting people for the first time, but the fact she was about to introduce strangers to her mom's life.

Knowing she would have to have documentation to back up her questions, she brought along a few of the more meaty journals—the ones with a good handle on incidents that transpired as well as drawings—which would show the progression of Astrid from friend to whatever she had become. For good measure she also brought along a few journals she hadn't even looked at yet in case they needed more information to reach a hypothesis.

Charlie passed rooms three-eleven, thirteen, fifteen, and finally reached seventeen. She knocked on the door, which was already cracked open with Def Leppard playing inside.

Cassandra came to the door and greeted Charlie. "Hey there, girl. Glad you could make it. Jared, this is the chick from the group the other night I mentioned."

"Charlie, right?" Jared said with a smile.

Charlie nodded and greeted them both as she walked into the room. Sensing the informality of it all, she opted to take a seat on a bean bag rather than Casandra's bed.

"Can I get you anything?" Jared asked. "Coke, water, Dew, joint?" Jared chuckled at the last suggestion.

"Let's save that one for later, babe," Cassandra said, rolling her eyes. "Charlie, I've been filling Jared in on the meeting from the other night, but I'm sure I'm leaving gaping holes in the story."

"Yeah," Jared said, "I feel there's way more to it than even what you shared the other night. Am I right?"

Before responding, Charlie took Jared in. He had a wannabe slacker vibe to him, but she had a feeling it was a ruse. Her gut told her he was way more than meets the eye. Speaking of eyes, she couldn't help noticing that his were the most intense ice blue she had ever seen. His shoulder length, jet black hair set them off.

Realizing she had been staring in silence, she quickly spoke up. "Yes, layers and layers. I'm finding more every day. As a matter of fact, I brought some of the actual journals from my mom to share with you guys."

Unzipping the larger section of her pack, she pulled out a handful of journals. She also pulled out her recorder and asked if it would be okay if she used it. She explained she was a meticulously detailed note taker, and if she had to take written notes, she wouldn't be much of a contributor to conversation. The recorder, she added, would allow her to focus on the discussions then take her notes later.

Jared and Cassandra shrugged their shoulders as if to say, "No problem."

"Cool." Not knowing if they wanted to jump right into it, Charlie looked at them both and pulled out the first journal to share. "Now or never?" she asked.

"Totes," Jared said and maneuvered to Charlie's side. It was at that moment she caught a whiff of his intoxicating scent. She could tell it was natural, not like a lot of the boys her age who were dousing themselves in cologne. She cleared her throat as Jared gestured for Cassandra to join them.

Charlie retold the story of how her mom died and what the authorities concluded, letting them know that, except for run-of-the-mill issues and the migraines, her mom was very healthy. She explained how she found the journals tucked away as if her mom had been hiding them from the world. She did not bring up the money; that she would save for later. Opening the first journal, she showed the pair the initial stories of the friends. She shared the crude stick figure drawings in the first journal, then handed it to Jared before reaching down to her side to hit the record button on her mini tape recorder.

Jared mindfully flipped through the journal, and Charlie could see he was making mental notes. He leaned over to Cassandra to share some things with her. Seeing they needed more, Charlie continued in succession with two other journals, letting them know they were out of sequence, but the journals in between didn't show much progress, just more of the same.

Wishing she had taken them up on the Dew, Charlie watched and listened as the two discussed some opinions as to what had happened.

Cassandra flipped between several of the sketches. "It's interesting that Astrid's appearance changed. It's like she was attempting to deceive your mom, or at the very least, confuse her."

When they got to the part about the rescue, it was as if Jared had an electric current shooting through his body. The hairs on his arms stood up and his eyes widened as if he recognized something. He leaned forward, closer to Charlie.

Oh my, Charlie thought, and she tried not to be obvious that he was making her swoon.

"See this, here?" he asked.

Charlie nodded.

"I've read similar stories to this before! I don't think these are your typical imaginary friends. I mean, well, let me back up," he stammered, as if his thoughts were going too fast for his mouth. "Kids have imaginary friends, we know this. Most psychiatrists chalk it up to an internal need for belonging, or a coping mechanism, or just someone with a strong imagination. They typically show up around the same time as your mom's did. They also can be used by the child as scapegoats for learning what is right and wrong and avoiding punishments. What is most definitely different here is the way they interact with your mom. In particular, this *one* uncanny act of stepping in to save her. This is a characteristic of a guardian angel or—as most small children know them from fairy tales—a fairy godmother."

Charlie sat with what she could only assume was a gaping mouth, possible drool, and wide eyes. Whatever the combination, she knew she had to stop based on Jared's and Cassandra's tilted heads. Snapping out of it, Charlie tried to digest what he just said. "Guardian *angels*? Like, heaven and hell and God and the devil and—"

"Exactly", Jared cut in. "Different religions and different cultures have varying names for them, but their existence is far from fetch."

Cassandra piped in. "Are there more instances of things like this happening?"

Charlie shook her head. "Not really. Not rescues, at least." She considered the notes she had been taking. "What I have found curious is the timing of the rescue and the fact it wasn't Astrid who performed it. It was Anthony."

Jared stared at Charlie. "An even better question is: Why was Astrid the one to stay while the others float in and out quickly? What's her added value? It doesn't seem like your mom was getting anything but grief from her friendship with Astrid. Or, is there more?"

Charlie didn't confirm or deny his questions as she handed him the next journal. Instead, she added, "This is where it gets real weird."

Discussing the added mystery of the missing time and physical interactions, the trio lost track of time. They were brought back by the chirp of Cassandra's watch reminding her to take her insulin. "Oh, shit," she said. "We totally just lost two hours! I need to dose up and eat."

Jared added. "Is it okay if we take this on the road?"

All in agreement, Charlie clicked her recorder off to see that it was fortuitous timing. She needed to insert a new cassette, anyway. Gathering up the journals, the group slipped out into the evening sky and made their way through the campus. They took the time on their walk to detox from their investigation and shared a bit about themselves with each other. Cassandra was an art major, youngest of four, and the only girl. Jared was from Tennessee, the oldest of three, with younger sisters. That's one thing Charlie had wished was different, other than the obvious wanting her mom back. She wished she had siblings. There were obvious perks of being an only child, but right about then, it would have been great to have a clan.

They arrived at The Nines, which was slammed. Walking down the stairs into the restaurant, they got extremely lucky and spotted a booth which had just been abandoned. Charlie slid in on one side. Jared and Cassandra took the other just as a mellow busboy came to collect the dishes and give the table a way too ample a wipe down. After he turned to walk away, Charlie grabbed a napkin from the dispenser and swished it over the table to soak up some of the water.

She slid the wet napkin behind the salt and pepper shakers and handed Cassandra and Jared a menu from the rack on the wall. While looking at the options, Charlie looked up to see Jared talking with a way-too-perky waitress and felt a pang of jealousy. *What is wrong with you?* Charlie chastised herself. *This isn't you.*

Shaking her head to clear her thoughts, she heard Jared's voice come through as if she were in a tunnel. "Earth to Charlie. What do you want to drink?"

She looked up to see all three faces staring at her and stammered, "Coke, please." The waitress didn't bother trying to hide a dramatic eye roll as she turned away.

"Hey, it happens to the best of us," Jared said. "I've been known to space out from time to time."

Charlie nodded.

"So, what are we thinking about getting?" Cassandra asked.

Charlie looked back down at the menu and perused quickly. She hadn't decided by the time the eye-rolling waitress returned.

Jared must have seen the look of terror on her face. "Tell you what. How about we split a large pepperoni? Sound good?"

Cassandra nodded with eagerness, and Charlie was quick to mimic the motion.

With their order in, the group moved back to the hot topic of discussion.

"So let me get my brain wrapped around the totality of this for now," Jared said as he made circle shapes on the tabletop. "Your mom had several imaginary friends. All but one, Astrid, moved on in one way or another through her life. During this time, your mom experienced loss of time, forgetfulness, and took blame for things she did not do. Adults refused to believe her, which allowed Astrid to step up her game." He stopped and looked at both Cassandra and Charlie.

"Yes," Charlie said. "That's the gist of it. Like I said before, I've skimmed through what I'm calling 'the middle years', and nothing super important stands out other than Astrid's attempts to push my mom into things she wasn't comfortable with and my mom starting to have her migraines. That's why I brought this stack with me tonight." She slid out the three unread journals and placed them on the table. "These seem to be her high school years, based on the dates."

They each slid a journal in front of themselves to inspect. Charlie had the first of the three, with Jared's being next in the timeline, and Cassandra's the end. The journals were notably thicker and larger than their predecessors. So they didn't have to read out loud to each other, they agreed to skim and speak up if anything stood out.

The waitress popped by to let them know it would be a few more minutes and to offer refills. They all accepted, then simultaneously buried themselves in the journals.

Cassandra was the first to speak up. "It seems this journal leans on the darker side. There have been multiple instances of lost time, and your mom's health is definitely being affected by something."

Charlie, feeling odd not following her routine of documentation, took a moment to jot down the description of Cassandra's journal and the notes she stated. The silence continued, and as Charlie looked up from her reading, she noticed Jared staring at her. Her cheeks turned what she was sure were three shades of red.

"Hey," he said, "this one seems to hover between her sophomore and junior year. Your mom definitely was getting perturbed with Astrid, and seemed to have sort of banished her at one point. But what's really, really odd is this…" He slid the journal around for the others to see.

As he pointed to the page, Charlie immediately saw what he was referring to. The handwriting was *completely* different. Not only that, but the content seemed off topic for her mom to have written. The entry was indecorous. "*And*," Jared continued, "it seems in your mom's junior year, there was some sort of Carrie moment at her homecoming dance. Your mom wrote about how she was with the rest of the court waiting for their names to be announced when an unfortunate accident happened that no one could ever explain. Your mom was attacked and had a bunch of her hair cut off in plain sight of the rest of the court. One of the upperclassmen saw what looked like an animal on the floor behind your moms' feet, and when your mom went to turn to look, everyone gasped because her flowy ponytail was gone." No one saw anything, and each one of the court emphatically denied having touched your mom."

Charlie sat, flabbergasted. Her mom had never ever spoken about that to her. She immediately wondered if Mom ever mentioned it to her dad, then made a note to ask him as soon as she could. As Jared rounded the end of the story, stating no one was ever held responsible, the waitress sidled up to the table with their food.

Everyone pulled back their journals to allow for the plates to be set and room in the center of the table for the pizza. For the next few minutes, food preoccupied all their attention. By the second and third slices, they each had slid their respective journals back to focus.

With no other notable, stand-out moments appearing at a skim, they decided to wrap it up for the night. Charlie let them know she would continue working on a timeline. Jared offered to check in with a friend of his to see if Birdie's experiences were some sort of possession and why it could have affected her mom's health. The trio paid and said their goodbyes, with Charlie offering heartfelt thanks to them both.

CHAPTER SEVENTEEN
FLYING SOLO

After settling back in her room, Charlie grabbed a milk she had stashed from the dining hall and chugged it. Between the pizza, the stress of the journals, the story about her mom, and the flip-flops that Jared caused her stomach to perform, she needed to settle it down a bit.

The thing Jared was making her feel was new. She could honestly say she never had a true connection with a guy before. She could chalk it up to the high standards her parent's had set forth in the relationship category. She had always assumed it would eventually happen, but man, was she surprised when it did.

Needing to talk to Ramona, Charlie grabbed her phone and slid it over to her bed, allowing the extension cord to trail across the room. She dialed Ramona's number and assumed, due to the late hour, she may actually get her on the first try. As Ramona answered, Charlie gave herself a mental checkmark for being right. Filling her friend in on what had transpired since they last talked, Charlie went into detail about how Jared and Cassandra seemed the most promising avenue to help her figure things out.

Ramona interrupted her and said, "Jared, huh? Deets, puh-lease!"

Charlie described Jared and once again felt her stomach perform flips and her face flush. She finished with, "He's different and *so* flippin' hot."

Ramona squealed. "Maybe a weekend visit will be in the cards soon. You know, for the bestie's approval and all."

Charlie sighed. "He may not even be into me, so it all could be a moot point."

"Sure, sure. And I'm the queen of England," Ramona taunted.

Looking across at her clock, Charlie saw it was somehow already one in the morning and told Ramona they had to wrap up, as she was planning an early morning of research before class.

Charlie woke after a surprisingly restful night of sleep, something she hadn't had since her mom's death. Thoughts of Jared lingered in her mind. She was affected by the guy for sure. Continuing to lie under her covers, Charlie reflected on what they came up with so far from the journals. Deciding she wanted to get it down on paper as soon as she could, she sat up, slid on her slippers, and padded down the hall to confiscate a cup of the common room coffee.

Luckily, it was late enough that someone had already started a pot of java but early enough the masses had not sucked it down. Thankful that her journey had been quick and sans human contact, Charlie returned to her room and dragged her bags over to her desk. She systematically laid out the journals in a pile and added the voice recorder and notebook to the surface. She then leaned over, clicked on her radio, and settled into her research tasks as George Michael belted out "Father Figure".

Charlie removed the newer cassette from the mini recorder and inserted the micro cassette she had marked #1. She then pressed play and listened to the conversations between her, Cassandra, and Jared. Taking meticulous notes, Charlie couldn't help stopping to daydream every time Jared's voice resonated over the recorder.

Feeling satisfied with her transcription, Charlie compared her initial notes to what she had just put to paper and filled in any blanks. Reading the final draft, she felt good about what they had found out so far.

She took the last sip of her coffee and chose to stay put for a bit and perform some housekeeping tasks she had put off after her return. She grabbed a small box of Captain Crunch and a stashed banana and snacked on them while she piled her laundry into a bag, gave her room a quick dusting and sweep, and sealed up the trash bags that were starting to overflow. Taking the bags to the trash chute, she returned to notice that it was only ten-thirty. Knowing she had some time to spare, Charlie threw on some clothes, grabbed her belongings, and headed to the library to see if she could get any more information about angels, imaginary friends, migraines, or anything else that might be helpful.

After grabbing another coffee on the way, Charlie set up shop at a corner computer along the back wall of the library. Hopping in and out of various articles, she decided that approach may not be her best bet, so she stood and walked over to the card catalog.

As she was flipping through the index cards, someone on the other side of the cabinet said, "Cute top."

Her eyes darted down at the shirt she had thrown on, then lifted her gaze above the catalog and scoped the library. She could only see the tops of heads at her vantage point. Curious, she responded "Yeah, how would you know?"

Keeping her eyes above the cabinet, she continued perusing her surroundings while she waited for a response.

A full minute drug before she heard, "I'll show you mine if you show me yours" This was followed by a chuckle.

Charlie backed up and scanned from side to side, and just as she was about to give up, she smelled something familiar behind her and let out a tiny yelp as a hand touched her right shoulder.

"Hey, Charlie. Hope I didn't spook you too bad," Jared said. Then, he added in a whisper, "I saw you when I came in, but you were deep in your research, so I waited until it looked like you were taking a breather."

God, Charlie thought. *Even his whispers are sexy.*

She let out a deep sigh, which must have triggered Jared to think he was bothering her because he quickly backed up and said, "Well, um, okay. I'll let you get back to it, then. I just wanted to share some things I found after we wrapped up last night. But if you are busy, I'll bounce."

Flummoxed, Charlie quickly took heed of what was happening. "No, stay. Sorry, I spaced out."

"No problem," Jared said. "I got back last night and reached out to my friend, who studies possessions in his spare time. He gave me some insight on what we are dealing with. Based on his research, he feels that what falls under true possession does not fit what Astrid was up to. He said what she was doing was a transference of energy versus a corporeal and spiritual takeover. He did confirm, however, that just like a spiritual possession can cause physical harm to its host over a prolonged period of time, an energy transfer could cause a significant effect on the brain and wreak havoc on chemical levels, causing migraines and lost periods of time. He said he'd need more details to be sure, though. Are there any more journals we could go through?"

Charlie explained there were, and realizing how much time had passed, she apologized for having to cut him short, explaining she had a class she had to attend. Gathering their stuff, the pair walked out and set up a tentative meeting at Jared's place off campus pending Cassandra's availability for that night.

Totally distracted, Charlie headed into class and somehow managed to participate and retain information fed to her from her professor. With the banana and crunch having disappeared from her system, Charlie needed to eat again. She decided to kill two birds with one stone and ran back to her dorm to grab her laundry. As she threw the bag in Juicy, Charlie cursed the dorm machines for always being so unreliable. However, it was a bonus that the laundromat was only a block down from Dinos, her favorite wing place.

After tossing her first load in, she made her way to Dino's and ordered some hot wings and a Coke. Waiting for her order to arrive, she opened a blank sheet in her notebook and wrote down what she remembered from her conversation with Jared earlier. She was so engrossed in making notes in the margins, she didn't realize she had totally phased out. The clank of her wings hitting the table startled her back to reality.

She thanked her waitress, who didn't seem to care one way or another if she had and asked for a refill on her Coke. The obvious signs of a late-night party hung on the woman's face like a painting on a crooked nail. She returned with Charlie's Coke and asked in a very unconvincing manner if she needed anything else.

"No, thank you," Charlie replied, but then quickly added, "Hey, I have to run up to the mat and toss my stuff in the dryer. I'm gonna leave this here for a minute." The waitress nodded, then she walked away and slipped behind a metal swing door.

Charlie made quick work of the transfer and was back at her table just in time for her wings to reach a non-scalding temperature. Inhaling the spicy goodness, she had to give props to Dino's—they definitely knew how to make a wing.

Continuing her notes, she thought about what her and the others could go through that night. Charlie realized she still had those two odd journals, the ones with the aged covers and locks. *Definitely, want to explore those*, she thought. After sliding the last of the meat off the final wing, Charlie took a long swig of her Coke, made her way up to the register, paid, and laid two bucks on the table for the remiss waitress.

She gathered her clothes from the laundromat and zoomed back to her dorm. She tossed her sack on her bed and made quick work of transferring the clean items to their homes. Wanting to be sure to stay on top of her actual classwork, Charlie honed in on some study time. With the help of Casey Kasem, the time passed quickly, and before she knew it, the glow of the late afternoon sun streamed into her room.

Standing to stretch, she realized she had to pee and stepped to the bathroom. She washed her hands, splashed her face and thought back to the incident from the other day. The lump had subsided along with the pain, but how it happened still haunted her. She made a mental note to bring it up to the duo later.

Charlie wasn't hungry yet due to the wings, but knew she wouldn't last long without something in her stomach, so she decided to get changed and head out to grab something to tide her over.

Realizing that, for the first time in a long time, she actually cared what a guy thought of her, she took extra time to sort through her outfit options for the evening. Not wanting to look like she was trying too hard, she ended up choosing a pair of light pink Jimmy Z's. She looked for her Go-Go's t-shirt and came up empty handed. Ramona must have borrowed it. Sorting through her drawers, she found her Blondie t-shirt and decided that would work. After sliding into one of her oversized wool cardigans, Charlie packed the next set of journals, her notes, the recorder, and the two oddball journals in her large crossbody sack. Giving her hair a toss, she placed a bonnie bell in her pocket and slid out the door.

She locked up and realizing she didn't want to be a moocher, she skipped back in and filled a plastic bag with a sack of Doritos and a can of Pringles. Making her way over to the dining hall, she enjoyed the creative cafeteria chef's version of chili mac, then hopped in Juicy and headed towards the address Jared had given her.

CHAPTER EIGHTEEN
TWO HEADS ARE BETTER THAN ONE

Jared was Charlie's first acquaintance off campus, and during her drive, she envisioned what his place would look like. She imagined a bunch of bean bags and secondhand furniture with rock posters everywhere.

She pulled up to the house, got out of Juicy, and knocked on the door. She was greeted by Jared's roommate, who introduced himself as Gunther, and was surprised to see a cross between ultra-modern art déco and a hint of gothic revival as she entered the main living area. Gunther offered her a spot on a blue, crushed velvet couch as she handed him the bag of chips.

He said, "Well, let's get these in a bowl and grab you a drink then." His mannerisms suggested he was definitely not leaning towards girls in the dating department.

Charlie set her crossbody on the brightly colored block rug and followed Gunther to the kitchen.

"Jared's just finishing up a call. He'll be down in a minute. You want Coke, Mountain Dew, Yoo-Hoo, or water?" Gunther asked with a pleasant yet crisp accent.

Choosing the Mountain Dew, Charlie looked around the kitchen. A vintage black-and-white checkered tile floor was offset by very dark cabinets and more black and white subway tile leading up the walls. It was not exactly pristine, but was no pigsty either. So far, she was surprised by what she was seeing.

Gunther gave her a quick tour of the first level, pointing out a small hall bath complete with red walls and gilded oval mirror. She peered in quickly to find several goth sculptures donning the far wall above the toilet. She thanked Gunther and reclaimed her spot on the couch. Excusing himself for the night, Gunther explained he had a party to get to, something that area was never short of.

Charlie sat and perused the room, taking in the wall of books to her left and the curious mix of art surrounding them. There were reprints of Nagels sidled up to quotes from Edgar Allen Poe. Crows and other gothic creatures filled the spaces between books on the shelves. A well-worn mahogany and purple armchair was flanked by what Charlie assumed was a blanket knitted by somebody's grandmother. Various pillows in crushed velvet, fur, and satin dotted the room. On the far side was a large arched window, complete with a window seat and more pillows. Incense burners were scattered about along with open, well aged books.

Deep in observational mode, Charlie was startled clear out of her seat when Jared appeared beside her and said, "Hello." She laughed way too hard at her own clumsiness, feeling hot and sweaty with embarrassment.

Reaching out to help Charlie up, Jared locked eyes with her and just like that, she felt better. "Awesome," he said. "I see Gunther got you set up with a drink. And where did these come from?" He asked, grabbing a Dorito and popping it into his mouth.

"I came bearing chips," Charlie replied. "Figured we'd get the munchies at some point." After offering Jared a few compliments on the place, she asked when Cassandra would be there.

"Ahh," Jared said, then hesitated. "That's who was on the phone when you got here. She ended up having something come up, so she won't be here, but she said to take good notes." His eyes gave a soft charge of energy as he finished his explanation.

"Oh, okay" Charlie stammered. "By the way, I love the décor here. It's very eclectic."

"Thanks, but most of the credit should go to Gunther."

As she reached for her sack of journals, Charlie asked "Where will we be setting up shop?"

"If you are okay sitting here on the couch, we can sprawl out on the coffee table," Jared said as he turned to head to the kitchen. "I'm grabbing a drink. Are you ready for a refill yet?" His voice softened as he rounded the opening to the kitchen.

"No thanks, I'm all set," Charlie answered, a tad too loud, quickly softening her tone as she finished. "I need to tone down on the hard stuff."

Jared turned the corner with the most amazing, naughty smirk on his face.

Charlie took a mental polaroid so she could remember that moment for her mandatory phone call with Ramona later. They both sat on the couch, and Charlie reached into her bag and began to pull out its contents. She laid the journals on the table. Jared reached out to grab the one on top and grazed Charlie's hand. She was unsure if she let out an audible whimper or not, but Jared's face didn't let on either way.

"I brought my mom's later high school years and early college days. I also brought these bad boys," she said as she pulled out the two strange journals. "I found these hidden in an unmarked box in the attic. These seem to be much older and are actually locked."

Jared's eyes came up from the journal he had begun to scan through and, like a child at Christmas, they grew to a saucer-like size. "Wow. Those are definitely not in the same realm as what we have been dealing with. Do you mind?" he asked as he took the smaller one off the top.

"Not at all," Charlie said. "I was actually hoping you had some lock picking skills tucked in your magic bag." Her smile amused Jared, she could tell.

He stood, took the journal in one hand, and swirled the other around and around the perimeter of the cover, saying, "A la peanut butter sandwiches." When nothing happened, he added, "Hocus pocus." Again, nothing. "Alakazam!" he shouted as he let go of the journal and sent it crashing to the table below.

Charlie looked up at him with her hand on her chin in a thoughtful gesture and said, "It seems like you are a bit rusty."

"Have no fret, madam," Jared said as he turned and walked to a rolltop desk in a room opposite them.

Charlie heard him shuffling through a drawer and smiled as he returned with a bobby pin.

"I think I have it this time." Lifting the journal, he plopped on the couch inches from Charlie, inserted the tip of the pin, and said, "Open sesame!" With a turn of his wrist, the lock relinquished its hold on the journal. Jared slid the lock off the clasp and flipped the journal open. He muttered, "Hrmm… Aha… By Jove!" At the last, he turned the journal towards Charlie. "Would you like to explain to me how your mom came into possession of Astrid's journal?"

"Yeah, right," she said with a chuckle. "Very funny."

Lifting his finger and bringing it down harder on the inside cover, Jared pointed out the name inscribed on it.

To Charlie's surprise, Astrid's name was as clear as day. "Astrid Fayerweather," Charlie said in a soft hush.

Jared looked at her, tilted his head, and said, "Is this some kind of joke, Charlie?" No sooner did he ask it than he must have realized from the look on her face it wasn't.

"Please turn the page," Charlie said.

Doing as he was instructed, Jared flipped past two blank pages and came to the first entry. *Am I Truly Dead?* was scrolled in a delicate cursive at the top of the page, followed by paragraphs describing, in a child's manner, what he concluded to be a form of ascension.

Jared continued to read the contents to Charlie, occasionally looking up at her, as she had not spoken a word since he started.

Charlie's heart thrummed in her chest. The entry made no sense. "Jared, do you realize what this means? Astrid died and entered a realm in the afterlife?"

Jared, seeming stunned by what he was reading, nodded and said, "This has to be fiction. Your mom was creative. Maybe she decided to write a book in the style of a journal."

Charlie considered that and, against the reality they were facing, it seemed like the most plausible explanation. "Yeah, mom was always scribbling stuff down. Maybe she was preparing a book series. But, why wouldn't she tell me or Dad?"

Jared lifted his head from the pages of the journal and said, "Some people, especially the super creative ones, get self-conscious about their projects and keep them to themselves. I had an aunt who was a phenomenal painter, but we didn't know until after she died. She kept it a secret, thinking her parents and siblings wouldn't understand."

Charlie nodded. "Yeah, but my mom knew we always supported her work, no matter how unusual the idea was." Feeling a bit hurt, Charlie laid back against the arm of the couch and sighed. "Keep reading, please."

Jared did as he was asked and through the pages, they learned that Astrid Fayerweather was a girl of thirteen years. She was raised in the Massachusetts Bay Colony and after her mother died, she and her father moved to Rhode Island to escape the perception of witchcraft tarnishing the family name. Charlie started taking notes as they learned Astrid thought her fellow townspeople had murdered her. Both the reason and the memory were unclear, so Charlie placed a star next to a note to research the Fayerweathers.

She tapped her pencil as she pointed it out to Jared. He quickly agreed that they needed to hit the library as soon as they could to verify the information they were reading.

Hours had passed and Jared's throat sounded completely dry from reading out loud. He offered to get them something cold to drink. Charlie nodded and pulled the bowl of Doritos over. Jared returned with two unopened bottles of Coors Banquet. He set them down on the table and reached out to open them, but Charlie's expression must have given him pause. "Hey, is beer okay? I didn't think to ask. I just assumed."

Charlie forced a smile and said, "Yeah, it's fine. I drink, just not very often." She hoped her lie didn't show through her nervous tone. Charlie wasn't about to tell him she had never had alcohol. She accepted the small, cold bottle.

He popped his open, then lifted it up to hers and said, "Cheers. To the weird things in life."

Charlie nodded and took a healthy sip of her beer. The bubbles caught her nose, and she coughed lightly.

Jared smiled and gave her a knowing wink as he reached for a handful of Doritos. They conversed, nibbled, and sipped their way through the next twenty minutes, then turned their attention back to the journal. Taking turns reading the contents and making notes, they ended up with a few dozen additional questions that needed to be answered. Placing the lock back on the first journal, Jared reached for the second and removed the lock, this time with no pomp and circumstance. He confirmed that it was again Astrid's writings. About a third way through that journal, another big discovery hit them like a ton of bricks. In Astrid's handwriting was Birdie's name. Charlie gasped as if she had been struck in the chest. The paragraphs that followed from Jared's lips were a mumbled blur.

"The Master feels I am ready for my own charge, one that will be all mine. Unlike the others, I will be left to decide unilaterally regarding how to approach and help this soul. With the Master's help, I have been searching for just the right person, and today I found her. Her name is Birdie, and she is the cutest child. She's southern, polite, creative, pretty, and she wears the most beautiful dresses. She shall be my raison d'être."

"Well, fuck a duck!" Jared spewed. "So, with all signs pointing the same way, it seems, Charlie Bear, that Astrid was your mom's guardian angel after all!"

Charlie stared with her mouth gaped open at Jared.

"Was it something I said?" he asked.

"Huh? Oh!" Charlie said as she shook her head and pulled her hair from her ponytail to keep her flushed cheeks from being noticed. "My dad calls me that, that's all."

"What, Charlie Bear?" Jared repeated.

She nodded. "It's been my nickname since I was old enough to know what one was."

"Cool," Jared said, then lowered his head to keep reading.

A chiming clock rang midnight.

"Shit!" Charlie exclaimed. "Where did the time go?"

Jared must have picked up on her nervousness, as he asked her if she needed to go.

"Oh, no. Not at all. I just didn't realize how much time had gone by. Working on this with you made it fly by." Her stomach interjected with a loud growl.

"Well, it seems like your stomach disagrees with our marathon reading session. You hungry?" Not waiting for an answer, he stood up and continued, "Throw on your jacket. We're gonna take a walk."

She did as he said, and the two escaped out into the crisp night air. They walked until they reached Stewart Avenue. It was at that moment Charlie realized what he was up to. After another quarter of a mile, Johnny's Hot Truck stood before them like a watering hole in a desert.

Upon smelling all the aromas, Charlie's mouth watered. She hadn't realized how hungry she actually was. They approached the truck and perused the booklet-style menu. All the sandwich options one could hope for were offered, including Charlie's favorite, the PMP, or poor man's pizza. She was sure a small amount of drool escaped from her mouth as she read the description.

Making their way up to order, Charlie said, "I will take two PMP's and a bottle of Coke, please." Seeing a surprised look on Jared's face, she felt immediately self-conscious. Did she commit a dating faux pas? Of course, she didn't; this wasn't a date. *Shake it off, Charlie girl*, she told her inner moppet.

"Impressive," Jared said, nodding. He then ordered a Reuben on rye with Swiss and extra sauerkraut. He added his own PMP, and as Charlie reached for her pocket cash, he pushed her hand down and said, "My treat. I insist. I haven't had this much excitement in months." He winked again, and Charlie's stomach fluttered.

They chatted as they waited for their food. Charlie told him about Ramona and her most recent time back home. Trying not to bring the energy down by bringing up the funeral, she kept it light and told the story of the baseball game, being sure to emphasize she was helping her friend out and in no way was on an actual date. As she wrapped up, a guy who was definitely not Johnny let them know their order was up.

Charlie reached for the bag and Jared slapped his palm on his forehead and said, "Hey, man, I forgot the fries. Can you throw me a quick order down?" He slapped two bucks on the makeshift counter, and the cook let out a deep sigh, not making any effort to hide his disdain at the request. Minutes later, he lifted a tin foil pouch onto the metal shelf. Taking the bag from Charlie, Jared nestled it next to the three PMPs and his Reuben. They continued conversing on the walk back to his house.

Jared set the bag down on the coffee table between the journals and the bowl of Doritos, then sauntered to the kitchen and reappeared with two more beers. Charlie accepted but delayed taking a sip until she had at least one PMP in her system. For the next few minutes, eating took precedence over conversation. With one sandwich down, Charlie graciously took a big swig of the Coors.

Sliding the fries in her direction, Jared asked, "Ketchup, mayo, or are you a daredevil craving a mix of the two?"

Admitting yet again that she was not as hip as he seemed to be expecting, she said, "I've never had mayo on fries."

"Well, then," Jared said in a sultry tone. "We will have to remedy that ASAP." He pulled a napkin over and mixed Charlie her very own metchup mix, as he called it.

She wielded her fry as if heading into battle and slayed the metchup, carrying a large portion to her mouth. In doing so, she mis-calculated, and a small blob ended up catching on the corner of her mouth. With a reaction speed quicker than a tomcat chasing a mouse, Jared reached up and swiped the schmutz off her face.

"There. Got it," he whispered as he stared into Charlie's eyes.

Blinking, her reaction time being more sloth than cat, she leaned forward to grab a napkin and ended up head butting Jared straight in the nose.

With a yelp and a few choice curse words, Jared fell back on the couch as Charlie realized what she had just done.
"Oh my God. Can I help? Ice? Hot towel? Nine-one-one?"

Leaning up at the nine-one-one comment, Jared started laughing hysterically.

Charlie, too mortified to laugh, stood up to get him something cold to put on his nose when he stopped her.

"It's okay, really," he said as he grabbed hold of her wrist. Pulling her back to the couch, he leaned in and pressed his lips to hers.

When the shock of the kiss and all that had led up to it wore off, Charlie sat back, took a deep breath, and said, "Thank you."

"Umm, you're welcome?" Jared said with a chuckle. "I've never been thanked before."

Realizing what she had said, Charlie quickly corrected herself. "I meant, that was nice."

"Nice, huh? You're batting zero here, Charlie."

There it was again. That smirk. To work herself out of the embarrassing scene she just created for herself, Charlie lifted a journal and brought their focus back to it.

Before she could get a word in, however, Jared stopped her. "Hey, I think we're actually at a superb stopping point. How about we just chill for a bit, let my nose heal and your beer wear off, and pick this back up tomorrow?"

Charlie nodded, then helped him clean up before packing up to leave. Jared walked her to her car. Helping her with her bag, he leaned in and pinned her to the side of the vehicle for a goodnight kiss that was somehow forceful and gentle at the same time. Charlie's stomach flipped and her heart nearly beat from her chest as every muscle in her back tensed.

When he finally let her come up for air, he said, "Reevaluate your rating system and get back to me on where this one fell." He then shut the door.

Quickly winding down the window, Charlie looked up at him and nodded.

"You are okay to drive, right?" he asked.

After giving another solid nod, Charlie smiled, put Juicy in gear and took off towards her dorm.

CHAPTER NINETEEN
AND THEN THERE WERE THREE

Startled awake by the sounds of people in the hall, Charlie bolted upright. Dazed and confused, she attempted to make sense of what was going on and where and when she was. Looking at her familiar clock, she got her answer to where and when. It was 9:30 AM, and she was in her dorm room. What, was answered by memories of the night before. She smiled. Big.

Needing a coffee as soon as possible, she slid her slippers on and made her way down the hall. Returning with a hot cup full of goodness, she grabbed her phone, plopped on her bed, and called Ramona. It rang and rang until the voice machine picked up. *Odd,* Charlie thought.

The beep did its job and Charlie started to leave her message when a click sounded, and Charlie heard Ramona say, "Hold on. I'm here. Hold on"." There was another click, followed by a deep breath, then Ramona said, "Hey, girl!"

"Hey," Charlie said. "I have to say, that was a surprise. I think I've only gotten your machine one other time. Is the clan on vacation or something?"

Ramona laughed and filled Charlie in on the happenings at the Casa Lorenzo. "My mom's sister had to have a surgery, and Mom wasn't about to leave the two monsters here with me, thank God, so they all piled in the Wagoneer and headed out to Syracuse. But my bestie senses are tingling. You didn't call this early to hear that. What's up?"

Charlie confirmed that she had ulterior motives for calling and conveyed the events of the night before. The squeal that came from Ramona would surely have caused hearing loss if Charlie hadn't anticipated it and moved the headset six inches away from her head. When she brought the phone back to a reasonable position, Ramona was asking a ton of successive questions. For the next forty-five minutes, Charlie went into detail about the journals, the headbutt, and the resulting kisses.

"You gotta be on cloud nine, Charlie. This is amazeballs! When do you see him again?"

"We made plans to meet up at the library later today to research the Fayerweather's to make sure the journal is legit."

"I wish I could be there for… well… *everything*. Speaking of, have you figured out the cash yet?"

"Nope, not yet," Charlie said. "I was hoping I could get some insight from my mom's journals, but nothing so far."

"Well, I hope you figure it out. Good luck with that and Jared. I'm sure you have a lot to do, so I'll let you get to it. Bye, bestie!"

"Later, Ramona."

Deciding she needed real coffee, Charlie got dressed and headed out to a local coffee shop for an Americano. As she walked back, she noted she needed a heavier jacket on the next outing and shoved her hands in her jeans to keep them warm. The coffee did its job to energize her, but her stomach was rumbling. From the bookstore on her way to her dorm, Charlie bought a packet of Pop Tarts and snacked as she walked the rest of the way.

She entered her room as the phone was ringing. She answered, and Jared was on the other end.

"Hey, Charlie," he said in a playful tone.

"Hey, yourself," Charlie replied.

"So, Cassandra and I were wondering something. We have the sketches of Astrid, and we know what you look like, but we have no intel on your mom other than her journals. You don't have anything with you here at school that could help us put the complete picture together, do you?"

Charlie winced when he said *Cassandra and I.* She thought it was going to be just her and Jared again. Actually, she hoped it would be just her and Jared again, even though she knew Cassandra resurfacing was a possibility. Shaking off her disappointment, Charlie said, "Yeah, I've got some photos and stuff I brought from my last visit home. I haven't sorted out anything yet, but I can bring the box with me."

"Fantabulous news, Charlie. See you soon. And hey, I had a great time last night, even though my nose is disagreeing with that statement."

Wincing even more at the jab, Charlie replied with, "Me, too. Sorry about that. We're meeting up at Uris library, right?"

"Yep! See you down in the Fishbowl Lounge."

Charlie decided to wear the jeans she had on and, since they were meeting in the Fishbowl, do the layering thing. One never knew what the temp was going to be like in there. Slipping off her current shirt, she opted for her long sleeve Billabong under her Billy Idol t-shirt. Remembering the shivers from her earlier outing, she pulled out her puffy vest from the locker and tossed it on the bed next to her backpack. Checking her hair in the mirror, she decided there wasn't much she could do at that point, so she repositioned the twist, slapped on some mascara and gloss, then went to her closet to find the box of goodies to take with her.

After eating a handful of bugles and swigging down a quick Coke for an extra boost, Charlie double checked her backpack, zipped it up, threw on her vest, and headed out to Uris for the meetup.

At the Fishbowl, Jared and Cassandra sat at a long table under the windows. 'Jared's nose was bruised from the headbutt. In an attempt to hide her grimace, Charlie turned to look in a different direction, but she was too late.

"Check it out," he said, pointing with both hands towards the bridge of his nose.

"Nice handiwork there, Charlie," Cassandra added.

Lowering her head, Charlie mouthed, *I'm sorry* toward Jared.

He replied with a silent *I know* and a sultry wink.

Not wanting to seem like she was pairing up, Charlie sat beside Cassandra. Setting her pack down, she officially greeted the two and unzipped the contents for them to peruse.

"Jared filled me in on the surprise journals," Cassandra said. "Wish I had been there for that."

Charlie smiled and said, "Well you are actually in luck, because I didn't get a chance to unpack from last night. I still have them in here." She slid the one journal they completed in Cassandra's direction, then slid the second one to the center of the table. "This one, we only got maybe halfway through. And, here are the items I brought from home that I mentioned." She placed the box in the center between the three of them and lifted the lid. "Like I said, I was kind of in a daze when I filled this up, so I am not one hundred percent sure what's in here. I know there should be photos and maybe some of her sketches."

Cassandra, preoccupied with the journal, kept her head down as she made notes on a small spiral pad.

Jared gestured his right hand towards the box and his left towards the unfinished journal and said, "You choose."

Locking eyes, Charlie opted to choose the box from home. "I'll go through it first in case there's anything super embarrassing in here." She snickered.

"Good deal," Jared said as he opened the journal to where they left off. After sliding what looked like graph paper out of his knapsack, he started to take notes.

Charlie reached into the box and took out a stack of items. Separating the pictures, she listened as Jared and Cassandra commented on what they were reading. They stopped Charlie to read some critical points. Realizing she had more of a selection than she thought but no incriminating photos of herself thus far, Charlie interrupted the pair to share what she had gone through. "These first few," she said, "are my mom, Birdie, and her parents, Dorothy and Joseph. My friend Ramona and I think these were when my mom was about six or seven."

"Cute bonnet," Jared said.

"So, they were churchgoers?" Cassandra asked.

Charlie nodded.

"I figured," Cassandra continued. "These totally look like church clothes."

Continuing to share photos through the ages, Charlie eventually got to the photo she found in her mom's studio: the one from them on their last vacation together.

Cassandra slid the photo towards herself and said, "Yep, definitely the family unit. Fun stuff."

As she slid the photo in Jared's direction, Charlie noticed the color drain from his face. Gone were the blues and purples and greens, and in its place were shades of gray. With his eyes bulging out of their sockets, he picked up the photo to examine it closer. Blinking, he looked at Cassandra first, then Charlie, then pointed to the photo and asked, "Charlie, *this* is your mom?"

"Well, yeah," Charlie said. "That was her. Why? What's wrong?"

Cassandra piped in. "You look like you've seen a ghost." She then let out a nervous laugh.

She immediately stopped when Jared said, "I'm pretty sure I did!"

Snatching the photo from his hands, Charlie's face went flush. "Stop it! This isn't funny," she scolded as a small tear formed in her eyes.

"It definitely is *not* funny," Jared said. "Charlie… I swear on my mom and my sisters I *saw* that woman right there a few days ago, by the quads. She was walking around, looking lost. I noticed her because she seemed out of place between her age and the fact she had on a Go-Go's t-shirt. That's not something you would typically see someone's mom wearing."

The group sat in silence for what seemed like an eternity. Jared's leg bouncing was the only motion Charlie registered in her search for what to say next.

Cassandra beat her to the punch. "So, Charlie, you're *sure* your mom didn't have a twin? You know, weird things happened back then. People thought of twins differently, especially super religious people."

Charlie confirmed with a nod that her mom was an only child. Still trying to piece together what was happening, she laid her head down on the table and sighed. Jared reached out and touched her arm. At that, Charlie sat up and told them everything. "Okay. So, there is a lot I have not told you because I wasn't sure how to, or if it was even relevant or real. This may take a while, but I think after what you saw, Jared, it needs to be told."

Cassandra and Jared nodded, looked at each other, and brought their chairs closer to the table.

Charlie began. She went through the timeline after her mom's death, drawing a diagram of sorts to see if they could connect the dots. She finally had to open up about the woman she saw. The odd things that have happened to her. The missing items; the groundskeeper at the funeral home; and, for the first time outside of Ramona, the money. As the last word escaped her lips, Cassandra's and Jared's blank expressions betrayed they were at a loss for words.

Charlie turned her diagram in their direction and offered it as their next puzzle to figure out. However, Jared had overcome his shock and was ready to dive into specifics. "So, let me get this straight. Your mom, who had mysterious imaginary characters in and out of her life, except for the occasional migraine, was a healthy woman. She hid journals, years of experiences, *and* tens of thousands of dollars from you, her family, and seems to have a twin no one knew about. Do I have this right so far?" After Charlie nodded, he continued. "We have looked through her journals up to High School so far with no mention of money, so it seems logical that these missing periods of time and the money have to be addressed in the newer journals she wrote. Did you bring those with you?" Charlie shook her head from side to side. "Okay. Then I would say our best course of action today is to do the research we came to do on Astrid Fayerweather. Maybe she can shed some light on some things, maybe not, but I think to understand this as a whole, we need to do our due diligence with our research." Jared reached across the table and mouthed ,*It'll be okay.*

Cassandra volunteered to go to the computer section and see if she could find anything there on the Fayerweathers. Jared suggested he and Charlie finish reading the journal for clues then head down to the microfiche for their deep dive. Cassandra looked at her watch and said she had about two hours before she'd have to satisfy her blood sugar levels. They agreed to meet back in that spot in about an hour and half.

Charlie suggested to Jared that he comb through the first journal again while she read on, to be sure they didn't miss anything key, especially with the new information fully available now. He agreed, and they both read independently.

Finishing up, both Jared and Charlie took their notes with them down to the librarian, whom they hoped could pull the needed microfilms from the archives. As they approached the main desk, a woman in her mid-fifties looked up from a stack of books she had been inserting check out cards into. Her expression softened as the two explained what they needed assistance with. It was as if she lived for that. As they read from their notes, she wrote down keywords that would help her narrow down the sections they would need to start with. Tapping her pencil on the pad, she looked up at them and said, "I recommend you start broad. It seems you know the time frame and the city of the search, so let me pull the film from any local papers we have from then. I also recommend local birth and death records, if I can find them for you. Start with those, and we can expand based on additional information you come across."

Taking the word of the professional, the pair were told to head down to the microfiche section of the library, which was tucked away in the dark confines of a sub-basement. She would meet them down there with the media. Thanking her, the pair headed down to the dark confines of the sub-basement where, it seemed, old technology went to die.

Sidling up to the machine, Jared offered to take the helm, as he had a plethora of research time under his belt and, as he put it, "I can drive this baby in my sleep."

Waiting for the Librarian, Charlie asked Jared for more details about the woman he saw.

Minutes later, the librarian arrived holding several films. She did her duty and ran through the operation of the machine. Charlie figured this was strictly a CYA instruction. They thanked her again, and Jared inserted the first microfiche onto the glass tray and pushed it into the machine. He used the load tray to bring the items into focus, and the glowing screen soon displayed birth and death records during the time frame they were researching.

Searching for Astrid Fayerweather, Jared moved the tray up and down and back and forth while they both scanned the images. Charlie was the first to see the name Astrid. "There she is," she said, a little too excitedly.

Jared turned and gave her a smirk. "Good eyes." He did a few more slight motions to bring the information into focus and there it was: *Astrid Cora Fayerweather was born to Barnabas Fayerweather and Carolyn Anne Thompson on this, the Lord's day, June the sixth of sixteen hundred and eighty-six.*

Charlie wrote the information down in her notebook and urged Jared to search the death records for all three names. They found Carolyn first. Her date of death was in 1692 and the cause of death was listed as immolation. This made Charlie curious, so she placed a question mark next to the date.

Knowing from the journals that they would not find any documentation for Astrid or Barnabas in the Massachusetts records, they moved on to the film for Rhode Island. They found Astrid's next, and it listed her cause of death as drowning after being charged with heresy.

"Heresy?" Jared asked.

Just as she had done with Carolyn, Charlie placed a question mark next to Astrid's date of death and wrote, *Acts of heresy.* They could not find a record of Barnabas, which could mean he either moved on again or died later than the time frame available on the fiche.

Jared inserted the final film, which was a local paper from Rhode Island. It seems Barnabas was a big deal in that area. And so, it also seemed, was Astrid. There were articles about his business dealings and the new types of crops he brought to the settlement. Astrid's stories, however, were more nefarious in comparison. She made the news several times for the wrong reasons. She was linked to several calamities and mishaps as a young girl. It seemed from the articles she dabbled in potion making and herbal remedies, which weren't always reliable. The final and most interesting article went into detail regarding Astrid's criminal charges and her resulting death. It seemed she gave a remedy to a local family for their daughter's headaches. The family stated that for a significant amount of time, the remedies brought relief to their daughter, allowing her to enjoy a childhood she could not earlier due to sensitivity to light and sounds, to the point where she had been homeschooled for the two years prior to Astrid's help.

As Charlie and Jared read the article, they pieced together events which led the parents to believe that their daughter had been poisoned and that the poison, which masked the pain, eventually built up to toxic levels in her system, causing her death after a fateful dose. The article said the colony of Rhode Island was a safe haven for those who endured persecution due to false accusations of witchcraft and, therefore, did not condone such acts, going as far as to outlaw said persecutions.

However, it seemed Astrid's fate was sealed in a different way. The parents, in their grief, found a loophole and claimed what Astrid had done was heresy against the Church, and that *was* a punishable crime. Hoping to obtain a confession from Astrid of heresy, an overzealous townsman named Green pressed matters to an unfortunate end.

Astrid died at the hands of Green and a few other townspeople in the square centered on the Church grounds. She was pronounced dead after her inability to hold her breath for the length of time deemed appropriate.

"How is that *any* different from being charged as a witch and hung, drowned, or burned?" Charlie huffed.

Jared sighed. "Wow, that's a total mind fuck."

Looking at her watch, Charlie noticed they had somehow already been down there for over an hour and it was time to reconvene with Cassandra.

Jared turned off the machine, grabbed the film, and the pair made their way back up to see that the librarian who helped them was no longer on duty. In her place was a college student. Sliding the films across the desk, they thanked the mousy girl and turned to head back to find Cassandra was waiting for them as planned.

She had taken a different route in her research. A more current one, in fact. She explained she needed to know if Charlie's mom had truly been an only child, and she was able to find information on the Doucette family. What she found made Charlie's hair stand up on her arms. Birdie was, in fact, an only child, the only live birth to Joseph and Dorothy on record. There was a record of another child being stillborn, however. That was a male, and it was years before Birdie.

"So," Charlie said, "no siblings, but maybe a distant cousin?"

"Nope," Cassandra said. "I found the Doucette's only spawned boys, and the Charpiats, Dorothy's side, had females born into the mix but none that would fall into an age range close to Birdies."

"So, where does that leave us?" Jared asked. "They say everyone has a double somewhere, a doppelganger." He paused for a moment, his face screwed up in thought. "However, while that would be a one in a couple million shot, having one living in the same area would exponentially increase that to one in a hundred million or more."

With that, Charlie thumped her head down on the table and let out an exasperated growl. "What are we not seeing?" she cried.

"We'll keep at it, Charlie," Cassandra said, "but I need food, STAT."

With that, the three gathered their stuff and headed out to attain that goal, agreeing their destination would be a Greek restaurant called the Souvlaki House.

Since the walk took Charlie right past her dorm, she decided to make a pit stop and pick up some more journals for inspection. Cassandra and Jared continued to secure them a table. Unlocking her door, Charlie stepped into the room and headed straight for her pile of journals she had separated out. While compiling a stack, she noticed the light was flashing on her answering machine.

Upon pressing the play button, her dad's voice resonated from the speaker. "Hey, Charlie Bear, just checking in on ya. Things are definitely quiet here without you"…" After a slight hitch, he finished "…and your mom."

Charlie winced. She had school and a mystery to distract her from overthinking and missing her mom to that level. Her dad had work and an empty house. As he wrapped up his message, he let her know to call when she could.

Charlie grabbed a crossbody sack she had picked up at a festival and shoved the journals inside. Giving a quick scan to make sure she wasn't forgetting anything, she decided to check the box that she had found the other journals in again, just in case. To her surprise, she found another one that she hadn't even registered as a journal due to it looking more like a bible. Satisfied she had what she needed, she grabbed a jacket to ward off any chill she might get at the Souvlaki House. They were known for not having the best climate control, and being an older building, it was either way too hot or way too cold.

After a short jaunt, she entered the front door and looked around. Seated four booths back were Jared and Cassadra. Again, they were sitting on the same side.

Stop being silly, Charlie chastised herself. *They're just friends*. Making eye contact, she waved to them and headed their way. She slid into the booth, and moments later, a server set a Mountain Dew before her. "Who do I have to thank for this?" she asked as she took a large swig.

"That would be Jared here," Cassandra said. "He said he knows what you like." She finished with a wink.

"I said no such thing," Jared retorted. "I just remembered your fondness for the Dew from the other night, so I took a shot in the dark."

Jared's face turned a few shades of red. Giving him a smile, she said, "Well, either way, thank you."

The waitress reappeared and said, "It looks like your third showed up. Y'all ready to order?" The three of them nodded in unison. Charlie, who always gets the same thing there, ordered the Greek Salad. Jared got the chicken souvlaki and Cassandra went off menu and ordered a burger and fries.

As the waitress headed to put in their orders, Cassandra turned to Charlie and said, "Show us what you got."

Charlie reached in the sack and pulled out a journal for each of them. Then, in a slow reveal, she slid her odd find to the center of the table.

"Pray tell, what is that?" Jared asked in a horrible British accent.

"I honestly don't know," Charlie answered. "I had a hunch to look in the box that had the other Astrid journals and found this one in disguise."

Jared slapped his hand on top of it and slid it in his direction. "Well, let's take a peek." He flipped open the cover and skimmed the pages, flipping through them at an express rate.

"It seems like Jared here took the Evelyn Wood speed reading class," Cassandra teased.

Charlie guffawed and insisted Jared share with the class what he was reading.

"Well," he said, "it is definitely newer."

"Newer?" Charlie asked. "Like, current?"

Jared held up his hand as he read through four more pages. He then lifted his head and continued. "No, like maybe within the past ten years. There aren't any dates on this one to help me figure it out, but she references you being in high school."

Charlie's eyes widened. "She knew who I was? She was that involved in our lives?"

Jared nodded. "It seems like she watched you grow up, based on statements she makes." He trailed off as he read further and further. "Bingo," he exclaimed. "Here's something we can use." Reading aloud from the book he shared how Astrid used her powers to trick Birdie into withdrawing the money. The journal detailed instance after instance of Astrid using either some form of mind control, or worse, possessing Birdie somehow. Slowly, over time, she posed as Birdie and withdrew funds from the bank or simply pocketed cash customers had paid Birdie.

Anger rose in Charlie. Her mom had been both violated *and* stolen from. Astrid was proving to be a con artist extraordinaire. As they read, they also began to discover why she did it.

Jared surmised, "It seems as if she became discontent with her existence in your mom's world. Seems there was a bit of jealousy, perhaps." He went on to tell them it seemed as if she were leading a double life.

"Wouldn't she need a life first?" Cassandra said with a chuckle.

Jared didn't seem to register the attempted humor. "No. I mean, it seems like she had an initial purpose here on Earth, and somehow she got sidetracked or…" He read on, introducing them to who

Charlie figured was once Astrid's boss. She called him "the Master". She abruptly left him for someone called the Dark Magician. As he rambled through the next third of the journal, the waitress delivered their food.

Cassandra, not waiting, dug in immediately, and Charlie followed suit, but Jared slid his meal to the side to continue his recitation. "Here! The money. Charlie, I think we found something." He slid the journal around and offered it to her to read.

Setting her fork down in her salad, Charlie read the section he pointed out. "Sure enough," Charlie said, "it seems that Astrid needs money for something, and 'she was using my mom to obtain it."

"Fuck, she was," Cassandra said in total disbelief.

Charlie "continued. "If I am reading this correctly, the Dark Magician is the head of some cult and was working with Astrid to steal money from my mom." Pushing the journal away, she gnawed on a few bites of salad and stared off in thought.

Jared broke through the lingering silence. "Why don't we enjoy our food and take this stuff to my place to finish up?"

The girls agreed, even though there was no way Charlie could get the revelation out of her mind. Small talk ensued, and Jared teased Cassandra about having a hollow leg when she ordered a slice of the twenty-layer chocolate cake the restaurant had displayed in a round plastic case on the counter by the register.

"I have a fast metabolism," she said. "I'm taking advantage of it while I can, because if my mother is any indication, I will lose this superpower sometime in my thirties."

The trio laughed and continued light conversation while Cassandra gobbled up her cake. Splitting the check, they sucked down their drinks, piled the journals back in Charlie's sack, and headed out for Jared's place. From there, it was all uphill. Cassandra may have had a hollow leg, but she was not built for physical activity, Charlie noted. On the final approach, Jared ran ahead of them to unlock the door.

Standing back to let Charlie and Cassandra enter, he said, "And three, two, one…"

On one, Cassandra sprang like a cat towards the bathroom.

"This a typical thing?" Charlie asked, already guessing the answer.

"Sure is," Jared replied as he laid his hand on the small of Charlie's back and guided her to the couch. "Can I get you a Coke?" he asked as he slid off towards the kitchen.

"Sure, thanks," Charlie said over her shoulder. She emptied her sack once again, opened the old journal to the spot they left off on, and began to read out loud, skipping the mundane and skimming straight to anything dealing with the money. She read example after example of Astrid somehow getting her mom to pull out cash. As Jared rounded the corner with the Cokes, Cassandra reentered the room.

"There's something missing here," he said. "Do you mind if we start over? I believe in my speed reading, I may have missed something that may be important."

Agreeing the information was too important to skim over, they decided to take turns reading the journal from the start so they could hypothesize together. The girls voted that Jared go first, and as he began, Charlie cracked open her Coke and leaned back to enjoy the view.

Jared read from the journal, and Charlie took copious notes. The main points they would need to expand upon would be who the Master is, who the Dark Magician is, why money was needed, and what the endgame was.

Charlie had a hard time believing the murder of her mother was in their plans. None of what Astrid wrote revealed anything malicious towards her. It seemed the toll her actions took on Charlie's mother was unintended, and perhaps Astrid wasn't aware of the consequences.

Cassandra took the next turn reading, and they got some answers to two of the nagging questions. It seemed the Master was a high priest of sorts in a realm in the afterlife. Based on Astrid's writings, he took her under his wing and taught her the steps needed to elevate her soul to the highest plane. Being a guardian angel was one of the first steps in achieving that. It seemed she had dozens of charges over hundreds of years before finding Charlie's mom, and for some reason decided to never let go.

Charlie and Jared hypothesized that it may have had something to do with her dying so young and finding her mom at the age she did. She seemed drawn to the modern lifestyle of a young girl and wanted to have the experiences that came with that. The Master eventually paired her with others in a mentorship capacity as she achieved certain goals.

From what they could gather, she was warned early in her training about the Dark Magician. "So, that negates the cult theory,"

Charlie said. "He's not human. He has to be another entity in the afterlife, along the same lines as the Master, but darker."

As Charlie took over reading the next section, her statement was proven to be true. He was the dark equivalent to the Master, who honed in on weaknesses souls brought with them from their human lives and manipulated those desires and frailties. He was like a cat, watching Astrid and observing her with Birdie before he pounced. It seemed like he took his time and lured her in with promises of returning to life.

"Wait," Cassandra said. "Returning to life? Like, physical life?"

Charlie read on and confirmed Cassandra's statement. "Yep. It seems he taught her dark magic techniques which would allow her to drain an individual's life force and assume their form."

"Fuck, Charlie," Jared said. "I think you just busted this wide open."

Charlie laid the journal in her lap, feeling like she was going to pass out.

Jared made it to her just in time to keep her from tipping over and landing on the floor. Holding firmly onto her, he said, "Deep breaths. In through your nose and out through your mouth." He chanted that over and over. "Cassandra, go get a kitchen towel, wet it, and bring it here, would ya?"

She did as she was asked and returned as Charlie's spinning head started to slow down. Jared placed the towel on the back of her neck and told her to keep going with her breathing.

Once she felt she could focus again, Charlie said, "My mom was murdered by an angel!"

"Maybe that's enough for tonight," Jared said, then insisted Charlie stay put, offering her the couch for the night. "This is a big pill to swallow, and I think you should have someone around just in case."

Cassandra nodded in agreement and even offered to make it a full-blown sleepover if it would make her feel better.

Thanking them, Charlie accepted the couch, but declined Cassandra's offer. They said their goodbyes, and Cassandra added she would work on finding any further information on the Dark Magician possibly lurking in any books on the paranormal. Charlie accepted the help, and they agreed to talk the next day and find some more time to meet up again. Jared led Cassandra to the door, gave her a hug, and waved as she started the short walk to her dorm.

Charlie was already flipping ahead through the journal again by the time Jared shut the door and turned around. "Hey," he said. "We agreed, no peeking."

Looking up like a kid caught with their hand in the cookie jar, Charlie slapped the journal shut and said, "You're right. I need to process this a little at a time." She set the journal down on the table and leaned back with the rest of her Mountain Dew as Jared disappeared down the hall.

His footsteps heralded his return with an armful of blankets, pillows, and a pair of shorts and a shirt. "Here you go. Can't sleep in what you've been in all day. Take these." He laid the stack next to her.

"Thanks," Charlie said. For about half an hour, they chatted about whatever came up naturally, avoiding the evening's topic completely. Jared stood and wished her a good night and let her know if she got up before him, just to leave everything there and he would take care of it. Agreeing, Charlie made the sofa up and fell asleep surprisingly fast.

CHAPTER TWENTY
SOMEONE TO WATCH OVER ME

A combination of light seeping in the bay window and a cushion spring poking into her back woke Charlie. She opened her eyes and, for a minute, forgot where she was and had a tiny what-the-fuck moment. Once the sleep cleared her eyes, she recognized her surroundings, groaned, and sat up.

Taking a quick inventory of her belongings on the coffee table, she quietly stood, retreated to the bathroom, got dressed, then folded both the clothes and the bedding. Setting everything on the corner of the coffee table, she swiped the rest of her stuff and slipped out the front door.

As she walked down the hill towards campus, she thought of two things: the need for coffee and her dream. The latter was still vivid in her mind's eye. She just had to decipher what it meant, if anything. Looking at her Swatch, she saw she had time to pop by the cafe in the Admin building.

She ordered an Americano and carried the scalding hot beverage to a small cafe table in the corner. After reaching into her bag for a notebook and pen, she jotted down what she remembered from her dream to figure it out. For the next ten minutes, she nursed her coffee so as not to scald her mouth as she scribbled in her notebook.

Content that she remembered most of the details, she sat back, dropped her pen, and enjoyed the coffee, which had reached the perfect drinking temperature. A huge smile came across her face when she thought of the night before and Jared. She was grateful she happened upon him and, of course, Cassandra too. They had both been integral in pushing her forward. She now had direction. She also had more questions, definitely, but also direction, none the less.

Charlie cleaned up her spot, tossed her trash, and headed back out towards her dorm. She wanted nothing more than to spend the next few days diving into what they had found out so far, but she still had classes and finals were just around the corner, so she decided the bulk of her attention had to be focused on school. "Not impossible," she mumbled to herself, knowing the hardest part would be not spending as much time with Jared.

Upon entering her dorm, she made her way up to her room. While she set everything on her bed, she decided to give her dad a call. She needed to see if he could pay a visit this weekend. She knew it was time to get him involved, and besides, she needed him to meet Jared.

Dale answered on the second ring. He said he had a few minutes before he headed to work, so Charlie made quick work of her agenda. She kept the details as vague as she could, making the visit seem more like a father-daughter get together than anything else. She slid in a mention of Jared, but Dale didn't offer the teasing she had anticipated. Saying their goodbyes, He confirmed he would come up early next Saturday and spend the day with her. Satisfied with their talk, Charlie grabbed her shower caddy and towels and headed down to the showers to get the feel of blue crushed velvet off her.

The rest of the morning was uneventful. A phone call from Jared checking in on her pleasantly interrupted the afternoon. She thanked him for the couch and use of the wardrobe.

He chuckled and said, "Don't mention it. You'd do the same for me, right?"

"Yeah," Charlie said, "except I'm not sure if you'd feel very macho sleeping in my fluffy kitty cat pajamas."

They both laughed at that thought. Jared confirmed he'd be around next Saturday to meet up with her dad if she needed him to. He also confirmed that both he and Cassandra would continue their research over the weekend. After saying their goodbyes, Charlie got back to studying and preparing for Monday's lectures.

As her stomach was the only one who was going to inform her it was time to eat, Charlie heeded its warning and headed down to the dining hall. That night was day number three in the spaghetti saga. Just like high school, day one was spaghetti, day two added chili powder to make tacos, and wrapping up the trifecta was a chili mac surprise. Luckily, chili mac surprise had always been one of Charlie's favorites. Getting a double helping, she added a few garlic sticks, a bowl of corn, and a double fudge brownie, which she planned to smother with the self-serve custard from the large machine in the corner. She decided to take time between bites to form her outline for discussion with her dad. She knew him. She had to approach this logically and not emotionally. Putting pen to paper, she came up with a list.

Marcus watched Charlie. *Such a sweet kid*, he thought. We need to get her through this. We need Astrid back on our side and Birdie in her rightful place. As he mentally prepared himself for what he was about to do, he couldn't help thinking about how the Master hates using that technique, as a rule, for he feels it's an invasion of a person's inner sanctum. Sometimes, it just has to be done.

He looked down at Charlie's notes and the list she had started. *She's on the right path*, he thought. We just need to give a little nudge. With that, he maneuvered her body and wrote a paragraph which would hopefully help her quest. *There*, he thought. *This should help her over the next hurdle.* Before setting the pen down, he replaced it with her fork and took one more delicious liberty before he released his bond. A dozen or so bites later, he gave control back to Charlie.

Lifting her fork, Charlie realized she had somehow inhaled both helpings of chili mac already. *Wow!* Time must have seemed to evaporate because she was so exhausted. Still shaking her head at the chili mac inhalation, Charlie stood up with her brownie, which she transferred from the napkin to a good size bowl located by the custard machine. She stood and eeny-meeny-miney-moed through her choices, landing on the center pull, which gave her a mix of both chocolate and vanilla custard. With her hefty helping, she set the bowl down in front of the topping bar and added fudge, sprinkles, and chocolate chips. Dessert spoon in one hand and bowl in the other, she returned to review her list. With her first bite of brownie, she almost choked. On the paper in front of her, in a handwriting that was not her own, was a message.

You're on the right path, Charlie. You need to find Astrid, but the Dark Magician is who you must be mindful of. Like our Master, he is powerful. But unlike our Master, he is dark and driven by the sole purpose of bringing about his own army of darkness. We are all here for you, even if you cannot hear or see us. We will do what we can to guide you, but you must find Astrid and attempt to bring her back to the light. Her decisions regarding your mother were desire driven and completely selfish. You need to get her to realize what she is doing is wrong and that her powers and purpose should be light driven. Good luck, Charlie. Continue to be open-minded and watch for clues we will hopefully be able to hand you through this process. Your mother's life will not have been taken in vain. She was chosen to do great things in our realm. We look forward to the day we can make this happen.

A series of numbers that made no sense to Charlie followed that paragraph.

Stunned, she immediately scanned the room for anyone who could have written it. Unfortunately, that time of night was for the in-betweeners: those who missed the main rush and were there earlier than the next mass of people, those who forget what time it was and would rush in with just enough time to spare.

Spooning her brownie concoction into her mouth, she stared in awe at the paragraph before her. *Shit. Fuck. Damn,* she thought. *Jared needs to know about this, but we agreed school comes first.* Fighting the urge to call him, Charlie finally decided to keep the message to herself for the time being. She also decided, however, to go straight back to her room and attempt to figure out what the numbers meant. Until then, she would enjoy her chocolate moment.

In her attempts to figure out the meaning of the numbers, all she gained was a headache. Deciding Tylenol and a mental break was needed, she grabbed a Mountain Dew, a bag of Doritos, and three of the little white capsules, then climbed into bed. Pressing the remote button, her TV came to life. She lost herself in a reality show and eventually dozed off.

CHAPTER TWENTY ONE
DECIPHERING

Preoccupied with the strange note, that evening was a blur, leaving Charlie little room for thoughts on Astrid, her mom, Jared, or her dad's visit. If her phone hadn't rung Sunday morning with Ramona checking in, she honestly wouldn't have known what day it was. After she filled in her bestie on what she learned since their last talk, leaving out the secret code, Charlie decided she needed to call Jared and fill him in on the whole shebang.

She dialed his number and got Gunther on the third ring. He seemed preoccupied and took way too long to get Jared on the line. A few seconds later, Charlie heard a clearing throat cut off Gunther's freight train of thought, and Jared asked, "Would that be for me?"

Apologizing, Gunther confirmed it was Charlie and passed the phone over to Jared. "Chello" Jared chimed. "How's your hiatus going?"

Charlie filled him in on general life happenings, then asked if they could meet up to go over some more things about her mom and Astrid. After a few moments of scolding for not taking a break, Jared took a breath and finished on a good note by saying he could come over that evening if she wanted. After confirming her dorm info and the time, they agreed to order a pizza and try to crack the mystery of Astrid.

Charlie passed the afternoon with uneventful laundry, a movie break, and a final inventory of her room. Looking around, she realized that other than her bed, she had no place for the two of them to sit. Desiring to avoid that awkward moment, she padded down to the common area and borrowed one of the old wooden chairs lined up against the coffee wall. Giving her room and bathroom a once over, she stood back and felt better about the visit.

Opening her desk drawer, she pulled out the flier for Vanzetti's Pizza for when it came time to order. Looking down at her outfit, she decided a quick spruce would be needed as well. Opting to stay in jeans, she changed from her oversized sweater into a comfortable Billabong shirt she had acquired on a family vacation to the Outer Banks of North Carolina. *Besides, the shade of blue sets off my eye.* She chuckled to herself.

Startled by a loud knock at the door, Charlie spun around so fast she had to catch herself from falling into the corner of her food locker. Steadying herself, she answered the door and, as if on cue, her knees went weak as Jared's smile appeared before her. Having never been so glad for the building's solid construction, Charlie white-knuckled the doorknob to not crumble to the floor.

"Can I come in?" Jared asked.

"Uh, um, sure," Charlie stammered as she gave an awkward arm swoop in the direction of, of all things, her bed. *Doh!* she thought, but before she could correct herself, Jared had already plopped on her daisy comforter and was making himself comfortable. *So much for planning ahead*, she thought, but couldn't help but allow an inner laugh.

Having found the Vanzetti flier, Jared grabbed it and said he was starving.

Charlie gestured at the phone on the bedside table, and Jared rolled across the flowery comforter to pick it up. Two minutes later, they had their order in and were ready to get down to business.

Charlie pulled the chair up to the bed, sat down on it, and laid out the research in front of them. "So," she said, "I have something to show you."

"You do, huh?" Jared asked in a taunting tone.

With possibly the most girly giggle she had ever uttered in her life, Charlie said, "Yep." She then slid the note she had received over to him and waited as Jared read the small paragraph.

His eyebrows gave him away. He was as intrigued as she had been. "Where did you get this?" he asked.

Charlie explained she had been writing a list to help her explain things to her dad while she ate dinner the night before. "One minute I was writing and eating dinner, then my dinner was gone, then I got up to fix my dessert, and I came back to find this. I have no memory of it, whatsoever."

Jared looked over the page again. "It seems that whomever or whatever wrote this to you is showing you how Astrid took hold of your mom. It seems to me we have to continue to research Astrid. Based on this note, her motivation is what may have created her link to the Dark Magician. Like, he senses deep desires, seeks out the individual's vibes, and uses them to his advantage."

He finally stopped to take a breath, and Charlie used this opportunity to speak. "I was thinking we should look into this first," she said as she pointed to the numbers. "Do you know what this could be or mean?"

Jared nodded and said, "It looks like a cipher of some sort."

"Cipher?"

"Yeah, like a secret code. Remember when we were kids, they had them on cereal boxes? Sometimes they would put rings in the cereal, and you would use them to decode messages? The military has been using ciphers forever in some shape or form. As a matter of fact, I think I may actually have one of my grandpa's old books on that topic. I can check for you when I get home tonight."

Charlie wanted to focus, she really did, but a hair dangling over his right eye was distracting her. She cleared her throat and looked at the clock to draw attention away from her reddening face. "So," she said, "this could be anything? Another message or a riddle."

"Well," Jared said, "based on the fact they took the time to write an actual paragraph here, I am thinking this is not an actual message, but maybe coordinates? This note mentions finding Astrid, so maybe he's giving you a clue on where to look. Do you happen to have a map handy?"

Charlie perked up at that idea. "I don't have any maps, but you know who does?"

Jared looked at her with a quizzical expression.

She blushed and continued. "Well, I mean, I know lots of people have maps, but my grandpa has *maps*." She emphasized the maps with an arc of her hands over her head. With that, she reached for the phone and dialed her grandparents' number.

Her grandpa answered with a sleepy, "Bauman residence."

Charlie said hello to her grandpa. "Were you already asleep?" she asked with a chuckle.

"Hey Charlie Bear! No, no, not at all. *Eleanor*! It's Charlie."

Within seconds, Charlie heard a second line being picked up, and her grandmother said, "Charlie. What a nice surprise. How are you, my dear?"

"Great, grandma. I actually had a favor to ask Grandpa."

"Oh?" Walter asked. "What can I do you for?"

Charlie said she had a puzzle she had to solve for a treasure hunt in one of her classes, winking at Jared. She went on to explain she had several numbers that she thought may be clues to a location.

"Oh, my Walter, this is right up your alley, hon," Grandma said.

Gone was Grandpa's sleepy tone. "Why, of course, my dear What are the numbers?"

Charlie read him the sequence.

He mumbled a few hmms and yups, then continued with, "So, if this is for one of your classes, then odds are it's a local location. Let me go get my map of that area. Eleanor, keep her busy."

Charlie and her grandma chatted about school, and Charlie let her know that her dad would be visiting Saturday.

"How lovely," Eleanor replied. "Any specific occasion?"

Charlie almost said no, but chose instead to take that moment to introduce Jared to her. She told her grandma about him, then handed the phone to him without warning.

"Hello, ma'am." Jared said as he cradled the handset between both his and Charlie's ears.

Charlie cringed as her grandma did what grandma's do. "Well, Hello, Jared. Are you a friend or a *friend?*"

Leaning back from the headset, Jared looked at Charlie and pointed with a shrug while he mouthed, *Am I a friend or a* friend?

Charlie blushed and held up two fingers to indicate the second option.

"Well, ma'am it seems I am a *friend,*" Jared said in a soft tone.

"Well, that is fantastic!" Charlie's grandma beamed.

"Ahem, what's fantastic?" Walter asked as reappeared on the call.

"Walter, honey, Charlie has a beau. Say hello, Jared"

"Hello, sir," Jared said.

"Well, I'll be damned," Walter said. "Congrats, Charlie! And it's a pleasure to meet you, Jared. I'll have plenty of questions for you later, son, but I do have that map I promised and am ready to crack this code for you."

Charlie and Jared sat patiently, listening as a pencil scratched across paper.

"Okay," Walter said, "it seems that these are indeed coordinates local to you. Do you have a pen and paper?"

"Yes," Charlie confirmed as Jared poised with both in hand.

"Okay," Walter started again, "it seems this is for an area and not a specific spot, so you are going to have to hoof it some to find the treasure you seek. Head to College and Dryden, then stay within a block or two radius of that, and you should be pretty warm. Do you know this area?"

Jared nodded as he wrote it down.

"Yes, Grandpa! We got it," Charlie said.

"That's my man," Grandma teased.

Charlie continued with small talk and reiterated to her grandpa that her dad was coming out to see her that Saturday.

"To meet the boy, I presume," Grandpa said with a chuckle.
As she was about to wrap it up with them there was a knock on her door. "Vanzetti's," a young man's voice announced sharply.

"Oh, Grandpa, our pizza is here. Can I call you next week?"

"Of course, Charlie," both grandparents said in unison.

"Have a wonderful date night," Grandma added.

As Jared turned around from grabbing the pizza, Charlie's stomach fluttered, and she blushed hard. Hanging up, she walked over to her locker and grabbed some napkins, then got a Coke for each of them from the fridge. "Sorry, I don't keep any plates here," she apologized.

"Who needs a plate?" Jared asked as he rolled a slice of pizza up into a tight cone and took an enormous bite.

Conversation ground to a halt as they both tore through the pie. With one slice left, neither had room for another bite, so Charlie set the box on her desk and slid up on the bed across from Jared. Leaning in to look at the notes he took from her grandpa, she was caught totally by surprise when Jared planted a kiss on her. A few minutes passed before they came up for air.

"Well, that was nice," Charlie cooed.

"Yes. Yes, it was," Jared agreed. "Now, do you know where this is?" Jared asked, pointing to the note.

"No, not by memory. I am more of a landmark type of girl. You know, McDonald's on the corner, across from the mini mart, that type of stuff."

"Of course you are," Jared teased. "I'm pretty sure this is up by North Quarry. We can go walk off this pizza if you are up for it?"

Charlie sat still without responding. That would mean the possibility of confronting Astrid. Was she ready for that?

"Earth to Charlie," Jared taunted.

"Uh, um, yeah. Let's do it," Charlie said. "Sorry, I was trying to decide if I was ready for what we might find."

"Totally get it," Jared said. "If you aren't ready, we can go tomorrow."

"No, it will eat me up all night if we don't go," Charlie said. After finishing up their Cokes, Charlie gathered a bag for their walk, then they both hit the *head*, as Jared called it, and headed out on their hunt.

As they walked through campus, Charlie asked whether they should include Cassandra. "I mean, she is part of the trio."

Jared shot that idea down, explaining Cassandra had a late-night art class and wouldn't be able to even if she wanted to.

Smiling, Charlie slid her hand down to his and was even more happy when he wrapped his long fingers between hers. They talked about her dad's visit and how hard it was going to be to tell him about everything. Charlie even took the time to recite the makeshift list she created as backup for his visit.

As they rounded a corner, Jared let her know the two-block radius would start on the next street. Not knowing what they were looking for, the pair agreed to note anything that might seem odd or of some importance. The night air was growing crisp again. May was approaching soon, but Mother Nature didn't want to let her cool grip off the Upstate New York area just yet.

Charlie shivered, and Jared pulled her in closer. They walked in silence, as if talking would have some effect on their sleuthing abilities. Charlie focused on the left while Jared honed in on the right. Nothing stood out. Being Sunday night, only a few college kids and a rogue tourist inhabited the streets.

Reaching the far end of their search area, they made a right onto Buffalo and continued their observations. The street had a few buildings with apartments above them. Charlie mentioned this to Jared, and they looked up to scope those out, as well.

Just ahead on the right was a makeshift church in an old storefront on the corner of East Seneca and Quarry. Above the front door was an old-fashioned iron sign with an angel holding the building number above her head. Jared poked Charlie and nodded towards the church. The pair stopped in the middle of the street and examined the corner.

Above the church were two additional levels, which could have been apartments or offices. Charlie pointed to the side of the building on East Seneca Street, where another door was marked with suite numbers.

Feeling her oats, Charlie walked up to the door and turned the knob. "What do ya know?" she said as she pushed the door open to reveal a set of stairs leading up behind the church.

"Shall we?" Jared asked as he held the door for Charlie. They entered and ascended the steps. Arriving at the top of the stairs, they found three doors along a hallway, one on the left and two on the right, with another set of stairs at the end of the hall.

Continuing towards the other staircase, they inspected the doors as they passed them. The one on the left was marked as an office, presumably for the church, and the two along the right seemed to be apartments based on the numbers mounted on them. Nothing stood out to them, so they continued up the next flight of stairs.

In the next hallway were five doors, two on one side and three on the other. As they inspected them, they could tell they were all apartments except for one, which was labeled a maintenance closet.

Charlie paused. Hanging on the door labeled *3-B* was a framed photo she recognized. Her mom had taken it on one of their summer trips to the Outer Banks. Two wild horses ran in the background as a baby posed by the ocean's edge. She remembered her mom saying they represented them as a family.

This was it.

With a nudge that ended up being more of a punch to Jared's arm, Charlie pointed to the photo and mouthed, *My mom took that.*

Jared mouthed back, *No fucking way.*

They both stood staring at it. After a minute, Jared tapped Charlie on the shoulder and pointed to the staircase. Nodding, Charlie followed Jared's lead, and the pair made their way back down to the street level. With a huge gulp of air, Charlie said a little too loud, "Jared! My mom took that photo. That has to be where Astrid is."

Jared nodded and said, "Inside voice here, Charlie. So, we know where she is. We have to be smart here and figure out our next steps. I say, based on your warning letter and with such a huge agenda, Astrid isn't going anywhere soon, so let's head back to your place, come up with a plan, and arm ourselves with more information."

Charlie gave Jared an exuberant hug and thanked him. As they walked back down Quarry, Jared looked at Charlie, tilted his head, and said, "Hey, Charlie, you know what I think our first step needs to be here?"

Not knowing, Charlie shook her head.

Jared stopped her and pointed to the sign above their heads. "Ice cream," he stated, and they laughed.

The sound of a bell signaled their entrance into the shop. Charlie opted for a double dutch chocolate in a waffle cone and Jared went for a peanut butter chocolate chip combo. "Cold weather be damned," Jared scoffed as they exited the front door.

Sitting here is a waste of time, Astrid thought to herself. *I should be out there looking for the money. The Dark Magician said he has a plan, but we don't have time! I can feel it.* She sighed and took another spoonful of her sundae, glowering at the ice cream shop from her seat in the corner. *It aches how much I want this. I was robbed of a life once, so I don't want to lose my only other chance.* As she licked her spoon, she took another deep breath and stopped herself from getting too introspective. What the Dark Magician had given her was a gift. He heard her desires, and he came to her to help her, like she had helped all those people over the centuries. This was her attempt to claim her reward for all of those years of servitude. Nothing meant more to her than experiencing a full life there on Earth.

A small tear formed in her eye as she thought about her mother. *This life is for the both of us, mama.*

CHAPTER TWENTY TWO
REVELATIONS

Situated back in the dorm room, Charlie and Jared had resumed their research at the bed. Charlie made notes on what they had just found, while Jared made a note to add research on the church to his list of things to look up. Talking through the timeline they had so far and what they found out more recently, the pair concluded they needed to fill in the middle—the "missing links" like money and motive.

"If we can figure out her motive, we may be able to find a way to reason with her," Jared said.

Agreeing, Charlie spread the last of the journals between them and said in her most ominous tone, "Herein lies the answer."

They chuckled, and each took a journal and started to read.

Jared had the first breakthrough with the money, startling Charlie by shouting, "Got it!" He slid over so the journal was in front of them both. "Look," he started, "see here?" He pointed to a page. "It seems the Dark Magician informed Astrid there was some sort of meeting place out west, a place where his devotees could live and thrive."

"Like a *cult*," Charlie blurted.

"Yeah, I guess kind of like that, but what would be their purpose other than to live amongst each other?" Jared asked. "Hold that thought, because here is where the money trail begins." He slid his finger down a few sentences to Astrid's documentation on how the Dark Magician explained how important money was to her and the cause. Over the next few paragraphs, he taught Astrid how to use the techniques she had learned from the Master to manipulate Birdie for short periods of time—periods of time where she could begin to fund her objective.

Flipping through the pages, they read as Astrid grew stronger in her abilities and was able to keep hold of Birdie for up to thirty-minute clips. This allowed her to use Birdie's identity to enter the bank and withdraw small sums of cash at a time without being noticed. She would then use Birdie to stash the money in the house in various places.

Charlie shivered as she read this. All the money was, in fact, her mom's. She still couldn't figure out how neither her mom or dad noticed, or maybe they did and just chalked it up to forgetfulness over the years.

They read on. Astrid used her powers to do more than shift money from place to place. She also took pieces of Birdie's life. There were dozens of instances where she stepped in and became Birdie for an event, an afternoon, or, towards the end, almost a full day. Based on Astrid's notes, this depleted her energies, and she would be gone for days at a time while she channeled what was needed back in to keep going. It seemed that her spying and small tasks were manageable, but the manipulation of her surroundings used a great deal of energy.

"She's an interloper, Charlie," Jared said.

"A what?" Charlie asked.

"Someone who's unwanted or unwelcome. She didn't belong. *Doesn't* belong. Astrid has her place in the afterlife, but her death means she doesn't have a place here among *us*."

Charlie let that soak in as she continued to read. Based on the dates of the journal, the pilfering of money had been going on for over a decade. It was at that moment Charlie's detective mode kicked in, and she grabbed her mother's journal from that same time frame. "Jared, let's compare these and see what we can find out. There has to be more clues to the truth. Who knows, they are probably buried between the two worlds."

The pair spent the next hour combing through the journals, comparing dates and stories. Complete mental exhaustion soon took over the duo.

Charlie sat back to look at Jared. It was ironic how not long ago, she was not even in a place to consider a relationship. It wasn't a blip on her radar. School was her focus. Then, her mom's death, leading to this mess of a mystery with Astrid. Then… there was Jared. People always have stories of the energy you feel when you meet *the one*. There was no denying that she felt that with him.

Leaning back in, she slid the journals out from under his nose and whispered, "Let's take a break." She ran her hand through a lock of hair drooping over his eyes
.

Jared nodded, stood to stretch, and looked over to the bedside clock. "Twelve-thirty?" he exclaimed. "Wow! Time just flew by."

With a disappointed huff, Charlie shuffled over to her mini fridge, squatted before the door, and stared blankly into the compartment. "Mountain Dew time?" she asked.

"Sure thing," he replied as he laid back on the bed and stretched out like a tomcat.

She carried two cans over and cracked the tabs. She sat next to him and took a sip, then slipped into the arm pocket he had created for her by his side. He planted a kiss on her forehead, and that was the last thing Charlie remembered before the bright sunbeam hit her straight in the eyes.

Bolting up, she startled Jared. "Whoa. Did we really crash?" he asked.

"Seems like it," Charlie said. Completely unaware of the time, she anxiously glanced over at her clock. *7:12 AM*. "Ugh." she said. "It's so early. If it's okay, I'm gonna set the alarm and we can go back to sleep for a bit before classes." Jared gave her a half nod and a moan before the snoring started. Charlie wasn't far behind.

The buzzing of the alarm made it official. The pair took their time waking and eventually sat up. Jared was the first to head to the restroom. Charlie could hear him splashing water on his face. He exited with his hair slicked back, drawing her attention to his piercing eyes. "Good morning," he finally mustered.

"Good morning," Charlie replied. "I have class at eleven. Do you have anything to rush to this morning?"

"The only thing I have to do this morning is inhale some coffee, preferably with some food."

"Coffee sounds good." Charlie got up and made herself mostly presentable, and the pair headed down to the dining hall.

As they inhaled their food and several cups of coffee, they put together a summary of what they found out the night before. "We got the money figured out. That leaves the motive," Jared noted.

Charlie was in her own world at that moment and didn't respond. She was trying to reconcile what they found with how to explain it to her dad when he visited. It was going to be one hell of a truth bomb.

"Charlie?" Jared spoke up again. "You okay? You were in another world there for a minute."

"Yeah", she replied, then filled him in on her thoughts.

They decided to put the mystery aside and get back to reality for the day. Giving her a peck on the cheek, Jared stood and announced he was going to bounce and let her get ready for her class. Charlie nodded, stood, and gave him a soul-energizing hug. Watching him walk out the dining hall doors, Charlie filled her cup one more time and allowed the caffeine to do its job.

The rest of the morning was normal: class, lunch, and a much-needed nap. When she woke, she gave Jared a ring and received the answering machine. Opting not to leave a message, she stood up and meandered over to her closet.

Lifting the safe over to her bed, she entered the combination and opened the box to reveal the money. "Jesus," she said to herself. "This is crazy. This kind of money is almost incomprehensible." Closing it up, she laid back and stared up at her ceiling, ruminating over possible motives. She knew if they could pin that down, they could reverse engineer a plan to fix things.

It was at that moment she remembered the note and decided to reach out to her helper. She was slow to start, as she was stuck on how to even ask for help. Was it like in the movies? Would she just talk out loud as if she were praying and hope they hear her? Or, should she go the *I Dream of Genie* route and yell out angel? Or crinkle her nose like in *Bewitched* and summon them to her?

Feeling a direct approach would work best, she said, "Hey! You, the guy who wrote the note. Are you there?"

No answer.

Would she hear an answer? She shook her head and continued. "Your help worked. We think we found her, and we have sort of an idea as to how she has been pulling all of this off. But we don't know why. Can you help us with why?" She lay there in silence, waiting for some divine revelation or a small sparkly entity to form before her eyes.

Nothing.

Turning on her side to look at her clock, she mumbled, "Thanks for nothing." Deciding to clear her head, she sat up, threw on a pair of sweats, and made her way out the door to go for a brisk walk along the water.

The Dark Magician did not like what he was observing. The girl was stirring up all kinds of problems for them. Her and her friends could be the undoing of his sinister plans. Calling to Astrid, he shared with her an idea to remove the obstacle from their existence. Once she acknowledged the Dark Magician's thoughts, he released her back into her own body. She had agreed Charlie needed to be stopped. However, he could tell she did not feel comfortable with removing Charlie from the equation entirely.

Returning from her walk, Charlie sets her sights on a hot shower. As she walked into her room, her hair wrapped in a towel, she saw the red number two flashing on her answering machine. "Man, I'm popular," she joked to herself. She pressed play on the machine.

"Hi, Charlie. It's Grandma and Grandpa. It's been eating your grandpa alive wondering if you won your treasure hunt game at school. Can you please give us a call when you can and let him know, so I can get a good night's sleep?" Charlie heard her Grandpa fussing in the background as her grandma giggled before hanging up the handset.

A long beep was followed by Ramona's voice. "Charlie! When are you coming home? I need my bestie. Pick up, pick up, pick up." There were a few sighs, then she continued. "Yo! Charlie? Last chance, homeslice. Okay, call me when you get this. Need to talk. *Bye.*"

Charlie slipped out of her robe and got dressed. Unwrapping her hair, she hung her head upside down and ran a comb through it, followed by a dollop of mousse and a quick flip up. She checked the mirror to adjust her part, hung her robe on the door, and shuffled back to her desk. Unzipping her backpack, she pulled out her notes from the lecture earlier and began to cross reference them with the textbook. After getting her money's worth out of her pink highlighter, she sat back and looked out the window.

Deciding to call her grandparents back before it was *Jeopardy* time, she dialed their number and listened as their answering machine picked up. "Hi. Bauman residence. We aren't home right now. Let us know what we can do for you at the beep."

"Hey, it's Charlie. Grandpa can rest easy. His mapping skills guided us in the right direction and we found our target. I'll call again later."

She hung up the handset, and before she could take her hand off, the phone rang. Startled, she took a breath before answering. "Hello?" she said in a winded voice.

"Well, hello to you," Jared said. "Did I catch you in the middle of *Sweatin' to the Oldies*?"

Jared was unable to contain his laughter, so Charlie waited for it to subside before she began. "Ha! No. You just startled me is all, Mister Smarty Pants."

They caught up before Jared asked if she had any new news.

"None, zip, zilch," Charlie responded. "You got anything?"

"Yes, and no," Jared said. "I was thinking about Astrid and this new character who left you the message. Obviously, they can see you, us, your mom, in our daily lives. Spying, so to speak. They clearly can use the written word to communicate, so we should be able to deduce that Astrid is capable of more advanced communication. I say you try and figure out how to use that. We may not be able to confront her in person yet, but we can try her at her own game. Whaddya think?"

Charlie sat back in her chair and tapped her pencil. "I… I dunno," she said. "I sorta tried that today with the one who left the note. You know, the whole talk and see if they answer thing. No answer, by the way. So, maybe that's not feasible."

"I see," Jared said. "Well, maybe there's more to it? Like, maybe you have to be in a certain mindset or in a certain time or place? Maybe you need someone with a connection to that side?"

"Like who? Should I call Kreskin?"

"How about just a good old-fashioned medium?"

"Yeah, because they are just out there floating around campus."

"Leave it to me. I may know of someone, but I have to verify and get permission to approach her first."

"Color me intrigued," Charlie said. "I defer to you then, sir. If you can figure this out, I am down for whatever we need to do to get this settled."

"Okay, sounds like a plan. I'll let you know if I make any progress." Jared then excused himself, saying he had a late art workshop he needed to get to. The pair said their goodbyes and hung up.

Deciding to give her way one more shot, Charlie sat up against her headboard, crossed her legs, and spoke out to her voyeur hoping for an answer. Seconds turned into minutes, which turned into almost a half an hour, and all she got was a tingling in her legs. Dropping them over the side of the bed to get the circulation moving again, she said, "Fine, then. I guess you don't wanna talk." She stuck her tongue out before standing to dress for dinner.

"She's spunky," Marcus conveyed to the Master. "Why is it we can't answer her requests?"

The Master explained, "Charlie will go on to do great things with her life, and in order to do those things, she needs to learn the techniques needed to grow her abilities and confidence. Reaching out to her now will stifle her curiosity and quest for knowledge. We must stand back and let her blossom. Many humans and souls will count on her over her lifetime."

Marcus nodded, knowing there were things he could never understand at his stage of development. He just hoped whatever she needed to do would happen before Astrid fully committed to the Dark Magician and his endgame.

Watching as Charlie made her way to the dining hall, Astrid decided it was time to put the roadblock into action. After she chanted a few choice phrases, a cold wind blew through the campus. She sat back and smiled. That would slow her down for sure.

CHAPTER TWENTY THREE
JUST WHO THE DOCTOR ORDERED

Making it back to her dorm, Charlie was completely miserable by the time she opened her door. The wind had chilled her to the bone. Complete fatigue and body aches began to take over. She wanted a hot tea or cocoa desperately, but couldn't bring herself to make the walk down the hall, so she opted for a few Tylenol and a Coke to wash them down.

As she waited for the pills to take hold, she slipped out of her clothes and into her warm, fuzzy kitty pajamas that she had threatened Jared with earlier in the week. Slowly making her way to the bathroom, she soaked a washcloth in the hottest water the dorm could muster, wrung it out, and hobbled back to her bed. Climbing under her covers, she clicked her remote and remembered that she had set her VCR to record a comedy show the night before. After pressing play, she laid back and enjoyed the show, wishing she had enough energy to actually laugh. That was the last thought Charlie registered as she dozed off.

Hours later, she woke to the sound of the static on the TV. Barely able to open her eyes, she moaned, glanced around her room, clicked her remote, and fell back into a deep, dream-ridden sleep.

Her slumber was interrupted by a raging fever. Charlie rolled over to realize that she had soaked through her pajamas and pillowcases and her hair was matted to her forehead. She groaned and coughed before realizing she had nothing to help with the cotton mouth she was experiencing. Glancing across to the bathroom, the trek there seemed impossible. *How can ten feet seem that far away?*

Sloth-rolling over to her other side, she attempted to focus on her clock. *5:30* came into focus first, then *PM*. She blinked and winced at the pain. *Did I just see a PM in the corner of her clock? Did I really sleep all day?* Opening her eyes again, she squinted to dull the pain. *Ugh… Yep. I did.*

With the coughing fit returning, she scanned for anything to help the desert that was her mouth. Behind the lamp was a familiar green can. But how was she going to get to it? She couldn't even lift her arm. Laying on her side, feeling completely helpless and hopeless, she inched her way towards the Mountain Dew. The clock ticked away one minute, then five minutes, then ten.

Around fifteen, she had extended her fingertip out just enough to get a sweaty pad on the can and successfully shimmied it over towards her. Wrapping her hand around the can, she went to lift it and realized it weighed as much as an anvil. Her thirst at that point outweighed the strain she was feeling, and she successfully maneuvered the opening to her lips and lifted the warm, flat Dew past her teeth and down her throat. *God*, she thought, *this may be the best thing I've ever drank.*

Not having the strength to put the can back, she released it off the side of her bed and cringed as it made a cacophonous clatter as it hit the tile floor. Rolling to a fetal position, she immediately fell back into a comatose state and slept.

Marcus worried about his newly appointed charge. She was very sick, almost inhumanly sick. He confirmed his worries with the Master and was given permission to intervene. Using some of his newly acquired skills and borrowed energies, he assisted Charlie.

He set her up with a few glasses of water on her bedside table, opened her pills, and set them within her reach. He held cold washcloths to her forehead and told her stories to pass the time. He heard her machine ring and record message after message from her friend Jared. He could hear the concern in his voice increase with each tiny speech.

Relaying that to the Master would be important, as he had the ability to reach out and place a sense of urgency in Jared's subconscious. Time in the human plane ticked away, and Marcus eventually heard footsteps approaching. The Master said Jared would soon be there. Marcus slid over to the door and used the last of his energies to release the lock before the first knock sounded, then he vanished.

"Charlie!" Jared said in a stern tone as he attempted another knock on the door. "That's it. If you don't answer me, I'm just coming in." Receiving no answer, he followed through on his promise and twisted the doorknob to let himself in.

The smell of sweat and stale air hit his nostrils. Charlie laid in her bed, hair matted and sweaty, and breathing heavy. He rushed over to wake her, but as soon as he touched her, he pulled back, alarmed by how hot she was. Deciding to first get some air moving in the room, he reached over the desk and cranked the windows open. The small openings swirled cool air into and around the room.

Next would be to try and wake her. He grabbed a small cloth that had fallen on the floor and wet it. After wringing it out, he carried it over and sat next to Charlie. "Hey, sleepy head," he said as he placed it on her forehead. "Can you wake up for me?" As he moved the cloth over her face and down onto her neck and chest, he saw the glass of water on her nightstand and lifted it to her dry lips. "Charlie, come on now. You're gonna have to wake up here."

With that, Charlie let out a soft moan. Jared placed his arm behind her head and sat her up a bit more, tipping the water to her lips again. This time, he allowed too much water to run through and her eyes opened wide as the liquid sent her into a coughing fit.

Jared continued to talk to her, still holding her upright, as she got her bearings.

She turned towards him and managed to ask, "Jared?" Then, another coughing fit took over.

"Hey there, you. Let's try some more of this." He lifted the glass to her lips again.

That time, Charlie sucked down the remains of the glass like a sponge. She gasped for air as she swallowed the last of the liquid, then mouthed a *thank you* to Jared.

He pushed her forward with one arm and piled her pillows behind her back to help keep her upright.

She leaned back and began to ask questions. "Why are you here? What time is it? What day is it?"

"What's the last thing you remember?" Jared asked.

"I went to dinner at the dining hall. Then I didn't feel well when I got back. That was right after we talked about you finding someone to help with communicating with Astrid." Seeing the look on Jared's face, Charlie could tell something was wrong. She tilted her head and said, "Spill it."

"Charlie, that was Monday. It's Wednesday! When I didn't hear back from you yesterday, I began to worry, but figured you were busy with class stuff since finals are coming up soon, so I let it slide. But when I didn't hear back today..." He trailed off, his eyes focused on something over her shoulder.

Using what little energy she had, Charlie turned her head in the same direction to find the number twelve frantically flashing on her answering machine.

"See," he said. "That is why I was concerned. I think I am at least nine of those. Do you want me to play them for you?"

"No," Charlie said. "Let's finish our talk first."

Jared stood up, took her glass to the bathroom, and came back with a fresh cup for her. Chugging that one as fast as the last, Charlie nodded and thanked him again.

"So, as I was saying," Jared continued, "I was worried about you. When I didn't hear back today, I got a feeling something was really wrong, so I came over. I can't believe you've been out for over two days. Is it the flu? It's not really the season."

Charlie thought a minute, then said, "I have no clue. It feels flu-like. I remember leaving here with wet hair the other night. By the time I came back, I had chills, then… nothing."

"I opened your windows to allow some air in here. It was quite ripe," Jared said. "You obviously aren't up for a shower yet, are you?"

Charlie shook her head side to side. "I don't think I could stand if I had to."

"Well, two days without food will do that to you. Do you want me to run down to the dining hall and grab you anything?"

Again, she thought too long. It was as if she were in a fog and her brain couldn't process what was going on— like she was drugged. "Yes, actually. I would. If you don't mind? Maybe some soup if they have any. And crackers and a ginger ale from the machine in the common room?"

"Sure thing," Jared said. "But first, let me get you set up with a little bird bath." He stood and walked into the bathroom. He returned with a plastic container from under her sink filled with hot water, a bar of soap, and a washcloth. He set the items down before her on the bed. He then grabbed a towel off her hook and a clean shirt and laid them within her reach. "You clean up a bit. Don't move. I will be back in a jiffy."

As he closed the door behind him, Charlie relaxed back on her pile of pillows in an attempt to gain some energy for the makeshift bath. Slowly, she dipped the washcloth in the water and rubbed the bar of soap, then began to wipe herself down. She then scooped her hands in the water and ran them through her hair, hoping to rectify the matting that had occurred. After drying off, she swapped her fuzzy pajama top for the dry t-shirt. She couldn't quantify how much better she felt, but she did feel better.

She must have dozed off, because the next thing she knew, Jared was sitting on the edge of her bed unwrapping a cup of soup, cracking open a can of ginger ale, and handing her a Saltine to nibble on.

"Thank you," she whispered.

"You are very welcome," Jared said. "If you are up for some good news, I would love to share something with you."

Charlie nodded as she took another bite of her Saltine. She really wanted some soup, but it was still hotter than hell.

"So, remember our last talk, when I said I may know someone who could help us communicate with Astrid?" Charlie nodded, and he continued, "Well, you can thank Gunther and his colorful family tree. He has an aunt who lives just under two hours from here in Oneonta and is a self-proclaimed psychic. She has a small business out there and, according to Gunther, has ways of communicating with other realms. He reached out to her on our behalf, and she is willing to meet with us if we want. What do you think? I was thinking Sunday since your dad would be here Saturday. But it's totally up to you, especially now that this is in the mix." He finished with a swirl of his hand at her face to signify whatever illness she had contracted.

Blowing on her soup, she took her time answering him. She was beyond exhausted, but was also excited by what he just told her. Taking her first sip of her soup, she savored the warm, salty goodness, then responded. "This is amazing news. If I can get this knocked out of my system, I am *so* ready to do this."

"Great!" Jared laughed. "Because I kind of took the initiative on your behalf and accepted. Her name is Kezia, and I told her we would be there about noon on Sunday."

They spent the next half hour catching up on the past two days as Charlie finished her soup. Jared then stood and hit play on her machine, cringing every time his voice came over the speaker. Charlie chuckled as each message played and his voice became more and more panicked. She winked at him as number six finished up. The next call was her dad confirming his arrival for Saturday. Then more of Jared and a final message from Ramona.

"Shit," Charlie said. "I never got to call her back on Monday. I hate to ask, but I am really not up for a phone call and I don't want her to start worrying too. Can you bring me the phone? I'll dial her up, and maybe you can fill her in briefly on what's going on here with my situation?"

"Of course," Jared responded as he stood and grabbed the phone off her desk.

"I must warn you ahead of time," Charlie began, "Ramona is a *lot* and she is going to attempt to pry. Shut her down quickly or I cannot help you. Okay?"

Jared looked at Charlie with a stern face and said, "Aye, aye, Captain." After following her instructions, said his goodbyes and promised Charlie would call once she was feeling better. He hung up and said, "Voila! Should we give your dad a call back too?"

Charlie shook her head. She didn't need her dad worrying about her being sick. Since his message was more informational than anything else, she decided to let sleeping dogs lie. Jared, seeming quick to pick up on her energy levels, took the plethora of items from her bed, straightened up her covers, and tucked her in. "I was thinking if it is okay, I might chill here for a bit in case you need anything else? I'll just find something on the tube."

Charlie nodded, smiled, and, before the first click of the remote, dozed off.

The sun acted as nature's alarm clock. Charlie shielded her eyes and slowly sat up. Still in somewhat of a fog, she looked around the room to get the lay of the land. To her surprise, Jared was still there, curled up on her beanbag on the floor at the side of the bed. Not wanting to wake him but desperately needing to pee, Charlie attempted to slide out of bed, not realizing how weak her legs were from three days in it.

As her feet touched the floor, her legs turned to noodles and collapsed under her, sending her crashing into Jared. Being woken up like that sent Jared into fight mode and, unfortunately, Charlie took a hit to the ribs that knocked the wind out of her.

As the pair lay sprawled across the bean bag and each other, the realization of what transpired must have hit Jared. "Oh my God! Charlie! Are you okay?"

Charlie was unable to muster a sound other than, "Ugh." She rolled over onto the tile floor.

"What happened? Why are you down here?" Jared asked.

"I… had… to… pee," she said, gasping. Still catching her breath, she added, "Legs… gave out."

"Oh, shit," Jared said. "You should have woke me. I could have helped you, you know that, right?"

She nodded. "Help."

He obliged and aided her to the bathroom.

"I'll be okay from here," she insisted, then slid the door closed behind her. He kept talking as she took care of her business, then she stood, wobbled, and squeaked out, "Help."

He entered the bathroom with his eyes locked on the ceiling, lifted her up, and placed her in bed.

Charlie swooned over that last gesture of chivalry and couldn't help but smile at him.

"So," Jared said, "I was going to ask if you were up for breakfast, but I am thinking you need to rest up a bit more and get your strength back. I think I know just the remedy for that. Do you trust me?"

"Indubitably," Charlie answered.

"Okay. Stay here. *Don't* move. I will be back in a flash."

Doing as he said, Charlie sat herself up against her headboard and looked at the clock. *Too early to call Ramona*, she thought. Taking a quick inventory of her room, she couldn't believe how much stuff had piled up during her convalescence. It was kind of embarrassing. Fighting the urge to clean, she instead reached over the side of her bed and snagged her backpack. She made a list of things she was going to have to catch up on. Top of the list, reach out to Tabitha for lecture notes. Outside of finals, her illness couldn't have come at a worse time. As she scribbled feverishly in her notebook, she barely heard the doorknob turn. What really got her attention was the smell of pancakes and bacon.

Jared walked in with a large brown bag in one hand and a cup carrier holding two large coffees in the other.

"My hero," Charlie exclaimed and dropped what she was doing. *Lists be damned when pancakes are involved*, she thought. She patiently sat and waited for Jared to serve her, holding the cups of coffee as he dumped packets of sugar in each, then cream. Setting them on the nightstand, she wriggled upright as he opened a Styrofoam container replete with the fluffiest buttermilk pancakes she had ever seen and four greasy strips of bacon. It was everything she could do not to drool all over her shirt.

"Whoa, girl," Jared said with a chuckle. "Let me get my fingers out of the way first!" He handed her a spork and a knife, and she began slicing up her stack as he opened his container, revealing a duplicate of hers.

The pair inhaled their breakfast, and after placing the trash on the desk, Jared grabbed the coffees and joined Charlie at the headboard. He kissed her forehead before handing her the coffee. "Well, good news is it seems your fever is gone."

Nodding as she took a sip of the nectar of the gods, she added, "I feel so much better. Thank you."

"Think nothing of it," Jared said as he laid his head on her shoulder.

After a few hours of channel surfing and recuperation, Charlie was feeling better, so much so that she desired a big girl shower. She poked Jared in the side to wake him.

"Hey, you," he said in a sleepy voice. "Sorry. I must have dozed off. I guess the bean bag wasn't the ideal sleeping arrangement after all. How are you feeling?"

"I think I'm ready to stand on my own two feet." With that, Charlie swung her legs over the edge of the bed and slowly stood, making sure not to let go of the bed until she was absolutely sure she wasn't going to fall. With all systems a go, she shuffled to the bathroom to pee and reappeared with her shower caddy and robe. "I am thinking I need a shower. Pretty sure I will be fine, as there aren't too many gymnastic moves involved, but could you hang here until I get back? Also, send for a rescue crew if it takes longer than say... ten minutes?"

Jared nodded as he slid back down on the stack of pillows, remote in his hand. "Enjoy," He called out as she slid through the door to make her way down to the showers.

Standing under the hot water, she couldn't remember a time where she felt more grateful to take a shower. "Okay", she said to herself, "there was that one time when Ramona puked on you after getting off the Tilt-A-Whirl. That was a shower for the ages." Letting the hot water flow over her, Charlie felt the muscles in her body relax. Cupping her hand, she filled it with extra shampoo and gave her mop a scrub. After a double rinse, she slathered a deep conditioner in to help with any knots she may have created over the past few days of not brushing. Feeling like a new woman, she gave a final rinse and made her way back to her room.

As she walked in the door, Jared whistled and said, "Squeaky clean."

She laughed and set her caddy in the bathroom. Grabbing a comb, she headed over to the edge of the bed and sat. While she combed her hair, she said, "I desperately needed that, but I'm exhausted now."

Jared sat up. "Well, that means I have a tidbit of good news. I have to jet for some classes, which means you can get some more rest. Although, I hope you have a set of clean sheets. I can help you change them before I head out."

Charlie pointed to her closet. "There should be a full set way in the back on the shelf."

Jared entered her closet for the first time, then immediately popped back out and asked, "Is that what I think it is?" Eyes wide, he waited for Charlie's response.

"If you mean the safe, then, yes. Yes, it is."

"How's about a peek?" He teased in a southern drawl.

"As long as you bring it over, you got a deal."

Jared lifted the safe and carried it over to Charlie. She entered the combo and opened the door so Jared could see the contents.

"*Wow!* So that's what thirty K looks like, huh? Not too shabby. Have you decided what you are gonna do with it now that we know how it came to be?"

Charlie nodded. "Yeah. I am going to give it to my dad Saturday after we talk. It is, after all, half his money, and I am sure he has expenses that piled up after the funeral." Closing the door, Charlie reshuffled the combo, and Jared placed it back in the closet.

He returned with a full set of Care Bear sheets. Before he could comment, Charlie gave him a *don't go there* stare. The two made relatively quick work of stripping the bed and reassembling a cleaner, less smelly version.

"Just leave those there," she said. "When I am back to myself, I'll run those through the laundry."

"You got it," Jared replied, complete with finger guns. "So, I gotta slide. You okay for the afternoon? I'll bring some dinner later if that's okay?"

Charlie nodded, climbed into bed, and reclaimed the remote.

"Glad you're feeling better there, chica," Jared said as he gave her a smile, then closed the door behind him.

Sliding down in between the clean sheets, Charlie heard Bob Barker's voice giving instructions to a contestant as she fell asleep.

CHAPTER TWENTY FOUR
RECOUPED AND READY

Waking to the theme song of General Hospital, Charlie let out a yawn and a big stretch. Thirst was the first thing to hit her. She got her bearings, shuffled over to her bathroom, and filled a glass with water. Sucking it down, she realized she needed more. Turning back to her room, she opened her mini fridge and pulled out a Coke. Cracking the top, she brought the can to her lips and immediately choked on the fizz that escaped into her nose. After taking a minute to get the tingles out, she took a big swig, grabbed her phone, and plopped on her bed.

After thinking about who to call first, she opted for her dad. He should have been home any minute and would be short and quick. She dialed and let the phone ring. Just as she was about to hang up, she heard her dad say, "Hello. hold on."

As she waited, she heard her dad's heavy breathing as he lifted the handset back to his face. "Hello?"

"Hey dad!" Charlie said. "You called?"

"Yeah, just wanted to check in and make sure we are still on for Saturday."

"Of course," she replied, then went on to explain the delay in her call.

Her dad made the typical analytical dad statements she was used to. There were reports of the flu in the area, be sure to wash your hands, cover your cough, stay out of confined areas and such. After confirming she was over the hump, he ended his diatribe with, "Well, I am glad you're okay, kiddo. How's Jared? Is he taking care of you for me?"

Charlie blushed. "Yes, Dad. He's good, and he has been a huge help."

Charlie confirmed their meeting place before they said their goodbyes. She hung up and took a swig of her Coke. Taking a look over at the TV, she caught an overzealous argument between Monica and Alan Quartermaine.

Picking up the phone again, she took a deep breath and dialed Ramona. *This will require some energy*, she thought. As the phone rang, she smiled, knowing Jared would be back soon, and quickly forgot that she had not yet reached out to Tabitha for her notes on the missed lectures.

As she was about to get up and write it down, Ramona's mom picked up the line and said, "Lorenzano Residence."

"Hi, Mrs. Lorenzano, it's Charlie. Is Ramona there?"

"Well, hello dear" Ramona's mom said with a crisp tone. "Ramona *is* home. Let me get her for you."

Knowing all too well what that meant, Charlie moved the headset a safe arm's length away just before Mrs. Lorenzano wailed, "*Ramona*! Phone!"

The phone clicked and Ramona said, sounding like an annoyed teenager, "Got it, Mom." After a huff from Mrs. Lorenzano, the tell-tale click of the phone being hung up signaled the girls were alone.

Ramona immediately launched into a long-winded ramble. Charlie watched the TV as her friend rambled, and it transitioned from afternoon soaps to local news. The sun lowered in the sky. It was a Ramona bender to end all benders. Charlie barely got in an occasional, "Uh huh. Yep." Laying back on her pillows, she set the handset cockeyed on her shoulder so she didn't have to hold it any longer. After getting through the boyfriend woes, the call continued as Ramona went into her next crisis, which consisted of her life goals—or lack thereof.

As Charlie sat up and drank the last of her Coke, a soft knock echoed from her door and the knob turned slowly. Jared peeked through the crack, half-obscured behind a sizable entering before him.

"Delivery!" he bellowed as he walked in, then winced as he apparently noticed Charlie was on the phone. As he set the box on the bed, he mouthed, *Sorry.*

Waiting for the slightest break in Ramona's rant, Charlie covered the handset, made the universal hand motion for yapping, and mouthed, *Ramona.*

Reading the signs right, Jared coughed, walked back to the door, knocked louder and shouted, "Delivery."

That gave Charlie the tiniest of windows to interrupt Ramona and explain she had to get the door. "Can we talk later?"

Ramona acquiesced and said her goodbyes, confirming a midday call for the next day.

Jared walked back over and took the phone out of Charlie's hand as Ramona's voice carried through the room, saying, "Got it." He then slid it on the cradle.

"Wow that girl can talk," he said as he moved the phone to the desk.

"You have no idea," Charlie joked. "She goes through existential crisis moments, and I am lucky if I can get a word in edge-wise." Her eyes were drawn to the mystery box on the bed. "What did you bring?"

"Hunan Garden." He gestured to the box in the most masculine Vanna White impression Charlie had ever seen. Pulling out the tiny containers, he recited what Charlie would swear was the entire menu.

Catching up on how their afternoons went, the pair dove into the food. Realizing neither of them had a beverage, Charlie slid off the bed and grabbed them Cokes. As she returned, Jared observed it seemed she was feeling much better.

"I am. In fact, maybe we could spend a bit of time tonight putting a plan of action together for our meeting with the psychic on Sunday."

"Sounds good," Jared said as he turned his attention to her movie collection. "Hey, is that *Silver Bullet* sandwiched between *Halloween* and *Lost Boys*?" Giving her the Groucho Marx eyebrows, he stood and yanked the movie from its spot on the shelf. He slid it from its sleeve and pushed it into the VCR, then joined her at the head of the bed and readjusted the cartons so they stayed within their reach.

As they relaxed and enjoyed the food and movie, Charlie filled him in on her talk with her dad and gave a rapid synopsis of Ramona's drama. Jared returned the favor, discussing his classes and a brief meeting he had with Cassandra in the quad. She had given him a bunch of notes on afterlife stuff and sent a message for Charlie to feel better.

"I didn't tell her about the psychic because I knew she'd want to go, and I think that two of us already may be one too many."

Nodding, Charlie asked to see the notes.

Jared smirked and said, "After Uncle Red and Marty capture the werewolf."

With the closing credits rolling, the pair took turns in the bathroom.

When Charlie re-entered the room, Jared had a stack of papers and his notebook in front of him. "Hey, I am going to review what Cassandra gave me and see if it's anything we can use regarding Astrid."

As they cleaned up, Charlie let Jared know she was going to check in with her friend in the morning regarding class notes then head to her analytical biochem lab. Afterwards, she was probably going to spend the afternoon cleaning and doing laundry. Jared acknowledged her plans and reminded her not to overdo it. Giving her a kiss on the forehead, they said their goodbyes and promised to check in at some point.

Sleep came fast for Charlie, and the morning alarm even faster. She realized she was not at one hundred percent yet and took her time stirring. Deciding she needed a real meal for breakfast, she loaded up her backpack and got dressed for the day. Before heading out the door, she gave Tabitha a buzz and asked if there were any notes that she missed from the past few classes.

Tabitha said one class wasn't too bad and was taken almost directly from the reading assignment. However, she said with an exhausted sigh, Tighman gave a hefty, nap-worthy lecture on the nature of reality. Tabitha confirmed she would set her notes outside her dorm room if Charlie wanted to swing by and grab them.

Agreeing she would, Charlie hung up and gathered her materials and dining pass. She remembered to dress for the weather by grabbing her jacket with a high collar. She maneuvered down to Tabitha's room to find a unicorn Trapper Keeper laying just outside the door. Scooping it up, Charlie began her walk to the dining hall.

Taking her time eating, Charlie copied the notes just in time to head out to her class. Thankful for the energy the food had given her, Charlie barely managed to make it through class. Knowing she still had a lot to do to prepare for her dad's visit, she made a beeline for the dorm, where she slid the notes outside Tabitha's door with a thank-you note.

Back in her room, she gathered her laundry into a bag, then she hopped in Juicy and made her way over to the mat near Dinos. Popping the sheets in the wash, she walked over to the restaurant and ordered a Coke and a large basket of fries. While she waited for her laundry to finish its first round, she read over several texts to bring herself up to speed on her classes.

Looking at the syllabus and her calendar, she gave a quick count of the days until finals. She couldn't believe the year was almost over. Just a few more classes left in sophomore year. She glanced at her Swatch, let the waitress know she'd be right back, and headed towards the laundromat to place her items in the dryer.

On her way out of the mat, she got distracted by a few of the local shops on the street and, doing what any girl with no actual income would do, window shopped.

She peered into a clothing boutique and stopped dead in her tracks. Standing between two racks, hastily shifting hangers from left to right, was Astrid. Charlie could not believe her eyes. *The nerve—no—the* balls *on this... this... woman? God, I don't even know how to classify her.*

Knowing she made a promise to not confront Astrid in person, Charlie stood quietly and observed her. It was heartbreaking how she was literally her mother's twin. There were significant differences in style and body language, but visually, she was Charlie's mother. Not being a violent person in the least bit, Charlie was surprised at the amount of hate that seethed from her heart. Deciding it was best to leave before she let her anger get the best of her, Charlie turned and walked across to Dinos.

Astrid had no clue why she was even in a store to begin with. Looking and not buying sucked. She felt her skin get hot as she thought about the money she had worked so hard for and how it was just sitting somewhere. *Soon,* she reminded herself, *soon the Dark Magician will get me to where I need to be, and I will never have this problem again. The life I want—no—the life I deserve will be mine.*

As she turned to look at a display on the wall, she saw herself in the mirror. After centuries of not having a form or reflection, it caught her off guard. She missed her hair and her eyes. The first thing she would do when she made it out west would be to rectify both those traits. She didn't mind Birdie's features at all, she just didn't want to be reminded of her at every turn.

With that thought, she turned away from the mirror and saw Charlie walking across the street. She realized her tiny curse had worn off. She could only hope that the girl got the message and would back down in fear of further retribution.

Charlie finished her fries and the second Coke she had ordered. After paying the waitress, she gathered up her belongings and shuttled back to the laundromat to retrieve her laundry. Not wanting to go straight back to her dorm, she decided to take Juicy on a small jaunt and enjoyed an hour of car karaoke before heading back to her dorm.

Folding her sheets like a pro, Charlie then made her way systematically around the ten-by-ten space cleaning, disinfecting, and all-around sprucing her room. Plopping on her bed, she decided it was time to take a well-deserved rest, so she sat back and closed her eyes.

She woke with a startled feeling, as if she were being watched. Shaking off the heebie-jeebies, she glanced at her clock just as her phone rang. Hoisting herself up on her knees, she stretched just enough to be able to reach it.

Before she could say hello, Jared greeted her. "Hey. Just checking in to see how you made out today."

She filled him in and reported that she was overall feeling much better. His response sounded so relieved she could imagine him smiling.

They volleyed information back and forth for a short bit before Charlie realized she had forgotten to tell Jared she saw Astrid.

"I can't believe it. I'm glad you took my advice and didn't confront her." Then, out of the blue, Jared asked, "Do you like Christian Slater?"

Thrown off by the question, she paused for what must have been too long.

"I'll take that as a no," he said. "I was only asking 'cause there is a movie coming out next week, and I would love to see it if you are up for it. Christian Slater is the lead in it, so I figured it would make up for the premise of the film."

Intrigued, Charlie asked, "What film, and what do you mean by 'make up for the premise'?"

"It's called *Gleaming the Cube*, and it's about… skateboarders." He inhaled after the last word. "Could you take one for the team and go with me for the promise of Slater?"

Charlie laughed and said, "For your information, I am totally into skateboarding. Ramona has brothers, and pretty much every kid on our street either skates or BMXs. As a matter of fact, this kid, James, who lived the next street over from me, built a wild half pipe in his parents' backyard. We used to go hang out and watch the cooler, more coordinated kids skate and break bones."

Silence took over the line. "Hey, you there?" Charlie asked.

"Uh, yeah, I was just pinching myself to make sure this wasn't a dream." As he chuckled he added, "So, it's a date then! We can pick a night after our outing on Sunday."

As they wrapped up their conversation, Jared agreed to come by her dorm in the morning, then they could take Juicy over to meet her dad for breakfast. They said their goodnights and hung up.

Sitting back on her pillow, Charlie smiled. A date. A real date. She liked that. Hopping up, she changed into her sleep shorts and shirt, washed her face, brushed her teeth, and slid back between the sheets. Clicking on the TV, she watched some of *The Bradys* before flipping the channel to catch *Perfect Strangers*. Something about Balki Bartokomous made her laugh.

Glad Charlie had recovered from the hex Astrid conjured, Marcus sat back and watched over her. The soft steering the Master had put in place was working. The next day with her father would be critical. His reaction could derail the Master's plans if not handled right. As being an optimist was kind of in his job description,

Marcus said, "It'll all work out." With that, he left Charlie to check on his other charges.

CHAPTER TWENTY FIVE
A DAD, A PSYCHIC AND AN ANGEL

Glad she had set her alarm, Charlie woke to the sound of the steady buzzing of her clock. She was so excited to see her dad, see how he was holding up, and share her news with him. The latter was more fear than excitement over how he would handle it, but she told herself it would all work out as she got dressed.

A soft knock on her door drew her attention. "He's nothing if not punctual," she said as she walked over to it.

"Good morning," Jared said, and as if reading her mind, he produced hands holding coffees. "I figured you'd need to pre-caffeinate before we got there."

Nodding repeatedly, she lifted one of the cups from his hand and paid him with a kiss—on the cheek just to be safe since she was sick.

"Just about ready," Charlie said as she walked into the bathroom and slid her hair up into a ponytail. Grabbing her coffee and her backpack she had filled the night prior, she motioned towards the door.

"What's in the sack?" Jared asked as he shut the door behind her.

"Oh, I brought a few choice journals and some of our notes to start the conversation. I figured we could see how that sits with him and introduce the deeper, more sinister stuff later."

"Ah, yeah. Good idea."

Sliding into a parking spot at the restaurant they were meeting her dad at, Charlie took a moment to shake off her butterflies. Not only was she nervous about telling her dad the information on Astrid and her mom, but also about him meeting Jared. Scoping the surrounding area, she saw her dad's Jeep a few cars away. Knowing him, he was already in a booth, all settled in. Turning to look at Jared, she took a deep breath and asked him if he was ready. Signaling he was, he gave her hand a squeeze before they both exited Juicy.

Jared opened and held the restaurant's door for Charlie as she shifted her backpack to her opposite shoulder. Before she even started to look for her dad, he stood out by waving them in from the expected booth.

"Last chance to back out," Charlie suggested.

"Never," Jared said.

Dale stood and gave Charlie a bear hug, their signature greeting. Stepping back, he squared up with Jared, stuck his hand out, and said, "This must be Jared. Glad to meet you."

The pair shook hands and Jared said, "Glad to meet you too, sir."

Jared hung his jacket from a hook on one of the booth's posts, then slid in first so Charlie could be across from her dad.

A waitress appeared, placed three glasses of water in front of them, and explained the menus were located in the napkin holder at the end of the table. "Can I get you anything to drink other than water this morning?"

Charlie and Jared opted for coffee, and Dale ordered an orange juice. With Jared being the closest to the menus, he took the initiative to pass them out as the small talk began.

"So, Jared. Tell me about yourself," Charlie's dad said.

While Jared went through the typical get-to-know-you questions. The waitress delivered their drinks and asked if they were ready to order. None of them had even looked yet, so Dale asked her to give them a few minutes. Jared wrapped up the question and answer session with, "And that's my life in three minutes."

Charlie snickered and turned her attention to her dad. "How are you doing, Dad? You look good. New duds too, huh?"

Verifying that he indeed had on new clothes, he gave her a similar synopsis that Jared had gone through, but the adult version and limited to current events since she knew the backstory already. "Your Grandma and Grandpa have expressed they think the house is too big for just one person. They hinted I should sell and move into something more befitting a bachelor." He winced when he made the last statement.

Charlie could tell why. He wasn't a bachelor; he was a widower. However, that moniker didn't suit him either, since he was still so young. "Dad, that is a decision you're going to have to make. I will miss the house and all the memories it holds of Mom, but in the end, it's just a place. You can find another and make new memories to add to those we have of Mom. Totally up to you, though." She ended her sentence with a brief touch on his hand.

"Hey, I know," he said with a sudden chuckle. "Let's figure out what to eat before the waitress gives up on us."

By the time the waitress made it back to their table, they each had their orders ready. Reading them back for accuracy, the waitress made a big check at the bottom of her notepad and twirled back towards the kitchen area.

"So, Dad…" Charlie began, hesitating.

"So… Charlie," he said, filling the silence.

"No, seriously, Dad. We need to talk." Taking a deep breath, Charlie started with the obvious knowns and the idea that her mom was healthy and that her death made little sense. Then, she dove into the rabbit hole and explained what had transpired since her mom's death, the journals she found, and the research she, Jared, and Cassandra had been doing.

Charlie kept her eyes on her dad to be sure she hadn't lost him in the details, and saw from the corner of her eye that Jared was doing the same. So far, it seemed he was following along. With her first set of explanations out of the way, she unzipped her backpack and pulled out a few of the journals. She opened them and explained how Mom had imaginary friends growing up, but they didn't go away. "Did you know that about Mom?"

His voice soft and measured as if he wasn't sure how to react to anything he'd just heard, Charlie's dad said, "I knew she had imaginary friends as a kid. Who didn't? But I had no clue she didn't outgrow them."

Charlie continued to give examples and ask questions. She explained how Astrid could manipulate Mom, leading to her blackouts and the forgetful moments they always chalked up to her being a free spirit.

Dale took a deep breath, but before he could respond to that last revelation, the waitress approached bearing a tray loaded with pancakes, eggs, hashbrowns, and an assortment of meats and toasts. After making quick work of the delivery, she asked if there was anything else they needed. Charlie and Jared both asked for ketchup, mayo, and hot sauce. Nodding, she retrieved said condiments.

"So, let me get this straight," Charlie's dad began. "Your mom has been plagued by ghosts her whole life?"

Jared jumped in. "No, sir. Not exactly. We believe, based on her journal entries, that Astrid is—well, *was* a guardian angel of some sort. At some point in Birdie's early adolescence, it seems Astrid began to covet what Birdie had. That might tie to the fact Astrid was murdered at such a young age." Stopping to take a breath, Jared looked over at Charlie.

She gave him an *it's-okay* look.

As he cut into his stack of pancakes, Jared continued. "You see, sir, from what we can gather, there is a realm, or possibly several, where spirits go when they pass on. Astrid's journals seem to suggest she was welcomed into one such plane where she was taken in as something like an intern and instructed on how to be an angel. We're still working on this theory. As a matter of fact, we are meeting with a psychic tomorrow to see what else we can find out." Jared looked down at the first, untouched bite of pancakes still dripping on his fork, then shoved them into his mouth, ending his monologue.

Dale stared at Charlie with an incredulous expression as he shook ketchup on his home fries.

"Dad, we get that this is a *lot*. We have had time to process this, and we still have issues believing what we are finding. But, we truly believe whatever Astrid was doing was somehow robbing Mom's life force, depleting her until she was so weak, spiritually and physically, that she couldn't fight back. I'm sure Astrid did something to cause mom's sudden death." There. She said it. Her dad's only response was silence. As she waited for him to say something, anything, she followed Jared's lead on the pancakes to distract herself.

With a complete hush over the table, the clatter of the forks and knives was almost deafening. Charlie looked at Jared for some release of the tension, who seemed to be looking for something from her. They both looked at her dad, who had not lifted his head from his plate.

Finally, as he picked up a slice of bacon, he spoke. "Well, this is *not* what I expected from my visit today. You know me, Charlie. I'm an analytical man. I have not, do not, and honestly never will believe or understand these flights of fancy. However, I must acknowledge the data you have presented. I have heard you both and what your obviously time-consuming research has produced. I'll attempt to understand. What I ask, for now, is that we enjoy our breakfast, move on with more pleasant conversation, and circle back to this at a later time." With that, he shoved the piece of bacon in his mouth and washed it down with his orange juice.

Charlie and Jared did as her dad wished, and they enjoyed their breakfast. They conversed over Charlie's classes, upcoming exams, and even a few spitball plans for the summer. Finishing up, Dale asked for the check, and the group slid out of the booth to make their way outside. Standing next to the Jeep, Charlie invited her dad back to the dorm. To simplify the parking situation, he agreed to ride with them in Juicy. As Charlie drove the short distance back to the dorm, she couldn't help but snicker as she saw Jared twisted like a pretzel in Juicy's nearly nonexistent back seat. Catching her, he stuck out his tongue.

The weather was great that day, so Charlie asked her dad if, after he inspected her dorm, he would want to go for a walk along the water. Agreeing, they entered the dormitory and headed up to Charlie's room. Dale took a seat at the desk, Charlie plopped on the bed, and Jared sank down into the beanbag.

"Not too shabby, Charlie Bear. This year's room definitely has more space than that shoebox you had to share last year."

Agreeing, Charlie mentioned the extra space was due to a lucky break she got with her roommate exiting the university early. She showed him what little she could, and they talked about everything and anything that wasn't Astrid or Birdie. Dale performed his fatherly obligations in grilling Jared on intentions and warnings that come with an only daughter. Jared took the pokes with lightheartedness.

It was at that moment Charlie stood and said they should think about starting their walk. Knowing she had never, nor could she ever, hide anything from her dad, she wanted to share something else with him. Jared sank back down into the beanbag as Charlie made her way to the closet. Exiting, she placed the safe on the bed and watched her dad's curiosity grow. Finagling the combination, she opened the door and began the story of the money.

Completely and utterly confused and dismayed, her dad sat with the most wondrous look on his face. He even asked Charlie several times where she *really* got the money from. She explained the story again, and it seemed to finally sink in with him.

"So," Charlie said, "this is obviously *your* money. Well, yours and Mom's. I really wanted to tell you about this sooner, but I knew you would need more information. So, I waited until I had it. We are still working out the real reasoning behind this. We hope to have this resolved tomorrow, as well. But, the money is yours to take home with you." Charlie let out a deep sigh of relief.

Jared also inhaled and exhaled, relaxing his shoulders back down to a normal height.

With that, Charlie closed up the safe and moved it to the floor, then they headed out for fresh air and their walk.

The trio spent the next hour enjoying the campus and small talk. As they neared the end of the walk, Charlie let go of Jared's hand and excused herself and her dad. As she watched Jared saunter over to a nearby oak tree, she giggled knowing he was being a show off in an attempt to seem deep in thought. Turning back to her dad, Charlie took her dad's hands and explained the feelings she was beginning to register for Jared. She felt her face get flush and then she heard her dad tell her that he couldn't be more happy for her, and he knew for a fact her mom would have approved of Jared, herself. Charlie listened as he continued on the dad advice trail which included the obligatory "take it slow, you have all the time in the world" speech. They finished up, Charlie nodded, and gave her dad a big bear hug. Signaling for Jared to join them again, Charlie beamed as Dale stated what a pleasure it was to meet Jared and reached his hand out for another shake. Sensing that Jared did not want to be a pretzel again in the bowels of Juicy, Charlie said her goodbyes to Jared who stated he was going to head out and catch up on some studying.

Charlie and her dad made their way back to Juicy. As she drove him back to his Jeep, he reinforced the importance of her getting the money in the bank as soon as she could. They would worry about long-term interest rates later. Giving him a final hug goodbye, Charlie kissed him on the cheek and said, "See ya soon, Dad."

Charlie sat and watched her dad pull off for his short drive home, stunned at everything that had happened in such a short time. He took the news well, or at least as well as could be expected. She knew his skepticism wouldn't allow him to accept the majority of it, but the fact that he was open to the idea meant the world to her.

In their brief one-on-one he also gave her his blessing regarding Jared. "Seems like a nice young man. Solid. Not a dreamer. Head on his shoulders." He then surprised her with his decision on the money. He explained that while the money had been his and her mom's, he knew if she were able, Mom would say the money should go to Charlie. He said she should keep it for whatever she needs or wants in the future, but made her promise it would go into a bank and not sit in her closet any longer. That was his one stipulation, and Charlie had agreed.

As she exited Juicy and walked back to the dorm, Charlie thought about the day ahead. Nervous was not a strong enough word to express how she felt, but she would have Jared with her, and it needed to be done. She performed a quick change before sliding in between her covers and fell asleep surprisingly fast.

Astrid fumed as she watched the day play out before her. Her fears about the money were confirmed. The girl had it the whole time, and was going to place it back into the confines of a bank. She had to come up with a plan fast. That money could not slip away, it just couldn't. Sinking back into her reality, exhausted from the energy she spent spying on the trio most of the day, Astrid cursed herself for having missed some key moments. She laid down to sleep knowing she would have to reach out to the Dark Magician for his help.

As the sound of the phone ringing made its way into Charlie's consciousness, she rolled over to see it was nine AM. Sitting up, she reached for the phone and was greeted by Jared's voice.

"Good morning, sunshine," he said.

With a small groan, Charlie replied, "Good morning."

"So, I wanted to make sure you were up and ready. I'm packing a few things for the day and will head over in like ten minutes, if that's okay?"

Charlie nodded, then realized he couldn't hear a nod. "Definitely," she said. "What are you packing?"

He explained Kezia had requested they bring a few items with them. He told Charlie to be sure to pack a few of the journals, especially Astrid's, plus a photo or two of her mom and anything else she considered significant memory-wise. She said she would, then they said their goodbyes, and Charlie hopped up to get dressed.

As she stood before her dresser, she opened the second drawer and contemplated what one would wear to see a psychic. Choosing to go with basic jeans, she dug deep in search of a shirt. Finding a Pink Floyd concert tee that had been her mom's, she slid into it. Turning her attention to her hair, she maneuvered to the bathroom to freshen up.

Marcus watched as Charlie prepped for the day. Knowing the events which would unfold would be key to thwarting Astrid and the Dark Magician, he performed a recitation for luck and understanding. Also, knowing Astrid would take full advantage of Charlie's absence, Marcus, at the bequest of the Master, needed to influence Charlie to take the money with her on their trip. As he watched her, he knew he was running out of time to accomplish his task. Deciding the only thing he could do on such short notice would be to just tell her, he honed in on his recent teachings and, for the first time, spoke to his charge, whispering in her ear, "You must take the money."

Charlie set her toothbrush back in its cup and shivered as she turned to her room. "Jared? Is that you?" She knew it couldn't be, but hoped it had been. Tiptoeing into her room, she peeked around the corner to make sure no one was there with her. She was completely confused, but knew what she had heard clear as day. Someone told her to take the money. She reached in the top drawer for a pair of socks and was startled by a knock at the door.

She twisted the knob to release the latch, then stepped back as Jared entered the room. "Hey, you almost ready?" he asked. He must have sensed something was off, as he asked, "Hey, you okay? Is something going on?"

"I… It sounds strange, but everything is strange lately, so here it is: I just heard a voice telling me to take the money with me today."

"Well, if that wasn't a sign, I don't know what would be," Jared replied. "With everything going on, I say we listen and take the money with us. You were warned for a reason."

As Charlie sat on the edge of her bed sliding into her socks and shoes, Jared walked over to the closet and lifted the safe from its confines and disguised it with a small blanket he found. Checking to make sure they had everything, the pair exited the room and made their way to the car. Charlie figured the best place for the safe would be in the small area behind the back seats. Securing the rest of their stuff, the duo started their journey to Oneonta.

Following the directions given to them, they exited the highway. Jared read the last stretch of directions, stating they were probably only twenty minutes away at that point. Looking at her watch,

Charlie saw that even with the twenty minutes added, they were going to be about forty-five minutes early. Agreeing they could both eat, they found a diner and decided to stop.

Plopping themselves at the counter, they ordered coffee and chose to share a breakfast special plate. They ate and drank. They talked about how they needed to go into the day with low expectations and how there was a very good possibility they would need to come up with a backup plan if it didn't work.

They finished up their coffees, Jared paid, and they made their way through the small town, pulling up just outside of Kezia's home with five minutes to spare. Jared looked up at the house and said, "Not what I expected. How about you?"

Charlie agreed the mid-century modern was not what she had been thinking of. However, what had she been expecting? A run-down cottage replete with a cobblestone chimney? She giggled at that thought.

"Ready?" Jared asked.

Charlie nodded. Making sure she locked up the car, she walked around and grabbed Jared's hand and they made their way up the walk.

After knocking on the front door, they heard a faint voice from the other side call out, "Coming." As the door opened, a small-framed woman with the most pleasant features stood before them. Charlie couldn't pinpoint it exactly, but she reminded her of what she had always thought the fairy godmother in Cinderella would look like as a real human.

"Well, you must be Jared and Charlie," Kezia said.

Charlie nodded and poked Jared in the ribs for thinking what she knew he was thinking.

"Come in, come in," Kezia said, standing back to guide them in her home. "We are going to be in the parlor today, just ahead on your right." Walking a few steps ahead, they turned to see the parlor. This *is more like it*, Charlie thought. The room was crowded but cozy. Bookshelves lined the side wall, with two windows flanking either side. Heavy burgundy fabric over them kept the daylight out. In the rear was a picture window and window seat, sharing the same fabric choice as the other windows. A round table with four chairs sat in the middle of the room. In the center of the table were what appeared to be stones and a few small books.

Guiding them to have a seat, Kezia offered tea. "Thank you," Charlie said, "but I just finished several cups of coffee and am at my caffeine limit."

"Same, but thank you," Jared added.

Chuckling, Kezia said, "But of course. If you change your mind, please let me know."

Charlie was having a hard time pinpointing her accent. Jared had mentioned Gunther told him she was not from the United States originally. Gunther's family was supposedly German, but Kezia sounded more Russian.

Tilting her head, Kezia looked at Charlie and said, "Slovakia".

With a baffled expression, Jared repeated, "Slovakia?"

"Yes, my dear. Your friend here was wondering where my accent is from. My family is Slovakian originally. They migrated to Poland, then Germany, and eventually here." As she finished her statement, she asked both to have a seat at the table. "So, Gunther offered little insight as to what you seek from our meeting today. Can you please fill me in?" She looked at Charlie as she finished her question.

Charlie began with what started this quest: the death of her mother. As she attempted to wind her way through the complexity of what they had experienced, Kezia stopped her.

"My dear, we have a visitor. An unwanted one, I feel. We must take a moment to protect our minds." With that, Kezia asked them to join hands with her as she began a prayer of sorts. Finishing up, she said they were free to have their discussions and asked Charlie to continue.

As Charlie finished, Jared added, "What we really need from you today is a way to communicate with the Master. We need to find out how to stop Astrid and figure out what really happened. We hope that, armed with the full story, we might come up with a plan to stop Astrid and the Dark Magician."

Kezia took a deep breath. "You will be dealing with strong forces if you are to attempt this. It could end poorly if you aren't careful. I need you to acknowledge this before I begin."

Looking at each other, both Jared and Charlie gave their consent.

With that, Kezia began. She picked up the stones lying in front of her and placed them in a small, purple, velvet pouch. She held it between her hands and chanted, then passed the pouch to Charlie and asked her to think about what she wished for. Then, she gave

Jared the same instructions as Charlie passed the pouch to him. With intentions out in the universe, Kezia reclaimed the pouch, opened the top, and spilled the contents onto the center of the table.

For the first time, Charlie noticed the stones had markings on them. As Kezia continued to speak in her native tongue, Charlie watched, not knowing what to do.

After a few minutes, Kezia placed her palms on the table and said, "Charlie, I have someone here who would like to speak. He says his name is Marcus. He says to tell you he was the one who whispered to you this morning."

Stunned, Charlie nodded in acknowledgement. *He has a name. Wow*, she thought. *This is real.* She looked over at Jared and arched her eyebrows.

Kezia continued. "He says he is a student of the Master and has been charged to be your protector—nay, he says to tell you he is your guardian angel."

Charlie nodded in acceptance as Kezia went on to relay messages from Marcus. After what seemed like an eternity, Kezia's posture and energy changed. Almost glowing, she announced she was speaking with the Master. She explained his role in the afterlife and how he was the one who had allowed Astrid to be part of Birdie's life. "He's apologizing to you, Charlie. He says it was his fault for not seeing the signs. Astrid was hand-picked by him, upon her death, because of her innate desire to help people, and her youth made her special in the world of guardian angels. He did not consider the desires that would arise from passing at such a young age. He should have sensed she was ripe for the picking for the Dark Magician."

Kezia continued to give a history lesson on the who, how, and why of their realms. She fed questions to both Jared and Charlie, and she relayed several questions they had for the Master. As Kezia appeared to grow weak from the ordeal, she began to share instructions for Jared and Charlie to follow to bring an end to the Dark Magician's plan for Astrid and to help her return to her true purpose within the Master's realm. Charlie's photographic memory chose this moment to fail her as she was left with just a few bullet points to follow - One: Find a way to lure Astrid to them. Two: Assemble as strong a team as they could, for they would need exponential energy. Three: Find a way to harness the energy in a way that wouldn't strengthen the Dark Magician. Knowing Jared was recording this visit, Charlie relinquished her attempts to keep up moments before Kezia's body slumped forward.

Not knowing what to do, Charlie sat still. Beside her, Jared seemed similarly paralyzed. Concern grew to panic as Kezia did not move. Seeing she was breathing, albeit shallow, Charlie continued to sit in silence. Time crawled until Kezia lifted her head and said, "We must have some tea".

As the group sipped their tea, Kezia averted her eyes from both Charlie and Jared. *This can't be a good sign*, Charlie thought.

Kezia set her teacup down on its saucer, steadied her hands on the sides, lifted her head, and finally looked at Jared, then Charlie. Not breaking her gaze, Kezia spoke to the pair, letting them know that the Master would be in touch and that he and Marcus would provide any and all assistance they would need to see this through. She relayed his final instructions on how to perform a protection spell that will keep Astrid from listening to them as they prepared for the event..

As she finished, Charlie drew in a breath and held it.

Jared cleared his throat and said, "Well, I think we need to get that down on paper, don't you, Charlie?"

Finally releasing the aforementioned breath, Charlie agreed and reached down into her bag for a notebook and pen.

Kezia repeated the steps of the Master's plan as Charlie logged the details. Charlie thanked Kezia, as did Jared. While Charlie packed up, Jared leaned over to Kezia to see if she was okay.

"I'm fine, young man," Kezia said. "I just need rest."

Jared handed her a hundred for her time and efforts. She grabbed his hand. "It is vitally important you follow through on the plan."

Jared stood back, flustered, and Charlie moved in for a hug goodbye.

Kezia added in Charlie's ear, "Marcus and the Master both said they are here for you. You have your own personal army of angels. Use them if needed, Charlie."

Charlie nodded and said, "Thank you."

CHAPTER TWENTY SIX
THE PLAN

The drive back was a quiet one. Even though Kezia had done most of the work, it was as if she had pulled from their energy somehow. Jared seemed to fight the urge to just lay his head back and sleep, which Charlie was thankful for since she was in the same boat and talking to him was all that kept her awake. The last thing they needed was to crash. Eventually running out of energy to carry on a conversation, Charlie did the best she could to keep their minds occupied with music. Unfortunately, there were not a lot of options on the long stretch of road, so she pushed in a mix tape she had made with Ramona. As she listened, she couldn't help noticing how ironic this playlist was. The highlights included "Wake Me Up Before You Go Go" by Wham, "Magic Man" by Heart, and "Abracadabra" by Steve Miller Band. On the third song, Jared poked her thigh and used what little energy he had to smile at her.

With the clock tower in sight, they knew they were closing in on the campus. The shared breakfast having worn off, Charlie knew they would need food to boost their energy level. It was going to be a long day; she could feel it. After making a few sporadic turns, she slid Juicy up in front of Dinos. Jared sat forward and for the first time since getting in the car and spoke. "You read my mind, Charlie." They exited Juicy and took a seat at a booth lining the front windows.

Astrid stared down at the pair. She knew they had gone out earlier, but something happened, and her power of sight was lost after they entered the home of the seer. Utilizing that time, she had gone to the dormitory to retrieve her cash, only to find they had taken it with them. They were toying with her. Something was up. Something that was not good.

Not wanting to risk Astrid or the Dark Magician hearing them, Charlie and Jared steered their conversations in every direction other than the plan. They both knew they would have to wait until they got to a safe space to actually talk. Inhaling their first plate of wings, Charlie mentioned they should give Cassandra a call and have her join them. They were going to need all hands-on deck. Jared agreed and pulled out his cell phone. Relaying that he would fill her in in person, Jared asked Cassandra if she was free in about an hour or so. The answer must have been yes, because Jared told her to be at his place and finished up by asking her if she had eaten yet.

Wow, Charlie thought. *I hit the jackpot with this guy. Always thinking about others.*

She smirked as Jared ended the call, and he said, "What?"

With a giggle, Charlie avoided having to answer that question. She instead steered the attention back to his conversation with Cassandra. "She's on board, then?" Charlie asked.

"Her exact words were 'color me intrigued'," Jared said as the waitress delivered their burgers. He added a burger to go on their order, and the pair sat back to eat in silence.

Arriving at Jared's, Charlie carried in Cassandra's burger and her backpack while Jared handled the safe. Excusing herself to the bathroom, Charlie set everything down on the coffee table as Jared placed the safe to the side of the couch, took his jacket off, and plopped down onto one of the oversized armchairs. Charlie then made her way down the hall, and by the time she came out, Jared was sawing mini logs. Deciding to let him be until Cassandra arrived, Charlie sat down on the couch and fell asleep herself.

In what seemed like only a few minutes later, the doorbell ringing jolted Charlie and Jared awake. Charlie sat upright as Jared shuffled to the door, opened it to reveal Cassandra, and let her in. He groggily greeted her and pointed to her burger in the box.

"Wow," she said. "What happened to you two?"

Knowing they couldn't answer until they performed the protection spell Kezia had provided, Charlie asked her to sit and humor her and Jared for a few minutes. Cassandra took her place on the couch and began nibbling on her burger. Charlie and Jared sat opposite each other at the coffee table and, following Kezia's instructions, laid half a dozen of the marked stones on the table and spoke the words written on the paper.

Once they were done, Charlie nodded to Cassandra and said, "Now we can talk." Charlie explained their trip to see Kezia and the protection spell.

"Ah," Cassandra said. "Like the cone of silence on the old *Get Smart* show?"

Jared looked at Charlie and laughed. "Yeah, I guess kinda like that."

Charlie slid her notebook further onto the table, being mindful not to disturb the circle of stones. The group freely discussed what needed to happen to bring Astrid back to the light and hopefully release Birdie's soul.

Cassandra nodded and broke it down to its bare bones. "So, all we have to do is lure Astrid in using Charlie and the money as bait; perform a spell to contain her; keep the Dark Magician at bay; somehow convince Astrid she *doesn't* want to be human; and release her soul from your mom's body, which will somehow do what? Trigger a cosmic shift and bring your mom back?"

Sighing, Charlie said yes to the first four, but clarified the plan was not to bring her mom back, but to release her soul from wherever it landed after her death. She explained what the Master told Kezia about how souls are held for a finite period of time while they were sorted to their final destinations. According to the Master, Birdie's soul was considered lost or in limbo at the moment, and if they could get Astrid to return to her rightful place, it would allow Birdie's soul to be free.

"So, wait," Cassandra said. "What will happen to the body?"

Charlie thought about that for a moment, and Jared was the first to chime in. "Well, from what I gather, the body that Astrid inhabits is *not* a real body, but an exact reproduction of Birdie. Astrid formed it over time through a close bond as she fed on Birdie's energies, creating an exact double. So, in theory, the body will just vanish."

Taking a moment to let that sink in, Charlie continued. "We will need to time this perfectly. We are definitely going to need some help. And, we cannot fuck this up. The Master conveyed to Kezia that he believes the key is Astrid's link to her mother, that her love for her mother will trump the desire to be human again. We just need to use that to our advantage somehow."

The group worked through the plan. Step by step so as not to forget anything which could cause a catastrophic failure. They realized they hadn't discussed when to enact the plan. Charlie pulled out a calendar from her backpack and looked at the weeks ahead. "I must secure the money tomorrow at the bank and somehow make Astrid think I still have it in the safe. We then need time to plan and gather the items and people we need." She paused. Sliding her fingers over the dates on the calendar, she noticed something and bolted upright. "Here!" she exclaimed as her finger landed on April twenty-first. "Look at what is significant about the twenty-first, y'all."

Jared and Cassadra leaned forward and smiled as they saw exactly what Charlie was referring to. That day was the full moon.

"Perfect," they all said in unison.

With the date picked and Charlie's initial tasks laid out, they assigned
Cassandra the responsibility of approaching Heather and Scarlett to see if they or the other group members would be interested in lending their energies to the cause.

"I have no clue how to approach them on this," Cassandra said. "Should be interesting for sure."

Jared would look for a location for their plan to take place. It would have to be secluded enough to not get interrupted, but large enough to house the number of people needed for the energy.

Confirming they had a good grasp on things for now, the group decided to call it a night and with that, Charlie scooped up the stones, and enjoyed a little rest and relaxation before disbanding.

Charlie woke the next morning, got dressed in a suit dress she felt was appropriate for making a thirty-thousand-dollar deposit at a bank, and made her way to Juicy. Having determined the money would be safer at Jared's overnight than at Charlie's dorm, she had to stop by to pick it up before heading to Citizens Savings Bank.

As she knocked on Jared's door, she heard a commotion on the other side and waited patiently for the knob to turn.

Looking like he was still asleep, Jared cracked the door and immediately shielded his eyes from the sun. "Get in here, quick," he said, backing away from the sun like he was Nosferatu. Once inside, Jared rubbed his eyes and ran his fingers through his hair, pushing some stray strands out of his face. Only after that did he give Charlie a good look, and he let out a construction site whistle. "Swanky," he said.

"Well, I couldn't very well walk into the you-know-what with the you-know-what in jeans and a sweatshirt." She said, "I figured I needed to present at least a façade of being an adult."

Agreeing, Jared walked towards the kitchen, gestured towards the coffee maker, and said they had to come up with better code. Charlie nodded in agreement.

Watching Jared maneuver around the kitchen preparing coffee, Charlie sat down in one of the kitchen chairs and fidgeted with her skirt. "I don't know how people wear stuff like this day in and day out. It's like a torture device."

As the pair sat and enjoyed their coffee, Charlie remembered they were possibly about to reveal a huge element to Astrid. "We didn't think this through," she snapped. "If she sees me go to the place, then she will know that the thing isn't in the thing anymore." As they sipped their coffee, they came up with a plan. A complicated plan, but a plan, nonetheless.

Jared grabbed the bag of stones and set them on the coffee table. They performed the incantation and were free to prepare the money. Heading upstairs, Jared returned with a small backpack he used for camping. They shifted the money from the safe to the bag, and in its place, Jared filled the safe with stacks of paperbacks from his bookshelves. They then walked through the plan.

Charlie would take the stones with her and perform the ritual in her car before she headed into the bank. Unsure if it would actually work, they hoped the barrier covered the person and not just the location. Looking at the clock, Charlie said she wanted to be at Citizens first thing so as to not draw attention to herself from the daily bankers. Deeming it was time to head out, she took a long, final swig of her coffee, stood up, and asked Jared to help with the safe and bag.

He let out a snicker and said, "Oh, the outfit turned you into a damsel, then, did it?"

She scoffed at him and said, "No, I am one hundred percent capable. I just wanted to give you your goodbye kiss out at the car if that's okay." Charlie grabbed the stones and the incantation as Jared panted like a puppy, slung the bag over his shoulder, lifted the safe, and followed Charlie out to the car. "May as well stick it in the front seat," she said.

Setting the safe on the floorboard of the passenger side, Jared slid the bag into the space behind Charlie's seat. "You're going to need the front seat for the you-know-what," he said.

Nodding, Charlie slung her arms around him and said, "Wish me luck." After giving him the kiss she had promised for his services, Charlie slid into the driver's seat and waved as she pulled off.

Parking in the lot two over from Citizens, Charlie leaned back in her seat and took a deep breath. She slid the stones out of the bag, made a small circle on the passenger seat, and read the incantation. She then exited the vehicle and grabbed the money. Walking to the bank's entrance, she looked around her to make sure she wasn't being followed.

Charlie then ascended the stairs, entered the foyer, made her way to one of the tellers, and said "I would like to open an account."

"Of course," the young girl behind the wood podium said. "Let me get the bank manager for you. You can have a seat over there."

Charlie took a seat at the desk donning a nameplate that read, *George Cambridge - Bank Manager*. Setting the money at her feet, she looked at her surroundings. *Banks always feel so overdone*, she thought. There was wood and marble everywhere.

As she brought her sights back to the desk, a man looking to be in his fifties walked behind it and introduced himself as, George

Cambridge. "Martha informed me you are looking to open an account. Are you a student here at Cornell?"

Charlie answered she was, however, she would not be looking for a student account. She remembered what her dad had instructed her to say and continued to explain that she would be looking for an account that would give her the highest yield on her deposit.

Giving her a curious look, Mr. Cambridge said, "Well, dear, unless the deposit is sizable, most don't worry about such things."

Having fun, Charlie asked, "Would thirty thousand dollars be considered sizable?" She watched as the color fell from his face.

He stammered, "Why, yes, I guess it would be. I must inform you, however, that due to our dear friend The Bank Secrecy Act, the bank will have to report any cash deposit of over ten thousand dollars. This is a duty of the bank and does not affect any further transactions on your behalf. I won't need to know where the money came from, if that would be a worry of yours."

"Not a worry at all," Charlie replied. Remembering what her dad had said: *It's none of their business.*

"Well, of course," Mr. Cambridge said as he pulled out a folder from his desk. "Let's get to it then, shall we?"

After spending the next twenty minutes crossing their Ts and dotting their Is, it came time for Mr. Cambridge to take the money to be counted. Again, Charlie remembered her dad saying that it was her right to be present when the bank counted it. Lifting the bag, she informed Mr. Cambridge that she would like just that.

"Of course," he said, taking the bag from her hands. He guided her to an area that housed a large counting machine. Mr. Cambridge called out to a gentleman sitting at a desk nearby and said, "Please get a count on the contents of this bag, with Ms. Bauman present, of course."

As the machine flicked out the bills at lightning speed, Charlie watched, nervous that Astrid had found a way past the incantation and was watching the procedure unfold. Confirming the deposit amount, the gentleman guided Charlie back to Mr. Cambridge's desk. After completing the signature cards and verifying her identification, he stood and stuck his hand out towards Charlie. Standing, she grasped his hand, and he recited a welcome-to-Citizens-Bank mantra.

Gathering her ID, a folder of paperwork, and her bag, Charlie exited the bank, glad to breathe in some fresh air. The bank reminded her of the funeral home, minus the dead people. Tossing the items in the car, she waited until she was a few blocks away before scooping up the stones and placing them in the bag. Next on her agenda was to secure the safe in her dorm and head to class.

The next few days resembled typical pre-Astrid days. They all attended classes like normal. Each worked on their tasks to prepare for the twenty-first. Cassandra had successfully recruited Heather, Scarlett, and half a dozen other members. Jared used a celestial map to pinpoint a location that would best suit their needs: a small field just outside campus. As to not draw attention to themselves, they continued to meet and discuss Astrid and the journals, feigning that they were stuck and unable to come to any kind of conclusion to keep her unaware they were up to anything. Time passed slowly and yet quickly at the same time. Jared and Charlie had their movie date. The Master and Marcus communicated with Charlie over crucial details regarding how they would fit in on the plan. Final papers were written, and study sessions were underway heading into finals. Charlie kept her dad informed of all things that were transpiring, but kept the bulk of what was happening from Ramona for the time being.

On the evening of the nineteenth, Charlie lay in bed with a hopeful, yet worried, feeling in the pit of her stomach. The plan was going to take a small miracle to work. It had so many moving parts, so many entities to keep control of. Good doesn't always triumph over evil, but it had to this time. Her mom's soul was at stake.

Burying her face in her pillow, she let out a scream of frustration, then decided to do something she hadn't done before, something she should have done when everything began. Setting aside any feeling of foolishness, she closed her eyes and spoke to her mom. She told her she loved her and missed her, and expressed how she hoped she could hear her, despite the likelihood being slim based on what she had learned from Marcus. Talking about how strange things had been since she passed, she said the world as she knew it had changed on both a fundamental and spiritual level. She shared how she wished her mom had felt comfortable enough to share more of that side of her childhood. She let her mom know her dad missed her terribly and would need some help to move on. Charlie filled her in on Ramona. She chatted with her about Jared and how happy she was that she found him. With tears in her eyes, Charlie then finished by saying she loved her and if everything worked as planned, her soul would be free to move on to the place it deserved to be. She ended with a sweet goodbye and fell fast asleep.

Early morning sunlight enveloped Charlie's room with such force that it was as if the universe was telling her to wake the fuck up. Sitting up, Charlie inhaled and with a slight hitch in her breath, then exhaled. Feet dangling over the edge of the bed, she gave herself a pep talk to get through the day. Standing, she began what would be the longest day of her life.

After class, she spent most of the afternoon gathering the items needed for the next day. With so many moving parts and entities involved, timing was crucial, so the group had agreed to have a final walkthrough of the plan at Jared's. Grabbing a quick dinner, Charlie returned to her room and gave him a call to confirm they were still on. With her confirmation, Charlie heaved her backpack off the floor and made her way to his house.

The group took time to create a mockup of the area, using Jared's living room floor to represent the field. Taking the stones out of the pouch, Charlie performed the ritual for the final time, and they went through each step in detail, confirming each of their roles and how critical it was to be as exact as they could.

The Master and Marcus had helped with a lot of the more obscure items, but the biggest potential for failure fell on whether Astrid would show up on cue.

Apparently sensing her concern, Marcus appeared by Charlie's side and reaffirmed the plan that he and the Master had come up with. They would lay the groundwork and make sure Astrid would show.

The team knew sleep was not going to be an option that night. They needed to be in place by two in the morning and ready for the divine hour, as the Master called it, the time when the boundary between the earthly dimension and the divine realm is the thinnest. It would not be a cakewalk, as it was also the time when the Dark Magician would be his most potent.

With everything theoretically in place, it was a waiting game. Looking at the clock, Charlie noted they had four hours before they would head over. Jared stood and made a large pot of coffee, which they quickly inhaled.

CHAPTER TWENTY SEVEN
THWARTED

Two in the morning arrived faster than expected. The trio gathered their gear and made their way out into the night. As they exited the front door, the light of the full moon shone down on them like a beacon in the night sky. Jared grabbed Charlie's hand and squeezed. Smiling at him, she knew he sensed her trepidation.

Arriving at the field, they began to set up the area. Gradually, the others arrived. Cassandra took them aside to make sure everyone knew their place and told them if they were going to back out, that was the time. Once they started, they would need each and every one's energy.

Charlie made a circle out of stones that Kezia had shipped to her just large enough for her and the safe. Like the bag of stones, they had the added benefit of being blessed by a shaman and would help protect Charlie from the Dark Magician, but only to a point.

Jared made a larger circle out of limestone, which, through their research with Heather and Scarlett, they had learned would encourage purification and bring forth innocence and positive thoughts.

Just outside the limestone circle, Cassandra had the others take formation.

With a few minutes to spare, Jared approached Charlie and knelt opposite her. Leaning in to not disturb the circle of stone, he gave her a kiss. Sitting back on his heels, he smiled and looked her deep in the eyes and, without words, let her know that she had this.

Charlie nodded as Jared stood and made his way to the outer circle. She then closed her eyes and called upon Marcus and the Master. Feeling Marcus's hand on her shoulder, she knew they were ready.

Charlie maneuvered the stones into place as those in the outer circle began to chant the spell. Then, as if out of nowhere, Astrid appeared. The Master had done his part and planted the seed that Charlie had buried the money earlier that day to conceal it from her.

As Astrid approached, Charlie squared up in her spot, hardly able to believe her eyes. Standing about one hundred feet from her appeared to be her mother. She knew better, of course, but her heart was outranking her brain at the moment. A deep warmth flowed through her as just seeing her mom again brought her such joy. It was then her brain caught up with her. Having discussed that very scenario with Jared and Cassandra, she had known it was going to be hard. However, it wasn't until she actually saw her mother's doppelganger walking towards her that she truly felt that their undertaking may have been an impossible task.

Through the din of the chanting, Astrid spoke, seething mad and with the energy of the Dark Magician flowing through her. "You little brat of a girl. You had to get in the way. I did *not* spend all this energy and wait all this time for you to muck things up. The Dark Magician has shown me what I can have, and I will have it. No matter what you and your little friends do, *his* plan will happen, one way or another. Now, be a good little girl and give me that money, and *he* may let you all live."

Based on what Marcus had told Charlie about Astrid and the Dark Magician, she knew it was more than likely not Astrid speaking. To stick to the plan, Charlie closed her eyes and welcomed Marcus to speak through her.

The voice that came through was not Marcus or Charlie, however. It was Carolyn Anne, Astrid's mother. Charlie smiled. The Master had figured out how to draw her from her realm, after all. That was amazing and returned a sense of hope to Charlie.

Stopping dead in her tracks, Astrid cocked her head, tears welling in her eyes. She parted her lips and breathed a soft, "Mama?"

"My dear Astrid, I am so sorrowful that I have been unable to speak to you until now. Please, listen to me, my sweet child. You must stop this. What you are doing is wrong. You have not yet gone too far, my baby. But if you continue on this path, your soul will be lost forever. Please trust me when I say the Dark Magician does not make promises he is not willing to collect on. You weren't meant for this life, Astrid. Like me, your time in this world was a finite one. You may feel you were robbed of the human experiences you crave, but you are meant for much greater things, things you cannot begin to understand, but the Master does. He chose you for a reason. Come back to the light where you belong. Give this soul you have imprisoned its freedom. Give this girl peace. I promise everything will be fine if you do."

Seeing Astrid waver, the Dark Magician pushed to break the energy field the Master and the others created. Momentarily stopping the chants, he telepathically reached out to Astrid and told her to hold steadfast, that she was so close to *all* the things she desired. "They do not understand you like I do. They do not know what it is like to have what we have."

Knowing that he must act fast, The Master released his energy from Marcus to strengthen the circle's defense against the Dark Magician. As the chanting began once again, Marcus weakened and released Charlie. The Master sensed the Dark Magician's connection to Astrid breaking.

"Mama, please come back."

With tears flowing down Birdie's face, Astrid realized what she needed to do. Closing her eyes, she fell to her knees and looked towards Charlie. Apologizing to her for what her greed put her and her family through, she looked up and called to the Master. A brilliant white light appeared and enveloped her, and she felt her soul fly free again.

Within moments, the corporeal form resembling Charlie's mother disintegrated. A blue dome of energy covered the circle, and Charlie heard her mother's voice one final time. "Goodbye, my sweet girl. You are destined for great things." With a flash, the field went black.

EPILOGUE

As Charlie closed the last of her boxes, she reminisced on how crazy sophomore year had been. She was looking forward to summer vacation with Jared. The pair had decided that a trip to visit his relatives and get away from it all was just what they needed. The added bonus of the money allowed any financial hurdles to drift away.

Setting the last box on the stack on the dolly Charlie flicked off her dorm light one final time. Exiting the elevator, she wheeled the dolly towards Juicy and found two loving smiles aimed her way. She smiled back at both men in her life as the sun's rays warmed her face and her guardian angel's hand squeezed her shoulder.

Marcus had confirmed her mother's arrival in the heavenly realm. Mom was where she was meant to be. Astrid, upon returning, began her training again and would observe for a while before being paired with another diva to ensure they wouldn't have a repeat of what had happened before. The Dark Magician would still be a threat to the seven realms, but such is the balance of good and evil.

Setting the last of the boxes in her dad's Jeep, Charlie turned and gave him a hug.

"You got everything?" he asked.

"Sure do," she said, taking Jared by the hand.

"Okay. Well, you two be safe and enjoy your summer." Dale gave Charlie a huge bear hug.

"You too, Dad. Tell Grandma and Grandpa I said hello and let me know when you find a house."

"Will do, kiddo. I can't believe I let them talk me into downsizing."

Jared shook her dad's hand and promised they would be fine. Dale then hopped in his Jeep as Charlie and Jared left to embark on their next journey.

"There goes our girl, Birdie," Dale said with a smile.

Coming Fall 2024

GEIST

Realms and Realities Series
Book 2

C.L. Merklinger

STANDING AT THE BOW OF a small sailboat, the clear water beneath her, Charlie watched in the distance as the silhouette of three dolphin fins came into focus. She smiled remembering what her mom had said about the dolphins and how they were considered a good omen when you were at sea. Watching the dorsal fins bob in and out of the water, shortening the distance between themselves and the boat she sprawled herself on a towel and slipped on her headphones. Relaxing as the breeze blew across her warm skin, she became increasingly aware of a huge change in the velocity of said breeze. Leaning up in an attempt to see what may be going on, she heard an alarmingly loud horn in the distance. *Funny, I don't remember seeing any other boats in our vicinity.* Again, the horn sounded. This time louder, and almost immediately, it sounded again. Snapping forward, Charlie barely had time to register a train that was approaching from the driver's side. The breeze from her open window swirled around her head one final time before they came to a complete stop in front of the train tracks.

"Welcome to the living, sleepyhead," Jared teased as he looked over at her.

"Looks like we may be here for a hot minute. This train seems to have no end in sight." Charlie nodded and uprighted herself in the bucket seat as Jared reached over and wiped the small pool of drool that had formed on her left cheek. "There, much better" he said as he winked.

"Thanks," Charlie said with a half smile. Yawning, she continued "So, where are we?"

"Approximately two hours from our destination. The last sign I saw placed us near Roanoke, VA. I took this exit so we could stretch and get some gas." Jared said, increasing his volume a bit as the train wheels let out a screech on the rails as it passed.

Charlie reached down by her feet and pulled up a warm bottle of Coke she had stashed earlier. Tapping the cap gently, she reached in the glove box and pulled out her rusty key shaped bottle opener. With slight pressure she released the seal on the cap and heard the all to familiar fizz releasing from its confines. Satisfied that there would be no foam over, she lifted the opening to her mouth and took a long swig. Gasping as the bubbles hit the back of her throat Charlie managed to choke out "Want some?" as she gestured the bottle towards Jared.

"No thanks, I'll hold off for something a bit colder." Jared said gesturing to his left to signal that the train was coming to an end shortly. "So, after that nap, I'd say you are glad we decided to split the driving, huh?" Charlie nodded. "Yeah, I didn't realize how long of a drive twelve hours really was. When we stop, let's take a look at the map again, then I can take over the last stint if you want."

"Yeah, and if there is a payphone, I should call my Aunt Tilde to give her an updated arrival time." Jared replied. The pair had realized early on in their summer escapades that mobile phones weren't very "mobile" unless you were willing to pay exorbitant usage rates to do so.

Staring out her window Charlie watched as they passed through the rural route. Their travels this summer had definitely exposed her to a plethora of home styles that you just don't see in the Rochester, NY area. Here, the range in home styles was more prevalent than anywhere they had driven through so far. From small ranchers and cape cods to log cabins and historical beauties, no two homes were alike. Homemade signs for fresh eggs and free wood were commonplace. So, it seemed, were abandoned vehicles of all makes and models.

Taking the last swig of her Coke, Charlie looked over at Jared and smiled. The wind was assisting his hair in a wild dance exposing his chiseled jawline. The summer had been good for his skin tone also. Charlie envied his ability to tan. His olive skin glowed with no effort other than just being. Charlie, however, had two modes, pale and burnt. This summer, luckily, she had managed to gain enough freckles to make it look like she was tan…ish. With summer soon coming to an end, she knew this would fade fast and she would be her normal ghost of a self by mid-September.

The clicking of the turn signal snapped her out of her introspection, and she looked up to see a small gas station straight out of a horror movie. The well-worn building was split into two sides. A small glass encased general store on one half and what Charlie assumed was a repair shop on the other. Two pumps sat out front and as Jared pulled in a bell dinged alerting the attendant inside they had arrived. A slight man in oil coated coveralls pushed through the door and Charlie watched as he shuffled towards them. The attendant got closer to the duo as they slid out of the car and stretched. Closing in on them, Charlie could see his skin was worn from what she would gather was too much sun, drinking or smoking. The latter was confirmed by the raspy "howdy folks" they got as he arrived at the pumps.

"What can I get for y'all today?" he said.

"We need a fill up, please, and a few items from inside too" Jared replied as Charlie squinted to read the oil smudged name tag on his coveralls. *Smitty.*

"G'hed and take a look see" Smitty stated gesturing towards the store with one hand as the other loosened the gas cap on Juicy. Charlie nodded and shyly asked if there happened to be a restroom she could use. Smitty nodded and said, "Look up on the counter next to the register, there's a key. Toilet's around the backside. Mind the low tree limbs as you head out back."

Jared and Charlie began their walk towards the store as Smitty slid the nozzle into Juicy. Opening the door, another bell jingled, and Jared gestured for Charlie to go ahead in. Scanning the room, Charlie made a beeline for the register and spotted the key Smitty had mentioned.

It was attached to a monkey wrench with a metal chain. *Kitchy.* Charlie grabbed it and excused herself as Jared slid open a cooler and began scoping out its contents barely registering the bell as Charlie exited the door.

Confounded by the sheer size of the key and its companion, Charlie nodded to Smitty as he yelped across the parking lot to her "See ya found it!" Turning the corner of the building, Charlie took time to scope out her surroundings. The area surrounding the exterior of the building was in just as rough shape as the building itself. Overgrown grass, unruly trees and bushes with thorns created a semi treacherous path for her. Narrowly escaping the teeth of one of the vines, she looked ahead and saw dozens of empty soda and beer bottles lining the ground in front of her. Gingerly hopscotching between them she reached her destination. A large steel door with a hand painted warning *Paying Customers Only - See Smitty for Key* hung ominously before her. Sliding the key in the lock she turned it to the left and heard the latch release. The sharp pungent odor hit her within seconds of doing so. Like a crypt being opened after centuries, the small room emitted a rotten and stale stench from its bowels. Holding back her first of what would be several retches, Charlie reached blindly around the corner in search of the light switch. Wishing she had a sleeve long enough to cover her fingers she felt the grimy nubbin and flicked it upwards engaging the most horrendous fluorescent light she had ever seen.

Squinting her eyes against the harshness she took a few steps forward and could hear her shoes sticking, then releasing, from the putty-colored tile.

Finishing her task at hand as quickly as she could, she debated whether washing her hands would create more germs than simply exiting the tiny petri dish. Her brain convinced her that anything else would be better than attempting to wash in the rusty sink, so she turned to back out of the door not wanting to touch the handle and about jumped out of her skin as Smitty softly asked her if she was finding everything to her liking. Unable to hold back the loudest *Fuck* she had ever verbalized, Charlie grabbed her chest and, in the process, dropped the key.

"I got that for you missy" Smitty interjected as he bent down to grab the lunk of a keychain.

"Thh..thhhaaank you" Charlie stammered. " You surprised me is all " she finished before making swift work of the obstacle course back to the front.

With Smitty in tow, she could feel her heart in her throat. Before she could reach for the handle of the front door, she was again beaten to the punch by Smitty.

"Ladies first" he said with a smile that showed off his shoe pegged, yellowed teeth.

 "Hey! Charlie! You'll never guess what I found!? Jared yelled from the back.

Not remotely in the guessing mood, Charlie looked up to see Jared holding up two bottles marked "Double Cola". Seeing the confusion on Charlie's face, Jared proceeded with a brief history lesson. "You don't see these anymore anywhere, especially in NY. These here are genuine Tennessee relics. Straight from Chattanooga! I promise you'll love it!"

With his head kin to a bobble head, Smitty fervently nodded up and down in agreement. "I tell you what, now. That there is some of the best fizzy you'll ever taste. Guaranteed."

And with that Jared armed himself with two more bottles and added it to the growing pile next to the register. "Anything you want to grab?" he asked Charlie.

Knowing she had to find something to at least rinse her hands with, Charlie stalked the shelves for the needle in a haystack. "No Phisohex I'm guessing?" Charlie asked, trying not to sound totally stuck up.

"Welp, gosh, no I don't reckon I've heard of that missy. Apologies" Smitty slid out with his southern drawl. "What's it kin too?" He quickly asked

Just as she was about to answer Charlie saw a small familiar brown bottle of hydrogen peroxide. "Nevermind, this will do" she said a bit too loud. Not knowing what was going on Jared titled his head in the universal sign for "are you ok?"

Giving a quick nod Charlie added the bottle to their pile as Smitty did some quick head math and punched the keys on the well worn register. "That there with your gas 'll be eighteen twenty three."

Handing Smitty a twenty, Jared said "keep the change" as he swept up their haul in his arms.

"Mighty obliged," Smitty slurred. "Y'all have a great day now, ya hear?"

The pair waved goodbye as they quickly maneuvered to Juicy.

"I have to pee like a racehorse," Jared said, ducking his head into the driver's side to set down the items. "But based on your reaction, I'm thinking I can wait."

Charlie said "wise move"as she leaned out the passenger door and squirted copious amounts of hydrogen peroxide over her hands.

"Hey, I almost forgot! I gotta call Tilde " Jared exclaimed "do me a favor and look at the map. I'd like to do the rest of the trip on back roads if possible. Can you see if that's a go?"

Nodding Charlie scooped up the map from between the seats and began to research. Nervously keeping an eye out in case Smitty decided to make a comeback.

A few minutes later the door to the driver's side opened and Jared informed Charlie that Tilde was "tickled pink" that they were arriving early. "Did you find our route?"

Charlie nodded and watched as Jared reached up to crank the convertible top. "Well that's perfect timing" he said as he exited the vehicle. Charlie sat and watched as he lifted the top up and over before tucking it in and engaging the clips. "Don't forget the cover" Charlie sounded off over her shoulder.

"Aye aye captain," Jared joked as he completed securing the snaps on the cover. Re-situating himself in the driver's seat, he placed his hand on Charlie's knee and said "next stop , Jonesborough."

THE AUTHOR

C.L. Merklinger the author of *Interloper* - The first Novel in the Realms and Realities Series, grew up with an insatiable appetite for reading and all things scary. Inspired by Horror Authors such as Ray Bradbury; Stephen King; Dean Koontz; and Edgar Allan Poe, she was also deeply influenced by great Mystery Character Authors such as Lawrence Sanders, Agatha Christie and Mary Higgins Clark. Following her passions for Horror and the Paranormal she pulls from her experiences as an Empath which inspired her to write this series. C.L. resides in the Chesapeake Bay area of Maryland where she dabbles in photography.

Interloper

COMPANION PLAYLIST

Listen Here!

Milton Keynes UK
Ingram Content Group UK Ltd.
UKHW012250110624
443988UK00005B/312